"**Do we have visual yet?**"

Javovich raised a thin eyebrow. "We do, and that was why I ordered that you should be roused."

"And?" Doltrane said, with a sharp intake of breath that was completely autonomic.

Fear, Katrina whispered. *It's called fear.*

"And you need to see this for yourself," Javovich said.

By Jamie Sawyer

THE LAZARUS WAR

Artefact

Legion

Origins

Redemption (ebook novella)

THE ETERNITY WAR

Pariah

THE ETERNITY WAR

WAR

BOOK ONE: PARIAH

JAMIE SAWYER

www.orbitbooks.net

Copyright © 2017 by Jamie Sawyer
Excerpt from *The Rule of Luck* copyright © 2016 by Catherine Cerveny
Excerpt from *Forsaken Skies* copyright © 2016 by David Wellington

Cover design by Lauren Panepinto
Cover illustration by Ben Zweifel
Cover copyright © 2017 by Hachette Book Group, Inc.

Orbit
Hachette Book Group
1290 Avenue of the Americas
New York, NY 10104
orbitbooks.net

Simultaneously published in Great Britain and in the U.S. by Orbit in 2017
First U.S. Edition: September 2017

Orbit is an imprint of Hachette Book Group.
The Orbit name and logo are trademarks of Little, Brown Book Group Limited.

The publisher is not responsible for websites (or their content) that are not owned by the publisher.

The Hachette Speakers Bureau provides a wide range of authors for speaking events. To find out more, go to www.hachettespeakersbureau.com or call (866) 376-6591.

ISBNs: 978-0-316-43322-8 (mass market), 978-0-316-43320-4 (ebook)

Printed in the United States of America

OPM

10 9 8 7 6 5 4 3 2 1

"Try, die, and try again."
Alliance Army Sim Ops motto

"If a job is worth doing, it's worth dying for."
Popular saying among Sim Ops operators

PROLOGUE

When the call came, the captain was dreaming of his ex-wife. Of a cabin they had shared on Ganymede Docks: a tiny cubicle that Naval Logistics had audaciously called "shared accommodation."

Katrina. That had been his wife's name.

Captain Erich Doltrane was still his.

It was almost gut-wrenching how the gossamer blonde of Katrina's hair—of a woman who had been dead for the better part of a decade—was replaced so suddenly with the austere grey of the starship's interior. Doltrane found himself roused from a dream in which it had been warm and bright, and into the dark reality of the Alliance Navy battleship. And not just any battleship: *his* battleship, the European Confederation starship *Hannover*. That fact carried an extra weight to it, somehow, because he knew that as captain the welfare of every one of the two-thousand-strong crew aboard the vessel was his responsibility.

He had been expecting the call, but that hardly made it any less terrifying.

"I'm up," he said, groggily. Knowing that the ship's internal comms system would detect his verbal response. Added: "I'm awake."

"Good morning, Captain Doltrane," came the smooth tones of the ECS *Hannover*'s artificial intelligence programme. It sounded almost *smug*.

"Is it?" he replied. The AI was a personification of the battleship's machine-mind, and Doltrane didn't trust a machine that was so obviously far beyond his own mental capabilities.

He struggled to throw off the shroud of sleep, and swung his tired legs over the edge of the bunk. Rubbed callused fingers at his eyes. He made a conscious effort to avoid looking at the data-slates piled on his duty desk, each filled with weird geometric designs and gut-churning alien symbology. The ship's warning siren wailed on and on in the background, echoing through the decks.

"There is an urgent alert from the command intelligence centre," the ship's AI said. "Alpha priority. Your immediate attendance is required."

"Of course."

Doltrane thought about how similar the AI's voice was to that of his ex-wife. Cold, calm, inexplicably collected. Both were, for all intents, dead.

"I did say immediately," the machine insisted, an air of urgency in its modulated tone.

"You're a bitch," Doltrane said, as he thrust his feet into his deck-boots, fastened the lapel of his Alliance Navy uniform. "I've already said that I'm awake."

"I do not understand your response, Captain Doltrane."

"You wouldn't. We're out here in the unknown, and you don't give a damn."

"It will not be the unknown for long, Captain. We have reached the coordinates."

The cabin's overhead LED lights flickered on as Doltrane stumbled to the mirror above a tiny sink in the corner of the room. Having his own wash facilities was one of the few perks of being captain of the European Confederacy battlecruiser.

"*Herr Kapitän*," came another voice, interrupting the alert tone: this time recognisably human. "If you're quite done sleeping, this cannot wait."

That was Lieutenant Javovich, and she sounded excited.

"I'm on my way, Lieutenant," Doltrane said.

He splashed warm recycled water over his face from the stagnant pool in the bowl. Confident that the comm connection was closed, he said, "This, Katrina, is what comes of chasing *ghosts* ..."

He could swear that he heard his ex-wife's voice through the airshaft above the sink: that shrill cackle of a laugh that had at one time amused him so.

The ship was by now light-years from the nearest human outpost, on the very brink of explored space. Three days had passed since the quantum-jump to the *Hannover*'s present location, and in that time Captain Doltrane had slept little. He couldn't shake the feeling that this was *verboten* space: that this was forbidden.

The ECS *Hannover* was currently deep within the Maelstrom, in a sector of turbulent space that Science Division had labelled as "the Gyre." Had it not been for the present Naval operation, Doltrane was quite sure that he would never have heard of the place. The Gyre was just one of so many stellar anomalies within the Maelstrom: statistically, a tiny and largely insignificant feature of the shattered realm occupied by the alien Krell. And yet, greater minds than Captain Doltrane's had ordained that there was something out here worthy of investigation ...

"But it isn't the location that makes this wrong," Doltrane whispered to himself.

It's the mission, Katrina whispered back.

The lack of sleep was getting to Doltrane. When he was a younger man, he had been more capable of working such long watches without rest. Things were different now, and he found exhaustion affecting him in many ways. He had been hearing things. Sometimes, just occasionally, even seeing things.

The walk from Captain Doltrane's cabin to the command intelligence centre wasn't far, but it seemed that whatever Javovich had to tell him simply wouldn't wait, and the younger lieutenant met him halfway. Pushing aside bustling sailors and over-amped Marines in full battledress, Javovich snapped a salute at the captain.

"Glad that you could make it," she said, with a blistering smile. A sixth-gen immigrant to the Vega III colony, she spoke with off-world accented German. "The ship has been trying to contact you for several minutes."

Javovich had a certain cold beauty to her features, and a caustic wit to match. She was impeccably clad, uniform immaculately pressed and pale blonde hair pulled tight beneath her service cap, despite the stressful circumstances. Doltrane found himself almost envying the younger woman.

"I've barely slept in three days," Doltrane said, increasing his pace towards the command centre. "I think that I'm entitled to a little shut-eye before ... before the event ..."

Doltrane's words trailed off. He realised, with some self-chastisement, that he was frightened. In some ways, being here, at the culmination of the battleship's mission, should have salved his anxieties. Instead, knowing what they were about to do—having read the reports on the subject—it just made him feel so much worse.

If Javovich noticed his unusual reaction, she didn't respond. Instead, the young lieutenant kept speaking. "We're running green on all systems. Command staff are on standby. We've reached the coordinates."

"As I expected," Doltrane said. "And the readings are the same?"

Javovich handed him a data-slate, which twitched with complex holographic info-feeds. Doltrane gave the slate a perfunctory glance; truth be told, he didn't understand much of what the Science Division team told him, but what he could absorb was bad enough. He handed the slate back to Javovich.

"They're the same," she said, referring to the readings. "Sixteen dead stars. Over a hundred dead planets."

Doltrane swallowed. "Dead Krell planets."

"Does that make it any better?" Javovich asked. "Planets are planets. Either way, the Gyre is dead."

"Do we have visual yet?"

Javovich raised a thin eyebrow. "We do, and that was why I ordered that you should be roused."

"And?" Doltrane said, with a sharp intake of breath that was completely autonomic.

Fear, Katrina whispered. *It's called fear.*

"And you need to see this for yourself," Javovich said.

Doltrane pounded into the command centre, registering the fully manned terminals and primed weapons stations. He passed an eye over the holo-displays, watched the tightly disciplined crew work. All had been handpicked by him for this operation.

Meanwhile, the command centre's view-ports were open, displaying the near-vista of the Maelstrom. Although

stars twinkled and shone out there, even Doltrane recognised that there were not as many as there should
have been. The captain tried to dismiss that thought as
ridiculous—because such an evaluation surely could not
have been made with the naked eye—but it was perni-
cious and invasive.

Doltrane paused at the tactical display. The view-
ports could tell only part of the story, and the ship's
scopes had assembled the rest as a holographic projection, refined the unexplained horror of it all down to
green wireframe images. Sterile and simple.

"As I said," Javovich muttered, "I thought that you
would want to see this for yourself."

Sixteen stars had been extinguished in as little as a
month. Sixteen living, breathing stars. The classification and other technical data pertaining to them scrolled
across the holo, confirming that those suns had not died
naturally. Each was now in the throes of a fast and painful demise: burning up their cores, sheeting out vast
coronas of exotic energy, consuming what should've
been millennia of power in a galactic instant...

"Good morning, Captain," said Science Officer Heath,
standing at Doltrane's shoulder.

The old captain almost jumped at the voice. "Morning, *Herr* Heath."

"Welcome to the Gyre. It is wondrous, isn't it?"

The *Hannover*'s computer had plotted the anomaly
in great detail. The worlds that had once orbited those
dying stars had been rearranged. The dead nubs of rock
were in a pattern, swirling inwards: like a huge spiral.

"I do not find it so," Doltrane replied, still staring at
the images.

The crew were mostly Euro-Confed, and as many as
Doltrane could justify were from German home-colonies.

There was no prejudice here, but Doltrane liked to be surrounded by a crew that reminded him of home. Science Officer Heath stood out as the only American—specifically, of Proxima Centaurian descent—among the command cadre. He was also, by far, the most unpopular senior official aboard the *Hannover*: a man whom Doltrane had fought to have removed from the expedition, to no avail.

The captain slipped into his command throne, and Javovich took her seat as executive officer beside him.

"Latest readings to my terminal, if you will," Doltrane said.

"Aye, *Herr Kapitän*," Javovich replied.

"They are most interesting," Heath pitched in. "The stars in question, had they naturally aged, would surely have become neutron stars or black holes…" Heath shrugged. "This was a deliberate act." There was now a fixed grin on his thin lips. "*Someone* did this."

"Or something…" Doltrane said.

"Can you imagine the power required for such an accomplishment?" Heath muttered. He shook his head in amazement. "And at such speed…"

"That is what concerns me," Doltrane said.

It's as though those stars were murdered, Katrina taunted.

Doltrane ignored his dead wife and instead examined the starship's flight data. As he expected, the *Hannover* was currently cruising towards the heart of the Gyre, taking readings from whatever was attracting the planets. Doltrane felt that gnawing inside of him again, a black hole forming in his stomach.

You shouldn't have come here, Katrina whispered.

"You think I don't know that?" Doltrane hissed by way of reply.

"I'm sorry, *Herr Kapitän*?" Javovich asked.

"I wasn't talking to you, Lieutenant."

"Are you feeling well, *Herr Kapitän*?" Javovich said. "Perhaps I should summon medical attention—"

Her voice was swallowed by the wail of a siren. Doltrane caught Heath's face—fatted by a lifetime of work in the labs, of a career spent safely in the Core Systems—dropping.

"Holy Gaia..." someone exclaimed.

"Stations!" Doltrane yelled, superfluously.

The tactical display snapped into focus. Space seemed wrong: as though its established limits had somehow been warped, been modified. Scanner returns began to pour in, began to—inexplicably—confirm the existence of *the enigma*.

Then he saw it.

This was why the *Hannover* had been sent out here. This was the objective. So vast and alien that Doltrane couldn't look directly at it. His eyes couldn't comprehend the enormity of it.

"It's firing on us!" Javovich said. Then, because even under pressure she was still a damned good officer, into her console she declared: "All hands, brace! Enigma is conducting offensive action—"

"Null-shield up!" Doltrane shouted back, knowing that he was giving the command too late.

The *Hannover* shook.

"The shields aren't responding," someone replied. "Something inside the Gyre—or perhaps some weapons we haven't seen before—is interfering with our systems—"

Another impact cut off the response. This was stronger, and damage readings filled Doltrane's console: a hull breach in the aft, a vented fuel cell on the engineering deck.

There are people on those decks, Doltrane thought.

Correction: *There* had *been people on those decks*.

"Weapons systems online," another officer declared. "Taking defensive action."

The command centre shuddered around Doltrane. He saw the *Hannover*'s plasma warheads igniting in space ahead, saw exotic gases chain-react to the explosions. Maybe, just maybe, they had caught something, but Doltrane wasn't sure at all.

Javovich pulled him back into the room as another impact hit the *Hannover*. "*Herr Kapitän*! We must sound the mayday!"

Doltrane shook himself awake. "Execute that command."

There was a deafening boom as something inside the *Hannover*'s spaceframe gave way. The scent of fire carried on the air.

"Why is this happening?" Heath yelled, spinning past Doltrane, scrambling for purchase in the evaporating gravity. "It wasn't supposed to be active!"

"We were wrong," Javovich spat back.

"This ship is no longer viable," said the AI, voice carrying above the developing chaos aboard the battlecruiser. "All personnel are to take immediate safety precautions, and abandon this ship. Evacuation pods are available on all decks."

"Go!" Doltrane yelled to Javovich. His eyes were pinned to the view-port, at the shape forming there.

"I can't leave you, *Kapitän*!"

"That's an order," he replied, with no conviction at all.

"We have to send a transmission!" Heath said, snagging the corner of the tactical display: floating there. "Someone has to know what happened out here—"

"Just go!" Doltrane shouted. "It doesn't matter any more!"

Javovich grappled a console, hauling herself away from the command terminal at which Doltrane still sat.

Another impact shook the spaceframe.

The thing outside had grown in proportion, had become so massive that it seemed to absorb space around it...

"You were so right, Katrina," Doltrane whispered.

CHAPTER ONE

JACKALS AT BAY

I collapsed into the cot, panting hard, trying to catch my breath. A sheen of musky sweat—already cooling—had formed across my skin.

"Third time's a charm, eh?" Riggs said.

"You're getting better at it, is all I'll say."

Riggs tried to hug me from behind as though we were actual lovers. His body was warm and muscled, but I shrugged him off. We were just letting off steam before a drop, doing what needed to be done. There was no point in dressing it up

"Watch yourself," I said. "You need to be out of here in ten minutes."

"How do you handle *this*?" Riggs asked. He spoke Standard with an accented twang, being from Tau Ceti V, a descendant of North American colonists who had, generations back, claimed the planet as their own. "The waiting feels worse than the mission."

"It's your first combat operation," I said. "You're bound to feel a little nervous."

"Do you remember your first mission?"

"Yeah," I said, "but only just. It was a long time ago."

He paused, as though thinking this through, then asked, "Does it get any easier?"

"The hours before the drop are always the worst," I said. "It's best just not to think about it."

The waiting was well recognised as the worst part of any mission. I didn't want to go into it with Riggs, but believe me when I say that I've tried almost every technique in the book.

It basically boils down to two options.

Option One: Find a dark corner somewhere and sit it out. Even the smaller strikeships that the Alliance relies upon have private areas, away from prying eyes, away from the rest of your squad or the ship's crew. If you're determined, you'll find somewhere private enough and quiet enough to sit it out alone. But few troopers that I've known take this approach, because it rarely works. The Gaia-lovers seem to prefer this method; but then again, they're often fond of self-introspection, and that isn't me. Option One leads to anxiety, depression, and mental breakdown. There aren't many soldiers who want to fill the hours before death—even if it is only simulated—with soul-searching. Time slows to a trickle. Psychological time-dilation, or something like it. There's no drug that can touch that anxiety.

Riggs *was* a Gaia Cultist, for his sins, but I didn't think that explaining Option One was going to help him. No, Riggs wasn't an Option One sort of guy.

Option Two: Find something to fill the time. Exactly what you do is your choice; pretty much anything that'll take your mind off the job will suffice. This is what most troopers do. My personal preference—and I accept that it isn't for everyone—is hard physical labour. Anything that really gets the blood flowing is rigorous enough to shut down the neural pathways.

Which led to my current circumstances. An old

friend once taught me that the best exercise in the universe is that which you get between the sheets. So, in the hours before we made the drop to Daktar Outpost, I screwed Corporal Daneb Riggs' brains out. Not literally, you understand, because we were in our own bodies. I'm messed up, or so the psychtechs tell me, but I'm not *that* twisted.

"Where'd you get that?" Riggs asked me, probing the flesh of my left flank. His voice was still dopey as a result of post-coital hormones. "The scar, I mean."

I laid on my back, beside Riggs, and looked down at the white welt to the left of my stomach. Although the flesh-graft had taken well enough, the injury was still obvious; unless I paid a skintech for a patch, it always would be. There seemed little point in bothering with cosmetics while I was still a line trooper. Well-healed scars lined my stomach and chest—nothing to complain about, but reminders nonetheless. My body was a roadmap of my military service.

"Never you mind," I said. "It happened a long time ago." I pushed Riggs' hand away, irritated. "And I thought I made it clear that there would be no talking afterwards. That term of the arrangement is non-negotiable."

Riggs got like this after a session. He got chatty, and he got annoying. But as far as I was concerned, his job was done, and I was already feeling detachment from him. Almost as soon as the act was over, I started to feel jumpy again, felt my eyes unconsciously darting to my wrist-comp. The tiny cabin—stinking of sweat and sex—had started to press in around me.

I untangled myself from the bedsheets that were pooled at the foot of the cot. Pulled on a tanktop and walked to the view-port in the bulkhead. There was nothing to see out there except another anonymous sector of deep-space. We were in what had once been known as the Quarantine Zone—that vast tranch of deep-space that was the divide between us and the Krell Empire. A holo-display above the port read 1:57:03 UNTIL DROP. Less than two hours until we reached the assault point. Right now, the UAS *Bainbridge* was slowing down— her enormous sublight engines ensuring that when we reached the appointed coordinates, we would be travelling at just the right velocity. The starship's inertial damper field meant that I would never be able to physically feel the deceleration, but the mental weight was another matter.

"Get dressed," I said, matter-of-factly. "We've got work to do."

I tugged on the rest of my duty fatigues, pressed down the various holo-tabs on my uniform tunic. The identifier there read "210." Those numbers made me a long-termer of the Simulant Operations Programme— sufferer of an effective two hundred and ten simulated deaths.

"I want you down on the prep deck, overseeing simulant loading," I said, dropping into command-mode.

"The Jackals are primed and ready to drop," Riggs said. "The lifer is marking the suits, and I ordered Private Feng to check on the ammunition loads—"

"Feng's no good at that," I said. "You know that he can't be trusted."

"'Trusted'?"

"I didn't mean it like that," I corrected. "Just get dressed."

Riggs detected the change in my voice; he'd be an idiot not to. While he wasn't exactly the sharpest tool in the box, neither was he a fool.

"Affirmative," he said.

I watched as he put on his uniform. Riggs was tall and well-built, his chest a wall of muscle, neck almost as wide as my waist. Hair dark and short, nicely messy in a way that skirted military protocol. The tattoo of a winged planet on his left bicep indicated that he was a former Off-World Marine aviator, while the blue-and-green globe on his right marked him as a paid-up Gaia Cultist. The data-ports on his chest, shoulders, and neck stood out against his tanned skin, the flesh around them still raised. He looked new, and he looked young. Riggs hadn't yet been spat out by the war machine.

"So we're being deployed against the Black Spiral?" he asked, velcroing his tunic in place. The holo-identifier on his chest flashed "10"; and sickeningly enough, Riggs was the most experienced trooper on my team. "That's the scuttlebutt."

"Maybe," I said. "That's likely." I knew very little about the next operation, because that was how Captain Heinrich—the *Bainbridge*'s senior officer—liked to keep things. "It's need to know."

"And you don't need to know," Riggs said, nodding to himself. "Heinrich is such an asshole."

"Talk like that'll get you reprimanded, Corporal." I snapped my wrist-computer into place, the vambrace closing around my left wrist. "Same arrangement as before. Don't let the rest of the team know."

Riggs grinned. "So long as you don't either—"

The cabin lights dipped. Something clunked inside the ship. At about the same time, my wrist-comp chimed with an incoming priority communication: an officers-only alert.

EARLY DROP, it said.

The wrist-comp's small screen activated, and a head-and-shoulders image appeared there. A young woman with ginger hair pulled back from a heavily freckled face. Early twenties, with anxiety-filled eyes. She leaned close into the camera at her end of the connection. Sergeant Zoe Campbell, more commonly known as Zero.

"Lieutenant, ma'am," she babbled. "Do you copy?"

"I copy," I said.

"Where have you been? I've been trying to reach you for the last thirty minutes. Your communicator was off. I tried your cube, but that was set to private. I guess that I could've sent someone down there, but I know how you get before a drop and—"

"Whoa, whoa. Calm down, Zero. What's happening?"

Zero grimaced. "Captain Heinrich has authorised immediate military action on Daktar Outpost."

Zero was the squad's handler. She was already in the Sim Ops bay, and the image behind her showed a bank of operational simulator-tanks, assorted science officers tending them. It looked like the op was well underway rather than just commencing.

"Is Heinrich calling a briefing?" I asked, hustling Riggs to finish getting dressed, trying to keep him out of view of the wrist-comp's cam. I needed him gone from the room, pronto.

Zero shook her head. "Captain Heinrich says there isn't time. He's distributed a mission plan instead. I really should've sent someone down to fetch you…"

"Never mind about that now," I said. Talking over her was often the only way to deal with Zero's constant state of anxiety. "What's our tactical situation? Why the early drop?"

At that moment, a nasal siren sounded throughout the *Bainbridge*'s decks. Somewhere in the bowels of the ship were cutting, the gravity field fluctuating just a little to compensate.

The ship's AI began a looped message: "This is a general alert. All operators must immediately report to the Simulant Operations Centre. This is a general alert…"

I could already hear boots on deck around me, as the sixty qualified operators made haste to the Science Deck.

My data-ports—those bio-mechanical connections that would allow me to make transition into my simulant—were beginning to throb.

"You'd better get down here and skin up," Zero said, nodding at the simulator behind her. "Don't want to be late." Added: "Again…"

"I'm on it," I said, planting my feet in my boots. "Hold the fort."

Zero started to say something else, but before she could question me any further I terminated the communication.

"Game time, Corporal," I said to Riggs. "Look alive."

Dressed now, Riggs nodded and made for the hatch. We had this down to a T: if we left my quarters separately, it minimised the prospect of anyone realising what was happening between us.

"You're beautiful," he said. "You do know that, right?"

"You know that was the last time," I said, firmly.

"You said that *last* time…"

"Well this time I mean it, kemo sabe."

Riggs nodded, but that idiot grin remained plastered across his face. "See you down there, Jenkins," he said.

Here we go again, I thought. *New team. New threat. Same shit.*

The UAS *Bainbridge* was a big old strikeship, and had been patrolling the Quarantine Zone for several months. Sure, we'd met some trouble on Praidor V. And we'd almost been deployed on Triton IV to counter a pirate ring. But neither of those had been hot deployments, and Jenkins' Jackals hadn't earned a combat extraction yet. The three-month deployment had started to drag, and the *Bainbridge* was spoiling for a fight.

On Daktar Outpost, she was going to find it.

I met Zero at the threshold to the Simulant Operations Centre.

"Where have you been, ma'am?" she asked.

"Sort of busy," I said, pushing past other operators.

"Come on. The team's ready to skin."

I was two decades and then some older than Zero, but she was undeniably the squad's mother hen. Although she didn't like her nickname—"Zero"—I expected that during compulsory education the names had been even less kind. She had the bearing of science staff more than of a soldier, and in her current role she was a little of both.

The SOC was filled with troopers, all eager to claim their slice of the glory. The chamber was subdivided into a bay for each squad on the deployment, with a science and medical team attached to every squad. Our corner of the SOC was taken up by five simulator-tanks, each marked with the Jackal dog-head symbol and trooper designations. Operators from some simulant teams—the Hayden Walkers, Jay's Angels, Phoenix Squad—were already climbing into their simulators, handlers giving the countdown to transition. Cross-operation statistics were displayed on a monitor overhead. That was like a speedball stadium scoreboard, showing the number of effective transitions and extractions per operator: Phoenix Squad in pole position, the Jackals on the bottom rung.

Four troopers in states of undress stood in the Jackals' dedicated operations bay. As I approached, they fell into a ragged line and saluted disharmoniously. They were greener than green, the freshest meat on the ship.

"As you were, Jackals," I said, with as much gusto as I could manage.

"Yes, ma'am," the group chorused back. Riggs winked at me, though no one else noticed.

It was hard to feel any enthusiasm when I looked at the group of misfits that was apparently my squad.

How little they looked like soldiers in their real skins. Not one of the Jackals was over twenty-five years, Earth standard, but then there was very little standard about them. Only Novak was of Old Earth origin, and his roots were so far removed from my own that we barely shared any common ancestry. The rest were Core Worlders— drawn from those planets that had become the heart of the Alliance territory.

In a futile attempt to shake out of it, I ordered, "Let's get stripped and mounted in two; I want transition in three." I began to undress myself, and a medtech came to activate my tank. As I worked, I called over to Zero, "Give me a summary of the briefing packet. What's the op?"

"Command believes that it's going to be an effective drop," Zero said, reading from her data-slate.

"A *combat* drop?" Riggs asked. He was half-undressed now. The callsign JOCKEY was stencilled onto his tank—a particularly literal name the rest of the team had thought up as a result of his background as a rocket jockey. Yeah, it had to be said that the callsigns left something to be desired.

"There's a ninety per cent probability of combat," Zero said. "Daktar Outpost stopped reporting two days ago. The reason for this failure has since been confirmed as a hostile takeover by the Black Spiral."

"Told you so," Riggs said to me.

"There are no prizes for being an asshole," I said, cutting Riggs down. I didn't want the rest of the Jackals getting wind of any private conversations I might be having with Riggs. "Then what's our assignment, Zero?"

"Captain Heinrich has assigned us to scout duty," Zero said. Her use of the word "us" was telling. Although she wasn't going anywhere, Zero's command console— from which she would remotely handle the squad, and would be our eyes and ears—sat in the middle of our SOC bay.

"Scout duty *again*?" asked PFC Gabriella Lopez. "Our last scout drop was a complete waste of time."

"It was a waste of time for everyone, Lopez," I said. "No one got any action on Praidor."

"At least the rest of the strike team got to conduct search-and-seizure," Lopez said. "All we got to do was freeze our asses off. That's scout duty for you."

Lopez had been recruited into the Jackals straight out of Army basic training, assigned to the team by the battalion's supervising officer, Colonel Draven himself. Twenty-something, and from a lifetime of privilege on Proxima Centauri. The callsign SENATOR had been stencilled onto her tank. Lopez was far from happy about that, but like I said: these guys were literal in their descriptions, if nothing else.

"You think they trust you with real combat-suit?" asked Leon Novak. He spoke Standard with a blunt Slavic accent, forming the words slowly and with intent. "And what do you mean 'again'? You have no deaths yet."

"*Transitions*," Lopez said. "The word is transitions, idiot. And I have six, just like the rest of you."

"Am not idiot," Novak countered. "Do not call me that."

"I'd say that was a pretty accurate description," Riggs joined in. "But you're wrong about one thing, Lopez. I have ten, actually. Let's not forget that."

"Those weren't combat extractions," Feng added. "So they don't count."

"You're all idiots," Lopez said.

She stumbled out of her fatigues, putting a hand to her breasts as though we hadn't seen all this before. Lopez was slight-bodied and beautiful, with a perfect golden complexion that suggested her South American heritage, and long dark curly hair that I couldn't recall ever having seen out of place. All of that was ruined by her personality. Lopez had a hell of a mouth on her, and she was hard work.

Novak sneered. "Whatever. Deaths, transitions, extractions. Is all same."

A small disc-shaped security-drone, silver and chrome, a couple of feet across, hovered at his shoulder.

"*Security protocol suspected during operation,*" the drone bleated.

Novak's callsign was CONVICT, and he was just that: a convicted felon and a life-termer, given a chance of reprieve out in the void. I wasn't sure of exactly what Novak had done to earn his term, but I knew that it must've been *bad*. So many military bases had been hit during the Krell War that the Alliance had found themselves with a serious shortage of simulant operators. They'd trawled the prisons for compatible recruits, had offered prisoners the opportunity to commute life terms to a period of military service. That was how Novak had earned himself a lifetime spot on the Programme, each extraction knocking a little time off his sentence.

Novak was an enormous, bear-like man, shoulders dominated by a winged skull tattoo that stretched across the blades. The word BRATVA was stencilled beneath in faded blue ink. The choice of word was a particularly bad joke, because this man didn't even know the meaning of the word "brotherhood." He was nothing more than an outcast from the Siberian prison-hubs—a killer that even the Russian Federation had been glad to disown. Whatever Command thought they had made Leon Novak into, this was the real man.

"Can the negative jive," I said. "We've got a mission, and that's enough."

"But it's a shit detail," Lopez complained.

"Someone has to do it," I said, "and we're the greenest team on this bucket."

"I am *ready* for this…" Feng said, bouncing on the balls of his feet. "I am *so* ready for this!"

Only Feng had any real soldier in him, and he wasn't even a free citizen. Technically, Feng was former Asiatic Directorate property. South Asian features, smooth-skinned save for the data-ports, covered in barcodes and serial numbers—dark-eyed and -haired, muscled in an unnaturally precise way. He was a man-child: born into puberty, direct from the clone-vats. The location of his "birth" in the Asiatic Directorate—Crèche Three, Crema Base—was stamped across the small of his neck, like a brand. He had been liberated by Allied forces from the same planet, and in many ways he was a poster-child for the new Alliance—a super-state willing to forgive the transgressions of the Directorate's political and military elite, and to strive towards a lasting peace for all humanity.

But whatever Feng's political heritage, right now he just looked like an over-excited kid. Granted, a kid who was about to be skinned with the absolute best in bio-technology, and about to be equipped with cutting-edge arms and armour, but still a child. He bobbed anxiously, nervously, as he was readied to mount the tank.

"Cool your jets," I said to the bay but really directed at Feng. "Just keep calm and we'll get through this."

Medtechs descended on the squad, and began plugging us into the simulators. I let the staff work but I knew the drill in my sleep.

Zero read more from the briefing. "All entrances to the outpost are locked down. You'll be supported dropside by the fire teams and heavier combat-suits. I've uploaded your objectives to the suit network; you'll have them as soon as you make transition. The Jackals' destination is Tower Three, located on the outer aspect of the base."

"This is real, people," Feng said, pumping his fists. "This is happening!"

"I hear that," Riggs added.

Zero gave me a watery smile, and I felt a pang of disappointment for her. I knew that she wished it was her going into the tanks, but we both knew that would never be the case. Zero's name was a joke, because she was less than that. She was a "negative," her physiology incompatible with the implants necessary to operate a simulant. As she watched us going through the procedure, there was something almost melancholy about her expression.

"Command expects the Black Spiral to be present in significant number," Zero said, continuing to read. "Captain Heinrich says that this is going to be hot. You should be aware that this is a joint—"

"More sorry-ass terrorists," Feng said. "I am on this!"

"We're doing what we do when we have no one left to fight," Lopez said. "We're killing each other."

"Those daddy's words, or yours?" Novak said.

"Fuck you, lifer," Lopez responded.

Zero seemed more agitated than usual, which in her case was saying something. "Ma'am," she said, "I really need to make you aware that this is—"

"No time, Zero," I said. "Tell me when I get back."

A respirator was snapped over my face, and a tech popped a bead into my ear. All that was left to do now was to get into the tank. It was already half-filled with blue amniotic fluid, quickly warming. My own callsign, CALIFORNIA, was stenciled in bold letters onto the tank's outer canopy.

"All good?" a medico asked.

"Affirmative," I said. I turned to check on the rest of my squad. Thumbs up all round. "Seal us in. You've got the formalities, Zero."

"Copy that, ma'am," she said. "Transition commencing in three...two...one..."

CHAPTER TWO

ON THE READY LINE

Understand this: when you operate a simulant, you're only doing so by a highly complicated method of tele-presence. The neural-link between the simulant and the operator is a purely technical procedure. Your mind remains in your real body throughout.

The whole process is technical, scientific, safe. That's the theory, at least.

The reality is *very* different. Believe me: it sure feels like your mind has been ported directly into the simulant-body. It's damned *spiritual*, and there's no amount of scientific explanation that will make me think otherwise. You become that body, and you wear it like it's your own.

How does this miracle of science actually work? Good question, but it's one very few can answer. The simulant tech was developed at the end of the Krell War—when the fighting was thickest, when it looked like we might be wiped out by the fishes—and exactly how and why it works is still a closely guarded secret. "Alpha-classified" doesn't even come close to describing the level of security. I got drafted into the Simulant Operations

Programme a few years after its inception, but I quickly learnt that where the tech is concerned you just don't ask questions.

The Jackals' simulants were located in a specialised holding bay aboard the *Bainbridge*, and I made transition into a waiting body. Jesus Christo, I'd almost forgotten how good this felt. I was more alive than ever, skinned up in a state-of-the-art simulant-body. Physically the skin was factory-fresh, loaded with more hormones than a lifetime of sex with Riggs would ever produce. Mentally, I meshed with the body as though I'd been born into it.

Simulants were force-grown from the operator's body. Produced in specialised farms, they reflected the very pinnacle of Science Division's dark arts. Only compatible with the genetic template of the original operator-donor, each body was much improved over the original model. The simulant was a representation of the operator at his or her finest: a snapshot of the user caught in their prime, without the baggage that real skins carried. Just like the Army Sim Ops recruitment campaign says—JOIN SIM OPS TODAY, AND BE EVERYTHING THAT YOU CAN BE! So Lopez's face was plumper, lacking the skin-sculpt of her real body. Novak's features were spartan without his gang tattoos, and so on.

"Transition confirmed," I declared into the communicator.

"Solid copy," Zero said back to me. "Jackals are operational."

My sim was already armed and armoured—the science team had taken care of that. I wore a reconnaissance-class powered suit, and the onboard AI programme recognised successful transition. WELCOME, the armour said. PREPARE TO ASSUME MANUAL CONTROL. The magnetic clamps holding the armour in place disengaged. I landed on the deck with a rumble, testing the suit's shock absorbers.

"You like the new armour?" Zero said.

"I'd prefer something heavier," I replied, flexing my arms, "but it's nice. A girl can't have everything."

Recon-suits were the lightest class of armour used by line simulant teams, and as a result they were sometimes unfairly referred to as "training suits."

"Your AI has made successful uplink to the battle-net," said Zero.

"Solid copy."

The recon-suit carried a complex sensor and intelligence suite, and as my armour came online an avalanche of data flooded the interior of my face-plate. The heads-up display—the HUD—filled with glowing holographics, info-streams, the ever-present bio-scanner. The data-flow gradually sank into the background, became a comforting undercurrent of battlefield noise.

That wasn't so for everyone. The Jackals were struggling to comprehend the wealth of information. Confused faces appeared behind their semi-mirrored visors.

"Cancel what you don't need," I said, nodding my armoured head. "You can always bring up new feeds once we're dirtside."

"This is more like it," Feng said, rolling his shoulders in the armour. "I am *so* ready for this!"

"Now you feel like a solider, yes?" Novak said.

"Anyone would feel like a soldier in one of these things…" Lopez said. In other circumstances, the look of amazement on her face would have been funny.

"Just don't let it go to your head, people," I ordered.

The hangar was filled with troopers, and the sound of boots on the deck, moving through the deployment hatch, was deafening. Most of the other teams were wearing the heavy shit: combat-suits employed by the frontal attack teams. Those were adorned with person-alised insignia, with death motifs and callsigns. Even though nothing that went down in a drop came back up, this was ritual—and if there's one thing that simulant operators cling to, it's ritual. As I stared down at my own suit, I realised that it was completely untouched. None of the Jackals' armour had been branded with insignia.

"Why aren't our suits marked up?" I asked.

"I assigned the task to Novak, ma'am," Riggs said.

Novak sucked his teeth. "Is not a soldier's job."

"A 'soldier's job' is whatever I tell you to do, and—" Riggs started.

"This is a bad sign," Lopez said. "We can't make the drop in unmarked suits!"

"Again, Senator, how would you know?" Novak said. "Is first combat drop, yes?"

Troopers from other squads passed us, making snide remarks on the open comms band.

"Watch it, rookies!"

"Fuck, you guys are already wasted."

"Shame about the new suits…"

"Jesus, Private Novak," I said. "Riggs is corporal. Like he says: when he tells you to do something, you do it."

Novak sort of shrugged in his armour, the servomo-tors humming as he moved.

"Maybe you should mark his record, ma'am," Riggs said. "Put some more time on his clock."

Riggs bumped shoulders with Novak, and the big Russian bumped back. Their armour produced a star-tling crash as shoulder-guards clashed. Inside a simulant and full armour, Novak was frighteningly large. Mon-strous, even. "Intimidating" was an understatement.

"Cut that out," I said, frowning at the pair. "There's

no time to do anything about the suits now, but I don't want this happening again. Just focus on the job."

Riggs wouldn't let it go. "You want to watch it, lifer. I could always send a report to the Parole Board myself."

"Fuck you," Novak drawled, in his usual semi-broken Standard, his accent making the words come out nasal. "You think I care about how long I serve?"

"Hey Novak," said Lopez, "are those blades regulation?"

The convict had at least six sheathes strapped across the plates of his armour—on his legs, his chest, even his arms. Each carried a knife of a varying length and size, both military-grade and more improvised weapons. I suspected that Novak knew how to use every one of them.

"What do you think?" he said, slowly.

Lopez huffed and pulled a face. "I think that you're an asshole, and I think that the Alliance should fire your Christo-damned corpse into the next available star," she said. "I notice that you had time to find those blades, when you should've been marking up the suits."

"Can it!" I said. "Officer on the deck."

"And what an officer…" Feng said, but fell silent as I scowled at him.

Captain Peter Heinrich—commanding officer of the strike contingent aboard the UAS *Bainbridge*—prowled an overhead gantry, watching the squads assemble far below. He was, as of now, the only real skin in the hangar bay: surrounded by tons of manufactured simulant skins. Was there something weird about the commanding officer of a simulant strike team being non-operational, incapable of using a sim? I certainly thought so.

"On the ready line!" he yelled. "That's it, people: form up, form up!"

Each five-man squad assembled in formation—just how Heinrich liked them—and occupied the better part of the *Bainbridge*'s hangar deck. Although Heinrich's gaze fell across every team on the deck, I felt its heat linger on us. The Jackals were at the back of the hangar, last in row. I looked down the line: even in simulants, they looked like four sorry sons of bitches.

"You're running out of formation, Jackals!" he shouted. "Get it sorted and fall in!"

"Fucking hell, people," I said, over my Jackals' closed communications channel. "How many times do we have to practise this shit?"

"By the way," Zero said, breaking in on the comms network, "Captain Heinrich noted that you were late to the bay. He's keeping a record of your attendance times."

So far as I was aware, Heinrich had never actually been in a combat zone, and he'd secured his role as CO through a combination of political wrangling and ass-kissing. Command had a way of doing that: assigning those with the least experience to the most important jobs. Heinrich's shipboard uniform was replete with medals for being "employee of the month" and "most annoying REMF." He was surrounded by a cadre of subordinate officers. They were all skinned and wearing combat-suits, keeping a tight cordon round the captain like the security detail of some particularly important diplomat.

"Listen up!" Heinrich barked. "This is not a drill, and you are not conducting a training exercise!"

"Someone ought to tell Jenkins that," one of the other veteran officers further down the line said over the general squad-to-squad channel. Tinny laughs filtered over the network.

"Fuck you guys," I said, eyes forward on Heinrich.

His bronzed brow creased again. Like Lopez, he was a Proximan, and rumour had it his background was almost as privileged. Heinrich shook his head, as though he couldn't even be bothered to rebuke me any more.

"All officers have been given an appropriate briefing package," he said, "but for those of us requiring the headlines, this is how it's going to go down."

The inside of my face-plate illuminated with graphics. The *Bainbridge* was fast approaching Daktar Outpost. The space station appeared as a glowing red dot on the screen, in a close orbit around the Shard Gate at Daktar 436.

"Daktar Outpost is a scientific research station," Heinrich continued. "Staffed by civilians, on last headcount it housed a hundred and six personnel. That was until two days ago, when the outpost stopped reporting. As of oh-six-hundred hours this morning, the station's AI reports that there are less than fifty personnel left on-base. The organisation known as the Black Spiral has since confirmed responsibility for a station takeover. The *Bainbridge* happened to be the closest Alliance Army asset, which explains our involvement. Just your luck, troopers."

To my left, Captain Ving raised an armoured glove in the air as though we were in a classroom.

"Yes, Captain?" Heinrich said, playing the role of patient teacher.

"Are we expecting hostages down there, sir?" Ving asked.

Ving was commanding officer of Phoenix Squad. His callsign was PHOENIXIAN, and he was an asshole. He currently held the record for the number of transitions across the Army Sim Ops Programme, and he also happened to be one of Heinrich's favourites.

Continuing the show, Heinrich gave a pantomime scowl. I suspected that Ving was a plant, that his question had been deliberately staged.

"Good question," Heinrich said. "The Black Spiral is holding the remaining station staff hostage, and has made certain demands as a condition of their release." Heinrich paused, and let that sink in, before continuing: "Among the group are a number of Alliance military officers."

There were mutters from the sim squads, the rattle of weapons against armour. The force of Heinrich's little speech might've been lost on me, but it had certainly had a stirring effect on some of the other veteran officers.

"Which begs the question," Riggs whispered over the comms channel, "who are these officers, and what exactly were they doing on a civilian outpost?"

"Cut it out," I said, glaring sideways at the corporal.

"We don't negotiate with terrorists," Captain Heinrich said, jabbing his finger in the air to punctuate each word. "It's not the Alliance way, and it sure as hell isn't the Army way. So this operation is simple. We drop to the station, and we secure it. Mission objectives have been uploaded to your suits." He pressed his hands into the safety rail of the gantry, leaned over into the bay. "Priority objectives are to secure the Shard Gate, and get the hostages out alive. Any questions?"

For a heart-stopping moment, I thought that one of the Jackals might have something to say, but to my relief they remained silent. Heinrich gave a self-satisfied nod from his ivory tower.

"Good. I want this done smoothly, and I want this done fast. Get to it."

There was a wash of commands over the shared comms-net, but mostly I heard Zero's voice: "Mission is a go. Lynx attack ships are ready for boarding."

Lynx ships sat in neat rows on the hangar's apron—a half-dozen assault transports. Haunched and armoured, stubby wings deployed, their cargo ramps open. Each squad jogged to their assigned transport. The Jackals behind me, I hustled into the waiting crew cabin of LYNX 06, our ship for the operation.

As I snapped the safety harness into place, my communicator chimed. PRIVATE COMM FROM CAPTAIN HEINRICH, the HUD said. I had no choice but to answer.

"Yes, sir."

"You're a damned disgrace, Lieutenant," Heinrich said, without preamble. "That outfit of yours is laughable."

"Yes, sir," I said. It was difficult to argue with him on that one. "Understood."

"When you get back from this op," he muttered, "I want to see you."

"Yes, sir."

The comms link cut, and overhead the amber warning strobe turned green—indicating imminent drop. The Lynx's cargo ramp slid shut, and we were sealed inside the hold.

"Earth's luck," Zero said.

"I'd prefer something better than that," I replied.

"From the look of these near-space scans," Zero said, "you're going to need it…"

"Thanks for the vote of confidence, Zero," I said. "California out."

"Lock in, people," Riggs said.

I heard the Lynx's two-man aerospace crew canting back orders to one another from the cockpit. No matter what Heinrich wanted to talk to me about, it could wait. I was about to do what I loved, and my blood had started to sizzle with excitement.

"Permission to launch in three…two…one…" came the voice of Navy Command.

The slow trickle of adrenaline had started. My breathing had become more intense, heartbeat increasing just ever so slightly.

It's been too long since I've felt this way, I thought.

"We're a go," the Lynx's pilot declared. "Hold tight back there."

The attack ship fired from the belly of the *Bainbridge* like a bullet from a gun, gaining speed as it hit the mothership's mag-rails, thrusters igniting. Multiple gravities pinned me to my seat.

"We're clear," the pilot declared. "Dropping to Daktar."

Launch diagnostics fluttered across my HUD, but I mainly ignored those. The suit could also read my squad's condition-status and that was of a lot more interest.

Of course, the Jackals had trained for this. No matter where they had come from, they were now Alliance Army. All soldiers had to complete Basic—Initial Entry Training, better known since the start of time as "boot camp"—and the Jackals were no different. They'd all done hostile-environment and hot-deployment courses, with varying degrees of success. They were also members of the Simulant Operations Programme, which made them the best that the Alliance Army could offer. The Sim Ops version of Advanced Infantry Training required several hundred hours of immersive VR interaction, in an effort to acclimatise operators to simulated death: far and above what was expected of a typical Army grunt.

But none of that made them ready. The drop to Daktar was *real*.

The Jackals were struggling, and their bio-signs showed it. Heartbeats and respiratory levels fluctuated wildly. The recon-suit was equipped with an onboard medical-suite, which would automatically administer combat-enhancing drugs to keep the wearer at peak performance, but even those weren't enough. Feng looked like he might stop breathing at any moment, and Lopez's pulse was so erratic that she was verging on cardiac arrest. Riggs, who had racked up dozens of drops as a Marine aviator, was shaking inside his armour; whatever his previous training, this experience was something different and so much worse.

Only Novak seemed untouched by the proceedings. He sat across from me, his pointed jaw set, face dancing with waves of kinetic force.

"Is good launch, yes?" he asked.

He looked far more menacing without the security-drone at his shoulder, and the glow cast by the ship's interior consoles made his face appear almost demonic. No one bothered to answer him.

I opened the command stream between my sim and my recon-suit. The armour used by Sim Ops was top-end shit; while it's not quite telepathic, it's pretty close. I could control several of my suit's facilities just through the neural-link, and I wanted to get a proper look at our destination. I thought-commanded my recon-suit to open the Lynx's external camera feeds.

A grainy image appeared on the interior of my HUD. Daktar 436 was a grey and featureless C-type asteroid, one of a few thousand in this sector, caught in the gravitational pull of Daktar Star. Data on the objective filled my HUD: the combined intelligence pool of all Alliance assets that were currently operating in the area. There was a sudden flash of light across the display.

"What's that, ma'am?" Lopez asked, peering at the image on her own HUD.

"A null-shield," I said. Frowned. "And it looks functional."

The null-shield was a ubiquitous piece of Alliance

engineering: a projected anti-energy field, designed to repel incoming weapons fire. The shield was particularly effective at dispersing laser-based weapons, but in a pinch could be deployed against railgun and flak munitions as well.

"Shouldn't that be turned off?" Lopez asked.

"Don't ask me," I said. "I'm not in charge." But that development was worrying, and Lopez had a point. I pulled up the briefing packet, and rapidly absorbed the contents via my suit's neural-link. Just another added advantage of being in a simulated skin. "Intel insists that they managed to switch off the station's defences on the approach. The base was equipped with a Class Three null-shield, and a full anti-aerospace defensive array."

"Is getting interesting, yes?" Novak said.

"Can we fly through the shield?" Lopez muttered.

"You worried we're going to get wasted by a damned null-shield?" Riggs asked, sighing. "Course we can fly through it. The shield won't be strong enough to repel something this big—"

"No, but they've hacked the defence array," said Feng, "and that will definitely be able to stop us..."

There were laser batteries mounted across the outpost, and they swivelled to track incoming targets from every angle. Feng was right: the Black Spiral had somehow hacked the outpost's automated defence systems. Alongside the Lynx attack ships, the *Bainbridge* had also launched her entire complement of robot fighters—automated drone-ships, light assault boats that carried limited offensive weaponry—at the outpost. The fighters were already meeting resistance, becoming tiny but brilliant stars as they reached the perimeter of Daktar's defence grid, within range of the laser batteries.

"Nothing is getting within landing range," Lopez said.

At the centre of the matrix of light sat a small, irregularly shaped asteroid—grey and dusted, honeycombed in places—moving so slowly that to the naked eye its spin was imperceptible. Closing at high speed, I could make out a trio of landing spires on the asteroid's surface. Those were Towers One, Two and Three: the strike team's primary entry points. The Towers were actually docking platforms, designed so that each could accommodate a dozen or more starships.

"Has anyone made it down so far?" Feng asked, almost superfluously. His early enthusiasm for the mission was quickly waning, replaced by grim realisation that all we could expect to find on Daktar was an early death.

"No," I said, hurriedly checking the strikeforce shared-intel pool. "It doesn't look that way…"

Just then, I received a battle-space update. Two teams had already made extraction: that is, the simulants had "died," and the operators made the jump back to their real bodies aboard the *Bainbridge*. Sure, the strikeship carried a stock of replacement sims, and more could be launched, but we only had so many transports, and those Lynxes were wasted. This was also a time-sensitive operation; unless the situation changed, those teams were as good as out of the fight. Bright flashes marked the demise of two more simulant squads—their transports destroyed before they could even make planetfall. Rapidly cooling debris showered near-space, and the nearest attack ships and robot fighters dodged to avoid being hulled.

The communicator bead in my ear chimed with an incoming message.

"This is *Bainbridge* Command," said a familiar voice: Heinrich. He liked to make these addresses himself, micromanaging the activities of every simulant squad under his command. "All squads should be aware that the area is hot. Expect heavy resistance until you breach the station."

"Man can stop stating obvious," Novak said, rolling his eyes. "Is FUBAR, yes?"

"The situation on the ground is fluid," Heinrich said. "Tactical objectives are currently being updated. Things are worse than we thought. It goes without saying that the Gate cannot be allowed to fall into enemy hands."

The Lynx's camera system glitched as it focused on the Shard Gate, straining to comprehend that area of non-reality beyond Daktar Outpost. Inactive at present, the Gate's interior was a deep bluish colouration: emptied of stars, hard light dancing around its edges. Even inert, the Gate still put out a constant wave of exotic energy.

"And we most definitely cannot have that..." Riggs said, mimicking the timbre of Heinrich's voice.

At its most basic, each Gate was a wormhole: a tunnel connecting two distant points in time-space. The Gates were abandoned alien technology, made by the Shard—a machine-species that had been largely absent from this sector of the Milky Way for the last few millennia. The Gates had the potential to revolutionise space travel, offering instantaneous transport across the Shard Network. Many had been mapped, made safe and predictable, but just as many remained unknown quantities. I could well see why Command didn't want the Black Spiral commandeering an operational Shard Gate...

I received a further battle-space update as another

transport exploded behind us. More simulant teams had extracted, with over half of the original strike team now neutralised. Our ship vibrated, shook; debris smashed into the flank.

"Fuck!" Lopez screamed. "We're hit."

Up front, the anonymous pilot—a simulant just like the rest of us—began shouting coordinates into his communicator. The co-pilot activated weapons systems, and flares of light sprang across the ship's flight path.

"Deploying counter-measures," she declared. "Tracking multiple threats!"

"Ease up," Riggs moaned. "Try pulling back on the acceleration—"

"You're going to have to bail out," the pilot yelled to me, plugging a respirator over his lower face. "I can't compensate for this sort of damage."

"But we're running scout duty!" Lopez argued. "We're supposed to land on the other side of the outpost!"

The irony that Lopez, just a few minutes ago, had been complaining about assignment to scout duty wasn't lost on me, but now wasn't the time to make a thing of it.

"Try telling *them* that!" the co-pilot shouted back, waving at the cockpit screens. "For terrorists, they sure know how to—"

Before she could finish the sentence, a beam of hard light slashed through the armourglass of the Lynx's cockpit. Had to be the laser array. The beam punched the co-pilot, went through her seat and then the ship's flank.

"Check your suits are sealed!" I ordered.

My body was tugged by escaping atmosphere, my recon-suit bucking against the safety harness.

"We're going down," the pilot declared. "This is Lynx Six, preparing for extraction—"

The view through the cockpit windshield span and span and span.

"Ready for impact," I said. "This is about to get real."

"You heard her," Riggs said to the rest of the team. "Get ready to bounce."

Jinking past laser fire, amid a zero-gravity storm of shrapnel and debris, the Lynx fell to the waiting asteroid.

CHAPTER THREE

DAKTAR OUTPOST

There are, contrary to popular belief, certain advantages to crash-landing in a vacuum. Sure, it's brutal, and if you want to be picky about it there's a very high probability that you won't be walking away from the mess that follows.

But while it isn't something I'd recommend, it also has benefits.

Namely, shit doesn't burn. And that was probably what saved us as the Lynx went down.

The pilots were both wearing simulants. Those skins are specially adapted, specifically designed to fly ships or die trying. The Aerospace Force uses next-generation simulants, which aren't anywhere near as durable as combat skins, but they sure are *fast*. Their senses are extreme: needle-sharp.

The co-pilot had extracted—there was no way she was coming back from full-vaporisation via a laser beam—but the pilot must've taken evasive action at the last moment, because he managed to pull up the Lynx's nose just before impact. That was a selfless but final act: in the split second that followed the manoeuvre, part of the cockpit's frame gave way and sheared the pilot in two, triggering immediate extraction. The Lynx—now pilotless—grazed a kilometre-long furrow into the rock.

Less than two seconds later, it came to a stop. Surrounded by a plume of grey surface dust: temporary cover for the downed ship.

It took me another second or so to get my jumbled thoughts in order.

"Is good landing, yes?" Novak growled over the squad's communication channel.

"Is good landing," I said back, on autopilot. The rational part of my brain was having some difficulty accepting that I was still alive.

"We are not dead, yes?" Novak said. "Is good."

"I've survived worse," I said.

My simulated body sagged in the safety harness, forehead pressed against the inside of my helmet. The diagnostics on my suit kicked in immediately and my medi-suite took care of any minor injuries I'd suffered. The medical tech was top-quality combat-gear, and my armour knew exactly when to give me uppers or downers. Had I been in my real body, I'd probably be a shaking mess right now, but inside the sim it was a different story. I felt the drugs hitting my system hard and fast, and threw off the vestiges of unconsciousness.

The cabin was drenched in red light from a security lamp set in the deckhead. Around me, the team were stirring in harnesses, bobbing in the micro-G of the asteroid's local gravity. The attack ship had landed at a forty-five-degree angle, the deck listing uncomfortably.

"Everyone alive?" I asked.

"Christo..." Riggs said. "I think I should've done the flying."

Another voice broke in on the comms. Lopez. Screaming. "I'm trapped!"

I thought-ordered the suit: UPPERS. IMMEDIATE.

Feng lurched out of his seat, crossed my vision. Full of twitchy movements. "I'll help."

Lopez's legs were caught beneath a weapons locker that had fallen from the deckhead, but as Feng pulled the crates clear it became obvious that she wasn't seriously injured. Riggs went to help, and the debris was quickly cleared. Then the uppers hit Lopez's bloodstream, and her breathing calmed over the comms channel. Her vitals stabilised too.

"I—I thought that I was breached," she stammered.

"Stay with it, kemo sabe," I said. "We've a long way to go yet."

My HUD rebooted and gave me a summary of our situation. SQUAD COMBAT-CAPABLE, it told me. The Jackals were—incredibly—in one piece.

"Combat-capable means mission-capable," I said to myself, unclipping the safety harness. "Up and out, everyone! Riggs, distribute weapons."

Riggs busted open the weapons locker, and tossed shotguns across the cabin. I scooped an A600 as it drifted past. It was a nice weapon: a tactical combat shotgun, cleared for use in a pressurised environment. Command wanted the Daktar Outpost intact, and breaching the outer hull with a plasma pulse wasn't compatible with that objective, so we'd been equipped with shotguns and fragmenting anti-personnel rounds.

"We need to get out of here," Feng said. "I'm getting readings across the board: the boat's drive is going to spill any minute."

He was poised at the cockpit door. It was open, and the two Aerospace Force pilots were dashed across the console: little more than red stains in flight-suits.

Lopez grimaced. "Look at the state of them."

"Someone want to check if Lopez shit herself on the way down?" Novak asked.

Riggs nodded. "Suits are sealed, keeps the smell in…"

"Fuck you," Lopez said. "Both of you."

"Any time, Senator," Novak said.

"Stow it," I said. "The dead don't care, Lopez, and unless you want to end up like them we need to get out of here. Riggs, do your job and get this sorry outfit into shape."

"Understood," Riggs said. "Novak! Get that hatch open, and Lopez: you cover him."

The Russian kicked at the Lynx's rear access hatch. The recon-suits carried manpower amplifiers that augmented the simulant's physical strength. While the man-amp wasn't comparable to that found on a suit of full combat-armour, it was strong enough. The ramp gave way with ease, revealed a stretch of stark, open landscape beyond.

"Form up on me," I ordered, bouncing out of the wreckage. "We need to get clear of the boat!"

Feng tumbled down the ramp, then froze, shotgun up, face scanning the horizon.

"Was it supposed to be like this?" he asked. "Place is a fucking warzone!"

The others paused as well.

It was hard not to be impressed by the sight. In a vast pyrotechnics display, the defence grid was making short work of the *Bainbridge*'s fleet, reducing the fighters and attack ships to molten slag. Like a deadly rain, pieces of debris flashed across the asteroid's face, appearing deceptively close to our position. This op was going south, and fast.

The Jackals scrambled across the rock. We'd dropped way off course, and our objective, Tower Three, was a good distance from our location. I needed new orders.

"*Bainbridge* in the blind," I said, talking as I bounced. "*Bainbridge* in the blind! Requesting orders. Do you copy?"

COMMUNICATION LINK UNAVAILABLE, my suit insisted. PLEASE RE-TRY LATER. I cycled through the available comms bands, trying to make contact with the rest of the strike force, but there was no response at all.

"No one can hear us," Feng said. He panted as he moved. "We're on our own down here."

"Is the *Bainbridge* safe?" Lopez asked. She flinched every time something cooked off above us. "Our bodies are on that ship!"

"Heinrich's up there," I said. "And we're still moving, aren't we? If the *Bainbridge* gets hit, we'll know it."

"Will hardly feel a thing," Novak taunted.

"Incoming!" Riggs interrupted.

The rock face beside him exploded, and reflexively I went to ground. The rest of the squad did the same, scramble-rolling in micro-G. Their response was hardly textbook, but at least no one died in the second that passed.

"Where'd that come from?" Lopez said, craning her neck to scan the horizon.

"Just stay down," I said. "Do as I tell you."

The asteroid had been worn smooth by millennia in space, and surface cover was limited to vague banks and troughs. The jumble of metallic towers and modules that made up Daktar Outpost appeared in the distance. Glowing icons indicated Tower Three, our objective, and from there several ruby-red lights shone.

"Snipers!" Feng yelled. "They've got snipers!"

More laser fire sliced the area.

"Activate stealth-fields," I ordered.

The recon-suits were equipped with an active camo package: a multi-sensory disruption field that was capable of avoiding detection by most known methods. Instantly, each of the Jackals became indistinct, their outlines invisible except for aura-flags on my HUD. Sinks in the backpack units locked in heat signatures, made us invisible to even infrared.

"Hold position," I said.

My suit tracked an explosive shell to my left, thrown in an almost lazy arc. A second after the warning, it hit the asteroid's surface. The impact threw up a column of dust and shrapnel.

"Right flank, double-time," I said. "Use your EVAMPs."

I got to my feet, and fired my EVAMP—extra-vehicular mobility pack—in a short burst. I was momentarily airborne, cruising the face of the asteroid, but also invisible thanks to the camo field. I landed. Rolled sideways, hugged the ground. The Jackals copied me, managing to outrun the detonation of another mortar shell, though only just.

"The snipers are using the mortars as range finders," Feng said.

"Good tactic," Riggs agreed. "It's what I'd do."

"Yeah, right," Lopez said.

I counted at least six targets on Tower Three. The tangos were pinning us down, using mortar emplacements from somewhere inside the outpost. The foot of Tower Three, where we were supposed to be going, was well-covered by multiple arcs of fire. It was a literal killzone.

"Have to think of another way in..." I whispered to myself. Before I'd properly formulated a plan, there was a brilliant bloom of light from the direction in which we'd come. The squad dropped low, their camo fluctuating to mimic the surroundings. New data flushed my HUD.

"That was Lynx Six," I said. "Cooking off."

"So?" Lopez asked.

Feng grimaced. "So, that means the Spiral will know where to find us, and they'll send troops."

I considered our options. The ground around us was already scored with mortar rounds and sniper shots. Our position was fast becoming untenable. I looked over the brow of the nearest undulation and could see that less than two hundred metres ahead there was an access point to Tower One.

"What're your orders, ma'am?" Riggs asked.

I made the call. There wasn't much of a choice here: either die trying to execute Heinrich's damned mission plan by moving on Tower Three, or make for Tower One and at least take down some tangos in the process.

"Change of plan," I said. "We're moving on that lock, and we're doing it now."

"But that's Tower One," Lopez argued. "Our objective was supposed to be Tower Three..."

"Tower One is nearest," I said, "so that's where we're going."

"But—" she started.

"Shut that shit down, Lopez. Tower One is our new objective."

Lopez went silent. Her disobedience wasn't acceptable, and I couldn't have her questioning orders out here: extraction could come at any second.

"Understood, Private?" I asked.

Lopez pursed her lips, but grudgingly said, "Affirmative."

I nodded. "I want you all to follow me. Short bursts on the EVAMPs. Try to stay low."

Two jumps later, chased by mortars and sniper fire, we reached the airlock. It was a large, circular portal, probably made to manually dock ground vehicles.

"A breaching charge to the seam would get us in,"

Riggs said, "but there are bio-signs on the other side of that lock."

I had my bio-scanner running on passive in a sub-window on my HUD. The scanner's sensor grid probed a hundred metres in every direction, capable of detecting all kinds of biological life-signs. It indicated several hot signals beyond the lock.

"Could be civilians," Riggs offered.

The scanner couldn't differentiate between good and bad guys, but I shrugged—a gesture that I doubted the rest of the team could see, given the activated camo package. "Just as likely to be the Black Spiral. They have control of the station."

"Only one way to find out," Novak suggested.

"Lopez, you're up," I said, nodding at her. "Put a breaching charge on the door seam: set it with a five-second delay."

"Copy that."

Lopez moved on the door, grasping the station's hull for limited purchase. She unstrapped a demo-charge—specifically made for breaching the thick, armour-plated hulls of space stations and starships—from her recon-suit. Slammed the mag-lock into place: activity light green.

A readout on my HUD indicated that Lopez's heart-beat had increased significantly, verging on hysteria. I caught her glove. Explosions above and around us reflected off her imperfect outline.

"Ease up a little," I said. "Keep cool and we all come out of this as heroes."

"I'm fine," she insisted. "It's all good. Honest."

"Stay that way, soldier."

"Hell, maybe Heinrich'll even give us a slap on the back..." Riggs said.

"I wouldn't go that far," I replied, with a raised eyebrow. "Are the rest of you ready for this?"

"As we'll ever be," Feng said.

I checked the arming stud on my shotgun. A reticule hovered on my HUD, superimposed onto the image outside. Suit and shotgun were slaved, working in unison.

"Right, let's do it. Lopez, activate the charge. Feng, Riggs: cover the hatch. Novak: ready to clear the chamber on the other side."

Novak's shotgun was up and aimed at the circular hatch. "Just say word."

"Go."

"Charge armed," Lopez said. She jumped back from the hatch, the rest of the Jackals falling into position.

The warning panel on the breaching charge turned amber.

"Don't bug out on me," I whispered over the comm.

"Wouldn't dream of it," Riggs replied.

The charge activator flashed red.

The explosive detonated and the seam breached. The lock gave way to decompression, a localised hurricane of debris and dust temporarily clouding my sensor-suite. Atmosphere vented from inside.

The gunfire started a heartbeat later, and we got our first glimpse of the Black Spiral.

Who were the Black Spiral?

They're murderers. Dissidents. Terrorists.

That was what the Alliance media called them. Maybe they were all of those things, maybe they were none, but those were just labels. Given that the Spiral's objectives remained unknown, the descriptions felt strangely inadequate. The organisation—if it could really be called that—had no specific agenda or manifesto.

The Spiral had appeared on a dozen planets and stations, spreading chaos in its wake, almost overnight. From the Core Systems to the Outer Rim, the Spiral made its presence known. Rather than one thing, it was many. The Church of the Singularity, the Iron Fist, the Frontier Independence Front: all of them had at one time or another declared affiliation with the Spiral. Each of those organisations was a threat in its own right—membership banned individually in the majority of Alliance territories—but together? Now that was something. It had been a long time since the Alliance had experienced terror on this scale.

Although I'd never fought them directly, I had been witness to the mess that the Black Spiral left behind. The bodies. The carnage. The pointless destruction. There were very few Alliance citizens who hadn't seen the newsfeeds.

Six months ago, they'd bombed Qua Remus: killed sixteen hundred civilians during a peace rally. Not long after that, the Spiral destroyed an Arab Freeworld colony ship en route to the Outer Colonies. Another two thousand civvies wasted. Most recently, the Spiral had attempted to poison Centauri Colony's water supply—an act that would've led to millions of deaths, had it been successful. There was no apparent rhyme or reason to the attacks. Nowhere was safe—anywhere and anyone in the Alliance was a target. American, Euro-Confed, African Union, Pan Pacific Compact. Hell, they'd even conducted the occasional raid on former Asiatic Directorate holdings.

When they struck, they looted. They usually took hostages, and often made demands. Those were rarely made public, but rumours abound that they wanted starships, materiel, and personnel.

Few had been captured alive, because most Spiral members would rather face the gun than an Alliance interrogation booth. But those who had been captured? They usually turned out to be nobodies. A broad cross-section of the Alliance citizenry, the sort of people that made up the bulk of a planet's population, that numbered billions across Allied space. Their only unifying feature was that each carried a burning sense of disaffection, so strong that it was capable of turning them against the very structures that had created them.

So, yes, the Spiral were murderers and terrorists.

But more than that: they were us. And right now, that made them the most dangerous thing in the universe.

"Covering fire, on me."

I tagged ten hostiles inside the airlock, hunkered down behind cargo crates and derelict vehicles. It took me a split second to assess the facts.

Lightly armoured targets.
Likely using stolen tech.
Probably shaken by the hull breach.

Inside a simulant, my time-perception and hand-eye coordination were vastly improved. Making the most of the sim's improved neural matrix, I moved fast. Vaulting into the lock, I swept the interior with my shotgun.

Made for use in vacuum, the A600 combat shotgun was fully automatic and drum-fed. It carried an inbuilt stabiliser, which made it almost recoilless: a perfect choice for a micro-G firefight. I caught a tango in the chest, and he or she—gender was pretty hard to determine from what was left—was thrown right across the chamber by the force of the impact. The next shell smoothly loaded and I fired again and again, frag rounds shredding light armour. Nothing says "you're dead" like a shotgun round to the face.

The Jackals followed me into the lock, and the space was soon stitched with gunfire.

Only Lopez stayed back, ducking behind a cargo crate.

All of five seconds later, the fight was over. Ten dead tangos floated across the lock. Not bad for first contact.

"Whatever those sorry sons of bitches were expecting," said Riggs, surveying the damage, "it certainly wasn't *us*."

"Good shooting," Novak rumbled.

ZERO INJURIES SUSTAINED, my suit AI told me. I quickly assessed the rest of the squad, and saw that none of the Jackals had been injured. The team cancelled their active camo, outlines instantly becoming distinct.

"Bulletproof…" Feng said, shaking his head. He grinned boyishly and his eyes became wide. "I am *bullet-fucking-proof*!"

"Don't let it go to your head, Feng," I said. Thoughts of invincibility were a common side effect of simulant operations. "Area is secure. Mag-locks on."

The boots of the recon-suits had magnetic soles. I activated mine and anchored to the deck.

Lopez emerged from behind the crate that had been her hiding place during the firefight, her face flushed with embarrassment. She snagged one of the dead bodies as it floated past and stared at the ruined face.

"Who was he?" she asked.

"Who cares?" Novak said. "Is dead now, yes?"

The tango wore a faded blue survival suit lined with flak plates, of a type used by mining teams. The Alliance insignia had been torn from the sleeve and another symbol painted onto the chest panel: a black infinity spiral. That was the Spiral's calling card, the closest thing the organisation had to a badge. Each of the casualties carried a crude metal icon of the same design on their belts, a private reminder of their affiliation. Lopez held the body for a long second, fascinated and horrified by our handiwork.

"Was this easier when they wore uniforms?" she asked. "When you were fighting the Asiatic Directorate, I mean?"

"Don't let Feng hear you say that," Riggs said.

I shook my head. "That was a long time ago."

"I wonder what they were doing in here," Lopez said.

"Waiting to die?" Novak offered.

"That's not what I meant," Lopez said.

Novak grunted. "Here." He pointed out a cargo crate at the mouth of the chamber. "Is like bomb, yes?"

The crate had been mag-locked to the deck, with the lid open. I floated over and peered inside. Recognised an industrial breaching charge—big enough to crack an asteroid's mineral seam. The activation panel was dark, but the various arming components were mag-locked to the side of the crate.

"We interrupted them," I said. A cold jolt ran through my system. "They were priming this charge, and we caught them in the act…"

"We need to call this in," Lopez said, shaking her head. "Captain Heinrich needs to know what's going on down here."

"How do we do that, Senator?" Novak grumbled. "Comms are down."

The Jackals had all come to stand around the open box now, were staring down at the oversized charge.

"They were going to blow the station," I said. "And everyone with it."

"That's cold, man," Riggs said, shaking his head. "But it doesn't surprise me. We are dealing with the Spiral here. I guess those officers are going to be wasted, for real."

Until now, the anonymous military brass had been someone else's worry, and I so desperately wanted them to stay that way. But if we were the only squad on Daktar, we were their only hope...

I pulled up the mission briefing again. Intel on the military contingent was short and to the point. Six officers had arrived on Daktar via transport shuttle, at some point prior to the takeover. I opened the file on the ranking officer, and his face was projected in holo on my wrist-comp. Hard-featured, with a shaven scalp and a tight, grey goatee beard. Eyes like sapphires. An Old Earther, Alliance citizen of the Russian Federation. Previously stationed in Moscow.

Name: Sergkov, Vadim. Rank: Major.

All other information redacted with the tag INSUFFICIENT SECURITY CLEARANCE.

None of the other officers' files would yield anything more than a poor-quality holo-picture, barely sufficient for identification.

"Whoever these guys are," I said, looking up at my squad, "Command doesn't seem very interested in giving detail on them."

I felt a familiar tightening in my chest. These guys weren't regular Army. I'd dealt with more than enough black ops types in my career, and I could smell one from a light-year out...

"Looks like he's one of yours," Riggs said to Novak. "He's Russian, I mean."

Novak grunted and shook his head. "Is *Moskvich*."

"He's what?" Lopez questioned.

"From Moscow," Novak said, twisting his upper lip in a sneer. "Not proper Federation." He slapped a hand to his chest. In the armour, the action was bone-crushing. "Me? Proper Russian. Old country, Norilsk." When no one immediately appeared to understand the relevance of the name, which I took to be a location, Novak sneered some more and added, "Is long way from Moscow. Is north: is real Russia."

Lopez raised an eyebrow and nodded back at the briefing image. "I didn't think there were many of them left," she said.

Riggs grinned. "Officers, or Russians?"

"Either," Lopez replied.

It was true that Russia and most of her Old Earth territories had taken a pounding during the Directorate–Alliance War. The Federation hadn't been directly hit, but the Directorate had deployed nukes in the 'Stans. To this day, decades after the engagement, the fallout still rendered many Russian districts uninhabitable. It felt inevitable that Novak had originated from somewhere that hellish.

"Well there's one, at least," I said. The holo snapped back into my comp.

"What are we going to do?" Lopez asked.

I thought about ordering one of the squad to extract from the simulants, to carry the news back to the *Bainbridge* ... But I quickly discarded that plan as a no-go. We'd be a skin down, and if I was right—if the Spiral were planning to sacrifice Daktar Outpost—I would need every trooper available.

"New objective, people," I said. "We're getting those officers off this station. The Control Room is two decks above us. That's where we're heading. We'll patch into the security system, and run a scan for the hostages.

"Lopez, Feng: get that airlock sealed. Riggs, Novak: covering fire on that corridor."

"We're on it," Feng said.

Feng and Lopez used sealant foam and a plasma welder to repair the hatch. As they worked, I called up plans of the station. A clean-lined schematic appeared on my

HUD—downloaded before we'd left the *Bainbridge*—and I plotted the route to the Control Room. Lopez finished sealing the lock, and my suit confirmed that the seal was good: that the base would retain pressure. I transmitted the new mission plan to the rest of the team. Their HUDs jumped with graphics as the info-stream updated, giving directions to the target.

"Roll out. We've got a job to do."

CHAPTER FOUR

FIRST CONTACT

Despite the initial resistance at the airlock, we found the lower levels of Tower One largely deserted. In fact, the place had an eerie stillness to it, as though the Spiral was concentrating its resources on the fight outside. Now that we were inside the outpost, we were running on the base's atmosphere supply. The air tasted salty and sweaty, carried with it the distant tang of smoke. The power had been cut save for the occasional security lamp, and the zone we were in was dark.

"Flares," I ordered.

"Copy that," Riggs said.

The Jackals followed his example, slapping chemical flares to the walls as they went. The fizzing lights dowsed the whole sector in an intermittent illumination that did nothing to dispel the sense of desertion. Feng attached a flare to the corner, then stopped as it lit the next section of corridor.

"You seeing this?" he asked.

The Black Spiral's symbol had been repeated everywhere, covering every bulkhead and hatch. The ever-decreasing black circles were almost hypnotic. The words REJECT THE LIE had been written on the closest wall in sloppy red paint.

"What lie?" Lopez asked, pausing in front of the graffiti.

"It's their thing," Riggs said. "Their leader—some asshole who calls himself the Warlord or something—says that you're supposed to figure it out for yourself."

This was just proto-religious bullshit. The Spiral had, in recent months, started leaving propaganda like this behind after their attacks, and I knew that we had Intelligence working on its meaning. So far as I was concerned it was just another terror tactic. I found it somewhat ironic that the Spiral had taken to leaving messages on the walls of a station that they intended to demolish.

"It's not our problem," I said. "Move on."

"Control Room ahead," Novak indicated, nodding at the hatch at the end of a darkened junction.

"Feng, Lopez: take those corners," I ordered.

Warning beacons flickered at the edge of my vision, tracking motion around us. I detected bio-signs at the perimeter of my scanner's range. There were people inside the room.

"Feels like trap," Novak said. He absently stroked one of the knives holstered across his chest, carrying his shotgun one-handed. "Smells like trap," he added, in an excited way.

In real life, his teeth were darker and had an almost jagged appearance: as though they had been filed. In his simulant, his teeth were bright-white and new. I wasn't sure which version I liked better. Not for the first time, I caught myself wondering exactly why he had received that life term.

"A drone would be nice," I whispered.

"Did you bring yours, Novak?" Riggs said.

"Fuck drone," Novak replied.

"We'll breach the door," I decided. "Get that panel, Novak."

The Russian nodded.

"On me," I said. Held up a fist. "Go."

Novak opened the door with a slap of his glove to the control.

The hatch peeled open, and I was met by a half-dozen figures in survival suits. They opened fire, rounds pranging against the deck and walls.

I brought my shotgun up.

FLASH BANG, I ordered my suit.

A single round fired from the shotgun's alternate ammo dispenser. A suppression grenade.

"Down!" I yelled.

My mags applied, I went to ground. As the grenade went off—throwing noise and light across the interior of the Control Room—my visor polarised in immediate reaction.

Lopez was a second too slow, and turned to run rather than drop to the deck. One of the tangos saw a chance and let loose a volley from his assault rifle. A round hit Lopez in the shoulder. I caught a brief glimpse of her face—contorted in pain. She yelped over the comm, twisted sideways, and hit the wall.

I was already up, spraying the inside of the Control Room with gunfire. Two more Spiral went down, the rest retreating behind consoles and terminals.

Novak lurched past me. He wasn't exactly graceful in zero-G, but what he lost in dexterity he made up for with enthusiasm. Over the nearest console in a heartbeat. There was a muted bark of more shotgun fire, then an unpleasant *schuck*ing sound as Novak got to work with one of his blades. A body sailed past me, suit slashed and torn.

Riggs took advantage of the tangos' shock and

pounded the chamber with shotgun rounds. Desks and chairs exploded. Two more tangos tried to dash into cover at the other end of the room, but Feng caught both.

"Room is clear," Novak said, stirring from his wet-work. Blood spattered his armoured chest. The Russian wiped a crude blade on the edge of a console, then methodically replaced it into its sheath.

"Impressive," Feng said.

"Disgusting," Lopez corrected. "You're lucky there are no news-eyes on us." She hovered near the hatch, her shotgun lowered.

"You okay?" I asked her. "You took a round back there."

Lopez looked at me with angry eyes. "I'm fine. It didn't breach my armour."

"You were lucky it didn't penetrate."

"I'm fine," she repeated.

Even if she didn't want to admit it, from the way her shoulder hung I could tell that the shot had hurt. When she saw me looking, Lopez righted herself and tried to shrug the injury off. From her bio-signs I knew that she was still mission-capable, and her medi-suite was already working to correct the injury, but her ego had been bruised.

"Be more careful next time," I said. "I saw what happened in the airlock. I can't afford to lose you out here. Every trooper counts."

"Understood," she said, with singeing belligerence.

I turned away and inspected the room. "Someone watch the door. Feng, get me a working terminal." As a former Directorate clone-trooper, Feng was the most technically adept of the squad. He liked to mess with machines whenever he got the chance. If anyone could get the systems running, it was him. "Access the surveillance system; try to call up the security-feeds."

"Can do."

The Control Room was long and rectangular, set into the side of Tower One. In usual circumstances, this was the main command centre for all three Towers, with computer consoles arranged in banks to face a view-port that stretched the length of the room. Someone had left the shutters open, and the port gave a view of space outside: the Shard Gate, sitting in the distance, looked disturbed in some way that I couldn't really explain...

Feng chose a computer and a seat. It creaked precariously under the combined weight of a sim in armour. He frowned and started jabbing at the console with fingers made chunky in his gauntlets.

"Do the terminals still work after what we just did in here?" Riggs asked, keeping watch over the hatch.

"They're made of sterner stuff," Feng said.

"Chinese-built and made to last," Riggs joked. "Just like you, Feng."

Novak grumbled a laugh.

Feng kept working. "You were *supposed* to be shooting at the Spiral, Riggs, not the computers."

Lopez raised an eyebrow. "Touché, Riggs."

"Here's what I've got," said Feng, turning to me.

A series of real-time surveillance feeds appeared in tri-D. Location names were assigned to each: PRIMARY LOCK, INTER-HUB JUNCTION and so on.

"Good job, Feng," I said. I swiped a finger at the last monochrome image, labelled TOWER ONE— DOCKING SPIRE. "Can you magnify that feed?"

"Affirmative."

Feng did as ordered, and the image bloomed in front of me. It showed the tip of Tower One. Several levels above us, the place looked to be a web of gantries and criss-crossing walkways. My suit began to paint icons onto the imagery as I watched, indicating the location of the missing officers.

"There," I said, pointing at part of the feed. "That's where the officers are."

"How do you know?" Feng asked. "I can't see anyone in there."

"All Alliance military personnel carry ID chips. Your suit AI interfaces with the station's."

"Really?" Lopez said. "Do we carry ID chips?"

"Didn't you listen to anything during induction?" Riggs snorted. "Of course you have an ID chip."

"You all do," I said.

"Even Novak?" Lopez queried.

"*Especially* Novak," I replied. "Let's hope that we never need to use them, but if you ever get trapped behind enemy lines it might be something you'll be grateful for." I turned back to the tri-D security feed and began to plot our route up the Tower. "Place is going to be a nightmare to assault," I decided.

Riggs suddenly snapped alert. "I've got readings…" he said. "Multiple signals on the bio-scanner. Closing on our position."

"Could be Riggs' civilians…" Lopez said.

There was only one way into the room—through the hatch we'd just used—and the signals were moving quickly in that direction. I kicked my mags, checked my ammo. Reloaded the shotgun.

"Get ready. Take up positions and keep eyes on—"

Then the hatch door slammed open, and the noose tightened.

If the Spiral had any sort of comms in place, by now they knew that they were facing an Army Sim Ops team. Most likely, they realised they were going to die in that room. But these guys were fanatics, not soldiers, and that didn't stop them. They had numbers on their side and they knew this station, knew that there was no other way out of this room. The only question was whether they were going to take enough of us out to stop our mission.

The initial wave was made up of sixteen armoured bodies. Carrying assault rifles, security shotguns, even a couple of flare guns. Pretty much any equipment that could be modified for offensive use.

A rifle barked in my direction and chased me into cover behind a console. Rounds slammed into the metal framework against my back. Machines spat sparks as gunfire slashed the room. A grenade sailed overhead. Exploded in the pit of the room, showering me with frag. Smoke started to cloud the atmosphere, reducing visibility.

TAKE EVASIVE ACTION, my suit warned.

"There are too many of them!" Lopez said, popping a round from her shotgun, then dipping back into cover.

Bodies tumbled past, but the corridor outside was pressed with new attackers.

"They've got a heavy inbound," Feng declared.

"How heavy?" I said. Even using the closed comms, the noise around us was blistering, becoming almost overwhelming, and I found myself yelling.

"See for yourself," Feng said.

A figure in a mining mech advanced down the corridor, a bright splash of yellow against the darkened interior. The mech's operator sat inside the pilot cabin, safely encased within an armoured cage, and gunned the controls. It fired pulses from a shoulder-mounted laser, strobing the chamber. The device was industrial, and short-ranged, but it was capable of breaching our armour.

The battle-space was closing around us. The press of bodies becoming tighter and tighter. Another grenade exploded, and I felt the shockwave of the blast wash over me. I wasn't sure whether that was the Spiral or the Jackals.

I shifted position across the chamber, took cover behind another bullet-riddled console. Snapped off a few rounds from the shotgun, and took out two more tangos.

Novak flashed past me, a blur of motion. One of his knives was plunged into the suited body of a terrorist. He pinned the struggling figure to the floor. Feng rose up from another terminal, firing his shotgun again and again, a snarl plastered across his face.

The Spiral were pouring fire onto us now. It seemed that no matter how many we hit they just kept coming.

"Prepare for extraction," I ordered the team. This was fast becoming a question of *when* rather than *if*.

I caught Riggs' face across the room. He looked almost relieved by the order, as though I was giving him permission to die. I found myself smiling at him.

But death didn't come.

There was an almost imperceptible lull in the fighting. In my real body, and without the sharpened senses of the simulant, I doubt that I would've sensed it. But in that microsecond, I realised that something had changed. Even Novak stopped his grisly work.

A whine of white static was building over the comm network. Filling my earbead, and my head. Too fast, or too strong, for my suit systems to properly counter.

"Oh shit…" Feng said. Eyes to the view-port. To space beyond the glass.

All faces—Jackals and Spiral—were directed to the window.

"Shit indeed…" I whispered.

My communicator was still awash with white noise, but a single looped message became audible.

"*Gate is open…All Alliance forces be aware: Gate is open…*"

The Shard Gate had taken on another aspect, and its black heart had become energised. Light began to dance across the Gate's surface.

A couple of the tangos crossed themselves, made pseudo-religious protestations of fear or respect—maybe Gaia Cultists or System Primarists—suggesting that at least some of them had a religious motivation for joining the Spiral. Or maybe not; when witnessing an event like this, there wasn't much distance between fear and respect. The Gate was an example of ancient, working xeno-tech—the likes of which we still didn't really understand. Active Shard technology had a universal effect, and even I felt a sense of dread. My heart raced, my breathing becoming fast and ragged…

But it wasn't the Gate's operation that was responsible for the reaction. It was what had come *through* that was causing it.

A Krell bio-ship.

Maybe because we had been so intent on killing each other, neither side had noticed the ship's arrival. Now it sat in tight orbit around Daktar 436, moving with a near-serenity that belied its destructive potential.

You spend enough time in and around human ships, you recognise nearly every pattern, every engine style, every spaceframe. Bio-ships were something completely different. I'd seen my fair share of them, but—at least to my eye—I'd never seen two that looked the same. Every ship was unique, and every one was alive. This one's shape was all wrong. Not a single sharp angle on the thing; it was covered in armoured plates that had grown and regrown.

A couple of the Spiral began to mutter profanities, in languages that I didn't understand. Those left in the room with us scrambled through the open door. None of my team gave chase: they were still entranced by the enormous alien ship.

The heavy mining mech retreated, servos whining as it moved off. There were shouts from further down the corridor, outside the Control Room. Gunfire began in the distance.

"How can *they* be on the station already?" Lopez asked.

I swallowed. "They're faster than you'll ever know."

The bio-ship's flanks flashed intermittently, discharging what could be mistaken for weapons systems, but something I knew to be much worse. One of the projectiles slewed past the view-port, so close that I could pick out almost every detail of the object. Spherical, armoured, studded with hooks. The ship was sending breacher pods to the surface. Krell boarding teams.

Space was soon filled with the pods in such numbers that Daktar's defensive grid was easily overwhelmed. Probably hundreds of Krell landing on Daktar. Greater women than me had spent the better part of their lives trying to understand the fishes, to predict when they would and would not turn up. The end result was that they were unknowable. The aliens were just that: alien.

The noise outside the room grew in volume. Shouts were replaced by cries, by screams.

The communicator bead in my ear had fallen back to static. I cycled the bands by thought-command, hoping for some scrap of information on what the Krell were doing here. Nothing. My throat was suddenly dry, constricted. I hated how the Krell could still make me feel green, even after all this time.

"Novak, get the door," I said. Could the Jackals detect the panic in my voice? I hoped not. "Seal us in."

Novak bounced across the room. Reached the control and slapped it. The hatch slammed shut.

I glanced around at the Jackals. My suit told me that every one of them was experiencing the same fear as me. I wished that the closed hatch blocked out more of the sound, because despite the three inches of reinforced plasteel I could still hear the screaming, the chatter of alien weaponry.

"Christo, sounds like a slaughter out there," Riggs said. He clutched his shotgun to his chest, fingers closed around the stock. "What are we going to do?"

"They're getting closer," Lopez added.

"There must be another way out of this room," Feng offered, although we all knew that there wasn't. "Maybe through the airshafts—"

Just then, there was an enormous rumble on the other side of the hatch. I braced.

A welt appeared in the metalwork.

"How can...?" Lopez started, but her voice trailed off, question left unasked.

"Away from the door!" I ordered.

The Jackals dropped back. Shotguns trained on the hatch now.

More welts appeared. More rumbling. More bio-signs.

My pulse beat faster and faster. The rush of blood to my ears was almost deafening.

I knew exactly what was coming.

The hatch buckled. Split. Like it had been nuked, hit with a breaching charge. There was a flash of light from outside, and a tendril of smoke languidly trailed into the Control Room. A body—ripped apart, survival suit breached—glided past.

Then another.

And another, but in several pieces rather than one.

A shape—a wet, grisly outline of a thing—emerged from the dark.

A Krell primary-form.

CHAPTER FIVE

THE TOWER

Six-limbed and massive, the Krell poised a pair of talon-tipped claws on the hatch and used another to grapple further into the hole. Empty, fish-like eyes scanned us, mouth open in an animal grimace inside its bio-helmet. It wore armour over a muscled body—plating that was contoured, looked like scales—and its webbed hands were encased in gauntlets. All of that tech had been grown rather than built, and some of it the Krell had probably self-produced.

I took in the detail in short bursts, trying to quell the rush of emotion that the alien's arrival caused in me. It had been years since I'd last seen a Krell, but old memories resurfaced immediately. I teased the trigger of my shotgun and fought my natural instincts.

"Hold your fire, Jackals," I ordered.

I had been at war with these aliens for the better part of my military career. I'd killed hundreds of them during the war, and in turn they had killed almost as many of *me*.

It wasn't the same for the Jackals, of course, because they had never fought the Krell. They hadn't seen the things that I had; for the entirety of their deployment the Alliance had been at peace with the Krell. Their experience of them had been second-hand, from vid-files and simulations. Even so, their anxiety was palpable, readable from their vitals.

"Going to have to find a bigger knife…" Novak muttered. His enormous shoulders rose and fell with each breath.

"I don't think any knife is going to help you against one of those," Riggs whispered.

"Activate frequency-beacons," I said. "And no matter what happens, do not shoot."

All five suit transponders lit on my HUD, distributing a tightbeam transmission across the surrounding area the likes of which I still didn't really understand. The freq-beacon was a product of the current peace. A sort of specialised friend-or-foe identifier. Science Division insisted that this tech would make us identifiable to the Krell Collective—that the aliens would be able to differentiate us from the enemy. I'd never had the chance to use it before.

"We're friendlies…" I said over an open comms channel.

With sweat breaking across my brow, I lowered my shotgun. I had to override the hind part of my brain, to work against the hardwiring that years of war had produced.

The Krell swivelled in my direction. The alien's face was scarred behind the bio-helm—a jagged welt that stretched from its slit mouth to a deep-set black eye. Made an ugly face even uglier. More vague shapes coalesced from the dark.

I recognised the aliens as primary-forms. The Krell had a strict and rigid caste system, with each and every specimen being born into its role. Primary-forms were warrior-drones, prolific within most Collectives. There were other, more diversified bio-forms within the majority of shoals—including secondary-forms bred solely for the carrying of organic weaponry, and larger leader-forms which acted as battlefield commanders. I was glad that we weren't dealing with some of the more esoteric off-shoots of the Krell genus…

After what felt like an age—but was probably only a heartbeat—words were projected onto my HUD.

<BACK UP. ASSIST.>

I nodded. "All right."

There was no perceptible change in the lead Krell's facial expression, but I had to assume it was making contact. Again, this was new technology—a xeno-linguistics package which Sci-Div had assured us would allow for direct communication with the Krell warrior swarm. What I found most disturbing was the idea that I didn't know *what* I was communicating with. I might be speaking to the warrior in front of me, or another alien further along the command chain could be using this one as a mouthpiece. Just one of the many complications of an alliance with an alien intelligence that relied on group consciousness…

The alien grasped the edges of the door panel and tore the metal framework with ease. I deactivated my mags and sailed onwards through the open hatch. The hole that the warrior had torn in the metal was easily big enough for the recon-suits to fit through and, dodging the jagged edges, I pulled myself into the waiting corridor. It was the scene of a massacre.

Six Krell primary-forms hung from the ceiling and walls. Except for the xeno with the scarred features, they were indistinguishable.

"My God," Lopez said. Her face was crumpled behind her visor. "They stink…"

She had a point. The odour was rank, overwhelming. Every breath felt like I was being invaded. That was the case even though the aliens wore full-body suits. Their tech exuded the same repugnant odour as their alien bodies, perhaps a by-product of organic construction.

"Use your internal atmosphere supply," I suggested, trying to hold my breath.

"Shut up, Lopez," Riggs said. "The fish heads can detect comms waves between our suits…"

"They can't understand though," she said. Added: "Can they?"

"You're not supposed to say 'fish heads' any more," Feng said. His voice quivered, the sense of unease that we were now fighting with the Krell—that they were our *allies*—impossible to shake.

<DIRECTION,> appeared on my HUD. <GIVE.>

Orders. They wanted orders. That I could do.

"Fall in," I said. "Follow us."

"We're … we're really doing this … ?" Lopez said.

Novak made a disapproving sound at the back of his throat. "Fucking fish heads," he said, except that in his blunt Slavic accent it came out sounding like "fugging."

The lead Krell twisted about-face, heading further into the station. The rest disengaged from their anchor-points. Using their webbed feet, they moved in the low gravity with an ease that I almost envied.

"Our odds of success have just improved significantly," I said. "We've got another chance to get those officers out. Let's show these fuckers how it's done."

Riggs made the Gaia sign over his chest. "Going to be hot and heavy."

"Just how the boss likes it…" Novak said.

"So I hear," Lopez replied.

United, simulant and Krell moved off down the corridor.

*　　*　　*

Tower One was almost a kilometre tall—the tallest of the three structures that made up Daktar Outpost. A hollow silo, sixty stories up and criss-crossed with gantries so thickly that visibility from the base to the tip was virtually nil. The structure was lined with external landing spars and docking berths upon which visiting transports could roost, with a series of lifts and cranes running the Tower's edge. The lower levels were filled with cargo containers, anti-grav buggies, empty maintenance mechs: plenty of cover.

Not that we necessarily needed that, because the game had *changed*. The arrival of the Krell had irrevocably tipped the balance of the battle in our favour, and the Spiral's discipline was crumbling. The sector around us was in chaos. Dozens of minor gunfights had broken out around the base of the Tower.

"Left flank," I ordered, spying motion among some crates. A sentry. "See to it, Riggs."

Before Riggs could react, one of the Krell primary-forms swooped forward. Seeing the alien at the last second, the Black Spiral agent lifted his assault rifle. The xeno was faster. The tango was shredded by claws and peppered with bio-weapons fire before he had a chance to shoot.

"Ah, thanks," Riggs said.

<EXECUTION,> the Krell replied. <ORDERS.>

The words floated on my HUD in a disarming way, and the scar-faced alien turned to look at me with those piercing, flat eyes.

"Hostages are up there," I said. My face-plate provided enhanced visuals of the Tower's interior but, again, I'd have killed for a drone or remote viewer. "At least according to the surveillance footage."

Riggs squatted behind the nearest crate, consulting

his bio-scanner. "I'm seeing multiple hostiles. Armed." He flagged targets on the squad display channel, bouncing his visuals to my HUD. "This isn't going to be easy."

Although we could only see them from below, a dozen tangos patrolled the gantries, covering the obvious paths of ascent with overlapping arcs of fire. They wore vac-rated armour, clasped heavy rifles to their chests. Riggs selected a couple of more obvious targets and identified them on the joint-squad battle-net.

"Are those *plasma* rifles?" he asked.

"Looks like it."

"How'd the Spiral get plasma rifles? Aren't those restricted weapons?"

"Try telling them that," Feng suggested.

These tangos wore the same ragged outer clothing as the rest of the insurgents, but something was wrong with this picture. These men moved differently, with a certain precision. At this range my suit couldn't read their vital signs, but these guys didn't seem phased by the presence of the simulant strike force or the Krell. That was something.

"They're trained," I concluded. "They're taking their time up there, and they aren't scared at all."

"That can change," Novak said. His shotgun had been lost in the fray back at the Control Room, and he was instead relying on his sidearm: an MP-600 Widowmaker.

"That's not all," Riggs offered. "Take a look at this..."

Far above us on the outer edge of the silo, nestled into one of the landing spars, was the outline of a ship. A small civilian-class transport vessel, of a sort found throughout the Alliance colonies. The ship's rear access-ramp was deployed, and the Spiral were loading crates into the cargo hold. Her nose pointed towards the hangar door as though she was ready to take flight.

Riggs breathed out through his teeth. "Typical black-market job," he said. "Her identification codes have been removed."

The Krell floated restlessly nearby. The xeno I'd taken to thinking of as their leader looked decidedly pissed off with the lack of activity.

<GO. WHERE.>

They're still soldiers like the Jackals, I told myself. *Only uglier.*

"We need to get here," I said, jabbing at my wrist-comp, at the map that showed where the hostages were being held. "That's our target. *Capisce?*"

I felt pretty stupid talking to the Krell in Standard, as I had no idea how much they could actually *understand*, but the suit was supposed to be running a translation AI, sending out data-packets that the xeno would then pass up the command chain. The alien just stared blankly at me for a long second. Was it communicating with the rest of its Collective? Taking orders from some other fish head further along the intelligence trail, aboard the bio-ship?

<RECOVER,> the alien broadcast back at me, <ASSET.>

Then all six of the aliens whipped about, and clambered onto the underside of gantries and walkways. They swiftly made their way up the Tower.

I evaluated the Jackals for a moment. They were battered and bruised, their armour covered in minor damage.

"Move up," I said. "Fast as we can, but stay hidden. Activate stealth-fields."

"Dumbshit terrorists," Novak grunted. "Never see us coming."

"Here's to hoping," Lopez said, disappearing as her stealth-field mimicked her surroundings.

The Jackals deployed. With the noise all around us, there was little prospect of being heard, and what with the activated stealth-tech we were almost invisible to the unassisted eye. The recon-suit's strength-amplifier made short work of the climb: what would've been impossibly tiring in a real skin became an annoyance in the armour.

Meanwhile, moving much faster than us, the Krell primary-forms slithered upwards. Despite moving so close to the Spiral's sentries, they remained undetected, their bodies appearing to merge with the surrounding structures in a similar way to our stealth-tech.

"I have eyes on the hostages," Feng said. He was by now several stories up the Tower, and had a clear line of sight to the location we'd seen on the surveillance camera.

I bumped his view-feed to my own suit, and saw what he saw. There were six figures on one of the central gantries far above us. Their faces were covered with cloth sacks, hands secured behind backs with plastic ties. All wearing Alliance Army uniforms, and forced to stand upright: back to back, in a group.

"There are more guards watching them," Feng added.

Three armoured shapes, carrying long-shot kinetic rifles, kept watch on the figures.

"I see them," I said. I thought-flagged the guards. If we were going to recover those hostages intact, we needed to take the guards down. "Novak, Feng: I want you to move into position and—"

Text suddenly scrolled across my HUD.

<ORDERS. EXECUTE.>

The Krell materialised on the walkway above me. There was a flurry of activity, a garbled cry. Then the three Spiral sentries were dead, bodies floating free of the gantry.

"Wait!" I ordered. "I need everyone in position before—"

"They're here!" a tango shouted.

Novak sprang from his hiding place, clambering onto another Spiral tango.

"Now this is work I like…" he roared, his laugh filling the comms line.

Around me, the Tower was suddenly filled with the sound of gunfire. Bright plasma pulses coursed the air. As though they were a single entity, the Krell fell onto the next group of Spiral agents.

<EXECUTE,> the alien blurted again. <ORDER—>

The xeno's body exploded in a bloody mess. It had taken at least a dozen direct hits to the chest, bio-armour ruptured. Fish guts spilled from the resultant wound. The primary-form floated past me. Dead. I bit back anger at the Krell's premature execution of the plan.

"Taking fire!" Feng said. He let out a garbled yell, body jerking in micro-G. I heard Lopez cursing sympathetically over the comm.

Feng's bio-signs flatlined on my HUD. His body span past, stitched by plasma bolts. As the stealth-field powered down, and he became visible, the Spiral reacted immediately. It felt like every tango in the Tower was firing at Feng's body.

And then it wasn't just Feng that the Spiral could see: it was all of us. Slugs spanked the metal gantries around me, tracers slashing the air.

"How can they see us?" Lopez asked, her voice rising shrilly. I'd lost her position—didn't even know where she was any more. "We have stealth-fields!"

"Just keep moving. Get up there!"

I fired my EVAMP and went up another level. The distance between gantries left me exposed, but I had little choice—

There was a tango on the walkway, and as I touched down he managed to loose a shot. The low-bore slug bounced off my plate like rain on a tin roof, ineffectual and impotent. The sucker behind the face-plate didn't seem to care: man was wired on neuro-agents, or had a death wish of some kind. I was close enough that I could see his glassy eyes, see the spittle on his lips.

"I don't have time for this!" I roared.

The shoulder of my suit met bone and tissue, and he hit the safety rail of the gantry on which we stood. Angrily, I threw the body over the edge, away from me.

"Riggs: prisoners! *Now!*"

"I'm there," Riggs said.

He had reached the top of the silo, where the prisoners were being held. Novak was trailing behind, covering his approach with his Widowmaker. I dropped onto a knee and popped advancing Spiral. Hoping to clear a safe zone around them, hoping that we could withdraw with at least some of the hostages alive.

"Objective secured," Riggs said, voice tinged with pride.

Riggs had the prisoners. His back was to them, shotgun blasting.

"I'm here too," Lopez said.

She was beneath us, moving up. Firing her EVAMP clumsily, bouncing between gantries.

"Docking lock is opening," the station's AI declared, voice barely audible above the din. "All personnel take immediate safety precautions…"

Another complication.

Air pressure was dropping. The hangar bay doors in front of the mystery transport were opening, and the Tower's atmosphere was escaping fast. Red emergency lamps strobed overhead.

"We need to get those people out of here," I said. The hostages would need respirators at the very least.

Riggs pulled free the bag covering the nearest prisoner's face.

Shit.

The prisoner's hands weren't tied at all.

Shit.

They were free, and they reached for the explosive-pack on his chest.

Shit.

Because the information I was receiving was so incomprehensible—because it made no sense at first—I took a microsecond to process it. Nothing more than that, but enough for the sham prisoner to react.

Riggs was even slower. His brow creased in abject confusion.

Big and dumb. Just how I like them…

In unison, the prisoners reached for their explosive-packs.

"Down!" I yelled.

Then the central hangar exploded.

With the hangar doors open, and atmosphere escaping, there was little to no oxygen left in the silo to burn, but the charge-packs carried just the right chemical combination to self-detonate. Perhaps that was another indication that the Spiral were more organised than Command had recognised. The resultant blast—which claimed the lives of the sham-hostages, as well as Corporal Riggs' simulant—was furious but short-lived.

Riggs had made a very rookie mistake—left his mag-locks on—and he didn't deactivate them fast enough when the bomb went off. Like a target on a range, he snapped backwards: folding. Both legs were broken in the ensuing explosion, and it was immediately obvious that no amount of medical assistance was going to salvage those limbs. He spiralled past me, weaponless, arms outstretched in a star shape. Hit the far wall, fifty or so metres distant, at speed, with enough force to shatter every bone in his body.

Dead. Dead. Dead.

Less than an hour ago, we'd been sharing my bunk back on the *Bainbridge*. Less than an hour ago, Corporal Riggs hadn't known what it felt like to die in combat. His eyes were wide, blood-filled, hands reaching out to me, fingers clutching at something that wasn't there. Even if this death wasn't real—wasn't final—it hurt all the same, and not just for Riggs. *Sorry Riggs*, I thought. There was nothing that I could say to make it any easier. I knew; I'd been there two hundred and ten times myself. *Better luck next time.*

It was probably experience that saved me. I triggered my EVAMP. In an uncontrolled jump, I sailed to the end of the catwalk. Caught the safety rail with one hand. A bone-jarring impact spread up my right arm—a shockwave of pain that went through the rest of my body. With a grunt, I snagged my arm around the rail and pulled myself up.

It was much worse than I'd thought. The network of catwalks and gantries had been torn up in the explosion, with debris randomly thrown across the silo. Splinters of sharp metal flew past me, and I just managed to dodge a railing that had been turned into a spear by the force of the explosion. There were bodies everywhere. Krell, simulant, Spiral.

But not everyone was dead. Every surviving tango was scrambling up the Tower, using all efforts to escape the dying structure. Their target: the Spiral's ship. Still in its docking cradle, the starship sat a level above me, ready to launch.

"Novak! Lopez!" I yelled, trying to recalibrate after the madness.

Something moved fast beside me. I swept my shotgun around—somehow, impossibly, I'd managed to keep hold of that during the explosion—and readied to fire again.

"Here!" Novak said. "Reporting."

He popped into existence on my face-plate, his outline flashing as he sailed past, his EVAMP thrusters firing intermittently.

"Grab something," I said.

"Trying," he snorted, hitting a safety rail and repositioning himself so that he was level with the ship. "Is not easy!"

"Lopez!" I called. I couldn't see her through the hurricane of debris. "Report!"

I was answered by a piercing scream over the comms line, and I recognised Lopez's voice. Her life-signs spasmed across my HUD, weak enough for me to know that she wasn't going to make it, strong enough for her to experience some pretty terrible pain. Novak met my eyes.

"Nothing that we can do to help her," I said.

Without hesitation, I silenced the comms channel. Did the same to Novak's suit so that he couldn't hear her either. Novak grimaced. Was I colder than even him? *He'll understand*, I told myself. *He's green, and eventually all of this will become second nature.* That was what watching comrades die had become to me. Just another day on the job.

"Stop that ship," I ordered. "Do whatever it takes!"

I activated my EVAMP in a short burst, and took

another gut-lurching jump to a higher position, Novak in tow. I was close to the transport's rear cargo bay now, so close that I could see tangos waving on their comrades, their faces determined behind the visors of their survival suits. The interior of the hold was lined with metal crates, stacked with cargo palettes.

And something else.

There were prisoners in there. Real, honest-to-Gaia hostages. The Spiral were hustling them, prodding rifles to survival suits, herding them onto the ship. One of the prisoners turned, and with my improved simulant senses I flagged a face. Beard, shaven head, hard features. A primary warning marker appeared on my HUD.

MAJOR VADIM SERGKOV.

Sergkov's expression was cold and neutral. Maybe that was because he didn't want to give the Spiral the gratitude of seeing him break. Maybe he was just a fool with a death wish. It was standard Alliance Army capture response: to remain in control at all times. Still, I wondered whether I would be quite so calm if I were in his position. The fact that the Spiral had equipped the prisoners with vac-capable suits meant that they wanted them alive. I considered the implications of that decision. Senior military officers, falling into the hands of the Black Spiral? That was bad news by all accounts. Whoever these brass were, they would be privy to high-level intel; their personnel files had been redacted for even my security clearance.

"Move up!" I ordered Novak. "Don't let them slow you down."

I fired my thruster. Launched to another gantry.

Novak threw a knife at the nearest Spiral. Although his aim was good, considering he was throwing a blade in micro-G, the homemade weapon was by now tarnished and blunted. The knife bounced off the tango's armoured torso. Lightning-quick, he threw a second at the same target. That found a home in the woman's chest: planted securely between two armour plates.

But it wasn't enough to stop her. She brought up a chunky plasma rifle—an older Alliance Army model—and peeled off a retaliatory volley. Bright bolts of plasma showered Novak. Punched through his suit.

What was left of his plasma-riddled body floated free of the gantry.

I bounced upwards, twisting mid-jump. Nailed the attacker with a blast from my shotgun. She toppled from the gantry. Gone.

Only me left.

Something else exploded in the hangar silo. On autopilot, I fired my thruster again. Landed right in front of the Spiral transport. The cargo ramp was still open, and a ragged figure waited there, surrounded by Spiral. I went to fire—

But that something that had exploded in the hangar?

With sick realisation, it occurred to me that it wasn't the hangar. It was *me*. My right shoulder was frozen, and I clutched at my shotgun with a weakening grip. More warnings on my HUD now, so many that the system looked on the verge of overload. The recon-suit's self-repair systems had initiated, were trying to seal a breach in my armour, but I could already feel the cold seeping in, breath escaping from my lungs.

Pain rippled through my right side. I snarled and held it back. My medi-suite fought to keep me operational. A few more seconds was all I would need.

A dozen red-dot laser sights flickered over my recon-suit. As with the rest of the Jackals, my stealth-field had failed. I kept the shotgun trained on the aft of the transport ship.

A figure paused at the ramp. Watched me.

"This can go down one of two ways," I said, activating the suit's general channel, trying to broadcast to anything that was in the immediate vicinity with a comms-net. Trying to sound like I wasn't dying. "Either you hand over the hostages, and stand down, or I blow your brains out."

The figure wore a full-powered armour exo-suit, the chest-plate adorned with a detailed version of the Spiral's eternity symbol. The exo was restricted, military-grade tech that would make him stronger, faster. Even so, ordinarily I'd have the physical edge on him, but right now I was in no condition to fight.

"Not today," the figure said. Male voice. Papery, dry. Thick with an accent that I couldn't place. "This is over, and we are leaving."

The helmet of the exo-suit was sprayed with a white skull motif, but through the glass visor I made out a furrowed, weathered brow and intense dark eyes. Although a respirator plugged his lower face, I got the distinct impression that the Spiral's leader—I had no doubt that he was in charge—was smiling as he addressed me.

He raised a hand. Waved something at me.

A sidearm. Alliance-issue. A PPG-17 plasma pistol.

"Shoot me, then," I said. "If you know how to use that thing, that is."

Mag-locked to the deck, I took a step forward. Could see all six military officers now. Stiff-backed and still: with a defiant dignity. That wasn't something I'd seen from Command before. Even now, Sergkov's face remained aggressively neutral. Whoever he was, this guy was a cold operator.

The Spiral's leader flicked the muzzle of the plasma pistol in my direction. When he moved, I noticed that he did so very carefully and with a measured gait. *This guy has had training*, I thought. *He knows how to use that suit.*

"I don't think we need to worry about that," he said.

He gave a barely perceptible toss of his head towards the men and women around him. The cargo hold was now filled with Spiral. Several of them had weapons trained on the military officers.

The threat was clear enough. The officers weren't simulants, and if they died out here it was for real.

Below me, Krell primary-forms were clambering up the Tower. In response, one of the leader's crew tugged at his shoulder. The leader backed away just a little. Placed a hand on Major Sergkov's forearm, as though escorting the officer.

The hatch to the ship began to close.

"You shoot," he said, over the comms again, voicing the threat now, "or you try to pursue: I will kill him. I will kill them all. You hardly know what we are capable of."

Again with the invisible smile. I was fast developing a dislike for this guy.

The Krell were advancing around us. Leaping between gantries, bio-fire flaring as they went. But the Spiral's leader showed no hint of concern or fear, nothing that would suggest this was anything out of the ordinary.

"Do not follow," he warned again, still speaking over the comms. "Tell your people this."

He lowered the pistol.

And I saw my opportunity.

I fired the shotgun one-handed, right into the open cargo bay.

The chief twisted. The exo-frame of his left leg pumped, and the motor silently whirred, giving him dexterity that few unaugmented humans possessed. He rolled out of the shotgun's threat radius. Instead, the round hit one of his bodyguards, and blew a hole in the man's vac-suit.

My suit's AI burst into my head, with such insistence that it was a red-hot poker through my skull. TAKE EVASIVE ACTION! it told me. TAKE EVASIVE—

The response from the Spiral was immediate.

A dozen kinetic and energy weapons emptied on my position. At this range, and under that much fire, I didn't stand a chance. Rounds impacted my torso, legs, arms. I tried to stand my ground, to get off another shot, but my hands wouldn't work any more. *Nothing* worked. Damned mortality was getting in the way. I was powerless to stop this.

The starship's ramp slid shut. Thrusters washed the interior of the docking bay, sending a backwash across the deck, making the gantry shake. The vessel lifted, nose towards the open bay doors. The Shard Gate was visible in the distance. Mocking me. The starship's engines lit blue-white and a wave of intense heat enveloped the surrounding area. Everything—and anyone—caught in the backdraft was vaporised.

That just so happened to be me. I didn't feel a thing, because pain on that level is impossible to process.

White.

CHAPTER SIX

FUBAR

Blue.

The neural-link between the sim and my real body was instantly severed. The white of the explosion faded. Was replaced by a deep, soothing blue. From instant danger, back to a place of relative safety.

I was in a familiar location: on the *Bainbridge*, floating inside my simulator-tank. Surrounded by warm amniotic fluid like an artificial womb. I sucked down processed air through my respirator, and tried to order my thoughts. I was in pretty bad pain—the human psyche is kind of screwy like that, and my real body was struggling to differentiate actual and simulated injury. As a counterbalance, a cocktail of pain inhibitors and nano-meds flooded my skin, calming me. That blunted the agony enough that I remained conscious.

Someone hit the release valve on my tank, and it flushed. Wet with sticky blue fluid, I dragged my ass out, blinking rapidly in the bright light of the Simulant Operations Centre.

I wasn't alone. Because the Jackals were so raw, they

were taking this a whole lot worse than me. There was vomiting, shaking, cursing.

"Remember your pain management," I said. "Breathe deep and the let meds work. Keep telling yourself that it wasn't real. The hurt will pass."

"That's easy for you to say, ma'am," Lopez said, shivering under an aluminium blanket. "You've done this before. That felt so real." She swallowed, shook her head. "I—I'm so cold…"

"So that wasn't hot enough for you, Lopez?" Feng asked, trying his best to sound clever. Although his sense of bravado was returning, he didn't look to be in much better shape than Lopez.

"Is it just me," Lopez said, "or do clones have a shit sense of humour?"

"It's not just you," Riggs replied.

Zero stood in front of my tank. Her uniform was pristine, but her freckled brow was creased.

"What happened down there?" she asked.

"Can't you at least let me get dressed before we start the debrief?"

"I need to hear it now, ma'am," Zero said, with an edge of determination to her voice that I wasn't used to from her. She passed me a fresh towel and some shipboard fatigues. "Take these."

"Thanks."

I struggled into the uniform but Zero hovered at my shoulder. "We were in the dark the whole time you were deployed," she said. "You weren't transmitting at all."

I shook my head. "We couldn't make uplink to the *Bainbridge*. What's the problem?"

Without feeds, the *Bainbridge* wouldn't know what had happened on Daktar. Hell, even the Jackals wouldn't know what had happened in the final minutes I'd been inside Tower One…

"Why the look?" I asked, realising that something was very wrong here.

"What look?"

"The look that you always give me when shit goes wrong."

"Yeah," Zero said, drawing the word out. Her body shook a little: another of her tells. "Maybe. I think it might help if you get your story straight."

I noticed then that several medics and operators were gathered at the nearest view-port. In such a hurry to look outside, some of the operators hadn't even bothered dressing after the tanks.

"She's really done it this time…" someone muttered.

"Done what?" I yelled. "What's going on?"

Zero tilted her head. "*That.*"

I pushed my way through the group to look through the port. Near-space was a tangled mess of debris. Daktar's asteroid belt had been thrown into disarray, with a mix of starship wreckage and shattered rocks drifting past the port. I picked out Daktar Outpost among those rocks, spied where I'd just died.

No, no, no…

I watched in sick fascination. At this distance, I could barely pick out the individual modules that made up the station, but the explosions were clear enough. They rippled across the base, and the operators and techs around me seemed to flinch in sympathy with each detonation. Very quickly, Towers Two and Three crumpled in on themselves, leaving only Tower One standing.

"Here she goes…" said another sim operator, Captain Ving of Phoenix Squad.

One of Ving's troopers began a whistling sound as Tower One gave way.

"Holy Christo," Lopez said. "Everything…everything is gone…"

"Is bad, yes?" Novak said. The Russian was dripping with amniotic, standing naked beside me.

"How many people were there left on that station...?" Lopez asked, her shoulders slumped.

Everyone down there was dead. The weight of it was crushing.

The other Sim Ops squads didn't find it quite so difficult. There was more whooping. Some gasping from the medtechs.

Riggs sighed and tried to put a brave face on things. "Most were already dead," he said. "The rest were probably on the Spiral's starship."

Despite the situation, I felt a wave of desire prickle over my skin as I looked on his naked body. Then, immediately, that was wiped clean with a wave of guilt, as another explosion rocked Daktar, and the crowd around me reacted in amazement.

My stomach went stone cold. A tight knot formed there.

"That'll be the outpost's plasma reactor," Ving said, knowingly. "Gone super-critical, I'd say."

The null-shield that had once protected the outpost from invasion briefly worked in reverse—holding the explosive force of the reactor's meltdown inside—but a second later that, too, collapsed. A rapidly expanding fireball spread across the face of Daktar 436.

Then there was nothing. The station was dust.

Various announcements sounded over the *Bainbridge*'s public address system, scrambling air support and recovery teams. The Aerospace Force would be going into the belt to search for survivors, but I knew that it wouldn't do any good. No one could've escaped that.

"This is a fuck-up, Jenkins," Captain Ving said. He gave me one of his most unpleasant smirks. "And it's on your head."

I couldn't think of anything to say that would make this any better, but Feng gave it has best shot. "We were trying to rescue the officers," he said.

"Leave it, Feng," I said, eyes still pinned to the port.

"Yeah, Directorate," Ving chided. "Leave it."

"You weren't there," Feng said to Ving. "Phoenix Squad didn't even make it into the station."

"Thank Christo we didn't," Ving muttered. "Tower One was our objective. You weren't supposed to even be in there, Jenkins."

"We didn't have a choice. There wasn't anyone else available."

Ving's chest shivered. A large holo-tattoo of a phoenix crossed his pectorals, and when he moved it made it look like the bird was alive. This was one of Ving's trademark moves—a crowd-pleaser for the ladies.

"That was *our* objective," he said. "We were supposed to be getting those officers out."

"You weren't doing a very good job of it," Riggs said. "We had no choice but to go into the Tower ..."

"No choice but to ignore your orders?" Ving said. "You're going to have to sound a whole lot more convincing in front of the court martial, Green." Phoenix Squad broke into a laugh, closing ranks around their CO. Ving shook his head. "Well, the intel was right. We suspected that Tower One was mined."

"Then why weren't we told that?" Lopez asked.

Ving glared at me instead of Lopez. "We had a target in that Tower, Jenkins. Public enemy number one ..."

I guessed that was the Spiral's leader—the man in the exo-suit—but I didn't give Ving the satisfaction of arguing with him.

Ving slapped a hand to the view-port with male bravado. "You weren't even supposed to know about him. Looks like he got away, thanks to Jenkins' Jackals."

The Shard Gate was visible through the expanding debris cloud. Now activated, it positively sparkled with fresh cosmic energy, and the Spiral's starship—rendered tiny by the distance—hit it at speed. A ripple of blue light as it went through, then it was gone. Onwards to wherever the Gate went.

"Why aren't we at least chasing that ship?" Feng suggested. "Are we just going to let them go?"

"You might want to get dressed first," Ving said. "Then, if you want to fly this bucket through the asteroid belt," he continued, turning to the rest of Phoenix Squad, "be my guest, Green. You're even more batshit than ol' Jenkins."

There was laughter, but it wasn't a good sound.

The spectacle done, the medtechs and other simulant operators eventually dispersed from the window. Left the Jackals with the mess.

"This isn't our fault," Feng said, although the intended meaning of his words—*this isn't* your *fault*—was pretty clear. "We had no choice but to assault Tower One. We should never have been in there solo; if Captain Ving's team had been doing their job, they would've taken their objective... I mean, we were running recon, right?"

"I don't think that Heinrich will see it that way," Zero said with a sigh. She looked down at her wrist-comp, the screen of the vambrace unit flashing with an incoming message.

"Is that who I think it is?" I asked.

Zero gave a reluctant nod. "Sorry, ma'am. General Draven is demanding the *Bainbridge*'s immediate recall to home base."

General Draven: head honcho for all Alliance military in this sector. He would only become involved if Captain Heinrich escalated this up the chain of command, and it seemed that was exactly what he'd done.

"It wasn't our fault," Feng insisted again.

"Doesn't matter whose fault was," Novak said. "Is FUBAR, as you Yankees say, yes?"

"Is FUBAR," I agreed.

The security-drone that by Alliance military regulation was required to follow Novak everywhere was back at his shoulder. Its single electronic eye fixed the Russian with its gaze.

"*Prisoner 675,*" the drone bleated in a high-pitched, monotone voice, "*return to quarters. Under Military Code 983 you are under limited release on a life-term service contract. Your mission has been aborted, and as such your licence requires immediate recall to the allocated barracks facility…*"

Novak grunted, and rolled his neck. His head and shoulders were criss-crossed with real scars from a life-time of criminality.

"Do as it says, Novak," I ordered.

Novak set his jaw, but didn't argue. He padded back towards the barracks, the drone trailing after him.

"It'll be okay," Riggs said. He reached out a hand in my direction, touched my shoulder.

I shrugged him off. Felt a hot flush of anger over my cheeks. "No, Riggs. It won't. All of you: get back to the barracks and remain there until I order otherwise."

Riggs gave me one of his best wounded looks, but I just turned away.

Nothing was going to get me out of this one.

Strikeships were expected to operate away from home-base for long tours, and as such the *Bainbridge* carried a full complement of post-op facilities. Unfortunately, that meant that I was scheduled for a complete hypno-debrief on the way back to base. I spent the better part of the journey in interrogation, as did the Jackals. Every shred of our intel would be pored over by the Military Intelligence service once we got back to base.

Despite the name, there's nothing particularly hypnotic about the process. It's just a direct neural-link, a smash-and-grab of your most recent memories. Although it's more reliable than a manual debrief, that comes at a cost: it gives you a headache that hurts a hella lot worse than a hangover.

I went down to Medical with the post-debrief ache ringing in my head. My express intention was to get something to soothe the pain, but that wasn't the only reason. The arrival of the Krell on Daktar was bound to affect some members of the Jackals more than others: I was worried about Zero.

But as I left the elevator tube and approached the Simulant Operations Centre, I heard a surprising sound. Laughter: gentle and genuine, carried above the hum of the air-recycling units. As I got closer, I corrected my impression. This wasn't laughter: it was *giggling*. Accompanied by two voices that I recognised.

I found Zero sitting at her console, Feng at the terminal next to her. As they saw me, both seemed to jump.

"Evening, ma'am," Feng said.

"Don't you have somewhere to be, Private Feng?" I asked, with only a half-serious tone.

Feng slid off the console. Pressed down the front tab of his uniform. He wore duty fatigues, the black dog-head insignia of "Jenkins' Jackals" printed on a tab on his shoulder, together with scant other achievement badges.

"Y…yes, ma'am," he stammered. "I was just, well…"

I raised an eyebrow. Feng's cheeks had turned a brighter shade of pink.

"And is the place that you need to be the Simulant Operations Centre?" I said. "Or somewhere else on the *Bainbridge*? We're done with the debrief for now."

Feng swallowed hard. "Well, I was supposed to…"

"The private was just requesting some painkillers as a result of the hypno-debrief," Zero pitched in, saving Feng's blushes. "That, and the recent extraction, were causing him discomfort. I was prescribing him something for the pain."

There was a little frisson between Feng and Zero that I hadn't noticed before. I wasn't sure whether I liked it or not.

"And you now have your painkillers," I said, phrasing the words as a statement rather than a question.

Feng gave a quick flick of his eyes to Zero, then nodded. "Yes, ma'am. I have them."

"And so there is, I assume, no reason for you to remain in the SOC?"

"That's right, ma'am. I'll be going."

Feng looked remarkably young in that moment. He squirmed under my gaze, and I could barely suppress a smile.

"Get out of here," I said. "Make sure that you're ready for disembarkation to Unity Base."

"Yes, ma'am," Feng said. He made a fast exit from the SOC, but not before offering a covert smile in Zero's direction. They were co-conspirators.

As soon as he was out of the door, Zero burst into laughter. A proper belly laugh—an unexpected sound from the young woman.

"Did you have to be so damned officious to Chu?" she said.

"So he's 'Chu' now?" I asked. "And was that *flirting* I heard on the way in?"

Zero was the closest thing that I had to a friend aboard the ship, among the team, and she and I could talk together unlike any of the others. Our shared record went back years. She had been my handler with my previous Sim Ops squad, and I'd insisted that she transfer to the Jackals when I took over their command.

Zero's cheeks now burnt. "What do you think of him?"

"I think that he's a moderately useful member of the Simulant Operations Programme, in the right circumstances," I said, adopting a mock-formal tone. "Why do you ask?"

"No reason."

It was pretty obvious what she was getting at but I chose to leave it there. I was hardly one to criticise what Zero and Feng did in their downtime, given the mess I'd gotten into with Riggs. Not even Zero knew about that.

Not that there was much to know right now. I had made the decision to call it off. Riggs didn't realise that yet. While fraternisation between a commissioned and non-commissioned officer wasn't exactly forbidden, if Heinrich found out about what we'd been doing, it would be something else that he could use against me. I couldn't let that happen. I figured that, given enough missed comms, Riggs would eventually get the message.

"Just be careful of Feng," I said.

"Why?"

I shook my head. Unsure of how to phrase it. "Isn't it obvious? He's a former Directorate weapon of war. A clone-trooper who would, if the universe had turned out a little differently, be fighting against us, rather than with us."

"That's a pretty narrow view, Jenk."

"I'm only telling you because I'm worried about you. As a friend, not your CO."

"I can look after myself," Zero said, warmly. "After what you went through, I know it's tough letting go of the past. But this is a changed universe. The Asiatic Directorate is gone."

"That's not quite true…" I started. While the Directorate was finished as a significant threat, there were still strongholds of purported support for the former military regime.

"The Directorate is shattered," Zero said. "And even if it were any kind of threat, Private Feng—Chu—*isn't* Directorate. They just happened to make him, is all."

Imagine the situation: Earth, divided by two superpowers—political blocs grown so vast that they left no room for any other authority. The Alliance: a conglomeration of superstates and power pacts that included the United Americas, the European Confederacy, the Pacific Pact. The Asiatic Directorate: comprised of Unified Korea, the Chino Republic, and almost every other bordering nation. Engaged in a war that lasted decades, that had been through so many cycles of hot and cold that the phrases had lost all meaning. A war which had claimed most of Old Earth in nuclear fire, and eventually spilled out into the cold of space. One side discovered the quantum-drive, and within months the other side had it too. The end result: Old Earth's animosities were suddenly spread across the galaxy, or at least that portion of it that the human race called home.

All of that changed with the discovery of the Shard Gates. By chance, most of them were located in, or bordered on, Alliance space. Time-dilation became a thing of the past. Almost overnight, the Asiatic Directorate collapsed. The war between us and them ended not with a bomb, but with the Gates.

I was lost in reverie for a moment, and it took Zero's voice to pull me back.

"He's a good trooper," she said.

"I know, but it's not just that."

"Then what is it?"

"He's different to you and me," I said, explaining

what Zero already knew. "Born into that body. He hasn't had the experience of growing into it."

Directorate clones had an accelerated rate of growth: a design objective, so that they would be ready to fight more quickly. Once they reached adulthood, as Feng had now, they slowed down and achieved a regular ageing rate. The technique was not without risk. Many liberated Directorate clones had personality defects—were subject to rage, depression, psychosis. Feng hadn't demonstrated any of those defects yet, but that didn't mean he wouldn't...

"Don't you trust him?" Zero asked, bluntly.

I rubbed the back of my neck and thought about it. I had every reason not to, given the history of my former outfit. Hell, I'd been involved in official and unofficial military actions against the Directorate for years. But try as I might, I didn't see the Directorate in Feng. I'd read Feng's interrogation file, and I knew more than anyone what he'd been through. He had been "recovered" from a crèche facility—from Delta Crema station—not long after his birthing. He'd never fought for the Directorate, and now that he was Sim Ops he never would. Of course, it still worried me that Feng might not be what he seemed.

I sidestepped the question, and said, "Just remember that Feng has a distinctly different upbringing to yours."

Zero smiled weakly. "I'm not so sure that's a bad thing," she said. "Now, to what do I owe the pleasure of this visit? Surely you haven't come all the way down to Medical just to interfere with my love life, or lack thereof?"

"Same as Feng. My head is splitting."

"Common side effect of hypno-debrief," Zero said, knowingly.

"Tell me about it. I've been through more than enough of them."

I flopped into a chair beside Zero. Half-empty coffee cups lined the terminal around her, filling the air with the smell of stale java. Zero's monitoring station was in the middle of the Jackals' operating bay: a command throne surrounded by tiers of holo-tabs and viewers, a post from which she could direct the war in relative comfort. She could be the ultimate voyeur in here, safe and sound aboard the *Bainbridge*.

"What have you been doing?"

Zero rummaged through one of the many drug cabinets around the SOC and produced a packet of meds. Tossed me a strip of ugly-looking tablets that carried numerous addiction and overdose warnings.

"I've been reviewing the data from the Daktar operation," Zero said. "Such as there is."

Zero was like this after every mission—would often review the available data-feeds, immerse herself in whatever was sent back to her command station. That sort of initiative is the sign of a good handler, sure, but Zero took it to a whole new level.

I popped a couple of tabs from the strip and swallowed them down with a mouthful of cold coffee. My head hurt so badly that the bitter aftertaste was a price I willingly paid.

Zero settled back into her chair. "What's the feeling on the ship then?"

I snorted a sound that I'd intended to be a laugh. "You're on it, Zero. You tell me."

"I've been kind of busy since the extraction," she said. "And I missed the last mess."

"And the one before that," I added. "But you saw how everyone reacted when Daktar went down. The vibe is pretty bad, Zero. I've petitioned Captain Heinrich for an audience, but he says this is now a matter for High Command."

"Maybe General Draven will surprise you."

"If the reaction on this ship is anything to go by, I'm in deep trouble. Place feels awfully lonely all of a sudden: every other Sim Ops team leader is avoiding me."

"Don't think that way," Zero said. "It really wasn't your fault."

"We've known each other a long time," I said. "Longer than the others. You don't have to tow the company line. Not when it's only us."

"Then take it from me that I'm not towing the line, Keira. You're a damned good trooper, operator, and officer."

"Really? Because from where I'm sitting, it looks like I have front-seat tickets to a shitshow."

"No one else could've gotten into that Tower in time. It's an achievement that you got into the outpost in the first place."

"I don't see it that way."

"You should, Keira. You really should."

Zero glared at the monitors, at the low-resolution images that looped across her screens. Ordinarily, if a mission went to plan, every scrap of data that the suits collected would be broadcast back to Command for review. That included the video-feeds from our armour. As we'd lost the comms link to the *Bainbridge* so early in the operation, only fragments of visual had been retained. Had she been sim-operational, Zero could've directly tapped into the feeds and relived the experience on Daktar Outpost. Instead, she was reduced to watching the streams manually, living the fight second-hand.

"You still wish things could've been different for you?" I asked.

Zero answered without pause, as though the response was automatic. "Every fucking day."

I raised an eyebrow. "Even on a day like today?"

"*Especially* on a day like today," she said. "I grew up wanting to be Sim Ops. I wouldn't even be here if it wasn't for you."

"Not this again."

Zero chuckled. "Hey, don't knock my one and only war story."

"Great," I said, more bitterly than I'd intended. "I managed to get a trooper to sign up for a branch of military service that she couldn't even undertake…"

Zero looked down at her bare arms, where the dataports would ordinarily be located. She still had bright scar tissue there. "That wasn't your fault either," she said. "How was anyone to know that I would be a negative?"

"Just bad luck."

"Just like today," she countered.

I was never comfortable talking about what had happened to Zero, so I changed the topic: "What happened to the Krell ship, back at Daktar?"

"The bio-ship jumped system," Zero said, "right after the explosion. Used the Shard Gate. Doesn't look like the ship took any damage."

"How were you with being, you know, around the Krell?"

"It was fine," Zero said, a little too quickly for a genuine reaction.

Even in the low light of the SOC I could see that a sweat had broken on her upper lip. She caught a few errant strands of hair, pulled them back from her face. While it was true that pretty much no one really *liked* the fish heads—that being in their presence evinced a universal foreign-body reaction that few humans, simulated or otherwise, ever really overcame—Zero and the Krell had proper history.

"It's okay to hate them," I said. "For what they did, I mean."

"Yeah, well, it was a long time ago."

"But those sort of memories... They're hard to forget. Even harder in your own skin."

"Honestly, I'm fine," Zero said.

That was the other thing about Zoe Campbell. She struggled to lie. She was the same with everyone, but with me the difficulty seemed more pronounced. Another aspect of our shared history. But I knew that Zero would let me know if she needed me, if she wanted to talk. She turned back to her screens. Better not to push it any further.

I stood from the terminal. "Thanks for the drugs and coffee."

"Anytime."

"And try to keep away from Feng."

"I'll try," Zero said. "But no promises."

CHAPTER SEVEN

UNITY BASE

The *Bainbridge* docked with Unity Base, and we disembarked. As I suspected, there was a security detail waiting for me.

"You've got priority orders to report to General Draven's office," a burly Military Police officer said.

"Can I get a shower first?"

"Nope."

A short walk across Unity and here I was: cooped up in Draven's waiting room, left to stew in my own juices. Great. What a way to end a military career.

Unity Base orbited 986-Udanis, a K-class star on the edge of the Former Quarantine Zone. It was home base for most of the military agencies operating in and around the Maelstrom—a launch pad for the Alliance Navy, the Army, the Marine Corps. A couple of million military types under one roof. Place was so named because it was supposed to be a monument to the lasting peace that had been achieved between the Alliance and the Krell. A plaee of hope, for a better future.

For me, it had come to represent anything but. It had

been here, six months ago, that General Draven had first given me command of the Jackals.

"They're a rough outfit," he'd told me, "and they'll need some polishing, but I know that you're the trooper for the job." As I had looked through their personnel files, scattered across his desk, I remember thinking that "polishing" was a very optimistic description for the task at hand. The operators that made up the Jackals were completely green, not a veteran among them, and their training records were far from good.

That initial shock had quickly turned to determination though. Determination to shape the squad into the best they could be. Determination to make them my squad, to make them into a decent fighting unit. *Great job you did there.* I mulled on that as I sat in the waiting room that adjoined General Draven's office.

Trying to do anything to get my mind off the inevitable ass kicking I was about to receive, I watched the tri-D viewer set into the table. The rate at which news spread in the Alliance seemed to be exponential: the worse it was, the faster it travelled. What had happened on Daktar was moving faster than light. The programme was Core News Network—Senator Rodrigo Lopez being interviewed by a glossy lipped reporter.

"*...joined today by an increasingly important figure in the galactic political arena. Thanks for speaking with us, Senator Lopez.*"

"*It's no problem. I only wish our meeting could've been in nicer circumstances.*"

Smooth-skinned, ink-haired, and charismatic in the extreme, Senator Lopez wore a dark suit, open at the neck to reveal a muscled chest. Quite handsome, really. The family resemblance was obvious: he had the same nose and cheekbones as Gabriella Lopez. Whether that was genetic, or as a result of the family surgeon, I couldn't say.

"I'm sure that's a sentiment with which many viewers will sympathise. You're referring, of course, to the tragedy on Daktar, to the loss of the Science Division facility stationed there."

"I'm referring to the loss of the Alliance staff stationed there, Roseti. There were one hundred civilian staff on that station. Questions are already being asked about the involvement of the Army in this fiasco. Specifically, the Simulant Operations Programme…"

"Here we go," I whispered, leaning in to focus on the feed. "And the figure was one hundred and six, if we're keeping count."

"Care to expand on that?"

"We're at a crossroads. We've never had it so good. The universe is changing—has changed—and for the better. The Krell threat is over. We're finally at peace with the only other alien race that occupies this corner of the galaxy."

"You say that, but what about the Shard? Isn't the existence of the Shard Gates evidence of their continued danger to Alliance security?"

"No one has heard from the Shard in over five years. That's a long time. We can't build military structures to protect against an enemy that is, by all accounts, dead. I don't call that good economics."

All shit arguments, but when you're sitting on one of the most profitable rocks in the Core Systems, they were easy to make. Senator Lopez had probably never been to the frontier and he certainly hadn't seen the things that I had. Hell, he hadn't seen the things that his own daughter had seen… For a man with his clearance level, I hoped that he'd read about them though. Which made his attitude all the more surprising.

"So what are you suggesting is the solution here?"

"Yeah, Senator, what are you suggesting?" I mimicked.

"Daktar was a disaster, and I place the blame on

the Simulant Operations Programme. It's a relic of a past age, populated by warmongers and veterans who still think that we're at war with the Krell. It's time that we started dismantling the old structures, started looking to the future. We've built super-soldiers out of these men and women—given them the power to ignore death, to be reborn again—and yet, when they start throwing their weight around, being careless with their guns and their bombs, we're surprised that innocents get killed. It's not hard to see how this situation arose, and it's not hard to see how it will happen again."

"Isn't your own daughter, Gabriella Lopez, a serving operator with Sim Ops?"

"I can't discuss her deployment. She's serving a compulsory term of military service, as is required by Proximan planetary law, before she can be considered for a political post—"

"There have been reports that Gabriella Lopez was involved in the Daktar disaster. Can you confirm that?"

"I'm not confirming anything. Her military deployment is irrelevant, and I'm not here to talk about her."

"Please…" I said, shaking my head. "This man is a hack."

"They say that he's going to be the next Secretary General."

The only other occupant of the room was an officer sitting over at the security checkpoint into General Draven's office. I'd almost forgotten about him, having been so engrossed in the newsfeed.

"They also say that talking to yourself is the first sign of madness," he said.

"So the voices keep telling me," I replied. The holo continued with another news segment on developments in the Asiatic subsector, and I tuned out. Famine, shattered nation-states, clone containment atrocities: blah, blah, blah. Same old story.

"Was she there?" the officer asked.

"Is this a test?"

"Just filling time," he said.

"She was. She's on my squad."

"That must be quite some responsibility."

"You haven't seen the rest of my team," I said, shaking my head. "She's the least of my worries."

"They say that Senator Lopez is a very powerful man, now," the officer said. He placed emphasis on "now" in a specific way, because everyone knew Senator Lopez's story of Venusian immigration to the Proxima Colony: how he'd apparently clawed his way up the ladder to become an authority figure in a notoriously power-hungry political environment. "I shouldn't imagine he'd be very impressed if his little girl didn't come home."

"I don't think that she'll be my problem for much longer."

The officer continued, "Did you know that Senator Lopez controls funding for this whole station, and they say his role on the Senate Committee will soon expand to cover responsibility for Sim Ops funding?"

"I had heard," I said. "And maybe his daughter will be something someday, but I'm not putting money on it."

"It's surprising that she's on Sim Ops, given that Senator Lopez seems to hate the Programme so much."

I sighed. "She requested the assignment, apparently."

The officer stood from his desk, perhaps responding to a silent alert somewhere. "The general will see you now."

"Marvellous."

I followed him through to General Draven's office.

*   *   *

General Enrique Draven stood before a large open viewport that overlooked Unity Base's main docking facility. The window controls had been adjusted so that it was half-opaqued, the glare of the local star just visible through the smoked plasglass, the occasional flare of a starship thruster muted by the effect. He continued to stare intently at the view as I entered the room.

"Lieutenant Keira Jenkins, as you requested, sir," the aide said.

General Draven didn't respond, but the other officer briskly withdrew, raising his eyebrows in a *good luck* gesture as he left.

I stood in front of Draven's desk. Got a jolt of déjà vu: it had been in this very room that I'd been given my command. Now, I threw a salute, simply because it seemed like the right thing to do. Draven ignored me. Just went on staring out of that port, his reflection visible against the glass. I let the salute drop after a few seconds of inactivity.

Just when the silence in the room began to border on excruciating, I went to speak. "Sir, I—"

"I fought alongside your father," General Draven said, speaking slowly and patiently, his voice a deep hardwood bass. "During the Deimos Campaign."

"I am aware of that, sir."

"Your old man ever talk about it?"

"Occasionally, sir."

"We were fighting the Directorate in those days," Draven said, still staring out of the port, hands clasped behind his back. "It was a dirty little war, Lieutenant." He paused, then repeated: "A very dirty little war."

"I've fought the Directorate, sir," I said. "I'm aware of the tactics they employ."

Draven continued as though I hadn't spoken. "The

enemy wasn't honest, but we knew them. We knew *who* we were fighting, and *why*. We lost good men and women in the tunnels on Deimos, and the Directorate made us pay for every inch of territory. But no matter the losses, we kept going. Do you know why?"

"No, sir. I don't."

"Because General Theodore Jenkins was the best commanding officer that I've ever served under."

Draven let that hang. The silence became uncomfortable again.

"Yes, sir," I said, just to fill the quiet. "I understand."

"Do you, Lieutenant?" Draven said. He turned his grey-eyed stare at me, fixed me with it. "Because I don't think that you do."

Draven was a tall, bulky man. Well-muscled in a way that only a regular rejuvenation regime could explain, his age tended to show the longer you were in his presence. The pressure of responsibility was revealed in the wrinkles that collected around his eyes, the back of his hands. The moustache that had probably started as a shield behind which the younger Enrique Draven could hide had become walrus-like and silver, and was seen as his defining characteristic among the Army units under his command. Which, it had to be said, was pretty much all Army-affiliated Sim Ops teams. Draven was the man so far as the off-world Sim Ops Programme was concerned: chief coordinator of the military efforts in the Maelstrom sector.

He pulled a chair from behind his desk and sat, leaving me standing right in front of him. Pinched the bridge of his nose with his forefinger and thumb. "You caused the loss of a hundred and six human lives—"

I couldn't take this any more.

"There were mitigating circumstances!" I said, speaking over Draven.

But he kept going, raising his voice until I fell silent. "…as well as the loss of six senior military officers, who are now in the hands of the largest terrorist organisation in Alliance history."

Draven stared at the surface of his smart-desk—piled with data-slates and other administrative tokens of his command—and shook his head.

"Captain Heinrich tells me that your squad wasn't even supposed to be in Tower One. Isn't that right, Captain?"

I heard a low cough at my shoulder, and turned to see Heinrich standing beside the hatch. Though his face was a picture of neutrality, his eyes didn't lie. He looked more than pleased with how the situation had developed: that this mess had been dropped in my airlock.

"As you can see from the mission plan, sir," Heinrich said, "Lieutenant Jenkins' squad was assigned to Tower Three. They were on reconnaissance duty. Captain Ving's team—Phoenix Squad—was assigned to Tower One. The mission plan specifically accounted for the fact that Tower One, and the rest of the outpost, might be rigged for detonation."

"The briefing packet didn't make that clear," I argued. "There was a lot that we weren't told about the operation." If Heinrich was going to hang me out to dry, then I had something to say about him as well. "For example, I wasn't briefed on the Krell's involvement in this mission."

Heinrich sighed condescendingly. "That information was restricted. I gave an oral briefing before the drop, sir. Lieutenant Jenkins was late to the SOC. She missed the warning."

I bit my lip. It was all true, but given the significance of that piece of information—that we were requesting backup from the Krell—Heinrich should've made damned sure that every simulant team was aware of it.

Heinrich went on, "Sergeant Campbell, the Jackals' intelligence handler, was fully aware of the circumstances of the joint deployment."

Cold realisation seeped into my bones. Zero had been trying to tell me something before we'd made the drop to Daktar. I now knew exactly what that had been: that the Krell were assisting with the mission.

"As a direct result of Lieutenant Jenkins' actions," Heinrich droned on, "the mission's priority target—the enemy asset codenamed 'Warlord'—was lost." He rolled his head in another patronising gesture. "We had a clear shot at him, sir. If Captain Ving had been allowed to get into Tower One, with the support of the Krell assault shoal, I'm sure that we could've taken him."

"Please download my debriefing," I said, exasperated. "As I've already said, the Jackals were the only ground asset in Tower One. We had no comms. What were we supposed to do?"

My outburst had the desired effect. Colonel Draven looked up sharply from his desk.

"Are you quite finished, Lieutenant?" he asked.

"I did what I thought was best," I said. "But yes, sir. I'm finished."

Draven's eyes shifted from Heinrich to me and back again. His expression remained stony and cold. "Continue, Captain."

Heinrich nodded. "We had intelligence, prior to the deployment, that a target of specific interest was present on Daktar." Heinrich leaned over the desk, and slid a plastic image across the surface. Even though it was a low-resolution capture, I immediately recognised the Spiral's leader: the man in the exo-suit. "I considered that deployment of a veteran team, such as Phoenix Squad, would present the best chance of both recovering the hostages and capturing the target."

"For your information, Lieutenant," Draven said, "Warlord is believed to be a member of the Black Spiral's ruling council. He may even be regarded as a leader of sorts. Given the disparate nature of the Spiral's organisation, I'm sure that even you can appreciate the importance of his capture."

In the picture, he wore a helmet, and beneath that his face was cloaked with filthy grey rags: bandage-like, wrapped tightly so that only his eyes were visible, but the armour was easily identifiable. I took in what detail I could from the image. I was now more sure than ever that the exo-suit was military-grade. An older pattern, for sure, but Alliance-issue. Powered armour was hard to come by, even for a well-organised terrorist outfit like the Spiral.

"Warlord is suspected of orchestrating dozens of attacks on Alliance holdings within the last year," Draven said, "many of which you've probably heard about."

One wall of the general's room was occupied by a wall-to-floor view-screen. He jabbed at a control on his desk and the wall became a monitor. A list of known operations, of other sightings of target Warlord, appeared there. Draven was right: I had heard of many of the locations and incidents. Whoever Warlord was, he certainly had blood on his hands.

"He was your real objective…" I said, looking up from the images. "Warlord; that was what the Daktar operation was all about, wasn't it?"

Draven and Heinrich and the rest of Command didn't care about Daktar or the civilians stationed there. They had wanted Warlord.

"As of right now," Draven rumbled, cementing my opinion, "that man represents the biggest danger to the security of the three hundred Allied worlds. So yes, I make no apologies for telling you that Warlord was our real target."

"It would've been nice to know in advance," I said. But even as the words left my mouth, I was very much aware of how ineffectual they sounded. That wasn't how the universe worked, and that certainly wasn't how the Alliance military worked. I added, hollowly, "I was using my initiative, sir. I didn't know."

"You can't do that any more. When I gave you command of the Jackals, you told me that you wanted to lead. That you wanted to make the Jackals into something better."

"I remember," I said. "I've been thinking a lot about that day."

"You're going to have to learn to lead that squad," Draven said, "and I think it's best that you go off-grid for a while. I've discussed the situation with Captain Heinrich. We, and Sector Command, feel that you should keep a low profile."

I could feel Heinrich's smile beside me, even if I couldn't see it. He radiated smugness like a breached energy core shedding rad particles.

Draven tossed a file of papers across the table. "Fieldwork is what you prefer, right?"

"Yes, sir."

Draven tipped his head in the direction of the hardcopy file. "That's your mission packet. The mission isn't glamorous, but it's all I can offer."

Any sense of relief I'd just felt that Draven hadn't stripped me of my command was quickly vanishing.

"What is it?" I asked.

"It's all in the briefing. Read it for yourself."

Reluctantly, because to pick up the papers felt as

though I was accepting the mission, I took the briefing. It was slim and light: a manila envelope sealed with the Alliance Army badge.

"You'll be gone for a while," Heinrich pitched in behind me, "and as such you'll be out of my direct command."

"Which should suit you fine, given your predilection for 'using your initiative,'" Draven muttered. "You're being assigned to the UAS *Santa Fe*."

I opened the packet and stared at the printed cover sheet. There was an awkward silence in the room as I read it. The words started to become jumbled after the first line, and my legs felt weak beneath me.

"You have twelve hours to get your business together," Draven said, as I looked up from the briefing.

"What's the destination?"

"The Maelstrom," Draven said. "But I'm sure that your new commanding officer will explain everything once you're aboard the vessel. As I understand it, your objective is to escort said military officer to designated coordinates, and remain on-ship for as long as required."

By assigning the Jackals to a starship, General Draven was writing a blank cheque. We could be gone years, with or without purpose. It wasn't a task for Sim Ops! Starship escort was a duty for the Alliance Marine Corps. Even regular Army would be better suited to the mission.

"This isn't a mission," I said. "It's punishment!"

Draven's expression didn't shift one bit. "You, and the Jackals, are to report to your assigned transport at oh-nine-hundred hours tomorrow."

"You can't do this! I'll take a court martial instead. This is so much worse."

"It's not your decision to make," Draven said. "Those are your orders. You're dismissed."

Next to me, Heinrich saluted briskly.

I left without the formalities, my face burning bright with rage. I needed to get out of there, and now.

I left the general's room with Heinrich in tow, and was surprised that it took him until we reached the sector elevator to comment.

"You're a disappointment," he said, "and I'm damned glad to get you and your team off my company."

"You know," I said, "for a senior officer in Simulant Operations, I often wonder why you hate the Programme so much."

Heinrich's face flushed. "Maybe you won't come back."

The elevator pinged, indicating that we'd reached Unity's crew decks, and I turned to walk out.

"Fuck you, Heinrich," I said, and only just managed to contain the urge to punch the sanctimonious prick in the face. "I'll be seeing you."

Heinrich watched me go.

That talk of my father made me think of what my folks back home, on Old Earth, would think of all this. It occurred to me that maybe I should phone them. My family would no doubt have heard about the disaster on Daktar, and would be following the newsfeeds. I could imagine their reaction: disappointment with their daughter's decision to enter Sim Ops being borne out once again. The mental image of their faces was enough to put me off that idea.

My father was proper old-school military, and my mother wasn't much better. Mom a teacher—working in the education centre base-side, Dad an Army man all the way up until his sixty-fifth birthday. My brother and I had been Army brats, through and through, brought up on Dad's stories of active service, and Deimos Campaign had been just one of many different episodes in his Army career. Strange, perhaps, that young Enrique Draven—a kid with a bad attitude and a worse moustache, as my father referred to him—had ended up outranking the mighty Theodore Jenkins.

A bullet to the abdomen had ended my father's aspirations of staying on the frontline for ever, and six months behind a desk on Old Earth satisfied him that becoming a REMF wasn't his calling. He'd left the Army with full honours, and the Jenkins family had transferred from San Ang Army accommodation to a suburb of the Lower State. Sure, it was nice and middle-class and we'd never had so much space. But that wasn't enough for Dad. The place wasn't *military*, and that was all that mattered.

I'd been fourteen years old then, and I hadn't really understood what the move had done to my father. Even through my later military service—and I'd only really joined the Army because that was what Ted Jenkins had wanted for his oldest child, eventually to become his *only* child—I hadn't really appreciated it.

But as I left General Draven's office, I felt a lot like my father. Maybe, now, I finally understood.

Once, he'd been someone great. A contender. Overnight, he'd become nothing, and now I was just the same.

I found the Jackals in one of Unity's many crew lounges. The facility was busy enough—a handful of Navy crew, some Aerospace Force pilots in Sims Ops get-up—but not rowdy, and the squad languished in a corner. The other occupants gave the Jackals a wide berth, as though they carried a lethal contagion.

That the Jackals were together at all was something. They didn't seem to like each other much more than they liked themselves, and most downtime was spent in private company. Come to think of it, other than Zero and Riggs, I had no real idea how the rest of the squad wasted their lives.

A round of beers sat in the middle of the table, untouched. I scooped one up as I approached. Novak went to follow suit, but his security-drone issued a violation warning. He swatted the drone away and slumped back, empty-handed. "No alcoholic beverages" was one of the many restrictions on his military contract.

The Russian eyed me carefully. "So?" he grunted.

"Steady, big boy. I've got news."

"What happened?" Riggs asked.

"I think that we have a right to know," Lopez started. "It wasn't just you who got burnt by that operation."

"And don't I know it," I said, with a sigh.

Lopez smouldered quietly. Of the whole squad, she looked the most different in her real skin. The real Lopez struggled not to look chic even in her combat-khakis, a spill of dark hair topping her head, her full face and lips speaking of a damned good body sculptor. She had a nasty pout, and when things didn't go her way she had a tendency to show it.

"I'm still commanding officer of the Jackals, if that's what you're asking."

"They didn't take away your commission?" Feng said. "Well that's something we should drink to."

"What about demotion?" Lopez followed up, with less warmth than Feng.

"No," I said. "They didn't demote me either."

"That's good," Zero said. Seeing Zero in the crew lounge felt a little odd; she looked out of place among the dirty beige wall panelling and beer bottles. This wasn't her sort of place at all.

"Then what happened?" Novak grumbled.

"New orders," I said. "Not just for me, but the Jackals."

Novak's mouth split in a grimace. "We have mission, but why are you not happy?"

There were so many tattoos over his face that there was barely any skin visible. He had a trio of metal studs bored into his forehead: body augmentations from his time in the gulag. He'd stripped his fatigues down to a vest that barely covered his enormous bulk, the fabric straining at his shoulders.

"It's not that simple," I said. I put the order envelope on the table, slid out the briefing pack.

"New orders has to be good," Riggs said, eyes lighting. "Another mission is better than being permanently recalled to home base—"

"Easy, trooper. We have new orders, but the good news stops there."

"Go on," Zero said.

"We're being seconded to a starship," I explained, slowly, trying to draw the sting out of my words. "The UAS *Santa Fe*. On escort duty. Destination: the Maelstrom." I swallowed. "Length of duty unknown."

The reaction to my news was immediate and expected. A round of curses and sighs spread round the table.

"Ah shit..." Riggs said. "The Maelstrom? That's some serious shit."

Novak sucked his teeth. "Is not good. Fish head country."

"Christo...!" Lopez exhaled. "You cannot be serious. We didn't have anything to do with your decision to go into Tower One!"

Feng shook his head. "We were all there, Lopez. We all knew that we were going off plan."

Lopez's eyes flared in my direction. "*She* was the squad leader! *She's* the supposed veteran! What would you know, anyway? You're Directorate!"

Feng hung his head, and said, "Fuck you, Lopez. That's not fair."

"What would a clone know about being fair?" Lopez asked. Back to me, she said, "I can't go into the Maelstrom!"

Feng nodded towards one of the media-walls, at the image that was streaming there. It was Senator Lopez's interview. The damned thing seemed to be following me around the station, haunting me.

"Why don't you call up daddy and ask for reassignment?" Feng suggested.

Lopez pouted some more. "At least I have a daddy."

I slammed a hand on the table. "Shut up, all of you. For your information, I tried to take a court martial, but General Draven refused my request." I looked around at the disparate collection of troopers that formed Jenkins' Jackals. "I'm sorry, folks. I shouldn't have taken you into Tower One, but it seemed like a good idea at the time."

The group fell quiet.

"You've got twelve hours to get your shit together," I said. "Considering that we don't know how long we'll be away, I'd suggest that you make the time count, and that you pack a second pair of underwear. But hear this: each of you is required to attend the main docks at oh-nine-hundred hours tomorrow morning, ready to board the *Santa Fe*. You might not like it, but that's our mission."

No one nodded, and no one agreed, but no one dissented either. That was the best I could ask for in the circumstances.

"Dismissed," I said, firmly.

The Jackals stood to leave and, heads bowed, filtered out of the lounge. As he went, Riggs made eye contact with me, lingered a little, but I gave him *the look* and he eventually followed the others.

Only Zero remained. Anxiety plastered across her befreckled features.

"I'm sorry about her," Zero said. "Lopez, I mean."

"She's no more under your control than mine," I said. "I'll see to her."

"I'm sure there's a good trooper under there somewhere."

"I'm glad one of us thinks so," I replied, swigging down another mouthful of beer. "I know that this— going into the Maelstrom—is going to be tough on you, Zero. I wouldn't do it for any of the others, but if you want me to ask for a transfer..."

Maelstrom meant Krell. Krell and Zero did *not* mix.

"I'll be okay," she said. "We'll be on a starship, right?"

"That's right. But I could still put in a word—"

"You mean do I want to leave the Jackals?" Zero said. She looked almost incredulous. "I dread to think what sort of a mess you'd get into without me. I'm with you all the way."

"You sure?"

"Couldn't be surer," Zero said. She put out her fist, and we bumped knuckles. "It'll be fun, right? An adventure. I could do with a break from all this desk work."

"I hear that, sister. I hear that."

What did I do for my last night in civilisation?

I knew what happened was wrong, even as I was doing it. I'd like to think that it was chance, that I did it on a whim, but I knew that wasn't true. I'd planned it this way, and I knew exactly what I was doing.

I went down to the barracks. Unity wasn't on a war footing—probably never would be—and as a result many of the troopers were given sole-occupancy quarters.

I stood outside his door. Finger hovering over the intercom button. Although, if I'm being honest with myself, there wasn't much indecision on my part. I pressed the buzzer.

Riggs answered the door, naked from the chest up. His short dark hair was scruffy and dishevelled, like he had been sleeping. The look was good on him.

"Ah, hi," he said. Confused. "I wasn't expecting to see you."

"I come bearing gifts," I said, revealing a bottle of New Ceti bourbon tucked into the crook of my arm, smiling as coyly as I knew how. Which, I admit, is probably not very coyly at all. "That is, if you're not busy…"

"Lieutenant, ma'am…" Riggs started, rubbing his eyes. "Is everything okay?"

"Fine," I said. "But call me Keira. Just for tonight."

Right then I didn't want to be a lieutenant. I didn't want to be called "ma'am" or suffer any of the trappings of command.

Riggs stood aside. Let me into the room. "Course, of course. It's just that I thought you said this wouldn't happen again. And since Daktar, well, I got the feeling that you'd been avoiding me…"

"Shut up, Riggs," I said. I took in the odour of his body; it smelt sweaty, as though he had recently been exercising. The scent made my mouth water. "Same arrangement. I don't want the others to know."

"You said that last time was *the* last time."

He looked slightly puzzled, a not unpleasant expression

on his face. I had a type, and Riggs—with his dumbass bravado—was exactly it.

"Maybe *this* is the last time," I said.

Riggs smiled. "Then I guess we'd better make it count."

"I guess so."

I shut the door behind me.

CHAPTER EIGHT

SANTA FE

"The *Santa Fe*'s in Bay Sixteen," the deck chief said, tilting his head towards the enormous hangar that comprised Unity Base's docking facility. "Papers ready for disembarkation, please."

None of us carried actual paper, of course. But the chief—a portly older man in an orange vacuum suit, wearing mufflers over his ears, and a light wand clipped to his belt—scanned our biometric dog tags.

Surprisingly, we had a full house. All of the Jackals—even Lopez—had attended for duty that morning, although with their crumpled fatigues and stuffed-away bags, they looked about as dejected as I felt. As planned, Riggs turned up late, trailing a comfortable distance behind me. None of the Jackals had noticed, and I'd feigned acceptance of his tardiness.

"You're all cleared," the chief said, checking off names on a data-slate. "Good luck, wherever it is you're going."

"Thanks, Chief," I said.

Zero wandered ahead of the squad. She was about the only member of the group who was exhibiting any interest in our surroundings. She indicated a berth.

The UAS *Santa Fe* was attached to Unity by an umbilical docking tube, the vessel's bulk visible through the view-ports.

"This must be us," she said.

I wasn't impressed. This was not what I was used to at all. The *Santa Fe* was so banal as to be almost lost among the sea of similar ships—nothing exceptional at all to mark her from any other vessels. Her battered hull was a charcoal black, scorched by the light of a dozen suns, and her name tag was barely visible. No national flag, no Naval identifier. Almost as though the Alliance was trying to disavow ownership of the vessel.

"Looks like a fairly typical Type 103 corvette," Zero said, with confidence. A corvette-class starship was the smallest of what could fairly be called a warship. "According to her public records, she was commissioned out of the Central Ventris shipyards in 2263. That makes her nearly three decades old."

Lopez let out an annoyed sigh. "She hasn't aged well."

"Except for those engines," Riggs said. "She's had a recent refit, I'd say."

"That your aviator training coming out?" I asked of Riggs. "How can you tell?"

Riggs seemed to take great pride in his knowledge of ship tech, and I often caught myself wondering why it was he'd chosen to transfer out of the Alliance Marine Corps.

"From the colouration of her aft," he answered. He added, more sharply than usual, "It's petty obvious, really."

As I examined the ship further, I realised that Riggs had a point. Although the vessel was still at some distance, the *Santa Fe*'s engine module—where her sublight propulsion system and quantum-drive were located—was shiny and new. Looked like it had hardly been used, with 986-Udanis' distant light glinting off the naked metalwork.

"It's a ship," Lopez said. Crossed her arms over her chest. "There's nothing interesting about it."

"She's gone by several names over the years," Zero continued, "and been assigned to—"

"That's great," I said, shaking my head. I had no doubt that Zero had researched the ship and could probably recount its full history, despite the length of time the vessel had been in service. "Shall we just board and sort out the rest later?"

"That's probably best," Riggs said.

Amid the bustle of utility robots and Navy men in mechanised loaders, we found ourselves in the *Santa Fe*'s main cargo hold. Soon after boarding, it became apparent that Lopez was wrong about the *Fe*. Much of the ship's interior had been replaced or refitted. Given the ship's age, that was pretty interesting. The air was thick with the smell of burning plastic and plasma weld.

Riggs approached the nearest gaggle of sailors.

"Jenkins' Jackals," he said, "reporting for assignment to the *Santa Fe*."

The group had been fussing over data-slates—no doubt conducting a review of the loading process—but paused when Riggs interrupted. One figure, who also happened to be the shortest, looked up abruptly.

"And you'd be?" she asked.

"Corporal Daneb Riggs," he said. "Army Sim Ops Programme."

The officer had the stripes of an Alliance Navy captain on her shoulder, but was much older than most working starship crew. She wore a dark blue service cap, which sat on top of a bun of silver hair, clasped at the back of her head with a miniature metal dagger.

"Whatever happened to shipboard protocol?" she asked. "In my day, you'd have asked for permission to come aboard. That, and you're late."

"No, ma'am," Zero said. "We aren't. We were scheduled to board at oh-nine-hundred—"

"Not by my itinerary," said the woman. "Are you telling me that I'm wrong?"

"No, ma'am," Zero said. She fidgeted and looked uncomfortable with the sudden confrontation.

The captain came forward, walking with a silver cane. Shorter than me, physically far less imposing. Her left leg was rigid, and I spied a metallic ankle at the hem of the woman's trouser: a crude Navy bionic. A handful of crew accompanied her.

"My apologies, Captain," I said. "Forgive them. They're green. Requesting permission to come aboard."

The captain curled her lip in my direction. I passed her our briefing packet, and one of the crew took it: gave a cursory glance over the detail. The officer nodded at the captain.

"Granted," she said, but glared at Novak. "I see that we have a lifer aboard. It's a shame that the Alliance has fallen so low."

Although the comment had clearly been designed to cause offence, it didn't work. Novak's hooded eyes remained impassive, and his drone hovered at his shoulder.

"He's approved," I said.

The captain sneered. "Lieutenant Yukio: get that man and his bags searched. I don't want any unauthorised weapons aboard my ship."

"Yes, ma'am," said an officer, jumping to a search of Novak and his away-bag.

Novak having failed to take the bait, the captain turned her attention to another member of the squad.

Her facial expression noticeably dropped, what little colour there was in her features seeping out like atmosphere from a hull breach.

"No, no," she said at Feng, "this really won't do. I thought it was bad enough that you'd brought a lifer aboard my vessel...But Directorate? Weren't you all put down in the camps where they found you? Hell, I'd rather share my ship with a Krell than a Directorate clone."

Feng's shoulders set back, his knuckles whitening as they tightened round the strap of his crew bag. I was very much aware that this could turn nasty.

"Let's hope that you don't have to make that choice," I replied.

"I'm not one of them," Feng said, through clenched teeth. "I don't know how many times I have to say this, but I'm not Directorate!"

The Navy officers exchanged worried glances. One of the younger crewmen stepped forward, blocking Feng's path to the captain. Feng was physically much bigger and probably stronger than the aged Navy officer. But if it came to a fight, there was no question of who I would be betting on...

"Steady," the captain said. Put a hand on her fellow officer's shoulder, and displaced him with the gentlest of touches. To Feng, she said, "I'm sure that someone out here believes you, even if I don't."

Feng looked sideways at me. His shoulders dropped. Probably disarmed by the grin across my face.

"She doesn't mean any harm," I said, nodding at the captain. "Trust me, her bark is far worse than her bite."

When he looked back to the captain, she was smiling too.

"It's been too long, Carmine," I said. "No one told me that I would be working under you."

"That's *Captain* Carmine to you, girl," she said. "At least in front of the crew."

I gave a brisk and genuine salute at the older woman. She waved it aside and flung her arms around me.

"Oh, I'm not your commanding officer," Carmine said. "But you'll meet him, soon enough. I just take care of the flying." She called over her officer cadre, indicated to the Jackals. "Get these troopers settled in. I'm sure they'll get used to me soon enough."

"Jackals," I said, opening my arms towards the squad, "meet Captain Miriam Carmine. Captain Carmine, meet the Jackals."

"You know the captain . . . ?" Lopez said.

Carmine frowned. "She's bright, this one. Do I recognise her from somewhere?"

"Maybe her daddy," Novak suggested.

"Hmmm," Carmine said, shuffling on her metal walking stick. "Probably. An old girl like me loses track after so many lovers . . ."

"I don't think he meant it like that," I said.

Carmine winked. "I might be old, but I'm not stupid. Come, come, Keira. We've got so much to catch up on. Anyone wants me, I'll be taking tea in my quarters with Lieutenant Jenkins."

Carmine grasped my forearm with an iron grip that suggested I couldn't escape even if I'd been armed.

"Come, my dear. Come."

I'd insisted that Zero accompany me for some moral support. She looked more than a little perplexed by the captain's presentation.

As Carmine ushered us into her cramped cabin, she turned to Zero and said, "Don't worry. I only mean half of what I say."

"The captain is an acquired taste," I explained.

"Much like a fine wine," Carmine said. She was basking in Zero's confusion. "Or a cheap spirit."

Carmine's cabin was hardly befitting of a senior Navy officer, but I supposed luxury was a foreign concept aboard a transport like the *Santa Fe*. The chamber was filled with bolted-down furniture, and we took up seats around a small desk. That was mostly dominated by tea-making facilities. The cabin, and Carmine, smelled of fresh tea leaves.

Carmine slowly *tap-tap-tapped* her way round the deck, sliding into a seat behind it. With the silver cane and the affected movements, she looked positively ancient, and I couldn't help but think about how long it had been since I'd last seen her.

"You haven't changed, Carmine," I said, just because it felt like the right thing to say.

"And you're a bad liar," she said. She flung her cap across the room, onto a poorly made bunk. "I'm older, and so are you."

"Thanks," I said.

"You can see it in your face, and I spied a few grey hairs back there in the dock."

Zero laughed. "I thought you two were friends?"

"Oh, we are, my dear," Carmine said. She set about activating the tea set, pouring steaming hot tea into a set of beaten metal mugs without asking whether we wanted it. "But even friends get older. So how have you been, Keira?"

I sipped at the tea. It was bitter, without milk, and very hot. "You don't know?"

Carmine smiled. Age lines spread across her cheeks. "If you're referring to Daktar, then of course I know. I suppose that'd age anyone. It's the biggest news this side of the Maelstrom."

"It wasn't our fault," Zero said.

"And who would you be, my dear?" Carmine asked. She pushed a cup across the table in Zero's direction and intimated that she drink it.

"Sergeant Zoe Campbell, ma'am," Zero said. "I'm the Jackals' intelligence and operations handler. Everyone calls me Zero."

"Welcome aboard the *Fe*, Zero," Carmine said. "You already know who I am, but everyone calls me 'Carmine the Carbine.'" She winked. "I pretend not to notice."

Behind Carmine, attached to the wall, was an ancient assault carbine. The pattern was one that hadn't been in service for decades. Carmine turned to look at the weapon. Her mechanical leg whirred noisily.

"What happened?" Zero said.

Carmine looked at me. "Can I tell her the story?"

"If you must," I said.

"The long or short version?"

I blew on my tea. "I don't think that we have time for the long version."

Carmine pulled a tight smile. "Listen to the girl, will you? Gets her own squad and she suddenly thinks she's General Draven himself!"

"Just get on with it."

"Well, Zero," Carmine said, rolling the words around her mouth in a theatrical way, "Keira Jenkins and I have known each other for a long time. Longer than she's been a lieutenant, in fact. We go back to when she was Legion, when she served under that irrepressible oaf Conrad Harris…"

"Lazarus?" Zero said. Her face illuminated at the name, in a way that I always found endearingly child-like. "You met him?"

"In the flesh," Carmine said. "Both real and simulated. The Legion used my ship as a base of operations during the New Ohio withdrawal. There was an evacuation order, you see, and the population were being shuttled into orbit. It was during the Krell War."

Carmine frowned, recalling the memory. "I was captain of the *Atran Prime* in those days. She was a good ship—served me well for almost five years. While we were ferrying civilians from the surface, the *Atran* was attacked by pirates. Boarded by two dozen of the nasty bastards."

Carmine tapped her leg. She shuffled around the edge of her desk, so that Zero could see what she was indicating, then pulled up her left trouser leg. The fabric snagged on a skeletal frame made of dull metal, and with some difficulty she pulled it to her knee. It was a poor-quality bionic. The Navy, like the Army, rarely went in for cosmetics: so far as Logistics was concerned, if a prosthetic did the job then that was all that mattered. She limped back to her side of the desk.

"I've only met pirates once in my life," she said, "and that was once too many. Lazarus and his Legion were a little late on that particular rescue operation…"

"The pirates shot you?" Zero asked.

Carmine grinned at me. "You've got another clever one in your squad then? Yes, my dear, the pirates shot me. Killed several of my crew as well though, so I count myself lucky. Anyway, Lazarus and the Legion were on New Ohio. But when they became aware that the ship had been boarded they extracted back to the Simulant Operations Centre and cleared the pirates out."

I looked at Carmine across the table. "Except that's not quite how it happened, is it? You're making out that *we* saved *you*…"

"Which is precisely what you did," Carmine insisted.

I shook my head. "You lost that leg defending the Simulant Operations Centre, so that we could get the refugees off-planet."

Carmine stared down at her tea, at the ripples that danced across the dark surface.

"I'm old, my dear," she said. "Sometimes the details get lost in the telling."

"What's important is that you're the heroine of that story," I said. "And that's how Captain Carmine got her nickname. She used a carbine—one of the pirates' assault rifles—to kill their leader."

There the weapon sat: a Fabrique Multiworld MN. A proper antique, with a moulded plastic stock and a battle-scarred muzzle. I knew, without asking, that the carbine would still be capable of firing. That was Carmine. Ever-ready.

Carmine breathed out slowly. "That's not the only reason they call me Carbine. I have a fast mouth too. I like to talk, and the Navy don't like that in an officer."

I pointed at the wall. Sarcastically added, "Hence the medals, and all."

As well as the carbine, the walls of Carmine's cabin were filled with accolades. Merchant Navy shipping certificates, from her early career, sat alongside framed holo-medals and ribboned badges. Pride of place was a picture of six young women who looked so much like younger copies of Carmine that it was almost uncomfortable.

"How's the family?" I asked, nodding at the picture.

"Good," Carmine said. "Last I heard, at least. Difficult to keep track of them when I'm never home. Earth's a long way from the frontline. I try to call when I can, but tachyon-links don't come cheap..."

Carmine was an Old Earther, like me, and given the practicalities of time-dilation I doubted that she had much time to go back to the Core and conduct family visits. She was actually from California, her hometown not far from Low State where I'd grown up. I wondered if I would end up like her in my old age. Out here alone, sailing the stars without anyplace to call home. *There are worse ways to go*, I silently concluded.

"And what about you, Zero my dear? Where are you from? I can't place your accent."

"I'm Mau Tanis," Zero said.

"American or French?" Carmine asked.

"Bit of both. My father was French, my mother North American."

Carmine gave a little shake of her head, remembering the details. "Wasn't Mau Tanis the site of that Krell attack in '76?"

"Yes," Zero said, and with admirable calmness. "It was. I was eight standard years old at the time."

"You were there, weren't you?" Carmine asked of me. "With the Lazarus Legion, I mean."

"I was," I said. I swallowed. *Not everyone can be saved.* "Maybe I'll tell you about that another time, Carmine."

"Very well," Carmine said.

Although Carmine might put on the old lady façade, she was very far from stupid. She must've detected that she was stepping into a minefield. She gave new direction to the conversation.

"What about the rest of your squad? The 'Jackals,' eh? Who the hell thinks up these names?"

"Command," I said. "I was supposed to iron them out, but things haven't quite gone to plan…"

"How many transitions?"

"Seven apiece," I said. I didn't explain to Carmine that six of those had been in training, and that the seventh transition had ended up in this mess. "Except for Riggs. He has eleven."

"That's awful green, Jenkins. Awful green."

Although she wasn't Simulant Operations, and she wasn't operational like me and the other operators, Carmine was an old hand. She knew the Programme well:

you didn't get as many years under the belt as Carmine without understanding how fellow military agencies worked.

"The dark-haired one," she said, waving a hand in the air, "he's quite the eye-candy."

"Feng?" Zero said.

Carmine scowled. "Not the Directorate one. The muscly one."

"Corporal Riggs," I said. "Yeah, he's easy on the eye, I guess."

Carmine smiled with a knowing glint in her eye. I felt my cheeks prickle with embarrassment. She had an almost supernatural sense for this sort of thing, an ability to wheedle information out of people without even really trying. She'd probably make a good Military Intelligence officer.

She poured herself another cup of strong tea. "Like I said, I only half-mean some of the things that come out of my mouth. I only half-meant the things about that Chino trooper…"

"Feng's okay," I said. "He's been through an extensive debrief procedure, and Sci-Div say that there's no residual Directorate influence."

Captain Carmine's concerns echoed my own, but I wasn't about to give up on Feng. As Draven had told me: I needed to lead this squad if they were going to be anything. That meant giving Feng, even Novak, the benefit of the doubt. I knew that Zero would be satisfied I had defended Feng, if nothing else.

"I'll take your word for that, Keira," Carmine said. "You know I trust you."

"Leave it with me," I said. "But more pressingly, we were expecting some sort of briefing on our part in this operation."

Carmine finished her tea and set the cup down on the

table. "You and me both," she said. "But as you'll see, he isn't exactly the talkative type." She raised her eyebrows in another dramatic expression. "But then Military Intelligence rarely are..."

"He's Mili-Intel?" Zero asked.

"That's what I said. We've been running transport operations for him for some months now, on and off. The work's usually clandestine, and often seems to involve Simulant Operations. You'll probably want to check out the Sim Ops bay, down in Medical. It's quite something."

"What's our destination and route?" I asked.

"All I know is that the major expects us to make Q-space to North Star Station," Carmine said. "From there, new course projections will take us into the Maelstrom."

"Any idea about journey time?"

That was the big question for any trip into the Maelstrom. While the *Santa Fe* travelled through quantum-space, time would slow down. But for the rest of the universe it was business as usual, and the clock still ticked. That was the time-dilation effect of a Q-space jump. The only alternative was to use a Shard Gate.

"Faster than you'd expect," Carmine said. "We're running an experimental engine module."

"Like Riggs said," Zero added.

"So he's not just a pretty chassis?" Carmine offered. "The drive is fresh out of Science Division labs. Fastest Q-drive that we have in operation. Jump time is much reduced compared to an older module. Only a dozen or so ships have the drive, and until it is safety-approved it won't be rolled out across the fleet. We've been running the drive for the last few months, since this new CO took operation of my ship."

"What's he like? The CO I mean."

"He's okay. Far from the worst officer I've ever had on one of my ships." Carmine's face grew a little reluctant. "But this can wait. Launch comes first, and you should take a look around your new home."

Before I could dissent, Carmine had commed for an officer to her cabin. Almost instantly, as though she had been waiting outside the hatch, a Navy lieutenant appeared.

"This is Lieutenant Yukio," Carmine said. "She's my executive officer—my second in command. She'll look after you."

We got squared away with quarters as the ship launched from Unity's dock. I had my own cabin, midships, and the Jackals were allocated a communal barracks at the *Fe*'s aft. The rest of the Navy crew were housed on the same deck.

Lieutenant Yukio gave us a cursory tour of the ship. She was a small, muscled woman of indiscriminate age, with a tight cap of black hair. Dour and formal, she was from one of the Alliance colonies on Taiyo and explained that she had been on Carmine's crew for several years.

The Jackals inspected all of the decks that they would be expected to work on, and met most of the starship's crew. The *Santa Fe* was equipped with a decent-sized cargo hold, which housed a Warhawk shuttle for interplanetary flight, a subspace communications array, a zero-G gymnasium, and a scientific-medical deck. For a ship of her size, the latter was quite impressive: with a well-equipped medical facility, an automated-doctor for treatment of injured personnel, and a full Simulant Operations Centre.

"This will be for your use," Yukio said to Zero. "We don't have a dedicated medical staff aboard the ship—not any more—so feel free to make yourselves at home."

Zero beamed at that. "Nice. I hadn't expected to have the place to myself. What about simulant supplies?"

"That's all been taken care of," Yukio said.

She showed us down the corridor to another hold. The air carried that familiar charge of working cryogenics technology.

"Holy Gaia..." said Riggs.

The walls were lined with powered cryo-storage capsules. Each held a simulant, refrigerated and ready for deployment. My pulse quickened and my throat constricted. This was excitement, refined. The idea that I might get to make transition again sometime soon was nearly intoxicating. Old hands called it "the high": an addictive sensation that every simulant operator came to recognise.

"How many skins have we got in here?" Feng said, the sense of wonder thick in his voice.

Yukio gave a tight smile. "A couple dozen each."

There were copies of each Jackal, every working capsule stamped with a name and serial code. Everyone except Zero.

"This would make Senator sick," Novak offered. He snorted. "All money."

Feng nodded. "Must have cost a pretty Proximan penny."

"Then it's a good job he isn't here," Lopez said.

We paced the rows of iced simulants. *Novak's hooded eyes. Lopez's hair swimming like a sea-snake. Feng's boyish features in a deep sleep. Riggs' thickset shoulders and tanned skin.*

"What is *that*...? Novak said.

In the middle of the room, held in a charging cradle that vaguely resembled medical stirrups, was an enormous suit of battle-armour. Now my pulse was hammering triple-time. It felt like my heart was about to leap out of my chest.

"It's a HURT suit," I said. "I've read about these things…"

"HURT?" Lopez enquired.

"Heavy Utility Response Team," Zero explained. "As worn by deep-space salvage and rescue teams, mainly."

"Its use is highly restricted," I said, "and this is the first time that I've seen one in the flesh, so to speak."

The armour was three times the size of a full combat-suit—a true mammoth. The limbs and body were bulbous, up-armoured to such an extent that the wearer would be dwarfed inside. Helmet removed, the driver cabin was visible. Being a true mech rather than powered armour, the unit didn't rely on haptic responses like a combat- or recon-suit. The armour was cast in a dull metallic grey, devoid of camouflage patterning or any insignia—because it would be almost impossible to hide something that damned big—and both arms terminated in oversized kinetic cannons known as suit-guns. A pair of ammo drums were locked beneath the forearms. The suit's weapons package was completed with a grenade launcher across the shoulders—perfect for crowd-control. Meanwhile, an enormous M66 EVAMP was attached to the rear, so that the suit could keep moving no matter what the opposition.

It was a thing of beauty.

Riggs saw my reaction, and gave me a grin of approval. "You like, huh?"

"Hard not to, Corporal," I said, circling the armour. "If it comes to it, I've got dibs on this suit."

"Wouldn't have it any other way," Feng said.

Novak grunted. "Do not need armour to kill shit."

"While I agree, Private," I said, "trust me when I say it'll be a whole lot easier wearing one of these…"

"It was loaded just before you people came aboard,"

Yukio said, with a shrug, as though she really couldn't understand what all the fuss was about. She hooked a thumb towards the back of the hold. "*Those* are for you as well."

Several suits of dull grey armour sat behind the HURT, each hooked to a charging cradle. In comparison to the HURT suit, these armoured suits looked almost harmless, although I knew that was far from the truth.

"Those are full combat-suits," Zero said. "Looks like whatever happened on Daktar, *someone* still believes in us."

Riggs bolted across to the armour, touching the camo-coated exterior. The Mark VI combat-suit was synonymous with Army Sim Ops—standard issue for approved veteran teams.

"We finally get to play with the big toys!" Riggs said.

"Not without full training, you don't," I countered.

"Now all we need is a mission," said Feng.

Yukio smiled. "I guess that you'll get that soon enough."

"We're certainly equipped for it," Lopez said. Even she sounded a little excited by the prospect of using the armour.

There was a chime over the *Santa Fe*'s address system. Yukio cocked her head, waiting for the announcement.

"Mission briefing commencing in five minutes," the ship's AI said in an androgynous voice. "The following personnel are to attend the briefing room…"

CHAPTER NINE

RESURRECTED

By the time we arrived, the briefing room was already filling up. Captain Carmine had taken up a post at the head of the auditorium, a tri-D tactical display on the table beside her, and I counted all ten of the *Santa Fe*'s senior staff in attendance as well. Along with the Jackals, that made the chamber pretty packed.

"Simmer down," I said to the Jackals generally. Remembering that the squad hadn't attended many briefings before, I added, "No one speaks without my permission, all right? Let me handle it."

"Solid copy," Riggs said. "You've got this."

"I know Military Intelligence better than most," I said, trying to sound more confident than I felt.

The truth was that Sim Ops and Military Intelligence rarely mixed, and Mili-Intel's involvement in this operation almost certainly meant that there was more to it than we had been led to believe.

"Do not be so anxious," Novak said.

"I'm not."

"You look it," Novak replied. "Is obvious on face. Just stay calm."

I was almost embarrassed by Novak's surveillance drone, which hovered at his shoulder. It was like a brand: emphasising that Novak was a lifer, not a proper soldier.

"I give the orders around here," I said.

Novak gave such a small nod of his head that I barely saw it. "Yes, ma'am."

The briefing room lights dimmed and another figure appeared beside Carmine. That ability—to materialise out of the dark, without warning—seemed to be something that all Military Intelligence agents had, a skill that they learnt as recruits.

But as the shadow took up the briefing podium, face dipping into the light of the holo-display, my unease went into overdrive.

"Am I seeing things?" Feng asked. "Is that…?"

"You look like you've seen a ghost," Zero suggested. "Are you all right?"

"Maybe I have," Feng said.

"To those who do not know me," the Mili-Intel man said, "my name is Major Vadim Sergkov."

He looked the same as he had on the briefing packet at Daktar Outpost: an *exact* replica of the man I'd seen kidnapped by the Black Spiral. Lean-faced, Slavic-featured. Middle-aged, by Earth standard years; grey shaved hair barely covering the scars that sculpted his scalp. I saw now that he was tall and muscled as well.

"What I am about to say…" Sergkov began.

I couldn't help myself. I stood from my seat.

"I'm sorry," I said, with an idiot frown plastered across my face, "but how are you…?"

Alive, I wanted to say, but the word wouldn't come.

Sergkov glanced in my direction. "Lieutenant Jenkins, I take it?"

"Affirmative, sir," I said. "And if you know who I am,

then you'll also know that my squad and I just died in an effort to retrieve *you* from Daktar Outpost."

"Of course," Sergkov said. He paused, but offered no more explanation, as though what had just happened on Daktar was entirely natural, as though the operation had gone exactly as he had expected.

Temporarily disarmed by Sergkov's response, I went on, "Then I hate to ask, but how the hell are you here? You were in Black Spiral custody the last I saw..."

Sergkov's lips settled in an amused smile. By way of answer, he rolled up the sleeve of his khakis. His uniform was very meticulously arranged, with an especial emphasis on the medals and rank insignia on his broad chest, but my eyes were drawn to his forearm. *Dataport*. The major had standard Sim Ops plugs installed in his arms. He was operational, capable of using a simulant.

"I was resurrected," he said, simply.

"You were using a simulant on Daktar?"

The answer to my question suddenly seemed very obvious.

"That's right. Don't look so surprised, Lieutenant. You're a Sim Ops long-termer. You've been skinning up since before some of your team joined the military. You're aware that Military Intelligence uses simulants..."

"I am aware," I said, "but it would've been nice to know that the officer we were tasked with saving on Daktar Outpost was actually a simulant."

There were simulant divisions—able to trace their parentage back to the Army Sim Ops Programme—embedded in most Alliance military agencies. Simulant pilots, Navy crews, even law enforcement. But using simulants in the way that Sergkov had on Daktar: that was new to me.

"All of the officers were simulants," Sergkov said, his tone frustratingly nonchalant. "We were using next-generation skins. Virtually indistinguishable from a standard human template. That was an essential requirement of our mission. Military Intelligence has been tracking the Black Spiral for some time."

"So Daktar was a set-up?"

Sergkov evaluated me for a moment, eyes up and down my body. Not in a sexual way, but like he was trying to take the measure of me: a workman examining a tool, deciding whether it was fit for purpose.

"That's right," he said. "It was a set-up."

"The whole thing?" Feng chipped in.

I was so angry that I couldn't bring myself to rebuke Feng for speaking up. *Did Draven know about this?* I wondered. *Had this been another part of the wider plan?*

"Not quite," Sergkov said. "But my removal from the outpost was deliberate, if that's what you mean. I self-extracted shortly after leaving the station. The mission priority was to capture Warlord, but we failed to achieve that objective. The rest—the loss of Daktar Outpost and the scientific team stationed there—was, ah, *unintended*."

I could recall Major Sergkov's facial expression, as he was being hustled into the Spiral's starship, very clearly. At the time, that look of unerring calm had struck me as brave, as courageous, but now it made a lot more sense.

"Bastard…" Riggs said, under his breath so that only I could hear.

"Are we finished with the preliminaries?" Sergkov asked. "I'd like to get on with this briefing."

I was literally too dumbstruck to speak out, and Sergkov took that as assent to proceed. What more was there that I could say?

"As of now," he said, "all personnel aboard this ship are under the command of Military Intelligence. According to the Combined Military Charter, you are hereby seconded to my command."

Sergkov's bright blue eyes scanned the room, flinty in the low light.

"Consider this briefing classified," Sergkov continued, "with an alpha security classification."

"That's maximum security," Zero hissed to the Jackals.

Sergkov began tapping something on his wrist-comp. The electronic eye of Novak's drone dimmed and a blue light flashed on its hull. I'd never seen that happen before.

"Huh!" Novak said. "Drone has stopped recording."

"If this is so classified," Riggs said, "why are they letting you and Feng stay in for the briefing?"

"Quiet Riggs," I said. "We're all Jackals here."

Sergkov ignored us and proceeded. "Sensitivities surrounding the Daktar incident prevented me from properly briefing you before we left Unity Base."

The holo-display sprang to life, showing a highly detailed view of the Maelstrom. Jump points, shipping lanes in and around the Former Quarantine Zone, and the disposition of Krell space forces, all appeared.

"The *Santa Fe*'s destination is inside the Maelstrom," said Sergkov. "Into an area of space known as 'the Gyre,' located in the Rion-Declar Spur."

While it wasn't exactly commonplace, going into the Maelstrom had become routine enough. Science Division had acquired star-data from many sources now, had mapped the periphery of the Krell Empire. But the Gyre? This was something else. The Gyre was a well of stars on the far side of the Maelstrom, deep within Krell territory. Warning markers whirled about, indicating black holes, stellar rifts, unexplored tranches of wild space.

"This is imagery of the Gyre six months ago," Sergkov said. He jabbed a finger at a control. "This is the Gyre now. When we first began examining this sector, it contained almost two hundred stellar bodies. Within six months, that has reduced to sixteen."

The well of stars had become denser, with more stellar matter clinging to the heart of the spiral. So much seemed to have disappeared. Planets, stars: everything. The Gyre was collapsing in on itself, and pulling all nearby planetary bodies into its dark core.

"It isn't just stellar bodies that are being affected. Several Krell space assets have also gone missing. Prior to this event, this region of space was heavily populated by Krell forces. We've been monitoring their traffic. In some cases, these disappearances suggest the loss of sizeable war-fleets. Mostly from the Red Fin Collective, but also the Silver Gill and Blue Talon."

"We're spying on our allies?" Feng asked.

"There's nothing new about that," Riggs countered. "And when the good guys look like that, wouldn't you?"

I recognised those names Sergkov had mentioned. The Krell didn't refer to themselves by those titles, but Science Division and other Alliance military agencies had tagged the Collectives. There were dozens upon dozens of different Krell Collectives, varying in size, threat and attitude to the Alliance. Names ranged from the vaguely threatening to the overtly comedic. But as the display indicated the location of the missing fleets, no one was laughing.

Not everyone was so familiar with this sort of knowledge.

"Red Fin?" Feng muttered.

Zero couldn't help answering. "The Red Fin Collective is the largest known Krell assembly," she said. "Prior to the Krell War, they held in excess of three hundred worlds."

Riggs sighed. "Trust you to know that."

Zero shrugged. "It's not expert knowledge, Riggs. You can read up on it on the ship's mainframe."

I knew that there was more to it than that, and resisted the urge to reach over and take Zero's hand in mine. *She's a big girl now, Jenk, and she has to stand up for herself . . .*

Instead, I simply said, "Maybe that's what Riggs should do. Maybe that's what we should all do."

Sergkov continued. "Since the end of the war, the Red Fin have been most vocal in their communications with the Alliance. They were instrumental in brokering the current treaty. We believe, although we cannot be sure, that they were also responsible for persuading some of the other Collectives to agree to the settlement."

Captain Carmine rapped her walking stick on the deck. "In short, the universe would be a far less pleasant place without the Red Fin."

"As ever," Sergkov said, "the captain speaks sense."

Zero prickled at that, but held her tongue.

"Can't we just ask the Krell what's happening?" Lopez suggested.

"That was what we attempted to do. When the stellar anomaly in the Gyre was initially detected, the Alliance Navy dispatched an expedition with the express objectives of investigating the Gyre and making contact with the Red Fin Collective. That ship was called the *Hannover*."

The display showed an image of a starship, as captured by a remote camera-feed. The ship looked like a typical Navy battlecruiser—a lot bigger than the *Santa*

Fe, but also slower. I estimated that she carried a couple of thousand crewmen.

"She's a European Confederation vessel," Sergkov said. "Equipped with a full offensive and defensive weapons package."

"Nice," Riggs said.

"What happened to her?" Carmine chimed in. Her face looked especially drawn in the light of the holo, and I knew what she would be thinking: she didn't want her ship ending up like the *Hannover*...

"That's what we're going to find out," Sergkov said. "We know that she reached her destination, in the Gyre, but shortly thereafter she went dark."

"No communications, no nothing?" Lopez said.

Sergkov shook his head. "No nothing, Private."

"Fishes cannot be trusted," Novak piped up. "I tell you this for long time."

I was surprised when Sergkov gave the lifer a response. "Perhaps, comrade. But if knowledge of the *Hannover*'s disappearance becomes public, it could destabilise an already precarious peace."

Both Novak and Sergkov were Russian Federation, but whereas Novak's accent was rough and jagged, Sergkov's was smooth and cultured. Despite their shared country and planet of origin, they seemed very different.

The occupants of the briefing room stirred, began to talk among themselves in confusion and concern. Carmine hushed the chamber, although I could see that the disclosure was causing her no less anxiety.

"What do *you* think happened to the *Hannover*, Major?" I asked, rousing from my seat. I noted that he had strategically avoided answering Carmine's question.

"There are a number of possible risk factors associated with an expedition into the Maelstrom," Sergkov said. "Engineering failure, erratic quantum tides, a dissident Krell faction...Even an internal influence."

"Ah, the Black Spiral..." Carmine said. "A group with which we are all familiar."

Sergkov nodded. "Perhaps. The Spiral has been running interference operations along the Former Quarantine Zone for some time."

More indicators glowed on the map: Daktar was just one of several locations that had been hit by the Spiral. There had also been attacks on Novo Selo, Decais Bay, and a mining station on Yibres.

"I recognise some of those locations," Zero said, frowning at the display, "but not others."

"There's good reason for that," Sergkov said, in answer to Zero. "Reporting of many of these incidents has been suppressed. The Black Spiral have been most prolific in the last few months, conducting raids on several sites of interest to Science Division." He raised an eyebrow. "Many of those attacks have involved gaining access to Shard Gates. We're not yet sure why that is the case."

"So what's our flight plan, Major?" Carmine said, focusing on what her role in this mission would be.

"We will depart immediately to North Star Station," Sergkov explained, the map beside him updating.

There were some sighs around the room. Located in the Drift, North Star was one of the most remote stations in the Alliance. That was a quadrant that bordered the FQZ—densely packed with asteroids, part of the Great Barrier that encircled the Maelstrom. The computer graphics only hinted at how dangerous this sector could be to passing ships: in the Drift debris ebbed and flowed like a living thing, as though the sector's tides were controlled by some unknown galactic force.

But although there were great risks to anyone exploring the quadrant, there were also great rewards. By way of example, a stable Shard Gate sat in the midst of the asteroid belt.

"On North Star we will acquire personnel essential to this mission," Sergkov explained. "We will then use the Shard Gate at North Star to jump further into the Maelstrom. That'll place us within quantum-jump range of the *Hannover*'s last known location.

"Lieutenant Jenkins will be responsible for mission security. Our objectives will be to conduct recon, gather intelligence, then withdraw and report to Alliance High Command."

"Sounds too easy," Novak said. "Is not good."

"Don't worry, Novak," Riggs said, with a grin. "I'm sure there will be some stuff to stab along the way."

Novak pulled a face. "Can only hope."

The briefing went to break, but Sergkov held up a hand for quiet.

"When we reach North Star, Lieutenant Jenkins and Sergeant Campbell will accompany me onto the outpost. I thereafter have two options: either allow you some downtime on-station, or confine you to your quarters until my business is concluded."

The Jackals fell quiet. The idea of a few hours' free time aboard North Star Station? Even I could recognise the appeal, given that we would be sealed on this crate for Christo knew how long...

"My squad can be trusted," I said. Under full hypno, I doubted that my answer would be the same: I was aware that the response wasn't entirely truthful.

Sergkov nodded. "I hope so, Lieutenant. My business on North Star is essential to this mission."

"Understood."

*   *   *

Major Sergkov made himself scarce as the briefing ended, leaving me with a plethora of unanswered questions. Carmine, to her credit, waited behind, wearing her own confusion like a badge.

"I didn't know, Keira," she insisted, as we left the briefing room. "I…I didn't know that he was your objective on Daktar."

"No reason that you should, Captain," I said. "It's above your head."

"So I'm 'captain' again now?"

"There are crew around," I answered, shrugging. "Like you said."

"We're friends, Keira," Carmine said. "I mean that. I'm not keeping anything from you."

My use of her formal rank seemed to irk Carmine, just a little, and I registered that. I'd worked with Military Intelligence before. They were a shadowy organisation, and I didn't trust them. As for Carmine? Her reaction to my words suggested that she was genuine. Even though I hadn't seen her in years, I thought that I could still read her well enough. I slowed my pace so that she could keep up, the *rap-rap-rap* of her stick on the deck a reminder that she had seen brighter days.

"I expect that Military Intelligence deliberately kept the agencies in the dark about the full extent of the Daktar operation," I said, thinking this through. "I doubt that you were in the 'need to know' category."

"There was nothing in the media to indicate that Major Sergkov had been on Daktar. We've been pursuing the Black Spiral for the better part of six months, but they're a big organisation…"

"I know," I insisted. Put a hand to the back of my neck and rubbed, realising how bizarre this whole situation was. "I believe you."

Carmine seemed relieved by that. "Good. I'll be on the bridge, if you need me."

"Copy that. Are you coming aboard North Star?"

"Not if I can help it," Carmine said. "I'm too old for that shit." She raised her thin eyebrows, nodded back down the corridor. "I could do with some more hands in Engineering, if you can spare them. We're still a day out of port, but we need to get this ship ready to dock again."

The Jackals trailed behind us. They bickered and argued among themselves, comfortably oblivious to the implications of what we'd just been told. Only Zero was absent, no doubt back in the SOC. *Only she really knows what war means*, I thought bitterly.

"They're still green enough that they remember Basic," I said. "Some makework won't do them any harm."

I called the squad to order, and put Riggs, Feng, and Novak under the captain's command.

"Follow Lieutenant Yukio," Carmine said. "She'll show you what needs to be done." To her own crew: "The rest of you need to get this ship inspection-ready for when we dock with North Star."

I nodded at Feng, Novak, and Riggs. "You heard the lady. Jump to it."

"Copy that, ma'am," Riggs said.

The Jackals disappeared into the ship. That left Lopez and me alone in the corridor.

"Hey," she said, almost furtively. "Can I speak with you, ma'am?"

"Trooper to CO?" I asked, somewhat surprised. "Or Lopez to Jenkins?"

"A little of both, maybe."

"I'm not sure that I like the sound of that, but we're alone now. You talk and I'll listen."

Lopez squirmed slightly. She fiddled with a ringlet of

dark hair as she spoke. "I just wanted to say sorry. About how I've been acting."

"Go on," I said, slightly enjoying Lopez's uncomfortable presentation. Lopez had been acting like a brat, but at least she seemed to realise it.

"Back on Unity," she said, starting again, "I know that I was being a bitch. I...I shouldn't have reacted to this mission like I did."

"Damn straight. You're a trooper, Lopez. You're in the Army now."

"Yeah. I know."

"Sometimes we get asked to do shit we don't want to."

I felt a lot like I was talking to a kid, but I chided myself when I saw the holo-badge on Lopez's chest. She had seven measly transitions under her belt, and no prior military experience. If I was angry with anyone, it should be with General Draven for giving me command of this outfit. Lopez *wasn't* much more than a kid.

"Things were different back on Proxima," she said. "My father...he didn't exactly agree with me signing up."

"Senator Lopez?"

"He's an okay guy," she replied. "Sometimes, at least."

I shook my head. "I've wanted to ask you a question myself, Lopez. If your old man is so against the Programme, why are you here?"

Lopez grinned sheepishly. "My father wants—wanted—me to follow in his footsteps." The way that she corrected herself made me think that perhaps Gabriella Lopez wasn't so keen on a career in politics. "He wanted me to go into government, like him. Only way you can hold those posts is by doing civic duty."

"Right," I said, understanding a little more about the girl now. "And I guess you chose the *wrong* civic duty, at least so far as Senator Lopez was concerned?"

"That's right. He wasn't keen on me joining the Army, but it was what I wanted." She paused, and pulled a plastic data-clip from the breast pocket of her fatigues. Showed it to me. "Before we left Unity, he tried to contact me. Novak and Feng might think that I tried to pull in some favours, but honestly: I didn't."

I sighed, slowly. "Senator Lopez offered you a way off the squad?"

"That's right. He didn't contact me directly, but then again he never does. He has *people* to take care of that." She laughed, an acid sound. "His office left me messages—*lots* of messages. They promised that, if I wanted it, they could get me a REMF position in the Core."

REMF: rear-echelon motherfucker. This was a different side to Lopez, maybe one that I hadn't appreciated before.

"You weren't tempted to take his offer?" I asked.

"No, I wasn't. You look surprised by that."

"No disrespect, Lopez, but you haven't exactly made a secret of the fact that you don't want to be on the squad..."

"I didn't even answer the messages."

Her face had taken on a hard expression. More Lopez that I hadn't seen before, and I kind of liked it. The senator had been most vocal about closing down the Sim Ops Programme. But his daughter, small and dark-eyed and anxious, was of a different breed. What she'd just told me chimed in some ways with my own history. Ol' Teddy Jenkins had wanted me to be Army, but he'd been equally disapproving of my decision to go into Sim Ops, insisting that it wasn't *proper* military. I had a newfound respect for Gabriella Lopez.

"You didn't need to tell me that," I said.

"I did. I've been a bitch, and I know it."

I shrugged. "I can take it. I've got broad shoulders, and I'm your CO."

"I wanted to tell you now," Lopez said, "because I figured that I can't be sure what we'll discover out there." She waved at the wall beside her, indicating space outside. "We could be walking into another media shitstorm."

"I get you," I said. "Thanks for the heads-up."

CHAPTER TEN

NORTH STAR STATION

Over the next day or so, we made a series of quantum-jumps through the Former Quarantine Zone. The ship's AI declared that we were about to jump, and the two-minute warning siren filled the air. Boom. We delved deep into the quantum. Less than a second later we were back in real-space, and light-years had passed. That's the reality of a Q-jump engine.

Into the Drift. Closer to the Maelstrom.

The Jackals collected on the *Santa Fe*'s bridge, watching our progress. The squad was eager to get off-ship, even if it wasn't going to be for long.

Small and cocoon-like, the bridge sat at the *Santa Fe*'s nose. It had a half-dozen crew stations, equipped with holo-screens and viewer modules that looked like they were the product of the First Space Race. Padded flight couches, of the type used during launches under high-G, lined the walls. A tactical display filled the crew-pit, showing computer-generated graphics of space around us.

"Hey, boss," Novak started. He rose from his chair with a creak, his tattooed head almost grazing the deck-head. "I lose drone now, yes?"

Novak's drone had recommenced recording as soon as Sergkov's briefing had ended, and it continued to follow him everywhere.

"Are you ever going to get tired of asking that question?" Riggs asked. "I'd say that the universe is a safer place with your every move being tracked, lifer."

"I ask again," Novak said, staring levelly at Riggs.

"No, trooper," I replied. "You're not losing the drone. You know the rules."

"I guess Novak's grand plan of escaping from Alliance custody while we're on North Star has been scuppered," Lopez joked.

Novak didn't see the funny side of it at all.

The surveillance drone hovered just beyond his reach. The machine had received its fair share of abuse, but Novak well knew that if it were damaged, or if it otherwise became inoperable without my permission, he would be in breach of his military contract: would suffer a penalty against his remaining sentence.

"How long do you have left on that sentence anyway?" Lopez goaded.

Novak scowled. "Not your business. Need more transitions."

"Do you know how many you'll have to do before they release you from the contract?" Feng said.

"Is many," Novak grumbled. "Is too many."

"Approaching North Star," Carmine said. She sat in her command throne, surrounded by a nest of screens plugged into the ship's mainframe. "Bring us in nice and slow."

"Aye, ma'am," said another officer. "Cutting thrust control."

"Get me a visual, if you will."

"Sending it to your console, ma'am."

North Star Station appeared on the tactical display.

"That's it?" Lopez said. "Hardly looks like the last bastion of humanity that people make it out to be…"

"Who says that about North Star?" Carmine asked. "Because I can tell you, there's very little humanity down there."

North Star was a military bunker floating in space. At first, its black hull was barely visible against the dark, but as we got closer I made out more detail. It was a vast, sprawling mess. Structures had grown from the flanks of the station proper: a shanty town of space habitats, linked together with air-tunnels and atmospherically sealed corridors, enlarging the base's footprint. The station's stamps of ownership—an Alliance Army emblem, together with a United Americas flag—had long since faded. Words had been printed over them: LAST STOP BEFORE THE MAELSTROM. REFUEL, KICK BACK, AND CHILL OUT.

"Someone has a sense of humour," I said.

"Place used to be a listening post, during the war. Now, military discipline is a little more lax."

Sergkov stood at my shoulder. The guy had a thing about sneaking up on you; I hadn't even heard him enter the bridge.

"Major," I said. Went to salute.

"Stand down. No need for the formalities any more. You're in Mili-Intel now."

"Yes, sir."

North Star had numerous docking bays, and dozens of starships swarmed around the station. Most were older-pattern Alliance vessels—I noted a United American vessel, and at least one ancient Pacific Pact sun-jumper—but others were so ancient that I couldn't identify their ownership.

"The station has an official military garrison of thirty-five Alliance Military Police officers," Zero reeled off. "They're supported by an unlisted number of corporate marshals."

"When the war finished," Sergkov said, his hands pinned behind his back as he glanced down at the display, "ownership of the station was handed over to the North Star Corporation. Hence the name."

"What was it called before then?" Riggs asked.

"It didn't have a name," Sergkov said, without looking up. "Just a numerical designation."

"That figures," Lopez said. "That's one ugly base. It makes the *Santa Fe* look beautiful."

Carmine glowered. "The *Santa Fe is* beautiful!"

"Just keep telling yourself that, Carmine," I said.

"The aesthetics are irrelevant," Sergkov countered. "We won't be here for very long."

The Shard Gate—North Star's reason for existing—filled the display now. Not physically, because this Gate wasn't spatially large. Instead, it threw exotic particles across near-space like an acid shower on a wet SoCal afternoon. The *Fe*'s scopes and sensors were going haywire, trying to compensate for the background noise that the Gate generated. I could feel my temples pulsing, the beat of some distant alien drum driving me onwards.

"That Gate doesn't look much like the one at Daktar," Riggs said, his voice dropping.

"Very few of them look the same," Carmine said.

Zero rocked on her heels in a sort of trance. "The Gate's official designation is NS-756. When they first found it, during the war, Sci-Div thought that it was a natural phenomenon."

"They thought *that* was natural?" Lopez asked.

Zero shrugged. "So they say. Lots of the Gates work that way. Hidden in plain sight. It's the best camouflage, I guess."

From a distance, NS-756 looked almost stiletto-thin: a vertical slit in reality. It was surrounded by a dozen or so heavy frigates, ships tasked with protection of our end of the Shard Network.

"The Gate isn't the only thing out here we need to be wary of," Carmine said. "Ensure that navigation's tracking those rocks."

"Aye, ma'am," Yukio said. We were in a vast asteroid belt, and the tactical display was alight with thousands of new objects. "We're also picking up several unregistered civilian vessels in the Drift. Do you want those flagged as well?"

"Don't bother," Carmine said. "Not unless they get too close."

"What are those ships doing out there?" Feng asked. "Mining the asteroids?"

"They aren't mining," Carmine said. "Didn't they teach you anything in that Directorate crèche?"

"I'm not Directorate," Feng said, the annoyance clear on his face.

The old captain either didn't register Feng's anger, or if she did, she simply didn't care. Distractedly, continuing to direct the docking procedure, she said, "It's what they find out there, in those rocks, that keeps bringing them back. There are Shard remains in the belt."

"Surely not actual Shard?" Lopez asked, wide-eyed.

"Of course not!" Carmine said. "You really are quite vacant, aren't you, my dear?"

"Cut it out, Carmine," I said. "You're enjoying goading my people a little too much."

Carmine smiled to herself. "The prospectors are

looking for xeno-tech, my dear. Alien weapons. Explorers go out there in little asteroid-jumpers, nothing more than powered boats. Usually, all they find is barren rock."

"But just sometimes," I picked up, "they find more. When the Shard disappeared from this end of the Milky Way, they left behind a lot more than just the Gates."

"And whatever they find," Carmine said, "they get to keep."

"Has anyone ever found anything valuable?" Feng asked.

"Not likely," Carmine said, with a chortle. "Bits and pieces, sure, but nothing significant. I doubt that they ever will."

I hope they never will, I echoed.

Sergkov brooded beside me. "No one has found anything that helps us understand who, or what, the Shard really were," he said, his voice a bass rumble across the bridge. "That's the real question."

"But more than enough civilian prospector teams have died trying to find out," I said, "before anyone gets any ideas about going on their own little treasure hunt."

Riggs grinned. "Wouldn't dream of it, ma'am."

I'd been avoiding Riggs for the better part of the journey. This was possibly the longest time we'd spent in the same room since we'd boarded the *Santa Fe*, and I noticed his lingering eye contact: like he expected something from me.

"We won't be there long enough for that," Sergkov said, putting a formal end to any such suggestion.

"*UAS* Santa Fe," a console crackled, "*this is North Star Station Traffic Control.*"

"We read you, NSS Control," Carmine said. "Adopting standard holding pattern."

"We've got your signal on the grid," Control said. *"Business or pleasure?"*

Carmine snorted. "Since when is there any pleasure this far from the Core?"

"I hear that, Santa Fe. I hear that. Just make sure that any tracking software is offline while you're in that holding pattern; don't want any fireworks on the way in."

"Copy that."

"You're cleared for docking in Bay Twenty. Have a better one."

A few minutes later, the *Santa Fe* docked directly with North Star Station, and parked up in an empty berth. The Jackals and Major Sergkov left behind the Navy crew, and boarded the station.

North Star's arrivals hall was an open concourse crammed with gaudy market stalls, selling everything from prospecting supplies to narcotics to chemical enhancers. The scent of so many unwashed bodies mixed with that of fried foods and liquor, a wall of odour that was nearly overwhelming. Many of the crowd bore religious symbology—from the robes of dedicated Gaia Cultists, to the ominous icons of Singularity Preachers.

"Isn't the Church of the Singularity supposed to be banned?" Lopez asked, almost naïvely.

"That's right," Zero replied.

"But out here," I said, shaking my head, "anything goes."

This was where the flotsam and jetsam of the universe ended up…Prospecting for xeno-tech wasn't the only reason to come to a station like North Star. Those that were desperate for somewhere to hide from the prying eyes of the Alliance authorities also called this place home. It wasn't much of a life, but it was better than the alternative.

Sergkov pressed on through the mass of shoppers and new arrivals, towards the immigration gate. That was a requirement of Alliance law, but that didn't mean it was taken seriously. A half-dozen Military Police officers—a decent portion of North Star's serving security detail—lounged at a booth, cradling shockrifles, wearing graffiti-covered vac-armour. They looked like they couldn't care less. Instead, a small figure in a grubby Customs Union uniform emerged from the bustling crowd and expressed an interest in us.

"Ah, new arrivals!" said the man, speaking in a strangely high-pitched voice. "Officers, please ensure that these people submit to station registration."

The base official was pale-fleshed and chubby, with bare strands of grey hair covering a shiny scalp. His uniform had faded from bright yellow to a milky beige.

"My name is Officer Crawley Gravid, but everyone calls me Craw. I'd like to make your stay here as comfortable as possible." He turned to the MPs. "Come on, come on. Let's get the new arrivals registered."

With marked reluctance, the Mili-Pol officers stirred from their languor.

"Guess it's been a long time since you registered any new arrivals," I said, making it clear that what I really meant was *it's been a long time since you did any work*.

The Mili-Pol sergeant grinned. Only his head was visible inside his uniform, but his chin was double and unshaven. "You read that right, Lieutenant. This is the ass-end of the universe. Name's Byers. I'm pretty much the law out here."

"That's nice to know," I said.

Sergeant Byers scanned our biometrics. "Hey, you guys are Sim Ops."

"That's right," I said. "Observant and handsome. Not a package you see very often."

"Witty and shitty," Byers said. "Again, not so common these days. You Sim Ops guys still around? It's been so long since we've seen anyone from your branch, we figured that they'd disbanded the Programme."

"Is this really necessary?" Sergkov protested. "We're on a timetable."

Byers sighed. "That's nice for you. But if Union guy says I should register you, I register you."

Major Sergkov reluctantly submitted to the immigration checks. I was unsurprised when a different name appeared on the Mili-Pol officer's scanner screen, but the trooper was satisfied with the result and moved on. The Customs Union man was a little more vigilant. His features fell as he read the text from the unit.

"You must be the, ah, major," he said. Swallowed.

"That's right," Sergkov said.

"The Union received your communication."

"As I intended."

The little man wrung his hands. How long had it been since North Star had received any attention from the rest of the Alliance? An aura surrounded the Customs man, as though he was suddenly dealing with high-ranking dignitaries—as though he was dealing with the Krell High Council itself.

"They're all clean," the sergeant said. Looked back over at Feng and Novak. "The lifer had better keep his drone switched on at all times. If I had my way, I wouldn't let the Chino onboard, but hey, what do I know?"

Zero put a hand on Feng's forearm, in an attempt to rein him in. It worked and he stood firm.

"No weapons on you, Novak?" Riggs said, with a grin. "That is a surprise."

"Is rules, yes?" Novak said.

"Is rules," I replied. "Let's get on with this."

The Mili-Pol checks had been cursory, and I was sure that Novak had a home-made shiv or two somewhere on his person. On that basis, I was eager that we move this along without any further investigation.

"Read this," Byers said. Tapped a handwritten placard that had been nailed to the immigration booth window. "No weapons at any time. Place is real old, real shaky."

"We've a fully pressurised environment out here," the Customs Union man said, as though having a "fully pressurised environment" on a space station was some sort of luxury. "A stray bullet could cause all manner of complications, and that simply would not do!"

Sergeant Byers nodded. "Pressure seals aren't what they used to be, and we don't want to risk a hull breach."

"Neither do we, Sergeant," I said.

Byers pulled back his lips. His teeth were stained brown by nicotine and caffeine abuse. "Then we understand each other, Lieutenant Jenkins. We don't want another incident like Daktar."

Riggs groaned. "And there was us hoping that you might not be up to date with current affairs..."

Lopez wasn't wrong to warn me of what we'd find aboard North Star Station; the place might've been on the frontier, but like most deep-space facilities it had a communications array, and thus it had news. VOTE SENATOR LOPEZ! a wall-display declared. VOTE CHANGE! MAKE IT HAPPEN! His image danced to life.

"*I promise to cut defence budgets. The war's over, and we need to move on. What do you say to an improved colonisation programme? To new worlds, a new life, and a new tomorrow?*"

"Yeah," the sergeant said, "we know who you are, Lieutenant, and we know who she is too."

In an unsuccessful attempt to conceal her identity, Lopez buried her face in her fatigues. I doubted that many in the Alliance would fail to recognise her.

"All right, that's enough of this," Sergkov said, cutting through the chatter. He nodded at Craw. "I need to see the Fleshsmith."

As soon as that name was mentioned, the atmosphere shifted. The reaction was as sudden as an airlock opening. Both Craw and Byers went rigid.

"Of course," Craw said. "Of course."

Byers patted the stock of his security-issue shockrifle. "We can take you down there," he said. "But Craw here will have to come too."

Craw nodded. "The, ah, Fleshsmith...He is quite particular about receiving visitors..."

"He's expecting me," Sergkov said.

"Are you, ah, all going?" Craw said. I was starting to get a serious vibe about this Fleshsmith, whoever he was.

"My squad won't be attending the meeting," I said. "They'll need a decent bar. Somewhere quiet."

"I can arrange that," Craw said. "If the rest of you would be so kind as to follow me..."

Sergkov and Zero started after the Customs official. I turned to my squad. "Remember what I said. You can be trusted."

"Solid copy," Riggs said.

"Keep comms on, and report to Carmine every hour. Zero and I will keep you updated on the progress of this meet."

Riggs nodded. "I got it already."

"He has rules," Sergeant Byers said as we went. "Strict rules."

The Mili-Pol security detail led us deeper into North Star, and the place changed around us. Colder, dirtier, smellier. Tight corridors. Abandoned hab-modules. Viewports that were scratched and patched and looked barely capable of holding back the vac. The architecture became almost archaic. The isolation pressed in like an insanity.

Byers continued. "You don't look at the Fleshsmith. You don't make any fast movements around him. You don't report what you see here. That last one he takes especially seriously."

We passed through another checkpoint. We had already been through several, and at each of them Craw and Byers were both required to scan palms before the sealed hatch would let us pass. Zero and I exchanged loaded glances. It was pretty obvious that Customs Officer Craw was far from being just that.

"He's one of yours, I take it?" I said to Sergkov.

"That's classified," Sergkov replied.

"I help where I can," Craw said. Turned to me and grinned—a smile that looked like it would shatter at any moment. "But as the major says, that's classified."

We arrived at an armoured hatch, surrounded by surveillance cameras. Unlike the rest of North Star, this door looked new and well maintained: as though someone was doing their best to keep people out. *Or perhaps the other way round*, I thought. A squirt of anxiety hit me—the feeling that this wasn't *right*...A familiar scent lingered on the air, just beyond the range of my human senses. Before I could place it, the hatch opened. Beyond was an enormous cargo hold, the extremities in shadow.

"Who did you say we're meeting again?" I asked of Sergkov.

The major stood with his back ramrod straight. "I didn't," he said.

"Do you think now might be a good time? I mean, who in the Maelstrom goes by the name 'Fleshsmith'..."

"The asset," Sergkov said, adopting formal Mili-Intel terminology, "is somewhat eccentric."

"And will he mind you describing him like that?" Zero asked.

Sergkov shrugged. Byers and Craw stopped in the middle of the hold. Byers' hands were on his shock-rifle, his eyes darting around him like he expected to be attacked at any moment. The station creaked and groaned, the stresses of artificial gravity playing with its ancient structure. Seriously spooky shit.

"Oh, do please drop the theatrics," a voice said, echoing around the hold. "Sergeant Byers is having fun with you."

Byers' face told a different story. There was no fun there.

A cargo elevator came into view, chemical engine roaring as it descended. The platform stalled just before ground level, the miscellaneous chains and rigging used to lift it swaying noisily. A figure stood on the edge of the platform, watching us very precisely, the dark circles of a pair of glasses peering back from the gloom.

Beside me, Byers had already started retreating. Craw was at his side.

"If you've quite finished with Sergeant Byers and me," Craw offered, shifting from foot to foot, "we'll be on our way. I mean, ah, this place tends to affect my sinuses..."

"You're dismissed," the speaker said, hands pressed to the lift's railing as though he were addressing us from a pulpit.

I stood my ground and looked up at the haggard figure.

"You're Fleshsmith, I take it?" I asked.

"That's right," the figure said, with a rigid grin that failed to expose a single tooth. "But you can call me Dr. Skinner."

CHAPTER ELEVEN

THE FLESHSMITH

Dr. Skinner drifted among the detritus of his laboratory, and we followed closely. To have been left behind in that shadowed hold would have felt like becoming lost in the dark for ever. The place was cavernous, with only specific sections lit by glow-globes.

"Forgive the use of the local MPs," Dr. Skinner explained, "but I have to take security very seriously. Of late, North Star has become inundated with pirates operating out of the Drift. Many would be very interested in the work that I conduct here."

Sergkov nodded. "Military Intelligence has been tracking some of them."

"Not well enough," Skinner countered. "There are rumours of insurgency across the Drift. Stories of the Black Spiral and a man they call Warlord."

"We've already met him," I said.

"Is that so?" Fleshsmith asked, without turning to look at me. "Much to my chagrin, he's conducted raids on several nearby facilities. I've found that securing decent-quality whiskey this far from the Core is now nigh-on impossible..." He laughed to himself, and I didn't like the sound much.

Sergkov coughed. I got the distinct impression that the Mili-Intel man was scared. "You can cut the small talk, Doctor. You know why I'm here."

Dr. Skinner paused. "Don't be so curt, Major. I don't get many guests out here. Even the two MPs who usually guard my lab seem to have disappeared, although fat lot of good they were anyway..." The man shook himself, and I began to question his sanity: out here in the dark for God only knew how long. "How is your wife these days, by the way?"

Sergkov bristled. "Fine."

Dr. Skinner hit a control panel. An LED lamp suspended above him blazed to life, illuminating this portion of the lab. It was crammed with inert isolation-booths, robotic manipulators mid-operation of grisly tissue samples, and untidy shelves stacked with tools of alien appearance. Dozens of cryogenic capsules lining the walls, reaching into shadow.

Suddenly, I knew exactly how Dr. Skinner had acquired the codename "Fleshsmith."

Things lurked inside those capsules: homunculi-like shapes with warped faces and twisted outlines. All frozen, of course, but even in suspended animation the specimens were capable of generating an aura that was difficult to ignore. Zero drew closer to me, gasping sharply.

Dr. Skinner showed no apprehension. He was a tall, lean figure, aged in a ragged and unpleasant sort of way. His light hair was cropped short to his narrow head, his skin paled. He wore a tan smock, the chest panel splashed with iodine or the remnants of a bloodstain.

"Time for introductions," he said. "I already know you, Major, but who are these two?"

I stepped forward, determined not to let my anxiety

show. "Lieutenant Keira Jenkins, of the Jackals. Alliance Army, Simulant Operations Programme."

The Fleshsmith nodded. Satisfied.

"And this is Sergeant Zoe Campbell," I said.

"Everyone calls me Zero," she added.

"I think that I will call you Sergeant Campbell," the Fleshsmith said. "My name is Dr. Claus Skinner." Despite his name, which I thought sounded Germanic or Euro-Confed, he spoke with a stiff British accent. He waved a hand around the room, at the summation of his works. "And everyone calls me Fleshsmith."

"I've worked with the Doctor for many years," Sergkov said. "That Mili-Pol officer was having some fun with you. As you can see, Dr. Skinner has few rules."

"I was once a pioneer," the doctor muttered. "When it mattered."

"Dr. Skinner was one of the directing minds behind the Simulant Operations Programme," Sergkov explained. "He was responsible for the creation of the simulant cloning technology."

"That so?" Zero asked.

When Skinner smiled, something froze inside me. "It was a lifetime ago. I've since become engaged in more pressing projects. Which is how I find myself out here, working all alone in the dark..."

He stepped in front of a rank of cryogenic pods. Illuminated by internal blue light, a thick frost on their canopies, the capsules hissed and wheezed as though they were living things. The sound was far from pleasant.

"Let me show you my latest work," the Fleshsmith said.

The pod beside Skinner opened, canopy lifting.

And just like that, everything changed.

That familiar scent in the corridor? It wasn't something that I had smelled often in my real body, thankfully.

That must've blunted my recognition. But now I could suddenly, and very precisely, identify it.

Krell.

"Cryogenic facility suspended," came the station AI's voice. "Please stand by for further information."

A xeno lurched out of the pod, trailing cables and dripping bright blue chemicals.

Zero didn't scream, didn't shout, but she quickly fumbled away from the nearest pod. Eyes pinned to the attacker, hands scrambling over benches and shelves and any other surface that she could reach—items clattering against the deck.

And me? Hardwired, primal instinct took over. An instinct that had lain dormant for a long time but that could never be unlearnt.

"Move!" I shouted, already doing the same myself.

Weapon. Fight. Survive.

My hand dropped to my gun holster—

"No weapons at any time. Place is real old, real shaky."

The recently decanted Krell shook free of the cables that had tethered it to the cryo-pod, and stomped its clawed feet on the ground. Spatters of glowing blue suspension fluid showered the lab.

Sergkov was either too old or too slow to react. He stood there, stupefied, as the drama unfolded. At his side, the Fleshsmith—or whoever the fuck he was—just grinned and grinned.

Dead. They're both dead.

Zero bolted between the shelves and benches. Something smashed in her wake, but she kept going. Head down.

To the hatch. Out into the corridor. Through the station to the waiting ship—

We'd never get that far. The Krell let out a pitched shriek, giving chase. Its stink hit me in the temples, so intense that it almost dropped me, so strong that I thought I was going to throw up. Maybe that and the cryogen would be enough to make me numb, so that I wouldn't feel it when the thing's claws and teeth ripped me apart.

Think!

I grabbed for something—anything—from the nearest bench. Fingers closed around a power-wrench. Battered and chipped but as long as my arm, with a decent weight behind it.

I had no choice but to fight.

I twisted. Wrench in my left hand, right against a shelf for balance.

Hit the power stud. The tool lit with bright sparks.

The alien was right in front of me. Where else would it be? Mouth open, fangs reflecting the scant light. Eyes like deep pools.

Time slowed to a near stop. It always did that in the end. Whether real or simulated, it's as though human senses are too blunt to properly understand the implications of death, and so the mind has to unspool time. To chop and press it, to process it differently.

The tool slammed into the Krell's head. Bounced off its skull.

Zero was screaming now. Reliving what she had tried to bury for over two decades of her life.

I pulled the wrench back. Painfully aware that I would not get another shot—that by the time this blow landed, the Krell would be on me.

"Desist."

Voice brittle, electronic. Sufficiently unnerving that I paused, wrench over my head, mid-assault.

In the pool of light cast by the cryogenic capsule, Dr. Skinner was laughing. It was a dark, self-contented sound.

"Desist," the voice repeated.

Still dripping cryogen, the alien towered over me. Its digitigrade legs quivered, head slightly cocked.

I tried to let go of the power-wrench, but my fingers wouldn't budge. I was already calculating how best to land the next blow, this time with enough force to break the xeno's skull...

"You see?" Skinner said. "Despite my seclusion, I have retained my sense of humour. Sergeant Byers isn't the only one capable of theatrics."

"Please, Dr. Skinner," Sergkov said, "was that really necessary?"

"They're on our side now," Skinner said. His shadow lingered beside the Krell bio-form, and I was aware of him even if I couldn't focus on anything but the alien. The Krell: that was all that mattered. The doctor drew a hand over the xeno's still-wet shoulder, where it had sprouted the tertiary pair of limbs. "My apologies. I do hope that the lieutenant and sergeant aren't too shaken by the ordeal..."

I swallowed. Looked back at Zero. She was on her feet again, and staring at the alien in a mixture of amazement and terror. It was an expression I'd seen painted on her features before, pretty much every time we talked about the Krell.

"You okay?" I asked.

"Fine," Zero muttered, voice sounding reed-weak. "I'm fine."

"Are you insane?" I said to Skinner, waving the power-wrench. "Letting a Krell bio-form loose on this station! We have no frequency-beacons—"

"Unnecessary," Skinner said. "As you can see, this bio-form knows full well the difference between human and Krell."

The alien's eyes scanned me impassively.

"Time for another introduction," Skinner continued. "Lieutenant Jenkins and Sergeant Campbell, of the Jackals, meet Pariah, of the Krell."

"We are allies," came a harsh electronic voice.

I laughed. Actually laughed. The voice, I realised, was coming from the Krell.

"Do not be alarmed," Sergkov said. "This Krell is different. This was why we have come to North Star."

As I finally managed to get my heartbeat under control, I noticed just how different this specimen was. A metal box was grafted to the alien's thorax, fused to its flesh. That looked like a speaker unit, and I assumed that was what the alien spoke from. The contraption looked suspiciously like back-street bio-technology, a close relation to the machinery Carmine had instead of a leg.

"As Pariah says," Skinner explained, "it is an ally."

"I'd say that was a good thing," I said, "but it really isn't."

"She doesn't mean it," Skinner said, turning to the xeno.

"It's a fish head," I said. "Do you think it gives a shit about what I think?"

"Lieutenant!" Sergkov admonished. "That isn't appropriate terminology."

"We do not understand 'fish,'" the Krell said.

Like most Krell, its posture was hunched, but while its physiology was familiar, there were subtle differences too. The head was larger, finned. A trio of nerve-staples—like Novak's prison studs—marked the alien's temple.

"Comparing the Pariah to a typical Krell war-form is like comparing a dolphin to a shark," Skinner said. "You must understand exactly what this specimen represents: the synthesis of Alliance and Krell bio-technology. It's a directed adaptation of the Krell genotype, Lieutenant."

While I'd never seen a dolphin or a shark in real life—
the West Coast's ecosystem hadn't supported that sort of
wildlife since before my grandparents died—I'd seen
plenty of pictures. When I was growing up, the education centre had been keen to explain that such things had
once existed in Old Earth's oceans, and I'd seen enthral-
lingly realistic tri-D footage of both. I vaguely remembered, in fact, that dolphins weren't even fish, but I could
well recall the intelligence that lurked in their features.
Looking at the deep, black eyes of the Krell bio-form, I
saw something like that here. The face carried some sort
of dignity with it, like warped alien royalty. I wasn't at all
sure whether I liked it.

"Project Pariah started a long time ago," Skinner
explained. "It was the reason that I left Simulant Operations. High Command and Science Division originally
intended to make contact with the Krell Collective during the war, when things looked most desperate. However, the work took longer than anticipated."

"We were created to make contact," the creature said.
Its mouth didn't move when it spoke, but every now and
again the thing's thin lips would twitch and a clicking
noise—alien echolocation—would emit from its throat.
"We are alone."

"The Krell…"—Sergkov paused as though searching for the right word in Standard—"*donated* a number
of specimens to Science Division. It has taken significant
resources, but the pariah-forms are the result. I'd remind
you that what you're seeing here is highly classified.
Project Pariah is a black op."

"So this is how Command makes contact with the
Krell?" Zero asked, the hesitancy thick in her voice.
"Using these creatures as a bridge?"

Skinner gave a small shrug. "It is more complicated
than a single bridge, but that is the basic principle. The

Krell Collective mind is like a massive, organic computer," he said. "Sci-Div has effectively extracted a single node from that network, and the pariah-forms are the result. The Krell have a form of deep comms—a sort of telepathy, as part of the Collective mind. Individuality is not only frowned upon, but it's dangerous."

"How did you make it talk?" I asked, still incredulous.

"The pariahs are created from a mixture of DNA," Skinner explained. "The result is a hybrid, if you will. It's a bridge, but with limitations. The Krell don't comprehend language as such, but pariahs are unique bio-forms. Because they still carry deeply ingrained biological imperatives, in the right circumstances they could act as a gateway to the rest of the species." The doctor sighed. "We've only been able to unlock a very small amount of information contained in the alien's head—in every cell of its body."

"Why don't we just ask *it* what happened to the *Hannover?*" I said, assuming that Skinner probably knew about our mission. "Hey, Pariah, what did your buddies do with our ship?"

The Krell bristled. A ganglia of barbels drooped from its mouth, and they flared angrily. "We are not of Red Fin Collective."

"Right, right, of course not. That would be far too easy."

"The Pariah is coming with us," Sergkov said. "As is Dr. Skinner. They will assist us with the next stage of this operation."

"You have got to be shitting me…" I said. Turned to the alien. "It's a Krell!"

I saw a dark ripple under the xeno's musculature, and wondered if that was a deliberate show of force, so that we knew just how easy it would be for the alien to escape from the lab.

"You're going to have to tell Captain Carmine about this," I said to Sergkov.

"She will do as ordered," Sergkov said, crossing his arms. "It's your reaction that surprises me. I had rather hoped that you might take the long view of this mission. Don't forget that I'm in charge here, Lieutenant. You're a Military Intelligence asset now. You, also, will follow orders."

I glared at Sergkov. "There are orders, and then there are *orders*. The whole crew deserves to know what they're getting into." I nodded at Zero. "Sergeant, I want constant surveillance on the Krell, and any change in its behaviour reported to me immediately."

The sheen of sweat on Zero's forehead was visible even in the low light. "Definitely."

"Our first priority is to secure the pariah-form aboard the *Santa Fe*," Sergkov said. "As well as assemble Dr. Skinner's laboratory."

"I've already packed up what I can," Skinner said, shuffling around the nearest bench. "Many of the other specimens donated by the Krell proved non-viable. They can be disposed of."

I noted Skinner's use of the word "donated," echoing Sergkov's. It made me question whether this had been a voluntary act by the Krell. The whole set-up reeked of an off-the-books, illegal project: the sort of operation that the Alliance might want to deny ownership or knowledge of at any time. But those thoughts were put to bed when I got a closer look into the unopened cryo-capsules...*The Pariah's kin*, I thought. The Krell in those capsules were the stuff of nightmares, and they didn't look like they had been created with much more than horror in mind.

Skinner caught me looking, and smiled. "Not all of my experiments have gone to plan, but needs must."

Sergkov was eager to get the mission back on track, and asked, "How long will it take to pack up your equipment?"

"A few hours," Skinner said. His eyes lingered on the failed experiments a little longer than was natural. "Maybe less. I have a cargo-loading droid around here somewhere..."

The doctor shambled into shadow, the pariah-form following after him like a loyal hound. Sergkov watched him go.

"Sergeant Campbell isn't right for this," I said under my breath.

Sergkov regarded me coolly. "We can't always choose the assets that we have to work with, Lieutenant. You know that better than most."

I took that to mean the Jackals. "At least none of them are xenos..."

"Is there a point to your insubordination?"

"Zero has a deep-seated fear of the Krell. There are warning markers on her service record. Making her work with one of them—it isn't right."

Zero stood close behind me. I could hear her breathing, heavy and frightened. In that instant, she was an eight-year-old girl again, and I wanted to do everything I could to get her out of here.

"Do you think that any of us wants to 'work with one of them,' Lieutenant?" Sergkov asked.

"Of course not."

"Then understand that I don't care what the sergeant's problem is, and that I want the *Santa Fe* loaded with Dr. Skinner's laboratory equipment within the next six hours."

At that moment, my wrist-comp pinged with an incoming message. RIGGS, DANEB. What the hell did he want?

"Go and assemble the Jackals," Sergkov said. "Prep them for the loading process."

I nodded. "Copy that."

Zero went to follow after me, but Sergkov waved her down. "Not you, Sergeant. I want you to stay here. Your scientific knowledge will no doubt speed Dr. Skinner's evacuation from North Star."

Zero looked at me, then at Sergkov. I could read the pain in her face. "Yes, sir," she said.

"You don't have to stay, Zero."

"I'm good. Promise."

"Make sure that you are. No more tricks, Sergkov."

I turned and stalked out of the lab, glad to put the wretched place behind me.

CHAPTER TWELVE

OLD RIVALRIES

"So let me get this straight," Riggs said, with an exaggerated frown. "We've come all the way to the edge of human space for a talking fish?"

I probably should've rebuked Riggs for his insolence, but he was only saying what I was thinking. I had explained the whole Christo-damned mess, just because it seemed so insane that it couldn't be real. The Jackals had listened dutifully, resisting the urge to comment until I'd finished the story.

"That's about the size of it," I said.

I'd tracked the Jackals down to a bar in North Star's visitors' sector. The establishment was occupied by a selection of the Drift's famous explorers: a bunch of off-duty prospectors still in vac-suits, and some civvie pilots wearing aviator gear. The air stank of disinfectant and piss—a particularly disagreeable combination, which I nonetheless willingly drank in simply because it was a good deal more pleasant than the smell of Dr. Skinner's laboratory. I could still taste that at the back of my throat, in every fibre of my fatigues.

"And are you all right now?" Riggs asked. "You're shaking."

I hadn't even realised until Riggs had pointed it out, but my hands were tremoring hard enough that everyone around the table could see it. I felt a lot like I did after a firefight, the adrenaline crash finally coming down on me.

"I'm okay," I said. Swallowed. "Major Sergkov says that it's safe." I was struggling to keep the image of the Krell—vaulting from its cryogenic capsule—out of my mind. "So far as those things are ever safe."

"But it's…" Riggs said, waving his hands around and searching for the right word, before settling on, "a *fish head*. And it actually spoke? Not just, you know, did that weird comms thing?"

"It spoke. I know what I saw, what I heard."

"I'm not doubting you," Riggs said, shaking his head. "But this… this is big."

"I didn't think that they could do that," Lopez said. "Have you ever seen one do that before?"

"Of course she hasn't," Feng said. "The XTs don't talk. That's kind of the point."

"Just asking," Lopez said. "Who died and made you the expert on fishes all of a sudden? You've seen, what, three of them back at Daktar?"

"I've seen pictures," Feng said, "and Krell tactical training was just one of the many things that I was born with already planted in my head." Feng bit his lip, and then proceeded to ask the question that had been on his mind since my arrival in the bar. "So you left Zero down there with the major?"

There was just a hint of accusation in his tone.

"Yeah," I said. "I did. She's under orders just like the rest of us."

Feng nodded but I could tell he wasn't happy with that

answer. How much did Feng know about Zero's background, about what had happened to her? I doubted that she had told him very much. Her history was a closed book: something that she preferred not to discuss until you really got to know her. If she *had* told Feng... Well, that meant their relationship—or whatever was happening between them—had moved on to a whole other level.

"Can I get you folks anything else?" asked the bartender. He was hovering around the edge of our table, trying his best to avoid clashing with Novak's drone.

"More drinks," I said.

After the Fleshsmith's dirty trick with the pariahform, I desperately needed a pick-me-up. And that was regardless of Major Sergkov's order to evacuate Skinner's lab.

"Anything particular?" the barman asked with faux politeness.

"Anything alcoholic will do," I said, slapping a universal credit chip down on the table. "Enough for my squad."

The tender was tall and whip-thin, wearing a worn grey vest that exposed veiny arms, tattoos that had faded to the point of near invisibility. He grinned at me, with a mouthful of gem-studded teeth. "You got some proper money, I can get you anything..."

When the credit chip hit the table, eyes and ears swivelled in our direction, money a homing beacon. Novak raised an eyebrow at a hooker poised over the bar— a woman dressed in a pair of red silk panties and not much else—and she began to saunter over to us.

"We're all good, thanks," I intervened.

The woman sucked her teeth at me, nodded at Novak. "You his keeper or something?"

"No, but I am his CO, if that's what you mean."

"Whatever."

The woman had the skin-tone of station-bred, an unpleasant pallor that she shared with the bartender. She turned back to the bar.

Novak grunted in disapproval at my intervention. "Maybe I make decision, yes? Is long time on ship…"

"You don't even have money, Novak," I said. "I imagine your friend over there would be less than pleased when she discovered that."

"Does the drone have to watch if you go through with it?" Riggs asked. "Reminds me of an old joke: a Russian, a Chino, and a Proximan walk into a bar…"

Novak slumped back into his chair. He gazed longingly at the table of beer bottles, all out of reach according to his terms of service.

"I thought that Gaians weren't supposed to eat or drink anything that isn't from Earth?" Feng said, nodding at Riggs' bottle of beer.

Riggs pulled a face. "You got it, but what can I say? I'm a bad Gaian. In a place like this, who knows where the shit comes from…"

"I really do *not* like it here," Lopez said, rubbing her arms across her chest as though she was trying to make herself look small. "I think I'd rather wait on the ship, if it's all the same."

I shook my head. "No can do, kemo sabe. You're staying put. This is team building. We have six hours until loading, and Captain Carmine can sort out the niceties. We're Army, after all, not Navy."

"Yeah, about Carmine," Riggs said. "That was why I commed you."

"Go on."

"I can't get through to her. The comms grid seems to be down."

"That's hardly surprising for a place like this," Lopez said.

Loading could wait, I decided. I was still too damned wired to worry about the next stage of the mission, and I needed something to blot out the still-fresh memory of Dr. Skinner's hall of horrors. The bartender placed a tray of drinks on the table, in glasses that looked as though they hadn't been washed in a very long time.

Riggs held up a drink. "To the Jackals," he said.

The whole group drank, except for Novak. I felt the sickly sour flavour hit my taste buds.

"Christo..." I said, wiping my mouth with the back of my hand. "This stuff really is awful."

"Feels good to get off the ship," Feng said. He rubbed his face. "I don't think that Captain Carmine likes me much."

"Carmine doesn't like anyone much," I said, "but she's one of the good guys. Trust me on this; if it comes to a fight, we'll want her on our side. She's okay. I'll change her mind."

"And how, may I ask," said Lopez, "is the mighty Keira Jenkins going to do that?"

"I was Lazarus Legion," I said. "I was a Legionnaire. I have my ways."

The Lazarus Legion was my former outfit, where I'd cut my teeth as a simulant operator. I felt an uncomfortable lump forming in my throat as I said those words. Thinking of the Legion brought back a wave of memories. Sitting in a bar, drinking, shooting the shit... The Lazarus Legion had been the most successful squad in Simulant Operations, and it had been with the Legion— under my former commanding officer, Conrad Harris— that I had learnt my trade as an operator.

"This was how Colonel Harris managed his people," I said, staring down at the half-emptied cocktail glass. "A good drink and a good talk."

It was probably the alcohol, but I was feeling more

than a little misty-eyed. Missions into the Maelstrom, discoveries like the Pariah Project: this was exactly what the Lazarus Legion had been all about. The table grew quiet for a moment, and the background noise of the bar seemed very distant. Even surrounded by my squad, by the detritus of the North Star bar, I felt an incredible press of loneliness on my shoulders. The idea of grabbing Riggs and taking him to one of the station's charge-by-the-hour rooms suddenly seemed more than appealing.

"What was Lazarus like?" Riggs asked. "I mean, we've all heard about what he did. But you knew the man, right? What was he really like?"

I snorted a laugh. "Conrad? He was an alcoholic, and he was an asshole. But he was the best damned officer I've ever known, and he was my friend."

"Captain Carmine knew him too, didn't she?" Lopez asked. "Lieutenant Yukio told us about it."

"Yeah. We had a mission together, years back now. That was how she got her metal leg. But you people don't really want to hear about Lazarus. All that happened a long time ago."

Everyone knew about Conrad Harris—callsign "Lazarus"—and what he had done for the Alliance. I didn't need to rehearse the stories that made up his legend: of how he had destroyed a Shard Artefact on Helios, fended off an Asiatic Directorate attack at Damascus, then defeated a Shard machine-mind at Devonia… Through their retelling, those tales had become more real to the Alliance than my genuine memories. The Shard Gate sat beyond the bar's battered view-port, reminding me of the things that Lazarus had done.

"Do you miss him?" Lopez asked.

"All the fucking time," I said, sighing. "But it barely matters now. The universe has changed. When I was

Lazarus Legion, we were fighting a different enemy. The Asiatic Directorate went down a year after we got back."

"Not all of them," Lopez said. "And I'm not talking about Feng."

"The Directorate would pay good price to get hands on you, yes?" Novak said. At first, I wasn't sure whether he was talking about me or Lopez, but then his eyes flitted in my direction. "Directorate never forget what Legion did. You are enemy of state."

"Daddy used to say that they were just sleeping," Lopez said. "The Sleeping Dragon, that's what Proximans call the Asiatic Directorate."

All of which was very true. Could an empire that large, that powerful, ever really die? I doubted it. I was quite sure that, if what was left of the Directorate got the chance, they'd make an example of me.

"Good thing that the only Directorate I know around here is Feng," Riggs said.

"It's funny," Feng said, "because people keep telling me that I'm Directorate. But I don't remember that time. The Executive made me, but I didn't even know them."

The Directorate Executive had been the war council responsible for implementing the cloning programme. They'd once maintained facilities on Old Earth, and had eventually expanded the operation across their share of the galaxy. All of that had gone down with the purported fall of the Directorate.

"I doubt Lazarus would've liked you much," I said to Feng, "but you're okay by me."

"Thanks, boss," he said, with a mild grin.

"When did they, ah, 'liberate' you?" Lopez asked.

"I was vat-born," Feng explained. "Genetically engineered to be bigger, badder, smarter."

"So I guess that the process doesn't always work out then?" Riggs said, playfully.

"Fuck you, Riggs," Feng said. "I was born in Crèche Three, Delta Crema Facility." He taped the back of his neck, where his serial code and birthing data were tattooed. "When the Directorate fell, things went to shit. One day we were being trained to become the latest generation of Directorate Special Forces…" He shrugged, searching the table with his eyes as though looking for answers. "The next, everyone who wasn't a clone just vanished. No trainers, no station staff, no nothing."

"Shit," Lopez said. "Must've been rough. Did you escape?"

"No way," Feng said. "Delta Crema is a hellworld. You can't set foot on the surface during sun-up, unless you want to be burnt to a crisp, and by night all air-traffic is prohibited. There's limited atmosphere. That's why they grew us there, on-station, so that we were safe from the Alliance." He looked at me, sideways. "The staff sometimes told us stories about the 'Bloody Demon,' about Lazarus. I didn't believe them, but it's hard to know what's true when your world is a single facility and a dozen other troopers-in-training…"

"They got you out though, eventually?" Lopez asked.

"Eventually is the word," Feng said. "The station was in lockdown. Turns out, everyone else had evacuated when the Directorate imploded. Most of the other crèches had been terminated by their handlers. Ours was either more humane, or he was a coward. Alliance troops stormed the base six days after we'd been deserted." Feng stopped abruptly, swigged from a bottle of beer. "Rest is history."

Riggs sucked his teeth. "Look at it this way," he said. "Things could've been a damned lot worse." Nodded across the table. "You could've been Novak."

"You want real horror," Novak said, "you come to prison. Delta Crema is nothing compared to gulag."

The Russian rubbed a huge hand over his forehead. Several words were tattooed in old-style ink onto his knuckles, all in Cyrillic script, and I wondered what they meant. I'd assumed that most of Novak's markings were gang tattoos: he would be a good fit for the criminal networks of many planets and space stations, as an enforcer or mob boss.

"What exactly did you do to get put in there, Novak?" Riggs enquired. "We're all very eager to hear."

Novak's drone began a steady chirp of warning signals, and the big Russian creaked in his chair. Although it had been Novak who had brought up the subject of his detention, his mood seemed to have taken a sudden nosedive. The aura of intimidation that followed him suddenly became more tangible, and everyone around the table could sense it.

"Fuck off," he said to Riggs. "Is not your business."

"Okay, I get it." Riggs waved his hands, open palm, in a defensive gesture. "The man doesn't want to talk about it. Chill out, Private."

"That's a real nice story…"

A gruff, cold voice intruded on our conversation. As one, the Jackals turned towards the speaker.

A huge man in a stained and worn-out aviator-suit— covered in patches from successful operations into the Drift—but otherwise far too large-framed to be a proper a pilot. The guy had an unshaven chin, with scars running the length of both weathered cheeks that told of a harsh life out in the belt. His considerable bulk was arranged across a barstool. The prostitute who had been shadowing Novak had draped herself over the pilot's shoulder, fiddling with a dirty-bladed knife, absently cleaning her nails.

"We're good, thanks," Riggs said.

The pilot's presentation screamed *Alpha Dog*. His eyes

were beads in his fat face, which wobbled as he let out a belly laugh.

"I don't think that you are," he said. "I don't think that you're good at all."

"No problem here," I said. "We're just finishing up, then we'll be on our way."

Negotiation first. That was my attempt at diffusing this standoff.

"Little late for that, ain't it?" Alpha Dog asked. "We got ourselves a situation here."

And that was what it had become: a situation. In an instant, it had developed from nothing to something. The tender slowly edged behind the bar. Eyes not on Alpha Dog or the prospectors, but on us. For the second time that day North Star's no-weapons policy hit home.

"So?" Alpha said. "What you got to say for yourselves?"

There were guffawed laughs across the bar. My skin prickled. I could feel the alcohol draining from my system.

Alpha Dog stood from his stool. "My friend here," he nodded at the hooker, "tells me that you haven't paid your entrance tax. That you have a nice shiny ship in dock."

"Yeah, nice shiny," someone else spoke up. Another figure was standing now.

"Thing is," Alpha said, his hooker friend hanging back, the knife still in her hand, "we don't got a lot of time for military types out here. The guard house keeps to itself."

The bartender nodded. "It does. It does."

"And I really do not like Directorate," Alpha said. "They pay double taxes."

"He's Directorate?" someone else yelled. "That fixes it then …"

Feng set his jaw. "Anyone want to make a thing of it?"

"Oh, we've already made a thing of it," the bartender

said, grinning with his jewelled teeth. "We don't like the Directorate round here. Not after what they did."

"We're just passing through," Lopez offered. I doubted that she had ever been in a bar fight before. "We weren't aware of any tax, but we can pay…"

She fumbled with something in her fatigue harness, but I shot her a cold glare.

"No," I said, firmly. This had gone too far. "We can't."

"You're paying taxes," said Alpha Dog. "And if not, the Directorate's gonna pay in blood."

The big man cracked knuckles. He wore heavy armoured gloves, of a type often lined with powered filaments. Those were illegal on most Alliance stations and worlds, and would certainly be in breach of station policy, but I doubted Alpha Dog cared about that. Special rules seemed to apply to locals.

Novak's drone broke the silence with a loud chirping, detecting the increase in the Russian's anger level. I caught his face in snapshot: the veins across his broad neck were tight, dancing like crazy.

"No taxes, asshole," he said.

I scanned the room. Ten men now, all standing between us and the door. The rest of the bar just waiting to wade in, if necessary. This was going to get real nasty, real fast.

"If you did bring a weapon," I said to Novak, under my breath, "now would be a very good time to reveal it."

Novak kept his eyes on Alpha. "You say no weapons."

I sighed in exasperation. "The one time you actually follow an order—"

But the locals started the show before I could finish my sentence.

The room erupted.

Glasses, chairs, and even—courtesy of Novak—a table.

I slammed a fist into Alpha's face. Felt something break in his nose, and sharp feedback through my hand. This would've been a whole lot easier in a simulant.

Alpha yelped, went backwards. Crashed into the bar.

The hooker was up, waving the knife in a deft arc. This clearly wasn't the first time she'd been involved in this sort of thing. Lunged past me.

"Lopez!" I shouted.

Lopez rolled sideways, still fumbling with something in her uniform harness. A pitcher of alcohol toppled over beside her, showering us both with glass splinters.

Two men were on Novak. Powered gauntlets sparked as punches connected with his chest and shoulders. He worked on through it, roaring like a bear and spinning bodies in every direction. A woman in space armour had Riggs, and was dragging him across an upturned table. He flailed as though he was unsure whether he should actually fight back. Feng was somewhere among the mess, but I couldn't quite be sure where—

A blow caught my jaw. Sharp feedback erupted across my skull, a lance of pain spreading across my jawline.

"Damn it!" I roared.

The force sent me sideways, crashing into a table. Something speared my ribs, immediately followed by the warm flush of blood being spilled.

"Jenk!" Riggs wailed, renewing his efforts to get free.

I shook my head, steadied the dizzying sensation that suggested I might pass out. It had been a while since I'd had any action—of the violent sort—in my real skin. I decided that I didn't like it so much.

"Fucking military assholes, coming out here and getting the best takings!" Alpha Dog remonstrated.

He grabbed me by the collar, and dragged me to my feet. As well as being significantly fatter, Alpha Dog was a good deal taller than me. He hoisted me upwards and I twisted—a fish on a hook. I thrashed my legs, managed to raise a foot. Slammed a boot into his groin. Hard.

Alpha screamed. Dropped me.

I felt my ribs. More glass had cut through my uniform, and bright, sticky blood seeped from inside, but the injury wasn't major. I'd live through it. I got to my feet, whirled about to avoid another punch. The attacker put too much force into the blow and sailed past.

Alpha Dog loomed over me. Flexing his fists, the filaments of his gloves spitting fat white sparks. His grin was gone: now he just looked angry. I imagined what a blow from one of those powered gloves would feel like. Not good.

"Things've changed out here," he rumbled. "Your Army doesn't mean shit to us any more—"

There was a muted bang, and his head exploded.

The bar froze.

Silence. Whatever rules the brawlers had set, killing Alpha Dog had obviously broken them.

All eyes trailed to the shooter.

I ranked the possibilities in my head. An Alliance Military Police patrol attracted by the noise. Captain Carmine or one of the *Santa Fe*'s crew, investigating the downed comms. Major Sergkov and Zero here to keep us on track.

Instead, Private Lopez stood there, a pistol in her hands.

The overweight gang leader slumped to the floor, hooker confidante poised over his body. Blood began to pool around him in a dark arc.

"Oh God, oh God, oh God…" Lopez was saying.

Her hand was shaking, which made the pistol's targeting sight jump. The weapon trailed limply in her grasp, clasped inexpertly.

The Jackals took that momentary pause in activity to

get to their feet. It was like someone had slammed the breaker, hit the reset, and allowed the squad to throw off their injuries.

"I … I … It was …" Lopez started.

"It'll have to wait," I said. My own voice was wet, and I realised that I had bled into my mouth. I thrust out a hand: "Gun. Now."

Lopez was more than willing to palm off the murder weapon, muzzle-first. I'd have to talk to her about that: it was bad gun discipline.

"Revtech-911K," I said. "It's a nice gun."

"I wouldn't really know," Lopez said, swallowing. She already looked green about the gills.

"No guns!" another patron blurted. "No guns allowed on-station!"

"Yeah," I said, retreating towards the bar's exit hatch, waving the pistol in as indiscriminate a manner as I could. "I heard that already. But aren't there also rules about robbing and killing visitors?"

The other occupants were recalibrating as well. Brawlers were getting back on their feet, shaking glass shards from their suits, readying for the next attack. Even with a gun, there were still far too many of them to contemplate taking down. We had to retreat, and fast.

The bartender saw what we were doing. I heard the snap of a shotgun being loaded from behind the bar.

"Get the fuck out of here," he said.

I pointed the Revtech in his direction. His was bigger: a badly maintained sawn-off shotgun which he held in both hands, aimed low. The grim expression on his face suggested that he wasn't going to fire immediately, but that he could change his mind at any time.

"That no-guns thing doesn't apply to you then?" I said. Backed slowly towards the door. "Just let me get my people and go."

The tender tossed his head at one of the locals. "Get that body out of here."

The bartender watched, shotgun trained on us all the way, as we made it into the corridor outside. I aimed the gun on him throughout, but my eyes were on the whole bar.

"Get the door control, Feng," I ordered.

"Affirmative," Feng said.

The door panels closed with a strangled groan. Relief was an understatement.

"Jesus, that was close…" Riggs said. "What the hell just happened in there?"

"It was a shakedown," I said. "Happens, sometimes. Stations like this are a long way from any real money."

"The Customs guy was probably in on it," Feng said. "He told us about this place. We should go find Zero and Major Sergkov."

"That's exactly what we're going to do," I said. My mind was already in overdrive planning the next step. "This way."

The Jackals scrambled through the empty corridors, putting distance between us and the bar. Although no one immediately gave chase, that didn't mean they wouldn't. The rest of the sector was about as downtrodden and disaffected as the bar itself, reduced to a virtual shanty of warren-like passageways and empty hab-modules. Completely deserted. Far quieter, come to think of it, than when I had last travelled this stretch of the station…

"Novak's hit," Riggs said.

The Russian staggered alongside me. The handle of a nasty-looking blade was plunged into the fat of his left thigh, pretty much to the hilt.

"Am fine," he said. "Can walk."

Dark blood stained the fabric of his fatigues, weeping

all the way to the ankle of his boot. I guessed that it hadn't caught an artery, because that would've felled even Novak, but the wound was bad enough to demand medical attention.

"You sure about that?" I asked.

"Yes, yes, can walk," Novak repeated.

Before I could order him not to, Novak pulled the blade from his leg. Lopez gasped and groaned "eugh" but the Russian wasn't bothered. As he held it, his expression became almost euphoric.

"Have weapon now," he said.

The drone watched on, recording the incident, chirping and chiming as it went. I knew that it wouldn't like what had just happened in the bar, and I predicted a penalty on Novak's service contract.

"Right, right," I said. "Someone get me local comms with the *Santa Fe*. Carmine needs to know what's happened here."

Lopez shook her head. "No can do, ma'am." She held up her blood-spattered arm, displaying her wrist-computer. The small screen was filled with a message: COMMUNICATIONS SYSTEMS OFFLINE. "Like Riggs said: local comms are down."

I activated my own comms unit, hoping to see a different result. Without comms, I couldn't even access North Star's mainframe, which meant no maps of the station. The same error message filled the screen.

"Maybe we can get comms online from that box," Riggs said. He pointed out a communications terminal attached to the wall further along the corridor. "We can call in the MPs. An escort off this coffin would be nice…"

The Jackals surrounded the terminal. In that instant, the silence around us felt wrong. I just couldn't explain why. I clutched the pistol tightly, scanning the empty corridor. No immediate threats—only trash collected in the corners, a couple of empty cargo crates stacked at the next junction—but something didn't feel right...

The comms terminal screen lit with an active connection.

"This is Corporal Daneb Riggs," Riggs said into the machine. "Alliance Army Sim Ops Programme. Requesting immediate support in sector T-89."

The comms unit hissed for a second. "Copy that. We see you on the grid." I spied an old-style security camera attached to the deckhead above us, and its electronic eye whirred as it focused on our position. "Stay put."

"There's a situation down here," he said. "We've been—"

Riggs' words trailed off as the station lights went out.

CHAPTER THIRTEEN

AMBUSHED

With no external view-ports, or any other significant source of light, it was pitch black in the corridor. The only illumination came from the running lights on Novak's drone, which continued to hover at his shoulder.

This is a trap.

I realised then what was happening. This sector was deserted, and deserted for a goddamn reason. It made perfect sense. What had happened in the bar hadn't been a random shakedown at all. It had been a set-up, an ambush, and we had fallen right into it.

We were in a stretch of corridor. One direction took us back into the bar, and the other led some way back to the docks. I heard noise from the junction, twenty metres in that direction.

"You people okay in there?" came a voice, echoing down the corridor. "Alliance MP response team inbound—"

"We're here!" Riggs shouted again at the dark.

"Down!" I yelled, dragging Riggs by the scruff of his neck behind an empty cargo crate.

There was a loud hiss, then the crack of a discharging

shockrifle. Blue lightning lanced the corridor, aimed exactly where Riggs had been standing.

"What—?" Riggs managed.

"Thank me later. Just stay in cover."

Had he been hit, he would've likely survived—shockrifles were mostly for non-lethal suppression—but he would've been out of the fight. Novak was already injured and I didn't like our chances of getting another casualty off-station. In fact, as I saw the green glow of low-vis goggles at the end of the corridor—at least three Military Police in full vac-armour, carrying shockrifles—I was less than impressed with our chances of getting off at all.

But Riggs couldn't accept that the Mili-Pol weren't on our side, and persisted in scrambling towards the junction mouth.

"We're here!" he shouted.

"We see you," one of the MPs called back. "Hold tight. Apologies about the misfire."

The shockrifle charged again, and once more I only just managed to drag Riggs into cover. In the dark, the flash of the discharging shockfrifle was dazzling: bright enough that an after-image was plastered across my retinas.

"Cut that out!" I barked. "Just keep down!"

I slammed my body to the wall, and the Jackals copied.

More shockrifle fire.

"Stay where you are!" someone yelled. "Security forces are inbound!"

I slid my head over the lip of the cargo crate, weapon up. Fired several rounds, got lucky with one. An officer yelped and collapsed.

"There's more where that came from," I shouted.

"I'll bet," said a voice I recognised: Sergeant Byers.

"They're supposed to be helping us," Riggs said. "This is insane! They're *supposed* to be station security!"

"Fuck security," Feng said.

In the distance, echoing through North Star's ageing air-recycling network, I strained to hear another noise. Kinetic gunfire. Maybe an assault rifle or machine pistol, followed by a short, piercing scream.

"Something bigger is happening on this station," I decided.

Emergency lights began to power up overhead, providing just enough light to see by. Small mercy—at least we could see who was shooting at us, but also more than that…

"Not again," Lopez said.

A crude infinity spiral had been painted onto the junction wall, the words REJECT THE LIE scrawled beneath. The black paint was still wet, dripping onto the deck.

"The Black Spiral…" Feng said, under his breath. "They're here."

I nodded. "I guess that they were waiting for the fight, using it as cover."

"How did they know that we were here?" Lopez asked. "We're supposed to be working for Military Intelligence!"

"Forget about all of that for now," I ordered. "We need to get back to the *Santa Fe*."

The MPs shouted to one another, coordinating their attack. Another shockrifle fired, and I saw shapes moving up the corridor. The MPs were suppressing us, would swarm us when they got close enough.

Novak's wet growl drew my attention. "Drone," he said. "I lose it."

I shook my head, angered at his timing. "Not this again!"

"Do not understand," Novak implored. "Drone is holding us back, yes?"

Novak's drone hovered at the edge of my vision. It had somehow escaped damage during the incident in the bar, and it was now bleating and whirring like crazy, attracting attention in our direction. Obviously didn't like the idea of being caught in the middle of a gunfight. Although there was no time to discuss the detail, perhaps Novak had a point.

"Fine," I decided. "Drone: command pattern beta-charlie-six-three-nine."

The drone had been programmed to recognise my voice, and that recitation was an execution prompt. Its single activation light flashed once.

"Confirm: offline command?" it said in a tinny voice.

"Do you think that this is a good idea?" Riggs asked, grabbing my arm. "Just think about this for a moment—"

"Confirm!"

The drone's anti-gravitic engine immediately went offline and it became an inert piece of machinery. Without the gravitic core to keep it aloft, the device fell to the deck with an empty *thunk*.

My action had another consequence. Novak's face was barely visible in the low light, but his expression shifted into a grin. Knife in hand, his uniform now saturated with blood, he looked positively feral.

"Thank you, ma'am," he said.

Then, before I could properly consider what I'd just done, Novak was up and running back towards the bar. As a final insult he scooped up the drone as he went. The Jackals watched on in stunned amazement; no one even bothered to challenge him.

"*Novak!*" I shouted. "What are you doing?"

But my attention was diverted by a kinetic round

slamming into the wall beside me. The MPs were advancing on us from one direction, and the only route out was back towards the bar, the way that Novak had run. That was no kind of option.

"He's gone," Riggs said, shaking his head. "The Russian's gone. I tried to say."

"Bastard was probably planning this all along," Lopez said.

"Damn," I spat.

Now he was off the lead. Armed with a knife, just as he liked, and caught on a space station in the midst of some sort of rebellion. Shit, he would probably get the next transport off-base, get a new ID and make a fast buck as a mercenary...

"Forget Novak," I said. "We need to move."

I checked Lopez's pistol. It was a short-nosed semi-automatic, carrying sixteen rounds per magazine. The display indicated that I'd already used six of those. How many targets were there out there? I scanned the junction ahead. Popped another couple of rounds at the MPs, trying to keep them in check, then bolted from behind the crate.

"This way," I ordered.

The Jackals doubletimed it across the intersection, chased by shockrifle fire, MPs yelling commands to stop. No casualties, although I felt the prickle of shock-fire discharge way too close to my neck. We ran without any military discipline at all.

I thought that I recognised this location. I knew where we were! Internally, I began to plot the route we'd need to take. Through the next junction, then into a concourse. Then the arrivals hall, and beyond that the docks. The *Santa Fe* was barely half a klick from our position...

"They're here!" came another voice.

The passage ahead was blocked by two more MPs in full armour. They stood at a door-control panel, ready to shut us in. As we approached, one trooper slammed a hand to the control, while the other brought his rifle to bear and began to fire.

There was no cover in the corridor at all. This was it: we had nowhere to go.

A shock-bolt hit Feng in the shoulder. He bawled in agony, was flung back against the wall. His body twitched with blue fire, and the scent of burning meat and melted plastic filled my nose.

"Someone get Feng!" I said. "Fall back!"

I fired Lopez's Revtech again and again. It bucked in my hands, unaimed and imprecise. No targeting software, no HUD—just me and the gun. The glass fragments in my chest stung like crazy each time I fired.

"We can't go back that way," Riggs said.

Of course, he was right. There were more troops closing from the other direction, their boots hammering against the deck.

We were trapped.

I raised the gun and fired.

Heard a sickening *beep*: the gun warning me that the magazine was empty.

The MPs stopped firing and advanced on us with weapons raised, the door still open behind them.

"They're contained," said one. He had a Spiral insignia on the chest of his armoured suit, black sprayed on grey, only visible as he came towards us. "We've got them—"

There was a flurry of motion somewhere above. The hatch of an airshaft fell loose from the ceiling, almost directly above the officers' position.

The Jackals closed ranks, back to back.

"Who's there?" the closest officer managed, just as something landed on top of him.

Novak.

Even if the MP was armoured, Novak was bigger and a lot heavier. His boots came down hard on both shoulders, and his weight knocked the man to the ground. The first MP just crumpled, his suit producing a startling clatter as it connected with the deck.

The second trooper brought his rifle up, cursing, going to fire.

Novak rolled off his victim, stamping down on the soldier's back. Then he landed on both feet. Let his legs take his weight, despite the injury to his thigh. He was carrying something, holding it in front of him like a shield.

The drone.

Shock-fire hit the machine, sent sparks across the corridor. It did nothing to slow the Russian down though. With a bear's bellow, he hurled the drone. It hit the officer squarely in the chest, and hard: with enough force to shatter his sternum. That accounted for the sickening crack as the man collapsed backwards.

The officer Novak had jumped was back on his feet now, stumbling away, shocked and surprised by the assault.

But Novak hadn't finished yet.

He flipped the knife, blade-down, and stabbed. And stabbed. And stabbed.

Military Police armour wasn't direct-combat rated, but it was heavy enough to withstand most small arms fire. Right now, Novak was a heavy weapon. He directed each stab of the blade with frightening precision, to where the armour joins were weakest, putting his considerable strength behind every blow. The MP gave a distorted groan—air escaping from a punctured lung, perhaps—and then he, too, slumped to the ground.

Novak wasn't done. He lurched over the trooper he'd caught with his drone. His knife punched into the MP again and again.

There had been two MPs there one minute, wearing full armour, and the next there were none. A thief in the night had replaced them with sacks of inert meat, their suits pierced at the neck, shoulder, wherever there was a weakness in the armour.

"Was that necessary?" Lopez said, trying to avoid looking at the dead bodies.

Novak shrugged. "We go now. Is this way."

Just a short while ago, the arrivals hall had been a bustling hub of commerce, but now we found it utterly deserted. Stalls and shops had been sealed up for the fight, no one risking exposure to whatever was happening on North Star. The arrivals gate was abandoned.

"What the fuck was that back there?" I asked Novak, as we ran.

"Seemed best thing to do," he said. "No time to explain plan. Do you have any bullets left in gun?"

"No," I confessed. "I don't."

"Then I was right," he grunted. "We would all be dead if I had stayed put."

"He's probably right," Feng said, gasping out the words. "Thanks for the assist."

The big man had his arm around Feng, and was helping him keep pace. The shock-bolt to Feng's shoulder had seared a ragged hole through his uniform, exposing a patch of blackened flesh. That Feng was still walking was something; maybe all of his talk about improved clone physiology had some truth to it after all.

The pair made an unlikely team: the Russian and the Chino clone.

"Just tell me what you're doing, next time," I said to Novak. "I thought that you were deserting."

Novak grinned. "Maybe was. Maybe was not."

The *Santa Fe* sat in the berth, her running lights flashing, the thrum of an active starship engine filling the chamber.

"Isn't that just the sweetest sight," Lopez exclaimed, rushing ahead and into the docking bay. "Friendlies inbound!"

The corvette's rear cargo hatch had been deployed, ramp touching the deck. Captain Carmine stood there, grim-faced, surrounded by a dozen fresh corpses. She had a carbine at her hip, but she raised the weapon when she saw us. Waved down three other sailors who were manning the hatch. They were armed with shotguns.

"What the hell's happening, Jenkins?" Carmine shouted. Sounded like she was maybe over-compensating as a result of close-range gunfire.

"We're under attack," I said, scrambling up the ramp. "Jackals, get inside!"

"Where's Zero?" Feng asked Carmine. "Has she made it back yet?"

"No," she said. "You're the first. Comms are down."

"We noticed. You saw some action too?" Riggs said.

Carmine nodded. "These brutes tried to get onto my ship without permission. Killing them seemed the only option." She patted the carbine. "Feels just like old times."

I noticed that Carmine had broken out her antique carbine: the weapon that had last seen action on New Ohio. She handled it expertly, and I could see from the nature of their injuries that several of the casualties had been her doing.

"You lost anyone?" Carmine asked.

"Not yet, but Novak is hit, and Feng took a shock-bolt." The Russian grinned. "Is flesh wound."

Gunfire started across the station's dock. Rounds sparked against the *Santa Fe*'s exposed cargo hold, spanked the ramp.

"Get down!" Carmine ordered. She returned fire, the entire area turning into a criss-cross of kinetics. "This is no longer a safe place to dock," she said, "and as such we are leaving! Hatch, now!"

"Aye, ma'am," an officer said.

"Not without Zero!" Feng argued.

"For all we know," Riggs said, "she could be dead already, and you're not in a fit state to go anywhere."

The cargo ramp started to close. I could see figures advancing now—could see them running for us. Carrying heavier weapons, by the look of things. All of them wearing the same model of suit. *Old friends.* I immediately recognised the armour from the troops we'd seen at Daktar.

The Black Spiral hadn't just infiltrated the Alliance security contingent on North Star; they had come in force. It would probably have been easy enough to do. Civilian ships came and went out here all the time, and security was lax. How many of those civilian ships that we had seen on the way in had actually been Spiral transports? There could be hundreds of tangos on-station...

"We need to pull out!" Carmine said. "Get to the bridge! We can breach the station's defences and—"

"We're not going anywhere," I said. "Not until we have our people." I tossed the Revtech pistol to Lopez, and she caught it awkwardly. "Get that loaded and stay sharp."

Carmine turned to me with a harsh scowl. "This place is a warzone! You can't seriously be thinking of going back out there?"

"We're not going without Zero," I said. "She's Sim Ops, and she's a Jackal. Feng, with me!"

Simulant Operations Centre.

I slipped into the still blue fluid, and felt the sting of the amniotic against the open wounds on my ribs. There was probably still glass in there, but I had far bigger problems to worry about. Things that wouldn't immediately kill me? They would have to wait.

"You read me, Feng?" I asked, into my communicator.

"Copy that, Lieutenant," he said. "All your readings look good—so far as I can tell…Pulse is a little elevated."

I gave a bittersweet smile behind the respirator. "That's normal for an operator, Feng."

"Whatever you say."

Feng sat in Zero's command chair, glancing up at the monitors with an anxious look on his face. Fluid pumped into the tank, filling rapidly. I didn't need to see the monitors to know that my pulse was elevated, because I could sense it. I was getting the euphoria, the simulant-shakes.

I wanted transition, and I wanted it *now*.

"Maybe I should get into the tank too," Feng suggested. Part of his uniform had been pulled free from his injured shoulder, and an empty analgesic syringe sat on the console beside him.

"That's a nice offer," I said, deliberately misinterpreting him, "but we don't know each other that well just yet, Feng. I'm ordering you to stay aboard the ship. Have Lopez and Riggs reported yet?"

Feng's watery outline nodded. "Affirmative. The HURT suit is locked and loaded. She's ready when you are."

I opened a comms channel to Carmine on the bridge. "Captain? You read me?"

"I hear you," she said. "Whatever has happened to communications, it doesn't appear to be blocking local comms aboard the *Fe*."

"Good. I want you to remain on-station until I make exfiltration."

Feng motioned to me through the simulator's canopy. The readouts behind him were all in the green.

"Jenkins out," I said, before Carmine could argue any further. "Feng, send me in."

He nodded. "Transition in three...two...one..."

The world made that short, sharp shift that it always does when you make transition into a sim. Seconds later, I was in the *Santa Fe*'s hangar again. Standing in front of the closed cargo hatch, but in a brand-new body.

"I'm ready to do this," I said. "Open the ramp."

I rolled my simulated head inside the HURT suit's helmet, and liked the way such a simple motion felt powerful. My bio-engineered blood thrummed, hungering for combat.

Carmine audibly sighed over the comms. "You know best."

"I sure do," I said.

The cargo ramp lowered, and I started to take fire.

CHAPTER FOURTEEN

TARGETS NEUTRALISED

The HURT suit was an exquisite piece of engineering. Heavily armed and armoured, it was the epitome of a personal assault suit: a veritable tank on legs, the biggest and baddest class of combat-armour currently approved for use by the Alliance armed forces. There was enormous locomotive strength pent up in the suit's limbs, but the man-amplifier that powered the armour also made every motion feel like second nature.

"I'm outside," I said. "Reading multiple hostiles."

The HURT's combat systems came online, and my already-sharpened simulant senses became razors. A grid of complicated combat-schematics appeared on my HUD. Dozens of targets materialised across North Star's hangar, with threat-ratings assigned to each.

The HURT had an AX-10 assault gun locked to each hardpoint on the forearms. They were big weapons, capable of firing high-calibre, armour-busting kinetics—more cannon than gun, really. Each was supported by a complex array of servo attenuators that held them in place, and that would compensate for their ferocious recoil.

The Black Spiral began to fire on me, and the HURT's null-shield activated. Plasma and laser fire rippled across the energy shield, dissipating harmlessly. The occasional kinetic round punched through the shield, sure, but that was like gentle rain against the HURT's heavy exo-plating. The tangos were ants, their weapons a petty inconvenience to the might of the HURT suit.

"You there, Feng?" I asked, over the comms.

"I copy you," Feng said.

"What about the vid-feed?"

"Affirmative on that too."

"Then you might want to watch this."

I raised my arms, tracking targets.

I wondered, as I stood there absorbing fire from every angle, what enemy Sergkov had envisaged we would face when he'd requisitioned the HURT suit. It surely couldn't have been the Black Spiral.

I opened fire with the suit-guns.

My guns carried smart ammunition: jet-assisted rounds, with a rudimentary tracking system built into every projectile. Bodies exploded across my field of vision, chased down by bullet-swarms.

"Splash one," I declared, counting off the dead. "Splash two, three, four…"

I felt the gentle rhythm of rounds loading into the weapons from the ammo hoppers on my back. The guns had an incredible rate of fire. Craw's warning about North Star being a fully pressurised environment was long forgotten.

Two troopers launched themselves towards me, using their exo-suits to achieve sudden bursts of speed. Before either could get close enough for concern, I adjusted my aim. Both attackers jerked backwards, pulled on unseen puppet strings, and vanished in a red mist.

"Splash six, nine, eleven…"

TARGETS NEUTRALISED, my suit said. ARMOUR INTEGRITY: 100%.

Much to my disappointment, the hangar bay was clear. I hadn't even used the grenade launcher on the HURT's humpback rig. That would've been overkill, and I'm not one for being flashy.

"You catch that, Feng?" I asked.

"We saw it all," Feng said. He sounded about as excited as I felt. "Nice shooting."

"I think that I'm going to like this suit," I said. "Keep trying Zero on the communicator. Tell her that I'm coming for her."

"Solid copy," Feng said. "Good hunting."

Comms dropped shortly thereafter, but that didn't matter.

I proceeded to take the most direct route to Dr. Skinner's lab: the Black Spiral knew that I was coming, and there was something liberating about throwing caution to the wind.

I popped tangos everywhere. The HURT had an impressive sensor-package, with a sensitive bio-scanner the like of which I had never seen before. I tracked hostiles on decks above and below, and reacted accordingly. The suit-guns fired with sniper-like precision through the ceiling and floor, punching through the deck.

The whole of North Star had turned against us. Civilians, Military Police, prospectors: they were all in on this. This was something organised—not an ad hoc revolution. Even inside the invincible HURT suit, an icy shiver ran down my spine. Sergkov said that he had been tracking the Spiral, but had the Spiral in turn been tracking him?

I stopped thinking and kept shooting.

Fire spread through the station. Inside the HURT,

my vision wavered—black-armoured figures leaping out from the smoke. They were maniacs, fervent devotees to the Spiral's cause. Their calling cards marked every bulkhead and hatch.

REJECT THE LIE.

NO PEACE.

CLEANSE THE TANK.

I checked my timeline. Found that I'd been off-ship for less than a minute, and already I was in Skinner's lab sector. Glowing schematics on my HUD indicated that I had passed through the half-dozen checkpoints and security stations that marked the journey, but I had hardly noticed. Depressingly, none of those had been manned with Alliance forces.

I evaluated the scene. The hatch to Skinner's lab was sealed shut: coffin-like and resolute, although pocked with some heavy scorch marks. The HURT mapped the corridor, identified several bodies—still warm, but undeniably dead—outside the entrance. The components of a quadruped gun-bot were liberally strewn among the bodies—the lab's last-ditch defence, now spent.

The Spiral hadn't got in yet, so that was a good sign. According to the HURT suit's mapping programme, this was the sole entrance to the lab. I could only hope that Zero and Sergkov had sealed themselves in.

I paused at the hatch. What about Dr. Skinner? Was he in on the Spiral's plan, or was he the Spiral's target?

I lifted a hand. Despite its brute size, the HURT carried a deceptively delicate pair of gauntlets for precision work. I rapped an armoured knuckle against the metal door, while I activated my comms unit and searched for working bands.

"…answer! Is that you, ma'am?" came a familiar voice, static-tinged and excitable.

Zero.

"It's me," I said. "You going to let me in, or am I going to wait here all day? I've got hostiles on my tail."

Seventy-one seconds after I'd left the *Santa Fe*, I was inside Dr. Skinner's lab.

The place was a mess: papers and data-slates and breakable science shit scattered across the floor. I'd been wrong about the Spiral failing to get inside: fresh red blood—human blood—spattered the floor, and two man-sized outlines lay behind a bench, draped with opaque plastic sheets like funeral shrouds. When I opened the HURT's helmet and drank in the local atmosphere, the smell of dead flesh hit me immediately.

Zero bolted across the room.

"I knew that you wouldn't leave us behind," she said, biting her lip. The emotion was raw on her face, her eyes rimmed red with stress.

"You're a Jackal, Zero. I'd never leave you."

"I wasn't so sure," said Sergkov. "The nature of this event wasn't clear to us."

Major Sergkov and Dr. Skinner emerged from the rear of the lab. Both looked dishevelled, but relatively collected given the circumstances. Skinner's pockmarked face settled into an impression of a grin.

"A simulant, eh?" he said. "How marvellous. It's been a long time since I've seen one of those. A Mark 16 combat sim, if I'm not mistaken."

I nodded. "Affirmative, Doctor. My real body is aboard the *Santa Fe*."

"Excellent," Skinner said. "Most excellent."

"This is a new issue simulant," I said, referring to the "Mark 16" designation. "I thought that you said you'd been alone out here?"

Skinner shrugged. "I like to keep up-to-date on developments in the field, as much as I can."

"This will have to wait," Sergkov interrupted. He turned to me, looking immensely insignificant and tiny before the might of the HURT suit. "What's happening out there, soldier? Give me a sitrep."

"It's bad. The Black Spiral have infiltrated North Star. They have agents everywhere, and they've taken control of station security. North Star's a write-off."

Sergkov clamped his jaw, obviously displeased with my assessment. "Where's the rest of your team?" he asked.

"They're aboard the *Santa Fe*, holding the ship and awaiting orders. But I can't contact them: local comms are down. Probably being blocked by some form of jamming technology."

Zero swallowed. "We can vouch for that. We've been trying to contact you and the *Fe* since..." Her eyes trailed to the dead bodies. "Since *they* turned up."

"What happened in here?" I asked.

"Two Military Police officers attempted to invade my laboratory," Skinner said. "A man and a woman that I didn't know." He sighed. "I've been here a long time, Lieutenant. You get to know the same ugly faces."

I stared at the dead bodies, and something occurred to me. There was an awful lot of blood staining the floor. "I thought there weren't supposed to be weapons on this station...?"

"There aren't," Skinner said. "Although, in light of current events, I would suggest that particular policy is reviewed..."

"Then who killed them?"

"We did," came an electronic voice.

The Pariah was perched atop one of Skinner's cryogenic

banks, so preternaturally still that I hadn't even noticed it until it had spoken. The alien uncoiled its sinewy body and dropped to the deck with a loud thud. I realised something as the bio-form stood before me.

"You've got bio-weapons?" I asked. To Skinner: "You gave this thing guns, for Christo's sake?"

The Krell's long arms ended in twinned weapon-enhancements—bio-guns that were not much bigger than a Widowmaker pistol, but wickedly curved and spiked, machined of flesh rather than plasteel. The guns meshed with the creature's palms, giving the false impression that they were part of it. I'd seen that sort of bio-adaptation many times before; Krell secondary-forms were even purpose-bred to carry grafted weaponry.

"Barb-guns," the Pariah said. "Lethal to others at close range."

"Others?" I asked.

"*Humans*," Skinner said. "Pariah means that the guns are lethal to humans."

"Isn't that nice," I said. "You fishes sure are a hell of a species."

The Krell ignored the slight, if it had even noticed.

"In answer to your question," Skinner said, a defensive tone to his voice, "yes, Lieutenant, I gave 'this thing' weapons. All Krell have a genetic predisposition towards aggressive bio-adaptations. The weapons were self-developed, as was the armour."

The pariah-form came into the pool of light cast by the nearest glow-globe, and I saw that its frame was now significantly bulkier. It was wearing a full bio-suit: vac-proofed living armour that was almost as tough as a combat-suit. A sleek-looking, organic helmet was hooked to its back.

I shook my head in surprise. "It's your call, Skinner. It's on your head."

Skinner indicated to the other cryogenic capsules, all sealed but just waiting for activation. "The species has a proclivity for spontaneous mutation, and so many of my experiments have ended up with dangerous bio-enhancements. Take experiment TY963: a Krell pariah-form that sports a carapace three times stronger than the average bio-form. Now, experiment WQ623 is even more dangerous—having developed a shrieker cannon on its left limb...."

The capsules were internally lit, catching the Krell prisoners in bright illumination, demonstrating Skinner's handiwork. He might call this work scientific genius, but to me it was lunacy. These things were lethal. Although the Krell mutants trapped inside each pod were still frozen—bodies coated with frost-crystals, kept in deep-hibernation by a no-doubt potent chemical combination—I could feel their anger even now. I wondered whether these specimens were as rational-minded as the Pariah...

Sergkov tutted impatiently. "This is not the time to debate the ethics of the Pariah Project," he said. He nodded at a series of terminals set into the far wall. "Dr. Skinner's surveillance network suggests that the attackers are moving on this lab."

I stalked over to the monitors and assessed the situation. Dark figures were advancing through the trail of destruction I'd left behind me. It was only a matter of time before the Spiral breached the lab door, and although I could hold my own I wasn't sure how well I could protect the rest of the team. That, and there was no telling how long Carmine and the Jackals could hold out aboard the *Santa Fe*.

"We're going to have to find another way to the docks," I said, thinking through our options. "There's too much resistance in the main station. Is there any other way out of here?"

Dr. Skinner rubbed a hand over his chin. "There's a transit tunnel that leads down to the docks located at the rear of my lab. Several tunnels, in fact."

"Does anyone else know about that exit?" I asked, intrigued. The idea of a secret route off base, that would bypass the fireworks, appealed to me greatly.

"I don't think so," Skinner explained. "When North Star was decommissioned, many of the transit tunnels were sealed. But I insisted that this access point remained active, just in case I needed it one day."

Zero sighed. "One day has come all right…"

My sim-senses picked up an explosion somewhere else on the station, distant but close enough to cause me concern.

"We need to get my research material onto your ship," Skinner said, pulling at his jowls. "That's the priority."

"How much material are we talking?" I asked.

"We can use a buggy to traverse the tunnels," Skinner said. He shrugged. "It'll take a couple of trips, I suppose."

I laughed out loud as I watched the surveillance feeds. "There's no way that we're going to be able to make two trips, Doctor. I'm disposable; you're not."

"I can't leave this lab without my work. I can't let all of this," he waved a hand in the air, taking in the whole dirty operation, "fall into the Black Spiral's hands."

I glanced around the lab. My eyes settled on the malformed thing in the nearest cryo-capsule.

"There might be a way of solving this problem…" I suggested.

"If you have a plan," Sergkov said, "then I'd love to hear it, Lieutenant." The fact that he had very little authority over this situation was irking him, and his impatience was growing. "We need to get out of here, and now."

An idea was starting to form in my head, becoming more defined as the Spiral advanced on the lab—as their footfalls started to sound through the structures around us. But as I thought on it, I almost hated myself for considering it.

Needs must, I decided.

"I think that I have a plan," I whispered. I caught Zero's eye. "But you're not going to like it."

Turned out that North Star was criss-crossed with tunnels. Literally dozens of decommissioned rail lines, connecting all of the station's major facilities: the legacy of an outpost that had once housed a much larger contingent of military personnel. Most of the network had fallen into disrepair, but Dr. Skinner had made it his business to keep several tunnels active. He provided me with a map marked with cargo runs.

"These tunnels weren't on my schematics," I said.

"Not even the MPs were aware of most of these passageways," Skinner insisted. "They're not on station maps, and I've only ever used this tunnel to take receipt of, ah, sub rosa specimens." He pointed ahead, into the poorly lit tunnel mouth. "This route will take us to the main docks."

"And from there, it'll be a short bounce to the *Santa Fe*'s berth," Zero added. Her faux optimism was almost grating.

The cargo run was a large empty space that seemed to capture and amplify sound. The noise of approaching battle was now undeniable.

"We've got to move fast," I said, slinging the last palette onto the back of the buggy.

Skinner immediately set about lashing the cargo to the open bed. The small vehicle was loaded with miscellaneous science junk: a rag-tag selection of cryo-genics tech, a terminal server unit, some small storage containers which contained Gaia-knew-what.

"Are you sure that we can't go back for another load?" he asked.

"I'm sure."

"But I think that I've left some of my virology research behind. Perhaps if the Pariah could..."

"The lab is compromised," I said. "You know the plan."

"Yes, and I'm not at all happy about it. They are not weapons!"

"We've already been through this."

Skinner huffed, but did as he was ordered, and he and the Pariah settled into the rear passenger section. The buggy had six seats and had once probably been equipped with a gun hardpoint, but that was in a for-mer life, and now its rubber wheels were only used for transporting cargo up and down the station's transit route.

"Lab is prepped," Sergkov said, buckling into one of the front passenger seats and glancing back the way we had come. His eyes trailed to his wrist-comp, at the graphics that indicated a link to the lab's security sys-tems. "Let's hope that your plan works. Sergeant Camp-bell is driving. You *can* drive, can't you?"

Zero licked her lips and nodded. She looked desperate to get out of here, and I couldn't blame her. "Of course. We had aerocars on Mau Tanis before the fall."

"You were eight years old when Tanis fell," I said.

"I also picked up a little during Basic..." Zero insisted.

"Fine," Sergkov said, now staring into the darkened interior of the transit tunnel: our route out of here. The place stank of oil and burnt rubber. "Just don't get us killed."

I clambered onto the buggy's cargo bed, and its wheel-base sagged as the vehicle took my weight. From here, I had a pretty good vantage point down the tunnel, and I would be able to deploy my suit-guns at a distance. I hoped that I wouldn't need to use them.

Skinner stirred again, moaning to himself. "I need to go back. I can't leave those files!"

"Buckle in," I said, putting a gloved hand to his chest. The simple action almost winded him, and he unwill-ingly settled into his seat. "There's no time left. I mean it. The Spiral are advancing on the main entrance right now, and once they breach your lab..." I let that hang. "Start her up, Zero."

Zero powered up the buggy's engine. An electric hum reverberated down the tunnel, and two thin headlights penetrated the gloom.

The stretch of tunnel ahead was tight, long, and straight—featureless except for the overhead rail line, now redundant and unpowered. A small local-network map appeared on Zero's control panel, beneath the steer-ing wheel, and the HURT's sensor-suite tapped into the vehicle's primitive intel system. I snapped my helmet into place, allowing the data-stream to flood my neural cortex.

"Go," Sergkov ordered, slapping one hand on the dashboard. "Now."

"Solid copy," said Zero. The buggy moved off down the tunnel. "Is Chu okay?"

"He was last time I saw him," I said. I couldn't give Zero any more assurance than that. "He sends his love."

"Really?" Zero asked.

"No, but your reaction gave away more than it should."

"Concentrate on driving," Sergkov muttered. "You're carrying one of the premier minds of the Alliance scien-tific community."

Skinner smiled. "It's nice to be recognised."

The buggy began to build up speed. The Pariah bristled in front of me, lurching in the ill-fitting seat, perhaps reacting to our plan. Although it was almost sitting on him, Dr. Skinner showed no apprehension about being so close to the alien—

LAB BREACH, my suit said.

"Hold on!" I yelled.

There was a cavernous boom from somewhere behind us.

The transit tunnel shook with the force of the explosion. Debris and dust clouded the buggy's headlights, fat motes of dirt falling from above. Zero built up speed, driving faster and faster.

"You ready?" I asked.

"All that research . . ." Skinner whimpered.

"I'm ready," Zero said.

"Do it," Sergkov barked, as though trying to retain some modicum of command.

"Opening cryogenics pods *now*!" I shouted.

Back in Dr. Skinner's lab, the two dozen capsules holding his failed experiments suddenly opened. The Spiral were going to get one hell of a welcome committee.

TAKE EVASIVE ACTION, my suit insisted. XENO CONTAINMENT BREACH.

"They're free," I said. "Plan has been executed."

The effect was almost instantaneous. From the direction of the lab: screaming, the chatter of gunfire, alien shrieking. The noise carried off down the tunnel, echoing tenfold.

"We feel them," the Pariah said.

The alien's features twitched. Was it unhappy that its kindred, feral or otherwise, were being used as cannon fodder? It was hard to tell much from the alien's face, but Skinner was much easier to read.

"Such a damned waste!" he deplored. "Those specimens presented invaluable research opportunities!"

"I'll bet," I said. "But it was our lives or theirs."

"Kindred fight," the Pariah said, its electronic voice linking to my helmet in a way that I found disturbing: as though the creature's thoughts were being projected into my head. "More others come to lab."

"Tell your buddies to kill everyone who gets into that room," I said.

"Just make sure your friends don't come after us," Zero said, her hair whipping about as we drove. She looked terrified.

The Pariah said nothing to that.

"What's the range on this thing?" I asked Skinner. "The Pariah, I mean."

"Unknown," Skinner said. "I was still running field tests. The link to the collective consciousness isn't always reliable. You should be aware that the effect works both ways: it's a two-way mirror. In other circumstances this might be a disadvantage..."

The buggy lurched onwards. The tunnel sides were smooth but oppressively close.

"Half a klick to go, Zero," I said. "You're doing fine."

The HURT's sensor-package flagged the end of the tunnel as a glowing icon. There was a hatch that led directly into a disused hangar; I would have to dismount the buggy to manually open the shaft and let us through. My bio-scanner was effectively useless at this speed, and I couldn't tell whether there were hostiles beyond the hatch. Just had to hope that Skinner's intel was reliable—that no one else knew about the tunnels.

"Are you able to make uplink with the *Santa Fe* yet, Lieutenant?" Sergkov shouted, turning his head back in my direction.

"Not yet, but—"

"*Down*," said the Pariah.

"You talking to me, fish head?" I asked. "Because I don't like—"

But then an enormous force hit me in the chest, and the buggy pitched forward.

CHAPTER FIFTEEN

READY TO EXTRACT

I tried to make sense of what had just happened. It had been so sudden that, even with my sim-senses, I struggled to process it.

I'd been thrown from the buggy and hit the deck: *hard*.

My medi-suite ran a damage report: indicated that I was shaken, but otherwise unharmed. That was the organics taken care of. So far as my suit was concerned, ARMOUR INTEGRITY 100% showed on the HUD. My bio-scanner commenced a reboot—

Something swooped from above, and gunfire raked the ground next to me. I rolled sideways, simultaneously struggling to my feet. The HURT suit wasn't made with agility in mind.

Multiple shooters.

Positioned in the rafters of the transit tunnel.

I brought up the suit-guns.

WEAPONS SYSTEMS RECALIBRATING, the HURT insisted. ADVISE AWAIT COMPLETION OF DIAGNOSTIC PROGRAMME BEFORE—

I fired both guns. The tunnel lit with a swarm of

self-guided ammo. Without the suit's targeting suite, the gesture was token, but it would force any potential attackers to keep their heads down. Instantly, I knew that I'd done something right. An armoured shape fell from above, made a loud crunch as it hit the deck.

All of this took place in a second—a fraction of a second, maybe. For me, now under the sway of combat focus, time was slowing, becoming syrupy and flexible.

For Zero, Sergkov, Skinner, and the Pariah, it was moving at an altogether different rate.

The buggy careened forward. Zero fought with the steering, but panic gripped her. More gunfire sparked the deck, and as the buggy jinked to avoid being hit, Zero lost control. Her short, sharp scream was largely lost to the cacophony of weapons fire that filled the tunnel.

With a squeal of shearing metal the buggy collided with the tunnel wall. It rolled end over end, came to a stop twenty metres up the passage, upside down.

Now my suit was back online, bio-scanner functions had been restored. Behind us, from the direction of the lab, definite signals were pursuing. Fear rose inside of me like a hurricane. Those signals could be Black Spiral, or they could be the Krell mutants. Neither thought was comforting.

I dashed for the buggy. Cleared the distance in a couple of strides, and let my null-shield take the heat of enemy gunfire.

Zero was strapped in and upside down, held by the safety webbing, barely protected by the driver section roll-cage. Sergkov was beside her, struggling out of his seat. I couldn't immediately see what had happened to Skinner, but his precious lab gear was spilled across the deck, crushed by the weight of the errant transport. Smoke had started pouring from the buggy's engine module, its wheels still spinning.

"Stay down!" I ordered. "We've got hostiles coming

down the tunnel, and I'm reading bio-signs closing from the direction of the docks as well—"

Shapes were emerging from the smoke around us: troops in bulky exo-rigs. I recognised them as the Warlord's elite, as Spiral veterans from Daktar. They were making quick progress, plasma and assault rifles stuttering as they advanced.

The Pariah bolted past me. One of the tangos fell with a yelp, eviscerated by the Krell. The alien tore another in two with its shoulder-mounted talons. Tossing the body aside, the alien dodged a retaliatory volley of gunfire with ease.

"We are being ambushed," the Pariah coolly declared.

"No shit."

Another jackhammer blow hit me in the side. The force was immense—enough to stagger me, despite the HURT suit's gyro-stabilisers.

Without thinking, I brought my guns up. Explosive rounds stitched the corridor.

The attacker darted under my field of fire, moving with superhuman speed. Quite something, given that I was using self-guided ammunition. I lurched forward, and reactively punched out with one hand, grappled with the other.

I hurled the body against the tunnel wall with weight enough to kill a normal skin. But instead of doing the decent thing and dying, the attacker got back up, slammed a fist into my torso.

"*Mothhherrr-fffucker!*" I growled. "No one damages my armour!"

The armour plating to my chest had become warped: deformed in the shape of a *fist*. What could've hit me hard enough to damage reinforced exo-plate?

"You awake there, Lieutenant?" intruded a voice over my comms.

Warlord.

He wore the same armour as I'd seen him in on Daktar, suit covered in Spiral motifs, helmet sprayed with the image of a crude skull. But the armour looked more ragged, worn out, than before, with a dirty camo-cloak that gave Warlord a wraith-like appearance. A long-shot sniper rifle was strapped across his back. I decided that must've been responsible for knocking me from the buggy. Equipped with shield-breaker rounds, a weapon like that would be capable of breaching a HURT suit's null-shield.

Without answering him, I brought up my suit-guns to fire, intent on ending this.

But, shit, Warlord moved *fast*. Flipped across the tunnel. An impressive move, especially in an exo. The camo-cloak reminded me of those used by recon teams during grounds ops, and it whipped around him as he moved. He launched at me, fist connecting with my face-plate.

I took the blow full-on. The visor of the HURT suit rang with the impact, but didn't break.

Now I was getting angry. I tracked Warlord, brought my left arm up to shoot—

He parried the movement with his forearm. Diverted, my suit-gun sprayed the tunnel floor.

I twisted. Slammed a fist into Warlord's body—

He dodged again, narrowly avoiding another stream of smart rounds—

We traded blows, again and again. Every time one of us loosed a shot, the other countered it. Every time one of us went to land a blow, the other dodged or parried it. Warlord's suit was smaller, but fast; my armour was heavy, but slow. He was equipped with a micro-grenade rig on his forearms—but couldn't get a fix on me. Equally, every time I shot on him with my suit-guns, he managed to evade and move off.

Battle raged around me. On the HURT's HUD, I saw that the Krell were almost on us now, that any second the tunnel would be filled with Skinner's science experiment rejects.

"Zero!" I yelled, blocking another skull-shattering blow from Warlord's powered gauntlet. "Get out of here! *Now!*"

I managed to grapple his cloak, and yanked hard. Warlord slammed to the ground, on his back, but quickly evaded the curb-stomp I attempted with my boot. *Who is this guy?* I asked myself. No ordinary terrorist, that was for sure. He was putting up quite some resistance. Would I get the better of him? Probably. Already, I noted that his movements were slowing—perhaps suggesting that he was tiring. But would I get the better of him before the Krell broke out of Skinner's lab? I wasn't so sure.

"It doesn't have to be like this," Warlord said.

"How are you using my comms grid? It's restricted."

Icons on my HUD indicated that the comms grid was still secure, so I knew that Warlord wasn't hacking the network, but he was accessing an encrypted military channel.

"I have methods," he said. "We're not that different, you and I."

"I just want to get my people off this station."

"A noble objective," he said. "It's a shame that our paths must cross, Lieutenant. Things could've been different."

Warlord evaded another volley from my suit-guns, and hurled himself at me again. He landed a series of blows across my torso with machine-like precision, each fist threatening an impact like a railgun. My armour held.

Zero and Sergkov were stirring from the wreckage of

the buggy now, but the Spiral were surrounding them. There was nothing I could do to help them: Warlord was my focus.

"There's a darkness within us all, Jenkins," he said. "You've just got to learn to let it out. When the time comes, which side will you be on?"

"Not yours, that's for sure."

I couldn't see Warlord's face behind the visor of his helmet, but I could hear the sneer in his voice. "You sure about that? I was like you, once."

Another hammer blow from my HURT suit, another dodge from Warlord. That presented its own set of problems—how the fuck was he outrunning me? I was in a sim and a full HURT suit. He was a nobody.

"That so?" I asked. "Then what happened to make you such an asshole?"

"A lot. I'm surprised that you don't know."

"Why are you here, Warlord?" I said. Desperate to buy time for Zero.

"Because I wanted to speak with you," he replied. "Because you need to know what's happening out here."

"All I see is a bunch of tangos who want to see it burn."

"That's probably how it looks, but it's far from the truth. The Krell can't be trusted, Lieutenant. We're here to right a wrong."

"Then you don't need us any more," I said. *And done!* I jerked my head in the direction of Skinner's lab. "You can take it out on them."

The bio-scanner on my HUD flared with activity: a ragged mob of signals, swarming down the tunnel.

"Zero!" I said, over the comms. "The Krell are here! Get back!"

The Pariah must've felt the shift in battle as well. It hurled the body of a terrorist aside, then jumped towards the wreckage of the buggy. Took up a defensive position, bio-guns raised, back to Zero and Sergkov.

"They come," it said. "We must go."

Warlord froze. Eyes back down the tunnel.

I could've shot him then. Probably, I should have. But's it's very hard to make rational decisions when you're presented with that many fish heads.

They swarmed the tunnel.

I knew that there had only been twenty-four viable specimens in Skinner's cryo-capsules, but it sure felt like there were a lot more. They moved so fast, and they looked so wrong. The Krell predilection for mutation had spiralled out of control, each so very different: each the product of the Fleshsmith's warped scientific intellect.

The tangos barely got off a word of warning before the Krell fell on them.

The first was shredded by stinger fire, speared by a dozen rounds of living ammunition. He screamed, loosed his own carbine in the direction of the attacker. But the Krell had already moved on, thrown itself at another Spiral agent.

"Back!" one of the insurgents yelled. "Get back!"

Suddenly, we weren't the focus of the battle any longer.

Warlord launched himself into the conflict, as if unable to resist the opportunity to spill Krell blood. He left me with a parting comment.

"This can't go on. It's not peace. It's giving up."

COMM LINK SEVERED, my suit said.

"Whatever you say," I replied.

I retreated down the tunnel. Zero and Sergkov crouched beside the buggy, Pariah towering over them.

"Will they attack you as well?" I asked.

The alien stared at me impassively. "We are Pariah."

"I think that's a yes," Zero said.

I desperately wanted to tell Zero that we were going to be okay, that we were going to make it, but I couldn't bring myself to lie to her. I was going to wake up in the tanks with a bad hangover and another war story. Sergkov and Zero: they were the ones trapped down here for real.

"Secure the Fleshsmith," Sergkov ordered, waving at the rear of the buggy. "He's the priority."

But I realised that I hadn't seen Skinner move since the crash. I peered into the wreckage, found him upside down, still held in place by the safety belt. His arms hung limp at his sides, smock spattered with blood.

"It is dead." The Pariah observed the doctor's corpse with a slightly cocked head and a blank expression. Did the alien feel anything for its creator's passing?

"My suit confirms it," I said. "Body's already cold."

Sergkov's eyes flared with anger. "*Jopa!* He was for priority retrieval!"

"Least of our worries," I said. "Take cover behind me. I don't know how long I can protect you—"

A Krell bio-form—weeping ichor from a dozen wounds—dashed past me, lunging towards Zero. It was bigger than Pariah, wearing bio-plates that sprouted thorns. Zero screamed, recoiling from the enraged xeno—

The Krell was lanced by a bright plasma bolt. The seared corpse collapsed at Zero's feet.

A new signal appeared on my HUD, coming from the direction of the docks. A friendly signal, IFF and freq-beacon blazing.

"You look like you could do with some company," Feng said over my comms.

He bounced up the tunnel, using his EVAMP, and

landed beside the buggy. Wearing a full combat-suit, carrying a plasma rifle. Fully skinned and ready for war. He scooped up Zero from the wreckage of the buggy, and nodded in my direction.

"Shall we go now?" he asked.

"Yes," I said. "I think that would be a very good idea."

Under the cover of the escaping Krell, we emerged from the transit network and into the docks. Two berths on, and we reached the *Santa Fe*: just where I'd left it. The cargo ramp still kissed the deck, a warning lamp flickering in the ship's open guts.

Covering Zero and, by association, Sergkov, Feng bounced onwards. He wasn't wearing his tactical helmet, and his face was smeared with soot and stitched with fine slashes: the tell-tales of being too close to a frag grenade detonation. Although the injuries looked painful, they were skin-deep, not serious. Feng's improved simulated blood had already started to coagulate.

"How'd you find us?" I asked. "Those tunnels were supposed to be secret."

"I just followed the fighting," Feng replied. "Thought that you'd be in the thick of it."

"Always try to be."

Feng paused, then said, "I thought I'd lost you."

"I'm not that easy to kill," I answered.

"I wasn't talking about you, ma'am," he said. He sounded sheepish, which was a difficult thing to achieve in a sim.

Zero stirred under in his shadow, her body tiny in comparison to the armoured bulk of his simulant. Her uniform was in a state of utter disarray, a bruise beginning to develop on the line of her jaw.

"Maybe I'm not so easy to kill either," Zero said, with a bitter grin.

"Let's hope so," Feng said.

Alongside us, the Pariah leapt from surface to surface, adhering to the sides of cargo crates more like a spider than a fish.

"Who approved this transition?" I asked.

Now that we were at close range, I had a clean comms link to the Jackals, and got green signals for encrypted comms with the *Santa Fe* as well.

"That would be me," Riggs said. Also skinned and armed, plasma rifle to his tactical helmet. "I was using my initiative."

"We all know where that will get you," I said.

Riggs, Lopez, and even Novak were at the cargo ramp, all in sims, their armoured outlines easy to differentiate from the Spiral. The Jackals pounded North Star's hangar with suppressing fire, but it wasn't necessary: the Spiral were focusing their attention on the Krell, giving us a temporary reprieve. It was impossible to tell how long that would last, and we had to make the most if it. That was the thing about fanatics: they were easy to rout, but they got up just as fast.

As we made it to the pool of bodies surrounding the *Santa Fe*, Novak's face twisted into a grimace. He turned his plasma rifle on the Pariah.

"This the fish?" he drawled.

The Pariah flipped both barb-guns in Novak's direction, alien face mimicking the aggression of Novak's features. I was quite sure that both outcasts could kill each other in an instant.

"This is the Pariah," I said. "Play nice. For now, it's on our side."

The *Santa Fe*'s engines were hot, the running lights on her nacelles flashing in sequence. The spooling engine components were generating a low roar in the oxygenated atmosphere, sufficient to making my bones rattle uncomfortably even inside my armour.

Lopez started, "Captain Carmine's ready to evac—"

Her words were cut off by the whine of incoming gunfire.

"In!" Lopez screamed.

Black Spiral troops began to fill the deck behind us, and a grenade went off closer than I would've liked. Whatever Warlord's intent aboard the station, he was dedicating a lot of firepower to the operation. He wanted something on this base, and he was going to make sure that he got it. As I pounded onto the ship, my null-shield flashing with incoming fire, I caught a glance at the heaped bodies on the deck. I thought of Skinner, dead now, left behind. Had the Spiral come here for him, or his research? But now wasn't the time for answers.

The Pariah lingered behind, pausing at the foot of the ramp. The xeno fired both barb-guns, gunslinger style, into the advancing Spiral troops.

"We've got to go!" Riggs said. "There are too many of them!"

I grabbed the alien by the shoulder-guard of its bio-suit. It was deceptively heavy, even with the HURT's strength-amplifier.

"Leave them," I said. "Save the ammo."

"It can make more," Novak rumbled.

"Not the point, lifer," Lopez said.

"Everyone in?" Carmine's voice came over the comm link.

"That's an affirmative!" I said. "Go, go!"

"Glad to hear that you made it back," Carmine said. "I knew you would."

"Liar," I replied.

Her cargo ramp still deployed, gunfire pattering

against her hull, the *Santa Fe* began to lift off. It was a manoeuvre that I suspected was strongly against Navy protocol. The deck bucked and listed as the ship's engines activated.

"Lopez!" I yelled. "Get the cargo ramp shut!"

"Hold tight," Carmine said. "This isn't going to be my best take-off…"

"Just get us out of here," Sergkov said, reasserting his command. "On my orders!"

Carmine laughed throatily. "You're still alive too, huh?"

The *Fe*'s hold was dowsed in amber light as the deck-head warning lamps lit. A thin siren sounded across the hold, the deck vibrating beneath us. The cargo ramp shut with a resounding *boom*.

"We'd better get to the bridge," I said.

The Jackals, with Sergkov and the Pariah, spilled onto the bridge as the starship took flight, the entire space-frame bucking like a goddamn bronco. Without being instructed, the Jackals slipped into the crash-harnesses around the edge of the bridge, ready for gravity failure if we took a catastrophic hit.

I'd disembarked from the HURT suit, simply because it was too big to wear on the bridge, but the rest of the squad were still equipped with their combat-suits. No one was yet willing to give up the protection of the sim-ulant bodies, and as the *Santa Fe* accelerated out of the hangar, and the tactical display lit with incoming targets, I thought that we might well need them. A sudden move-ment from the Pariah, slinking at the edge of my field of vision, reinforced that belief.

"What the hell is *that*?" Carmine yelled, eyes still on the controls but poking a finger at the alien. "And why is no one shooting it?"

"No time, Carmine," I said. "No one shoots it until I give the order."

"No one shoots it at all!" Sergkov shouted at me.

"*You do not have permission to disembark from the bay!*" a static-riddled voice said from the comms console. "*UAS Santa Fe, this is North Star Traffic Control: pull back on thrust now!*"

Carmine stabbed at the console, her ship accelerating. "Oh, fuck you," she said, closing the channel.

"Maybe not everyone on the station was a traitor after all," Feng offered.

"Just go!" Sergkov ordered.

"What does it look like I'm doing?" Carmine said.

Traffic Control must've realised that unless they opened the docking bay doors, the *Santa Fe* was just going to go straight through them, because the dock was in vacuum, the bay doors now open. We cleared the chamber at significant thrust.

"Holy shit and Gaia on a brick ..." Feng said.

North Star spread out before us. The station sparkled with internal fires, with vented and crumpled modules. Everywhere, docking bays were open or punctured. The tactical display tracked targets all around—the remains of ships that had been caught in the station takeover, other fleeing vessels, the station's evacuation pods.

"Null-shields are active," an officer declared.

"Fusion drive is powering up," Lieutenant Yukio said, her display dancing with green lights. "We'll have control in less than a—"

A warning siren filled the bridge.

"Targeting lasers," another officer said. "Two ships. Portside."

"Are you tracking them back?" Carmine said.

"Affirmative," the officer replied.

The *Santa Fe* accelerated aggressively, away from North Star. On the display, more guns were turning in our direction. Two ships broke their positions, started after us.

"This is UAS *Santa Fe*," Carmine said into her console. "Unidentified vessels, please stand down. North Star is experiencing some sort of takeover event—"

"They're part of it!" Lopez insisted.

"Multiple targets," an officer said. "Closing fast."

The tactical display was very suddenly and very clearly filled with warning icons.

"What in Gaia's name?" Carmine cursed, as though her disbelief of the enemy action would somehow protect us. "Those are damned civilian ships."

What little detail the *Santa Fe* could glean from the enemy vessels surely indicated that the enemy ships *were* civilian-made. They were cargo-transports, although likely refitted: those vessels were usually unarmed, and few carried null-shields.

"*Weaponised* civilian ships," I said. "Can we outrun them?"

"They look like they have fast fusion drives," Carmine said. "I don't know if we'll make it through this mess…"

Six starships closed on us, but even more vessels were breaking away from North Star, and debris was fouling our sensor-suite.

"Our fusion drive is at 90 per cent," Yukio said. She paused, swallowed. "We could make for the Gate."

The Shard Gate sat ahead. It seemed to fill the view-port.

"Do it," Sergkov said, his voice now steely calm. "Take us in."

Carmine fumbled with her console, murmuring something to herself that sounded like a lullaby.

"Firing counter-measures," a weapons officer, whose name I'd never even asked, declared.

The display lit with detonations, as the *Santa Fe*'s laser defences caught incoming warheads. Still, we were one ship, and with so much enemy fire surrounding us, we couldn't go on like this. Laser fire raked our null-shield.

Carmine nodded. "Make it so. Bearing ninety degrees, full fusion."

"Aye, ma'am."

The *Santa Fe*'s main drive engaged. We moved towards the Shard Gate, falling between twin rows of gravity-buoys that marked the approach path, flashing red against the black of space.

"Here we go," Carmine said, licking her lips.

Then the *Santa Fe* accelerated hard, alarms wailing, and was consumed by the waiting Shard Gate.

CHAPTER SIXTEEN

HOSTILES

They say that the Shard were machines. From what little evidence we have of their original form, Science Division insists that they were a type of life-form that was born of a violent and completely alien ecosystem.

But what hell breeds machines like *this*?

Machines that feel.

As the *Santa Fe* went through the wormhole— that's still the best we can do to describe the interstellar Network—I felt a wave of emotion crashing over me. So intense and complex that I could barely comprehend it.

Colours, lights, visions of things that might or might not be real.

A string of stars blazing with such intensity that they must surely now be dead.

A trio of worlds that had once been green. Now no more than blackened nubs, trailing their atmosphere to the void.

Then nothing.

Nothing.

Only the endless expanse of space, and the cold— empty—reassurance that no matter what we did out here,

no matter what we did to each other, none of this really mat-
tered, and the universe did not care.

No. I couldn't accept that the Shard Network was
built by machines, that it was the result of an analyti-
cal or a logically ordered mind. The Shard Gates touch
something in us all, something dark and irrepressible.

As we entered Shard Space the *Santa Fe*, and everything and everyone aboard her, ceased to exist.

After such a brief, infinitesimal segment of time that it
could only be described by Science Division as "instant,"
we were back.

One moment we were in the Drift, on the edge of
human space.

The next we were in the Maelstrom, coordinates
unknown.

The *Santa Fe* erupted into real-space. The sensation
was nauseating but thankfully also brief. Maybe it was
easier on me because I knew what to expect; I'd been
through it a handful of times before. Even so, I couldn't
resist grasping the arm of my crash-couch—trying to
maintain some semblance of normality, to anchor myself
to reality.

Not everyone had such a painless reaction. Even in a
simulant, this was no easy ride.

Lopez was monumentally sick, pouring the contents
of her guts onto the deck. Given that she was in a simulant, and hadn't eaten anything in that body, that turned
out to be a stream of stomach acid and green bile. The
odour was strong enough that it made my own gorge
rise, and I stifled the urge to join her. Vomit splattered
her combat-suit.

Novak still had his eyes pinned shut, as though he was
frightened to look at the view-screens around him. The
image was vaguely comic: the trooper made enormous

by his combat-suit, but humble by the expression on his battered face.

Riggs shook uncontrollably.

"Can't stop falling," he murmured. "Just can't stop falling…"

"That's a common reaction to a Shard Gate translation," Zero said. She looked more excited than shaken— another experience to be quantified and considered. "Extreme loss of balance has been recorded in several cases."

"Why are we being affected like this?" Lopez said, wiping a hand across her chin. "We're in sims!"

"It's the crossover from the effect that the jump is having on your real bodies," I explained. "Look it up sometime. Turns out that the Shard aren't so bothered whether you're using a real or simulated skin."

"Yeah," Riggs said, "it fucks you up all the same."

"That's about the size of it," I said.

"You want me to break out the meds?" Feng asked. He slapped a hand to the chest-plate of his armoured suit, where the onboard medi-suite was located.

"They make you Directorate bastards out of better stuff than the rest of us?" Carmine said, voice gravelly but devoid of malice. "Why are you holding it together so well?"

Perhaps it did have something to do with his clone physiology, because Feng seemed the most collected of the Jackals. He shrugged off the comment; he'd just endured much worse aboard North Star.

"Better sense of balance in my real body," he said. "I was built to travel the stars for real. Maybe that's why it's not getting to me."

"Forget medication," I said. "Best we can do is extract."

"Check it out…" Novak managed, throwing an armoured thumb in the direction of the Pariah. "Does not like Gate much, yes?"

The xeno had coiled, snake-like, into a corner between terminals. Its eyes flickered open at the sound of Novak's voice. He hadn't even mentioned the creature by name.

"This is Machine Gate," the Pariah said. "We do not like it any more than others."

"He means us," I said, translating for the alien.

Carmine searched my face, looked at the Pariah, then back at me. "It's…talking? They *do* that now?"

"Just this one," I said. "So far, at least. We can explain later; it's an experiment. Is the *Santa Fe* operational?"

Although obviously dissatisfied with my truncated explanation of why a Krell bio-form was somehow capable of speech, Carmine nonetheless turned back to her terminal.

"Just about," she confirmed. "We've got full AI processing power, and the navigation module is online. Internal systems are shielded against the effects of a jump."

Around us, the bridge was gradually shaking off the effects of the jump through Shard Space. All of Carmine's officers were alive and functioning, which was all we could ask for in the circumstances. Without being asked, a couple of officers saw to the mess that Lopez had made, and she looked away with embarrassment as they worked.

"Confirm our location," Sergkov said, at Carmine's shoulder now. "This Gate has been fully mapped…"

The *Fe*'s sensors took a second to draw a holo-map of the sector. We were on the edge of a foreign system.

"We're in an explored but unlisted star system," Carmine said. "Four planets. A dozen moons. Uncolonised.

The Gate's emissions are fouling our sensors; it's going to be hard to get much more data without launching a sensor probe." She paused, pulled at her chin as though deep in thought. Something on the scan had caught her eye. "Take us towards that moon."

The identifier "NX-923" flickered on the map.

"Aye, ma'am," an officer responded.

"What are you doing?" Sergkov said.

Carmine snorted. "I'll take care of the flying, if you don't mind. Make it a hard burn, maximum thrust!"

"I'm ordering you to tell me what you're doing, Captain!" Sergkov said.

"Easy, Major," I said, hand on his shoulder. "Let the captain work—"

"Incoming signal!" an officer yelped.

The Gate was receding fast as the *Fe* made burn across the system, darting for the cover of the nearest moon.

Sergkov took my advice and fell silent.

Three, four, five ships appeared through the Gate. Fusion drives lighting like miniature stars, streaking across the map.

"Ships from North Star," Zero said.

"No shit," Lopez whispered.

"Don't worry, Lopez," Zero said. "They can't hear us. There's no need to whisper."

Lopez opened and closed her hands into fists. The hydraulics in her gloves hissed quietly. "I know that, Zero," she whispered back. "But it makes me feel better."

"Those are Alliance ships," I said, watching the magnified images on the scopes. We were still a good distance from the vessels, but I recognised them even at range.

"They're running with active weapons signatures," an officer confirmed.

"They're hunting," Riggs said. Also now whispering. Zero sighed and shook her head.

"Can we take them?" Sergkov asked.

"I'd rather not. We start firing weapons, everything in this system is going to know where we are. Could be anything out there: Black Spiral, Krell..." Carmine shivered. "How long until we reach NX-923?"

"Closing distance now," an officer answered. Swallowed. "This is going to be close."

The hunting party spread out. Their weapons systems were running hot—broadcasting like beacons, bright and loud.

"Someone give me a status check on our weapons systems," Carmine said.

Yukio worked at her console. "The missile tubes are locked and loaded," she said, "but the railgun isn't hot yet. To do that, we'd have to light up. I'm also getting a report of a damaged null-shield projector on the portside."

"Can't you initiate auto-repair?" Sergkov said, impatiently.

"I'm currently getting a red signal on the auto-repair package," Yukio explained. "Possibly damaged when we disembarked North Star."

"Someone will have to go outside and do it manually," Carmine muttered.

"Not during a fight they won't," I said, ending any discussion of conducting a complicated field repair under enemy fire.

The tac-display showed that the *Santa Fe* had now pulled into a tight orbit around NX-923. The moon was barren and rocky, lunar-like.

"All stop," Carmine declared. "And go dark."

Sergkov made a sound at the back of his throat, as though he was about to start asking more questions, but Carmine held up a bony hand to silence him.

"We need to make sure that we haven't been followed," she said.

The crew executed the order. Various stations around the bridge's work-pit went dim, indicating that the ship was running at minimum power. The fusion engine deactivated. The scanner-suite went passive. Energy emissions were shielded, held inside the *Santa Fe*'s stealth coil. I'd been on starships running dark before, and it's never a comfortable experience. This was no different: I felt incredibly vulnerable out here without shields or weapons. The SOC was one of very few modules that was still running.

"Near-space scan, please," Carmine said.

"Results on your console, ma'am."

Five starships spread across the system.

"Will they be able to see us?" Lopez asked.

"Space is big," Carmine said. "If we hold our position here, the moon should block any emission leakage. We're tucked in nice and tight; its gravity well should do the rest."

"*Should?*" Sergkov said.

Carmine gave a non-committal shrug, her uniform rustling. "Nothing is guaranteed, Major. Who knows what systems the Spiral have on their ships?"

"More than they should have..." Riggs said. "That's for sure."

Every passing second seemed to stretch out, last a lifetime. No one even moved aboard the bridge as we watched the enemy ships burning across near-space. Cold sweat trickled down my spine. I wore a neoprene undersuit, designed to interface with the HURT suit's control mechanisms, and I realised that it was bathed in damp sweat.

"Hostile Bravo is moving off," Yukio said.

The starship designated Bravo—actual name and serial code unknown—made a sudden and sharp braking manoeuvre. Just as suddenly, the ship then arced towards the Shard Gate, leaving a heat trail from her fusion engine as she went.

"She's squawking," another officer said. "I'm getting comms traffic between ships."

"Let's hope that someone is giving the order to break off," Carmine said.

I noticed that her mechanical leg was twitching rapidly, beating a staccato rhythm against the deck. Nervous energy.

Like hunting dogs, the Black Spiral ships nosed around the edges of the system. More data was exchanged between vessels. The information was in turn parsed and digested by the *Santa Fe*'s intelligence engine.

"Do we know what they're saying?" Lopez asked.

"Yeah," Riggs said, "they're saying 'Vote Lopez.'"

"Fuck you, Riggs."

"We might be able to crack their encryption later," Carmine said, "but now isn't the time."

"Hostiles Alpha, Charlie, and Delta are breaking off too," Yukio said. "Taking a course back towards the Gate. Hard burn."

Only Echo remained: a flashing blip, the closest hostile on the map. It was one ship, and maybe one-on-one we could take it, but we had no idea of its armament or whether it was still in contact with the rest of the fleet. If she found us, the ship would undoubtedly call in back-up.

Then, finally, Yukio said, "Echo is leaving. She's taking the same course as the others."

I allowed myself the luxury of breathing. Riggs and Feng bumped fists, hooting in triumph. Carmine remained on the sensors, Sergkov at her shoulder, assessing her every action and reaction.

"All hostiles off-grid," Yukio said. "The Shard Gate's energy emissions are reducing."

"Shit," Novak said. "Was close, yes?"

I realised that he hadn't spoken throughout the incident.

"Nice work, Carmine," I said. "You've still got it."

Carmine gave me a lukewarm smile. She opened her hand, and I noticed for the first time that she had a crumpled holo-picture in her sweaty palm: her daughters, young faces beaming back at a mother that they hadn't seen in years of real-time. Carmine quickly stuffed the holo back into the fold of her uniform, looking away from me with strained eyes.

Sergkov sighed. "If you have a plan, next time I would appreciate a little warning."

Carmine stirred from her command podium, Yukio at her side with the silver cane. The captain took it and wrapped it on the deck, noisily.

"Unless someone just died and made you captain," she said, her words deliberately acidic, the expression on her worn face not much better, "I'd remind you that I'm in command of the *Santa Fe*. There was little chance of us escaping that encounter without suffering significant damage."

Sergkov looked around the bridge, embarrassed that his authority was being undermined. I just watched on with interest: from experience, I knew that Carmine was not a woman to be messed with.

"And while we are discussing the free exchange of information," Carmine continued, "I would like an explanation for the presence of an alien entity aboard the *Santa Fe*."

She lifted her cane and pointed it at the Pariah—still wedged between terminals, its mass coiled and crammed like a sardine in a ration-pack. The xeno's eyes traced the metal implement, perhaps evaluating whether it was some form of weapon. In Carmine's hands, it probably was.

"I want that *thing* locked down," Carmine said.

Carmine didn't even react when the Pariah stirred from its hiding place, stood at full height beside the bridge hatch. The rest of her crew were perhaps made of weaker stuff, because several flinched away from the alien, giving it a wide berth. The Jackals bristled, ready to react, but the Pariah just stood there.

"This isn't the place, Captain," Sergkov eventually answered.

"Fine," Carmine said. "Main conference room it is, then." She nodded sharply in my direction. "Fifteen minutes. It will be a meeting of your command staff, Major."

Sergkov swept his gaze over the bridge, but nodded. "All right," he said, before turning and stomping away.

"Someone doesn't like his command being questioned…" Riggs offered.

"Stay out of it," I said. "I'll take care of this. The rest of you, get down to Medical and out of those sims."

"This is highly irregular," Sergkov said, before the hatch to the conference room had even closed.

"I don't give a damn what it is," Carmine said. She flopped, ungracefully, into one of the chairs set up around the main meeting table: where, in other circumstances, a proper command cadre would be assembled. "I had the decency not to embarrass you any further in front of the crew, Vadim. Now at least have the decency to tell me what the hell is going on."

Sergkov's brow furrowed, and I noticed that his face was still streaked with dirt. His uniform was stained by oil from the attack in the transit tunnel.

"This is a classified operation, Carmine. You're just going to have to trust me on this. I'm telling you what you need to know—"

"How long have we worked together, Vadim?" Carmine asked.

It struck me off-balance that she was suddenly using his first name, and I remembered Dr. Skinner's question about the major's family. I found it hard to accept that this man had a life beyond the mission.

"I don't see what that has to do with it—"

"Shall I tell you, then?" Carmine said. "Three years. Three years you've had me flying around the Drift and probing the FQZ looking for the Black Spiral. How many times have we found them?"

Sergkov worked his jaw. "That's not the point."

"I'll answer for you again, then: twice. We engaged the Black Spiral on Sigma Base nine months ago. Then we found them at Daktar."

"So what?" Sergkov said. "We have intelligence, the likes of which I'm not at liberty to discuss with either of you."

"And now you bring a talking fish onto my ship, without a word of explanation!" Carmine threw her hands in the air in exasperation. "What's happening here, Vadim?"

Sergkov dogmatically towed the Mili-Intel line. "It's *classified*."

"The Warlord was on North Star," I said, slowly. "He was on Daktar, as were you. Who is he, Major? Who is the Warlord?"

"Intelligence on the Warlord requires specific clearance."

"Bullshit," I said. "Warlord said that he was like me, once, and he told me that I needed to know what was happening out here."

Sergkov let out a long sigh, his shoulders dropping. He gave me a two-barrels glare and collapsed into the seat beside Carmine. Somewhere inside of him, conditioning came unstuck: a dam broke. I could almost see him working through this problem, figuring out how best to keep Carmine and me onside.

"Fine," he said. "You want to know? I'll tell you."

"That's more like it. See, that wasn't so hard, was it?"

"You're not funny, Lieutenant," Sergkov said. "'Warlord' is the intelligence designation of the Black Spiral's self-appointed leader. Not much is known about who he is now, but we know who he *was*. Clade Cooper."

That didn't mean much to me; I'd never heard of the name. But if Sergkov was in the mood for talking, I wanted as much information from him as he was willing to give.

"Go on," I pressed.

"He was Alliance military."

"Sim Ops?"

"No, thankfully," Sergkov said. "Sim Ops traitors tend to be few and far between, for what it's worth."

"I've known enough of them," I said, pushing uncomfortable memories aside. "But that doesn't tell me much. I'd guessed that he was military after what happened on Daktar."

His ability to interfere with communications—to access the Army comms-net, as he'd demonstrated on North Star—only confirmed that impression.

Sergkov continued: "Warlord was a serving Alliance Army Ranger, 1st Battalion. Special Operations. He made Sergeant. His team specialised in insertion missions across the Quarantine Zone and the Maelstrom. During the last war, he had quite the kill-count."

"And he did it all in his own body?" I asked, scepticism creeping into my voice.

Sergkov gave me a wicked smile. "Not everyone fights in a different body to that God gave them."

"Still, if it was deep insertion work—wouldn't it be easier to use a sim team?"

Sergkov's smile became fixed and glassy. "Not this sort of work, and not this deep. Cooper's Ranger team were the best at what they did: deep recon work, well inside the Maelstrom. The sort of work that few simulant teams can do, given the need for a base of operations. They used small, single-squad ships to monitor the movement of war-fleets, during the Krell War. They probably saved millions, if not billions, of lives—allowed us to evacuate warm bodies from the Outer Colonies while they remained that way."

I frowned. "Sounds an awful lot like suicide to me…"

"Coming from you, is that some sort of accolade?" Sergkov said. "Warlord's squad was called the Iron Knights, and much of his work was off the record." He sighed, shook his head. "Which was how he ended up where he did. "We—Military Intelligence—sent him and his team to Barain-11. A moon that was only relevant because of its proximity to a Q-space jump point. It was called Operation Pitfall. Contact was lost shortly after the Knights made planetfall. Sixteen days overdue, and Command thought that they had been wiped out.

"While that operation was underway, the Red Fin Collective launched an attack on one of the Alliance territories. Cooper's family was caught in the evacuation." He swallowed, and the colour seemed to drain from his face. "They were killed. Wife and two children—all gone."

"And what happened to Warlord?" I asked.

"He was taken prisoner by the Krell." Sergkov paused for a long moment, as though toying with guilt, or perhaps deciding how much he should tell me. "He spent two years in Krell captivity. Experienced something that the Krell call 'the Deep.' I suppose its closest description is a form of interrogation or torture. He could never forgive the Alliance for not sending in reinforcements to save his team, and never forget that his family had been killed while he was on that operation."

"How did he end up becoming leader of the Spiral?" I said. "Guy sounds more like a hero than the head of a terrorist organisation..."

"He went through rehab and extensive body surgery after his liberation," Sergkov explained. "But the last the Alliance knew of him, he was a broken man." Sergkov swallowed. "Then, a few months after his discharge from a rehab station on Fortuna, he turned up fighting for the Spiral. Whether he started the Black Spiral movement or just hijacked it, doesn't really matter. He's part of it, and with him on board they have leadership."

"And why were you tracking him, Major?" I asked.

"It...it's not relevant," Sergkov said.

Carmine shook her head. "We need to know *everything*."

But I already knew the answer to my question, because I'd heard enough to draw my own conclusions.

"You sent him there, didn't you?" I said. "You were responsible for sending Cooper to Barain-11, weren't you?"

Carmine's eyes widened with anger. She looked from me to Sergkov, then stayed there. A fraught silence stretched across the room.

"Well, did you?" Carmine asked, her voice rising in pitch.

Sergkov exhaled slowly before speaking again. I wanted Major Sergkov to confirm it, to accept it.

"I want to be the one to bring him in," he said, carefully, "because I started this. I gave him the mission. I sent him to that moon."

"Great," Carmine said. She threw her hands up in the air. "So this is personal."

"Warlord doesn't know," Sergkov said. "But his case—bringing him in—has become an obsession. A quest."

"And we're just caught up in your little vendetta," Carmine sighed. She shook her head, tutting to herself.

Sergkov wouldn't be cowed. "It isn't like that. I want to right a wrong. You have to believe me when I say that I don't know why the Warlord was on North Star. The Spiral attacks cannot be predicted."

"Did the Spiral want Dr. Skinner?" I offered.

"That's a possibility," Sergkov said. "Either him, or his research."

Both of which are now gone, I thought with some bitterness.

"Let's deal with what we know," I said. "Should we call in the attack on North Star?"

"We can't," Sergkov said. "You're under my authority, and if it comes to it, I'll take responsibility for the lack of report. Other Alliance forces may have been compromised."

This was like fighting the Directorate all over again. I'd been there, done that: and was quite glad that the cloak-and-dagger war was finished. The idea that the Spiral might be doing a better job of compromising assets than the Alliance's long-term nemesis... It didn't feel good at all.

"We continue with the mission," Sergkov said. He removed a data-clip from his lapel pocket and passed it to Carmine. "Everything you need to proceed with the next stage of the operation is on there."

Carmine inserted the clip into a console on the conference table. Astrogation files and other navigational material flooded her feed, a holo-map projecting from the desk. The name SAB RHEA appeared on the readout.

"That's the last known location of the *Hannover*," Sergkov said. "Whatever happened to her, we'll find some answers there."

Carmine assessed the data. "There are stable Q-jump points here, here, and here," she said, pointing out coordinates on the holo-map. "The journey will be several days." She shrugged. "Accounting for time-dilation, even with our improved drive, we're talking months of real-time."

"Then it's lucky that I don't have plans," I muttered.

"You and me both, girl," Carmine said. She turned to Sergkov. "Fine. I don't have much of a choice but to take you there, do I?"

"No," Sergkov said. His command façade was back up, game-face in place. "You don't."

"That Krell is your responsibility," Carmine said. "Whether it can 'talk' or not. We've more than enough to worry about out here, without a xeno threat loose on my ship. Understood?"

"The Pariah is an important asset," Sergkov said. "I'm eager that we field-test both its combat and communication abilities."

"Fine, but while it's on my ship, it follows my rules."

"We can use the brig," I suggested. "That has cameras, and it's big enough to act as a containment cell."

"Yes," Carmine said, nodding sharply. "That's what we'll do."

Major Sergkov didn't exactly agree, but said, "That'll be all."

With that, he turned on his heels and left the room.

CHAPTER SEVENTEEN

EVA

In Medical, the Jackals were receiving treatment for the various injuries done to their real bodies during the fight in North Star's bar. Since they had now extracted, those scrapes, bruises, and cuts had come back with a vengeance. I extracted from my simulant too, and Zero set about patching me up.

"Easy there," she said, a hand to my shoulder. "It looks like the stitches'll hold, but I'm no medical doctor."

A dish and tweezer arrangement sat on a metal trolley beside the couch. The dish was filled with bloodied shards of glass, each of which Zero had just painstakingly—and painfully—removed from my ribcage. A collection of nasty wounds to the left of my ribs was currently taped with amateur butterfly stitches.

"I'm good," I said. "They're only flesh-deep."

"Which is more than I can say for that injury to your chest..." Zero said.

I sat on the edge of the examination couch in my Army-issue underwear, bra crossing the black welt of a bruise that had appeared directly over my sternum. Had to be said, it was an impressive injury: I'd seen bullet wounds that looked less spectacular.

"It's not real," I said. "Warlord hit me when we were ambushed in the tunnels. He punched me with an exo-suit glove. Damaged the HURT suit."

My HURT suit currently sat in the charging cradle, the torso armour scarred by the dent that Warlord had caused. The damage was largely superficial—Warlord might've been strong, but he hadn't breached the armour—but the whole incident had shaken me.

I had told the Jackals some of what Sergkov had said—sufficient that they knew who Warlord was, and what we were up against. Unlike Sergkov, I didn't believe in keeping things from my team.

"Looks like you've been hit by a tactical nuke," said Riggs, inspecting my injury.

"That's not funny, Riggs," said Zero. "The injury *looks* real."

Although that was true, a scan from the auto-doc had confirmed that it was only simulated. The bruise was a stigmata—the result of the human brain's efforts to interpret injuries done to a simulant-body. More transitions you did, the more it happened. Science Division didn't really understand why. There was a lot about the simulant tech that Sci-Div still hadn't figured out, despite its extensive use throughout the Alliance armed forces.

Of the Jackals, Riggs had probably been the luckiest, having escaped North Star with only the occasional cut or bruise: nothing that would require more than a few minutes under the auto-doc. When my eye turned to Novak, I was reminded that things could've been so much worse.

"You going to pull through over there, Novak?"

"Will be fine."

Novak was in a black mood. Occupying one corner of the infirmary, he had assembled a collection of various bladed articles on a medical bench, and he still clutched the black-bladed weapon that had been lodged in his thigh. That was a big, ugly knife, with a hooked tip made for causing maximum injury. The name "ADRI-ANNA" had been printed along the blade—relevance unknown, the former property of one of North Star's hookers who was now quite likely deceased. The last time that I had seen that weapon, it had been planted in the chest of a traitor MP; I guessed that Novak must've retrieved it.

"Still enjoying your souvenir, I see," Riggs offered.

Novak simply sucked his teeth, eyes fixed on the arrangement of blades in front of him. Several were homemade—just pieces of broken metal and plastic, with tape-wrapped handles. The way that Novak looked at those things wasn't natural.

"You're going to need to give those up," I said. "I can't have you running around this ship with weapons, Novak."

"Why bother?" he said, looking up at me with red-rimmed eyes. "Is no point any more."

"What bug has bitten you?" Lopez probed. "Jesus, we just escaped from a space station full of Black Spiral agents, jumped through a Shard Gate, and managed to avoid being vaporised by a fleet of enemy ships."

"Drone is gone," Novak grumbled.

"I thought you didn't like the drone?" Lopez said, frowning. "Make your mind up!"

Novak shook his head. Fiddled with one of his blades. "Will suffer penalty on service contract. More years, yes?"

"Is that what's bothering you?" I said. "Listen, we can work that out."

There would no doubt be questions asked of me, as to my decision to deactivate Novak's surveillance drone. The fact that the drone, and its onboard memory, had been destroyed back on North Star might well mean that a penalty was applied to Novak's remaining sentence. I decided that it was better not to mention that: not until we made contact with the chain of command.

Novak was in the worst condition of all, and hadn't yet changed out of his ruined fatigues, or even received proper medical attention. Instead, he had a medpack taped high on his left thigh, over the stab wound. The dressing had already turned a dilute pink colour.

"I don't care what you say, you're going under the auto-doc," I said. "You were damned lucky that blade didn't hit an artery."

"Is not necessary," Novak said. "Is also just flesh wound, like you, yes?"

"Yeah, flesh and muscle," Feng said.

Feng didn't look much better. He had new fatigues, but the wad of medical dressing over his shoulder blade was visible at the open neck. He calculated his movements to shield the pain; I'd seen the burn injury caused by the shockrifle, and it looked plenty painful.

"At least we got transition under belt," Novak rumbled. He had scored his arm with a knife: seven long cuts scarred over, an eighth still fresh.

"You don't need to keep doing that, Novak," Zero suggested. "I'm keeping a record."

She had set up an ad hoc scoreboard on the SOC wall, and the glowing data-feed provided a modest morale-boost to the squad. Post–North Star, the Jackals, except for Riggs, had eight transitions apiece. Riggs sat at twelve. I had two hundred and twelve effective transitions. Jesus, I felt old.

"Time off sentence, yes?" Novak said, forcefully.

"You know your contract better than anyone," I said. "If it says you have time off your sentence, then you get it."

"Only another nine-hundred-odd years of penal servitude to go," Riggs said.

Novak settled back on the couch, satisfied with the figures on the board. As I looked at the mess of ugly tattoos across his face and legs, I caught myself once again wondering what it was he'd done to get this gig.

"We're several days from the *Hannover*'s last location," I explained, "and there's a lot to do before we get there." I, too, was back in command-mode now. "By rights, I should have you all up on breach of regulation: I didn't approve that transition back on North Star."

The squad went quiet. Every one of them, except for Zero of course, had made an unauthorised transition.

"I specifically told you to remain on-ship, Private Feng," I said.

Feng nodded. "I know. But shit was going down out there, and if I hadn't skinned up…"

"That's hardly the point," I said. "Are you trained in the use of the Class VI combat-suit? Or the M115 plasma rifle?"

Feng went quiet. There was no answer to that: the Jackals hadn't trained in that equipment at all. Daktar had been the closest they'd come to using proper kit. We'd been using recon-suits and shotguns back then, and it felt like a lifetime ago.

"It wasn't *that* different to the armour we used on Daktar," Lopez piped up. She shrugged her shoulders. "Used the same haptic feedback response."

"That armour is bigger, heavier, and meaner than a

recon-suit," I explained. "And I'm not saying anything about the M115."

"It's a hell of a weapon," Riggs said, shaking his head.

"Corporal has a point," Novak added.

"I'm going to let it go this time," I said. I nodded at Zero, who had remained quiet throughout the exchange. "But using the heavier tech is hazardous. We had real skins out there; the major and Zero could've been at risk."

"I didn't want that," Feng said quietly.

Zero gave a blasé shrug of her shoulders, which I could tell was for Feng's benefit. "I'd rather be wasted by a stray plasma bolt than be left with the Krell."

"It shouldn't have come to either of those things," I said. "But I'm serious about that equipment. It isn't for greens. We're going to use the time before we reach the *Hannover*'s coordinates to run simulations, for armour and weapons drills. I want you all to really learn to use those tools."

"Does that mean that we aren't green any more?" Riggs joked.

"It means that I don't want you killing each other by accident during the next deployment," I said.

Although she wouldn't be able to participate, Zero brightened up at the suggestion. "The simulator-tanks have a VR facility. I can set up some scenarios, if you want."

"Sounds good," I said. "Not only that, but I want the Jackals to assist Captain Carmine as required. Riggs, you draw up a duty rota. Whatever Carmine needs done, we're doing."

"Copy that," Riggs said, nodding. "That Warhawk shuttle in the hold needs to be prepped, for a start."

The Warhawk was a basic runabout shuttle, likely to be needed if we conducted any off-ship activity.

"You see to it," I said.

"What are we going to do about the, ah, *fish*?" Lopez asked me.

"It's going into the brig," I said, pulling on my fatigues and trying to avoid catching the stitches. "And I want round-the-clock surveillance on it. We'll run a watch-schedule." I paused. "An *armed* watch."

"Wouldn't want to trust Lopez with a gun," Riggs said, with a mild smile.

Novak rumbled a laugh. "Senator did okay on North Star."

"Yeah, about guns," I said, rolling my eyes in Lopez's direction. "We need to have a discussion about what happened back there."

Lopez bit her lip. "A formal discussion? As in, I need an HR rep before we talk?"

Novak let out another big belly laugh at that, although Lopez clearly hadn't meant it as a joke.

"All of you, except Lopez, get out of here," I said. "You've got jobs to do."

The team sullenly filtered out of the infirmary, leaving Lopez and me alone.

"You brought a restricted firearm aboard North Star Station," I said. "Do you have any idea how dangerous that was?"

The rebuke sounded hollow before it had even left my lips, but Lopez hung her head and answered, "I have an idea."

"Smart ass," I said. Then sighed, adding, "Maybe it was kind of a stupid question. Where did you get the weapon from? Did you bring it aboard the *Santa Fe*?"

"Yeah," Lopez said. "My brother gave it to me. For protection, he said. I've had it since I joined up. I thought it was a good idea to have some backup, just in case."

"And you didn't think to request permission to bring it onto the ship, or the station?"

"I... kind of hid it."

I slapped Lopez's Revtech 911K down on the table. The gun's arming indicator blinked red, indicating that the weapon had been made safe. It was a high-end piece of equipment. The sort of gun that you bought when you had more money than sense: largely made of plastic-steel hybrid, undetectable by most scanning methods. Ownership alone was prohibited in twelve of the thirteen Alliance territories, and having it aboard the ship probably breached several interstellar statutes.

"It's a nice sidearm," I said. "Good range. With those rounds, it also has decent stopping power."

"I wouldn't know," she admitted. "That was the first time I'd fired it."

"Well, at that range it would've been hard to miss," I said, recalling Alpha Dog's destroyed head.

"Are we going to have a problem here, ma'am?" Lopez said, pursing her lips. "I know that it was wrong. I'm sorry. But if I hadn't brought along the gun, we would probably be dead—or worse—right now."

The girl had a point. "Do you have any more contraband that you want to report?"

"Nothing, except for maybe some more rounds in the barracks..."

I leant in to her. "Then here's your punishment: I want you to learn to shoot that thing, and keep it on you at all times."

Lopez's expression brightened. "Copy that," she said.

"In other circumstances, if we weren't surrounded by all this shit, I'd take a dimmer view. But as it turns out, you're right: the gun saved our asses."

She scooped up the pistol with a little more confidence than when she had handled it back on North Star.

"That's not the only punishment," I said, wincing again as I moved around the infirmary. "You've got first watch on the Krell."

"Q-jumping in T minus two minutes..." became a familiar refrain.

How many jumps did we make? I lost count. The *Santa Fe* plunged ever deeper into the Maelstrom's heart.

Carmine's estimate of "several days" turned into sixteen, subjective.

Sixteen days jumping around the Maelstrom, neither avoiding nor seeking the Krell's attention. Sixteen days sealed in the metal can of the *Santa Fe*. Sixteen days of wandering the empty corridors, thinking about what had happened back at North Star, about what could be happening elsewhere in the universe.

This far out from the Core Worlds, there were no newsfeeds, no relay-stations and no comms: we were on our own. Those planets became dim and distant, the glow of their stars paling. For all I knew, Senator Lopez might now be Alliance Secretary General. Simulant Operations could've been disbanded. And what of the Black Spiral? What of Warlord, of the man I now knew as Sergeant Clade Cooper? Sixteen days, allowing for the time-dilation effect of Q-space, was months of real-time.

I used the time to work on the damaged HURT suit. Cooper had put a crater in the chest armour, and I wasn't going out in the armour unless, and until, it was repaired. The work was decent, honest labour, and it was a task that gave me some focus. Several hours later, and the HURT suit looked good as new: sitting in its charging cradle, ready for the next deployment.

As promised, there were endless armour and weapons drills: both simulated and actual. I suspected that the Jackals even started to enjoy the daily manoeuvres. None of it was practical experience, of course, but that wasn't the point. The Jackals were beginning to function together as a *team*. The shift was slight, and gradual, but it was something.

"You should run some field tests with the Pariah," Sergkov suggested one day, as he watched us coolly from the corner of the Simulant Operations Centre.

"We're good," I said. While the Jackals ran their VR sims, Carmine had assigned one of her crew to guard the alien.

"The xeno doesn't have a neural-link," Sergkov said, "but I know that Dr. Skinner was working on it."

"A Krell that can make uplink via the simulators?" I asked with amazement. That idea was plainly terrifying.

Sergkov gave a non-committal lift of his shoulders. "As I say, nothing was finished. Dr. Skinner had great plans though. The Pariah was central to many of them."

I towelled myself dry, eager to break this conversation. "Well, we're doing VR runs in here. The Pariah can't play."

Sergkov shrugged. "Perhaps we should set up a training room in one of the cargo holds. It wouldn't take much effort."

"Like I said, we're good in here."

Sergkov had been a shadow since we'd left North Star. He ate mess in his quarters, kept tabs on the Pariah, and occasionally enquired about journey times. Only made his presence felt when necessary.

"You know," he said, "the Pariah saved me and Sergeant Campbell on North Star. You saw what the mutant specimens did, how out of control they were."

"Sure," I said. "But do you really know what's going on in the fish's head?"

Sergkov crossed his arms over his chest. "My point is that it didn't side with Dr. Skinner's failed experiments. Doesn't that show you something? Had it wanted to get away, it could've? That's all I'm saying."

"Fine. It saved your ass. It saved Zero's ass. I admit it. Happy now?"

Zero manned her console, trying her best not to get involved in the conversation. Since we'd taken the Pariah onboard, she had been almost as reclusive as Sergkov: making the SOC her safe place. Like she was frightened to walk the corridors on her own.

The conversation was interrupted by a chime from the ship's PA. It was Carmine, on the bridge.

"You down there, Keira?" she asked.

I opened a comms channel. "I copy," I said. "Just running some simulations."

"Lordy, at this rate those Jackals will learn to shoot straight by the end of this journey."

"Here's hoping," I said. "What's the issue?"

"As you know, the ship suffered damage to the port-side shield array when we left North Star," she explained. "For whatever reason, the auto-repair module can't fix it."

"So you want someone to go out there?"

"Got it in one."

"We'll see to it."

"Carmine out."

Sergkov had a mild smile plastered across his face as he listened to the exchange. I toyed with the idea of sending him out there—preferably without a space suit—but decided that fate was a little too kind. Riggs lingered nearby, as though he wanted to talk to me about something, but I avoided making eye contact with him. How long had it been since we'd last had a proper conversation? Well before North Star. I nodded over at Lopez, still drying herself from immersion in the tank.

"Lopez, you're with me. We've got a job to do."

"Do you ever notice the way that Daneb—Riggs, I mean—*looks* at you, ma'am?"

The main portside airlock was located at the aft, and Lopez and I were anchored at the outer hatch. We wore full EVA space suits, and the cold of vacuum was already teasing at my extremities. The suits were an unflattering bright orange, standard Alliance units with glass-globe helmets and magnetic locks built into the heavy boots. We carried vac-proofed repair kits on our backs: plasma welders, rivet guns, personal anchors.

"Not especially," I said over the suit-to-suit comms. "It's just the same as he looks at you, or Yukio, or any other woman."

Lopez laughed, dragging a partly assembled pressure-pump from inside the lock. She almost lost control of the heavy industrial tool but snagged it as it drifted past.

"No," Lopez said, shaking her head. "It's different. I think that he has a crush on you."

I turned away. "That's the last of the equipment. You can seal the lock."

"Copy that," Lopez said. She activated the hatch control, which silently slid shut, locking us outside the vessel.

I activated the comms channel to the bridge. "Captain Carmine? This is Jenkins. You copy?"

"Affirmative," Carmine said. "Aren't you done yet?"

"We've only just started. I'm reporting that we're outside the ship. Thanks for your assistance, by the way."

"My crew's got more than enough on their hands."

"And I'm not a repair tech, so I'd say we're about even."

"Just get that shield projector fixed."

"I'll comm you when we're done."

"Copy that."

I activated the mag-boots on my suit and stood on the hull. Lopez did the same, and we paused for a while. It took a second or so to get used to the shift in perspective.

"Whoa," she said. "Kind of a different world out here…"

"Or lots of them," I said.

Space was filled with star patterns, many of which— given time—I could probably name. The idea that the Maelstrom was that familiar to me was a little perverse. I was pretty sure that I couldn't do the same for the Core Systems or many other Alliance holdings.

"Still, it's sort of nice," Lopez said.

"You okay? Tell me if you're feeling panicked."

The suits didn't have bio-monitors like proper armour, and I felt vulnerable not being able to read Lopez's vitals. If she freaked out in the vac, by the time I realised it'd already be too late to do anything about it.

"It's not that," she said. "When I was growing up on Proxima Colony, we used to take holidays on the high-orbit stations. It was kind of a family tradition."

We plodded across the outer hull. With no tether lines, and in zero-G, it was necessary always to have a foot in connection with the hull, acting as a magnetic anchor. Around us, the landscape of the *Santa Fe*'s hull was bleak and mainly featureless, broken only occasionally by antennae and sensor masts.

Lopez kept talking. "They had domes like you wouldn't believe. Big as cities, supposed to be like the Venusian Cloud Habs."

I felt a smile tugging at the corner of my lip. "I think that's just hype, Lopez. I once knew someone who lived on one of those Cloud Cities. He had family there. Turns out he didn't have such a good report on them."

"For those that could afford them, Proximan star-domes are pleasure cities. You can get anything up there; everything has a price." She was doing a pretty good job of keeping pace with me, despite the chatter. "Daddy would send us up there for summer breaks. Pay for me and my brothers to do whatever we wanted. The domes can be reconfigured, you see. They can be made to look like whatever location you want. My brothers would usually go for trips to Fortuna, to other pleasure planets."

Something squirmed in my stomach for a moment, and before I could stop myself, I said, "I had a brother, once."

"But not any more?" Lopez asked.

"Directorate. Back when they were a thing."

"What happened?" Lopez said, a little apprehensively.

"Got wasted," I said, bluntly. No point in dressing it up. "When they bombed Low State. He was in Diego District at the time."

"Jesus. I'm sorry."

I shrugged—not an easy thing inside the suit and laden with gear. "Don't be. It is what it is."

"You've never mentioned it. How does Feng make you feel?"

I sighed. I'd maybe had a change of opinion about him. "He's not Directorate. I've fought them. I know them, and I know he isn't them. And no, he doesn't know about what happened."

"Probably better that it stays that way."

My suit's HUD was superimposed with graphics that identified the damaged shield projector was ahead. Set into the hull, the projector appeared to be a mushroom-head, studded with black mirrors that would ordinarily throw out the null-shield into surrounding space. Such a simple device, but the loss of the single projector had caused a chain reaction that effectively disabled the port-side null-shield.

"What did you pick?" I asked. "The star-dome simulations, I mean."

"I always picked war-stories."

I raised an eyebrow. "Really? That doesn't sound like you."

"That's what Daddy used to say. He got so angry that I wouldn't do one of the proper simulations that I eventually started lying. I'd tell him that I'd been to Fortuna with my brothers." I could hear the smile in her voice, as she added, "In the end, Josef and Patrico ratted me out. Daddy stopped me from using the domes. Last time I saw either of my brothers was on one of those high-orbit stations. Josef gave me that gun. Said it was for personal protection."

"Josef's your brother, I take it?"

"Older brother. I was the middle child."

"What did your family think about you joining Sim Ops?"

"I'd already taken the aptitude test, and I knew that I could handle the implants. Daddy wasn't very pleased."

"I'll fucking bet."

"I told him why I took the posting."

"Why was that?"

Lopez sighed like she maybe didn't want to tell me, but then obviously decided that she would after all. "I told him that this was the safest way to do my military service. That this way, I wouldn't be in any *actual* danger."

I laughed. "That hasn't really worked out so well."

"I know."

"You want to do the honours and open the plate? You've got the pressure-pump."

"Sure," Lopez said.

She leaned forward, over the nearest array. Although the vac-suit's HUD wasn't as advanced as that of a combat-suit, it was good enough to show what needed to be done. Lopez's fingers caught at the edge of the panel, and she deployed the pressure-pump around the nearest bolt.

"Ready when you are," she said.

"Do it."

The first bolt gave way with a puff of escaping atmosphere—

Then, suddenly, the world turned to white and noise.

I was thrown off the hull of the *Santa Fe*.

A lance of pain pierced through my left arm, the limb closest to the ruptured panel. The suit, being engineer- rather than combat-issue, took a second to track the damage and begin sealing the breach. That was enough time for my ears to prickle with escaping pressure—

Not again.

I spiralled across the hull. Arms outstretched, gloved fingers grabbing uselessly for whatever handhold I could grasp.

Lopez's pretty brunette head—her features filled with shock, a frozen sheen of blood over her lips— floated past me.

Her head, I realised with grim certainty, was no lon- ger attached to her body.

To confirm that point, Lopez's orange-clad frame span by too. Spread-eagled, it bounced against the hull—thrown by the force of the explosion—and then out into space.

"Lopez!" I shouted, on automatic, cursing myself that she was already dead.

I slammed into a hull panel. Caught a safety handle. Pain bloomed across my shoulder blade.

The cause of the explosion suddenly became clear. There had been a pressure build-up behind the shield array, and removing the single bolt had allowed it to escape. Such a simple thing. The array was erratically firing now, sending a barely visible network of light across the ship's flank.

"Jenkins!" a voice roared in my ear, piped in through my comms bead. "Jenkins! What the hell is happening out there?"

The voice had been repeating variations on that monologue for a few seconds now. I swallowed blood that had built up at the back of my throat—pretty sure that something new was busted inside my chest—and answered.

"I'm here," I said. "I'm still here."

"What's happening?" It was Carmine, her tone urgent and insistent. A useful anchor on which I could focus, to stop me from giving in to the pain. "The power grid is fluctuating like crazy."

I grappled with the safety handle. Steadied myself. The world still felt like it was spinning, and I wished for a dose of anti-vertigo drugs from a proper medi-suite, but my stomach and head were settling. That was a whole lot better than being sick in my space suit.

"Something's blown out here," I answered. "The shield's pressure seal is gone. That was why it wasn't working."

"Whatever the damned problem is, you've got to fix it!"

"No can do," I said, drolly. "Lopez is gone."

The array crackled silently, arcing energy discharge. Meanwhile, my suit reported an unpatchable leak from the damaged arm. Unless I got inside on the double, I'd be as dead as Lopez. Her orange body was a barely visible splash of colour against the darkness of space now, vanishing quickly.

"I—I can't move my arm," I said.

There was noise behind Carmine's voice. The bridge was getting busy, crew becoming excitable. How bad was this energy overload? The projector showed no prospect of reducing power discharge.

"Stay with me!" Carmine said. "I'm sending help."

"I—I need to…" I started.

A shadow appeared on the outer hull. Moving fast. *Scuttling.*

At first I thought that I had imagined it. Space could do that to even the most disciplined mind, and mine was hardly that. But as the shadow came closer, I realised exactly what it was.

The Krell pariah-form used any available anchorage point on the hull to move. It had no mag-locks, and it wasn't until the thing was virtually on top of me that I actually noticed it was wearing armour. Its bio-suit encased almost every aspect of its body—so perfectly in tune with the XT's musculature that it looked to be an extension. The creature lurched past, barely turning in my direction, face covered by another organic apparatus.

By the time it had reached the damaged projector, and the arcing blue light had diminished, I was already being dragged into the black. The xeno turned to watch as I finally gave in to the pain, my cold fingers dragging against the hull as I fought for purchase.

OXYGEN LEVELS CRITICAL, the HUD said, in bold, flashing text.

I gasped a final breath, and then darkness came.

*   *   *

"Goddamn it, Sergkov! What the hell was that?"

I conducted an emergency purge on the simulator-tank and opened the canopy. Then I stepped out, still hooked to my tank, before the hood was fully up.

Sergkov stood at the hatch to the SOC, leaning against the bulkhead. His nonchalance was obviously feigned, the smile on his face meant for me.

"What?" he asked, in his droll Slavic accent. "The Pariah offered to help."

I strode purposefully across the deck. I jabbed a finger—still wet with amniotic—into Sergkov's smug face.

"I told you to keep your pet on a lead. That does not mean allowing it free rein of the starship!"

"And I told you that I am mission commander," Sergkov said. "Which means that you have no authority to counter-mand my orders. I wanted a field test for the Pariah."

Lopez stirred beside me. She'd already dismounted her tank, and was wrapped in an aluminium sheet, shivering and twitching like an addict recovering from cold turkey. She had a particularly vicious injury to her neck: a deep, red laceration, in exactly the same place as her simulant. Of course, that body was currently drifting somewhere in deep-space. Lopez's eyes were unfocused and jittery.

"That hurt..." she muttered. "A lot."

"At least you've got another transition under your belt," Feng said.

I shook with anger. "And who's guarding the Pariah?"

"Major Sergkov said to let it out," Feng said.

Feng and Novak were standing around the SOC monitor station, watching what was happening out-side the ship via the external cameras. The imagery was grainy and mostly monochrome—interrupted by chain lightning that still danced around the hull—but a shadow was just visible against the bright backdrop.

"Incredible," Feng said. He was almost hypnotised by the vid-feed. "Way that thing moves out there. No mag-locks, no survival gear."

"Is fucking fish head…" Novak added. Groaned as he repositioned his leg to get a better view of the monitor.

Sergkov smiled some more. "I could've sent Privates Novak or Feng into the tanks," he said, "but the Pariah seemed more appropriate, given the urgency of the situation."

"That thing is *Krell*, Sergkov," I argued.

Sergkov shrugged. "So? The alternative was to wait for you and Private Lopez to recover." He nodded down at Lopez's snivelling form. "With all due respect, I don't think that Private Lopez is going to be fit to make an-other transition for a while."

"I'm fine," she managed. She tried to get to her feet, but the strain of that simple action showed on her face.

"You don't look that way," Sergkov said. "Had we waited, the shield battery might have become fully depleted."

The Pariah was impervious, or at least resilient, to the energy discharge. From this angle, it looked like the XT was right in the middle of the miniature lightning storm—a fat spider in the heart of a web of light.

"It's doing it…" Feng said, watching the readings on the SOC console. "Fucker is actually shutting the breach down."

"And it knows which relay to shut down *how*?" I asked.

"Because I told it so," Sergkov said. "The relay sche-matic isn't complicated, and—"

"And you thought that telling the Krell how to fix, or sabotage, the *Sante Fe* was a *good* idea?"

Sergkov's expression glassed over just a little. "We're all on the same side now."

"Tell that to the *Hannover*," Novak said without humour.

The alarm that had been sounding since I'd decanted from the tank abruptly silenced. At the same time, the Pariah deactivated the relay. The vid-feed showed no motion save for the xeno's twitching form, never quite at ease.

Sergkov stooped over the console and activated a communication channel. Speaking into the mike, he said, "*Santa Fe* to Pariah. The relay is safe. You can come inside now."

"We are moving," came the machine-voiced response.

"*Santa Fe* out," Sergkov said.

I shook my head in disbelief. "Now it has its own communicator as well?"

"That wasn't my doing," Sergkov said. "You can thank Dr. Skinner for that."

"I would, but he's dead."

Sergkov rolled his bottom lip. "It repaired the shield projector. That could've been a major hindrance to this operation, and now it's fixed."

"That's not my point!" I started.

"Then what is? The Krell War is over, Lieutenant. Things *have* changed."

"So people keep telling me," I said, sighing with annoyance and...something else?

I hated to admit it, but was Major Sergkov right? I was angry with myself. I didn't want to understand why or how the Pariah had just helped us, because I was part of the old world.

Sergkov straightened his uniform. "As you were, troopers."

I watched in silence as he left the SOC.

"Major is one arrogant prick," Feng said, eyes still on the monitors, the Pariah now clambering back into the airlock and aboard the ship.

I looked around the SOC. "Where's Corporal Riggs?"

Novak slung a thumb towards the hatch. "Down in shuttle bay. Said wanted to see you."

CHAPTER EIGHTEEN

THE SHUTTLE

Despite the air-scrubbers working at maximum power, the ship's corridors had started to develop an unpleasant odour. Maybe it was mental rather than olfactory, a by-product of my natural antipathy towards the Krell, but the whole ship smelled like fish. That was all I could think as I wandered into the shuttle bay.

"Hello?" I called.

My voice echoed around the hold, bounced off the metal walls. It was dark, the rectangle of light behind me cutting a shape across the polished deck. The Warhawk shuttle sat alone on the apron, ready for launch. Behind me, the hatch that led back into the *Santa Fe* hummed shut.

Scratch the dark. Place *was* lit. The Warhawk's portside access hatch was open, spilling a soft glow that barely illuminated the hangar.

I stepped forward. Wings of anticipation fluttered in my chest. It was that smell, I decided. It always put me on edge, and while the Pariah was on the ship I was never going to feel at ease.

"Hello?" I called again. My throat tightened. Angry

that I was letting this stupid situation get the better of me, I swallowed it back and added, more angrily, "Report!"

For no reason other than unbridled curiosity, I took a few steps closer to the shuttle door.

I heard music. Something gentle and guitar-driven: the sort of shit my dad used to force me to listen to as I was growing up. He played it to Mom, and she insisted that it was romantic. A pang of homesickness welled up inside of me. I was tired and emotional. Today had been a long day.

"Report! I'm not sure what this is supposed to be, but I've had enough already—"

I reached the shuttle's hatch.

The warm light from inside was created by a handful of glow-globes, installed around the shuttle's passenger cabin. The deck was padded out with some survival blankets, made almost cosy. In the middle of the nest was an upturned cargo crate: an improvised table filled with open ration-packs that had been arranged as though this was an actual dining table.

Riggs stood just inside the cabin. Biting his lower lip, rubbing the back of his neck with one of his big hands.

"I..." he started. Paused, like he was unable to read my reaction, and then began again. "Sort of wanted to see if you wanted some time on our own..." His Adam's apple bobbed as he gulped back nerves. "I hope it isn't too much."

I glared at him through my eyebrows, scowled. "What the fuck is this, Corporal?"

"It's a stupid idea," he said, taking a step back from me. "Sorry, ma'am. It's just that you've been avoiding me, and what with North Star, and then the repair job— and, well, I don't blame you, but..."

"Are we in high school?"

"No," he said, shaking his head. "We're not."

"Am I your date, and is this prom?"

Riggs stared at the ground. The Warhawk's cabin looked an awful lot like an oversexed teenager's attempt at romance.

"You are not, ma'am," Riggs answered. "Negative to both."

But when he did manage to bring up his head and look at me, he was probably surprised to see that I was smiling.

"It's ridiculous," I said. "And I hate it."

"I'm sorry," he said again.

"But I'm touched by the effort."

And just like that, my promise to let this thing with Riggs go—whatever was really happening between us—was broken.

Riggs grasped me in his arms. Natural endorphins began to pour through my bloodstream, began to buzz in my head. Without even thinking, as our bodies entwined, I switched my wrist-comp to silent. Didn't want what I knew would follow to be interrupted.

"I wanted to do this for you, ma'am."

I went rigid and glared at Riggs again. "Call me Keira."

He nodded and I folded into him.

What followed was sweaty, torrid, and animalistic.

In short, it was very much like the night of my high school prom. The Warhawk's cabin had a lot in common with the back seat of an aerocar, reinforced by the plethora of sharp corners and jagged edges, and the fact that there never seemed to be enough space. Eventually—exhausted and spent—we both collapsed in a heap on the deck.

Riggs had scooped me into his arms—those big,

muscled arms that promised everything was going to be okay—and instead of fighting him, I just let it happen. More than that, if I was being true to myself: I *wanted* it to happen. It felt good to give in, to surrender, if only for an hour or so. It was like I was parking First Lieutenant Jenkins at the door, and allowing myself to becoming Keira for just a little while. Which was the real me? One was the simulant: a battle-scarred body made for war. The other was the operator: soft and vulnerable. One could be hurt, the other was impervious.

I lay back on Riggs' chest and felt the throb of his heart against my head, the gentle rhythm of his breathing.

"Have you been avoiding me?" he asked, quietly.

"No talking."

"I'd like to know," he said. Not confrontationally, but with a bit of insistence in his voice.

I sighed. "Maybe. I'm not sure that this is right."

"But you do like it?"

"Of course I do."

"Then it's right. I know that it's what *I* want, and if you enjoy something this much then it can't be wrong."

"You're infatuated, Riggs. You're a Gaian, I'm an Earth-girl. You're a corporal, I'm a lieutenant. Just because you like all of those things, doesn't make it right."

"That's pretty cold, Keira," Riggs said. He sounded more disappointed than angry though, and his arms remained wrapped around me.

"That's how things have got to be," I said. "That's how things are. What do you think Captain Heinrich would do if he found out that I was sleeping with my first officer?"

"He doesn't need to know," Riggs insisted.

"Then what about the rest of the squad?" I thought of Lopez's words, as we had been on *Fe*'s hull. "I think that they suspect."

"And does that matter either?" Riggs shrugged. "These things happen. You already know about Feng and Zero."

"This is different, Riggs. I don't want them knowing about us."

The armour was coming back up. As though a maggot were eating at my insides, I could already feel remorse and regret beginning to gnaw away at me. I stirred beside Riggs. Despite the blanket on the deck, it was hardly a comfortable environment, and now that we were finished the air inside the cabin smelled stale with sweat and the odour of the uneaten ration-packs. The words EARTH PRODUCE: GAIA CULT APPROVED had been stamped across the lids. As a Gaia Cultist, Riggs wasn't supposed to eat anything that wasn't the produce of Old Earth—a pretty ridiculous religious stipulation if you asked me.

"I should go," I said. "The others will wonder where I am."

"Stay for a while," Riggs said.

"There's too much to be done before we reach the coordinates—"

"Nothing that can't wait. One of the others will cover your watch."

He snaked an arm around my naked waist. Tenderly pulled me towards him. The private war going on in my head—between vulnerable and armoured—reached perfect equilibrium for a second, and I rolled on top of Riggs and let it happen. But instead of going for another round, Riggs dangling mod looked almost sad. His smile faltered.

"Are you okay?" he asked. "I know that this has been hard on you."

Don't let him go there. Don't let him in. You need that armour back.

"I'm fine," I said.

"We can talk instead, if you want to. It might help."

"You've said that already."

"I just want you to know that I'm here for you."

"I thought that we covered this on the *Bainbridge*," I said, icily.

"You also said that was the last time, Keira. And there have been a couple since . . ."

"Are you complaining?"

"Of course not. It's just that I'd like . . ."—he grimaced, chewing on the words, his brow creasing in frustration at not being able to express himself as he'd like—"well, in my head, I'd like this to be more than it is."

"And I've already told you: it is what it is. There's no point in trying to change that."

I rolled off Riggs. Felt the prickle of cold air on my skin, and the endorphin crash that comes after good sex. Armoured Keira was definitely winning the war now, and I was mentally building up the list of tasks that needed to be done before we reached our destination.

"All I wanted to say is that I'm here for you. After what has happened with the Krell, with North Star . . ."

"Sure thing," I said. "Talking Krell isn't exactly something I thought I'd experience on this mission."

Riggs laughed. "I hear that, but it wasn't what I meant."

I started to dress. Pulled on my fatigues. Strapped on my wrist-comp. "Then what do you mean? Spit it out, Corporal."

Riggs sighed. "I'm not sure. The Pariah is freaky as all hell, but something else is niggling me."

"Such as?"

"Such as, how did the Black Spiral know that we were going to be on North Star Station?"

"Chance," I said. Began to pull my deck-boots on. "They operate throughout the Drift. This is their country, not ours."

"You believe that?" Riggs said. "Space is pretty big. There are sixteen border stations along the FQZ. North Star might be the most remote, but why did they pick there?"

Riggs stirred and, still naked, clambered through to the Warhawk's cockpit. It was spacious enough to accommodate two simulants in combat-armour, and even Riggs' muscular frame was dwarfed by the control console. He called up a holo of near-space, showing the entirety of the Maelstrom's border.

"Three of these border stations have access to Shard Gates," he said, pointing to his research. "Two are closer to Daktar than North Star."

"What's your point? There's no way that the Spiral could've known that we would be on that station."

"Unless," Riggs said, turning to me so that his face was half-concealed by the green glow of the holo, "someone tipped them off. The intel must've come from us. From the *Santa Fe*."

Scanning the imagery, I wondered if Riggs had a point. It *did* seem terribly coincidental that the Spiral had turned up at North Star. The more I thought about it, the less credible it seemed. The idea that the Black Spiral had chosen the same location as us by mere fluke...

"This is a serious accusation."

"I'm not accusing anybody," Riggs said. "But I wouldn't even raise it with you unless I thought it was worth considering."

Now that the facts were laid out like this, it was pretty hard to argue with them. The Spiral turned up on North Star because someone had told them that was where we would be. They hadn't gone after the Pariah until we had arrived, and even then...

"They wanted us alive," I whispered. "That, or they wanted our intel."

"Maybe," Riggs said. "But they wouldn't know that unless they had someone on the inside."

"What are you thinking?"

"Feng is former Directorate. Novak is a lifer."

"They're Jackals," I said. But even as I said it, I realised that I wasn't speaking with conviction. As terrible as it sounded, did Riggs have a point here? Something opened inside of me, and I felt myself standing on the edge of a precipice, the brink of an abyss. There would be no return from this point. I swallowed, said, "Feng isn't Directorate."

Only this time, unlike when I'd had this same conversation with Lopez on the *Fe*'s outer hull, I didn't feel so certain.

"Like Carmine says: who knows what they put in his head?" Riggs replied, staring at the holo. "And back on North Star, I really thought that Novak was going to run."

"But he didn't. He came back."

Riggs lifted his shoulders and held them there, as though undecided. "Yeah, but maybe that was only because he knew that he had no other choice. Like I said, I'm not making accusations. But can you really trust anyone on this ship?"

I exhaled slowly. The urge to climb back into the simulator-tanks, to make everything all right again, was becoming more intense by the second.

"Except for me, I mean," Riggs added, giving me his best hangdog look.

"Keep this tight," I said to Riggs, patting his shoulder in what I hoped was a comradely manner. "Sub rosa. Don't share it with anyone."

"Solid copy."

My mother used to have a phrase: *everything changes, but nothing is ever different*. Seemed about right from where I was standing. I'd fought against the Asiatic Directorate more times than most Sim Ops troopers, at least those who were still in one piece. Old rivalries sometimes died hard. Was whatever we were chasing in the Gyre worth upsetting galactic peace for?

Riggs stood and reached for my waist, but I pushed his hand back.

"I've got something else to tell you," he said, haltingly. "About us. I've been meaning to say it for a while."

I finished dressing. The inside of the Warhawk was suddenly too small, claustrophobic even, brought on by the press of the decks, and the mingled smells in the small space. I needed out.

"It can wait, Riggs," I said.

"It can't, Keira. Who knows what we're getting into out here?"

"We're executing the mission," I said. All business now. I could tell where this was going, could see on Riggs' handsome face that he wanted to open up. I just knew that it was going to be something emotional, something that I couldn't handle right now.

He started, "I want to tell you—"

"No," I said. "Don't say anything. Don't say another word."

"I need to say it."

"No, you don't. This isn't what you think it is."

Riggs' face dropped: gave me that wounded puppy look that was disgusting and cute in equal measure.

"Get dressed," I said. "Get this place cleaned up, and don't let anyone see you leave."

"Copy that," Riggs said.

Tomorrow, Carmine promised, we would be at the coordinates. Whatever happened to the *Hannover*, in less than eight hours we were going to get some results.

That night passed fitfully. I had dreams, which was nothing new. I topped up on the sedatives—took double the dose that the medtechs had recommended, but knew that I could take it. Soon I'd be back in my simulant, and all of my blunt edges would be sharp again.

But the drugs did little to help me this time. Though I slept, all I could think about was Riggs' disclosure. Was there an infiltrator on the ship? Too many suspects, and too little intelligence on which to base a proper case. Surely not Captain Carmine: we had history together, and she was a good Alliance officer. But I knew nothing of her crew. Had they been vetted by Major Sergkov and Military Intelligence?

And what of the shadowy major...I doubted that he would sabotage his own mission, but his methods had been suspect so far. The decision to lay over at North Star wasn't beyond criticism: why couldn't we make the collection of the Pariah somewhere less prone to infiltration?

Worst of all was the suspicion that the one of the Jackals—*Jenkins'* Jackals: my squad—might be a traitor.

I saw each of their faces, and knew that none was above suspicion.

Try as I might to defend Feng, how deep did his Directorate loyalty go? Perhaps Carmine was right about him. Perhaps his dedication to the cause ran deeper than we knew. Riggs had mentioned Novak too, and he was an obvious weak link. Whatever I'd said to Riggs, I had genuinely thought that the Russian would run on North Star. In a restless sleep, I replayed the incident in my head. Was his decision to come back for the squad just covering for something else?

And what about Lopez? Not an obvious suspect, but a possibility nonetheless. She carried a potential streak of conflict as strong as Feng's, but in a different way: Senator Lopez wanted Sim Ops shut down. What better way to do it than leave yet another destroyed space station in our wake?

In the end, I gave up on sleep, and took an extra watch on the Pariah.

Feng was on duty, sitting alone at a guard station that wasn't much more than a console and a chair, one of the *Santa Fe*'s shockrifles laid across his lap. He'd been on watch for a while, but Feng didn't seem any less frosty, and I noticed that his rifle was armed. No chances taken where the Krell were concerned. Still, Feng looked glad to see me when I arrived.

"Evening, Private," I said. "I'll take this watch."

"Are you sure, ma'am?" said Feng, although obviously grateful for the offer.

"I'm sure," I said. "Scram. Just stay away from the SOC."

"Zero still down there?" he asked.

"Where else would she be?"

"Good point," Feng said.

"How has our friend here been behaving?"

"Take a look for yourself."

The brig was a small, confined space, with a single containment cell. A null-shield extended across the length of the chamber, allowing an unhindered view inside the cell. That had started small and featureless, but the Pariah had made the place its own. The Krell had nested inside the chamber. The walls ran with something like mucous, rivulets of moisture coalescing in an unnatural pattern. The Pariah sat in one corner, limbs folded around itself, battle equipment randomly scattered across the cell floor. Feng's console was filled with multiple camera angles of the inside of the cell, ensuring that nothing the Pariah did would go unseen. *Maybe spending so much time with Zero is beginning to have an effect on him*, I thought.

"Go get some shut-eye, Feng," I ordered. "I'll take it from here."

"Solid copy."

I took up the post. The Krell didn't give any perceptible response to the change of guard. "You asleep in there?" I asked the Pariah.

The alien didn't move, but said, "We do not sleep like others."

"Of course not," I said. "That would be too easy."

The cell lights had been dimmed, and the alien's eyes were barely visible in the dark. It seemed to be watching me. Feng's console had been set up so that some views of the cell were in infrared, and I noticed how little body heat the creature seemed to shed.

"Do you know how many of your kind I've killed?" I asked the alien.

"We do not know," it said.

"That's probably best."

"Does that matter?"

"So you're some kind of XT philosopher now?"

"We do not know 'philosopher,'" the alien replied. "Or 'XT.'"

"It means extraterrestrial. Like outside of Earth."

"Understand 'Earth.' Is homeworld."

"That's right," I said. I didn't feel entirely comfortable with the alien knowing about Earth, about what our homeworld meant, but I quickly decided that it didn't really matter. Old Earth was a nuclear shithole. The Krell wanted to bomb it? They were welcome to try.

"Dr. Skinner told us about Earth," the Pariah said, twitching its limbs. "Like Kindred Reef Worlds."

"That's probably the closest thing you'd understand," I said.

"We have never been there. We will never go there. We are Pariah."

"Do you miss Skinner?"

The alien paused, then said, "Define 'miss.'"

"Do you think about him?" I asked, tapping a finger to the side of my head. "He was your creator, the man who made you. You spent time with him."

"We are," the alien said. "That is all."

Talking to the Pariah was a lot like trying to reason with a crude AI. Not just the way that it spoke—that electronic voice-box made it feel a lot like a machine—but the nature of its responses. Struck me as little actual reasoning going on behind those dark, alien eyes. The creature was just a big organic machine.

"I wanted to say thanks for the save," I said. "For going outside the ship, earlier today."

The alien regarded me impassively. "We did as asked."

"You didn't need to do that though."

"We did as asked," the Pariah repeated. "Other requested."

"That'd be Major Sergkov," I explained.

"It is leader-form?" the Pariah offered.

A leader-form was probably the closest analogy within the Krell caste-structure to an Alliance officer, although leader-forms enjoyed the perk of being able to mind-control their lesser troops in a way that I was sure Sergkov would appreciate...

"I guess," I said. "Sort of."

The alien poked a talon towards me. More inquisitively than threateningly. "It is different to Sergkov-other."

"You mean that I'm different to Sergkov?" I touched a hand to my chest. "I'd hope so. For a start, I'm female."

"Sergkov-other is not?"

"Major Sergov is male," I said. "He's also an ass. But then most men are."

So far as we were aware, the Krell were sexless. Was

the Pariah any different? Impossible to know whether Dr. Skinner's experiments had messed with the alien's genome, and this really was not a subject I wanted to discuss with the alien.

The Pariah craned its neck. "We do not know 'ass.'"

I permitted myself a tired laugh, and shook my head. "You don't need to know, P. You don't need to know."

The conversation—if you could call it that—ended there.

I sat up the whole night-cycle. The Pariah barely moved at all.

CHAPTER NINETEEN

INTO THE GYRE

Early the next day-cycle, we were inside the Gyre.

Carmine scrambled all crew to the bridge, and the place was once again packed with personnel. The Jackals assembled around the tactical display—all except Zero, who had remained in the SOC—while Sergkov paced the chamber with barely restrained frustration.

"We're here," Carmine declared, as blunt as ever. "And the Sab Rhea star system isn't."

"Run through this for me again," Sergkov said. "If you don't mind, Captain."

The Gyre spread out before us: a twisted spiral of planetary matter and stellar debris, an ever-decreasing coil. At the very heart of the conglomeration was a super-massive black hole—the result of dozens of collapsed stars—pulling everything into the churn.

"See for yourself," Carmine said. "We're currently inside the Gyre, although only just, and the Sab Rhea system isn't here."

Carmine was hard-plugged to her console, and she'd been that way, mostly, since we'd fled North Star. Her old face displayed the edge of exhaustion: black bags hung at her eyes, her mechanical leg twitching. That, I'd noticed, was a sign she was on edge. Right now, her leg was moving positively non-stop.

"What do you mean by 'isn't here'?" Sergkov pressed.

"It's gone. *Everything* is gone."

The tactical display demonstrated where Sab Rhea had once been, with comparative imagery. According to historic analysis of this region, the sun had once held sixteen satellites. The *Santa Fe*'s AI considered those and spat out a lengthy stream of data on them, together with tach-scope pictographics.

"Maybe we're in the wrong place..." Lopez muttered. "Could there be an error with navigation?"

"That's not possible," Carmine said. "I've checked it myself, and our location is confirmed by scope. This is all that's left."

An expansive swirl of debris and matter—a purple, mist-like swathe—claimed most of Sab Rhea's space.

"Ship's sensors are having difficulty getting through it," Carmine said. "But it looks like asteroidal debris. I can't tell whether it's new, but it wasn't there when this system was last imaged."

"Why don't you just ask *it*?" Riggs said, nodding to the back of the bridge.

Sergkov had insisted on the Pariah's presence on the bridge, but it had stayed quiet throughout the approach to Sab Rhea. Although it was deceptively easy to forget that the alien was even there, I never lost the feeling that it was listening to everything: a potential spy in the camp, gathering intel. *And not the only one*, I thought as I looked around the bridge.

"We cannot assist," the Pariah said.

Lopez stared at the tac-display. "Can you sort of, you know, sense any other Krell out here?"

"We cannot," Pariah intoned. "This place is Red Fin territory. We are not of the Red Fin Collective."

"So you guys call yourselves by those names as well?" Riggs asked.

Pariah tilted its head towards Riggs, before answering, "We are of Kindred. We are using words that others understand."

"When the *Hannover* was last here," Sergkov said, walking the display, "the Sab Rhea star was still burning. This is *fresh* damage."

"It likely had millennia of energy reserves," Carmine said. "At least, according to those data-files."

"Couldn't the Gyre be to blame?" Riggs suggested, pointing at the heart of the stellar phenomena.

The Gyre turned away in the centre of the map. The more I looked at that hypnotic spin of dead matter, a terrible sense of familiarity came over me. *I've seen that image somewhere before*, I realised. The Gyre looked very much like the Black Spiral's insignia: like the badge that they plastered over the stations and ships they attacked...

"I doubt it," Carmine said, bringing my train of thought back to the present. "The Gyre is reckoned to be stable, and our readings don't suggest any change in its condition. It would take the Gyre thousands of years to pull Sab Rhea in."

"What is that thing, anyway?" Lopez said, referring to the Gyre.

Carmine shrugged. "Lots of stories to tell about the Gyre, when you have time to hear them. They say that it is a failed Shard Gate. Something massive and terrible left over by the Shard, when they upped and left this end of the universe."

Sergkov tutted and rolled his head in annoyance. "None of which is confirmed," he rebuked. "And none of which is helpful. Keep your rumours to yourself if you will, Captain."

I flagged a location at the heart of the stellar cloud that had once been the Sab Rhea system. "Can we run a targeted sweep deeper into the cloud? If the *Hannover* went down, she may have fired her evacuation pods. Those carry broad-frequency distress beacons."

Carmine paused before answering. "We can try it, but what with so much fouling of the sensors any beacons out there will be seriously muted—"

"We're picking something up on the scanner…" Yukio said. A look of determined concentration dawned on the lieutenant's face.

"Follow the scanner return," Carmine ordered.

Silence descended over the bridge. The tac-display was scattered with static, the *Santa Fe*'s scopes becoming so clouded that we had virtually no visuals at all. Space around us was swamped with exotic particulate…

"It's definitely a generated signal," Yukio said. "I…I think that it's Alliance pattern."

She patched the audio beacon through, and we listened to the pulse of an electronic signal.

"That's an Alliance distress beacon," Riggs said. "I'd recognise that anywhere. I used to run evac when I was with the Marines."

"How far out?" Sergkov asked.

"We're almost on top of it," Carmine said, still focused on her data-feeds. "Can't see a damn thing through this shit!"

Carmine's terminal began to chirp. A siren whined across the ship's PA system.

"All halt," Yukio declared. "Gravitic drive holding in position."

The *Sante Fe*'s spaceframe shuddered, and ahead of us *something* emerged from the sea of debris.

"Oh shit…" Novak whispered. "Fish heads…"

A Krell bio-ship appeared on the scanners.

"All sensors, maximum power!" Carmine suddenly interrupted. She threw off the vestiges of fatigue and became almost hyper-alert: as though she'd made transition into a simulant.

"Aye, sir," a staffer replied.

The next few seconds passed in a sort of frenzied blur.

The Navy crew ran all of their tests, did their scans, and the *Fe*'s scopes and scanners strained to amplify the visuals until they were clear. But at this distance, there was little that the sensors could really tell us: bio-ships were made for stealth and emitted very few detectable readings.

"Your signal—the distress beacon—is coming from *inside* that ship," Carmine said. "The vessel must be acting as a barrier. All that bone and gristle… That's why our sensors didn't detect it earlier."

The *Santa Fe*'s intelligence engine had assigned the identifier *Azrael* to the bio-ship, and the name currently floated alongside the vessel's holo-image.

Sergkov nodded. "She was seen on Askari during the Krell War."

The *Santa Fe* carried a local copy of the Navy's intelligence database, and it quickly provided us with everything that had been collected on the ship. The *Azrael* was ancient, venerable, and had been encountered by the Alliance many times before. She had some impressive kill-stats, her history steeped in the blood of human–Krell engagements. Red Fin Collective apparently—in recent years assigned to a defensive fleet mustered in the Sab Rhea system…

"The signal could be from one of the *Hannover*'s evac-pods," Sergkov said.

"It has to be," I said. I couldn't see any other explanation for a human distress beacon emanating from *inside* the bio-ship. "There could be survivors in there."

"Ship is not right," the Pariah added.

Everyone turned to look at the enormous bio-form. Its skin had gone oily, and the musk it emitted was almost overpowering.

"Can it communicate with the bio-ship?" Lopez offered, talking about the Krell while also trying to avoid looking at it.

"We cannot communicate," the Krell voiced. It writhed its limbs, producing an almost wet sound as it moved. "Ship is not of our Collective."

"Any other nuggets of wisdom you want to share on that topic?" Riggs said, attempting to goad the alien again. "What exactly is the point of having this thing on the ship if it can't actually communicate with the other fishes?"

This time, the alien snapped about, its two taloned forearms raising like shoulder-mounted battle cannons, directed at Riggs. Fully deployed, the alien's limbs grazed the deckhead.

"Whoa!" Novak said. "Easy, fish."

The crew scattered away from the alien; only Sergkov remained in proximity. But the second passed, and the xeno's limbs gradually sagged. Breath caught in the thing's chest.

"Ship is…wrong," it said again. "We want to know why."

Sergkov looked up at the alien, making eye contact. "You'll get your chance," he said.

"And how exactly are we going to do that?" Riggs asked. "If the fish head can't speak with the ship, I mean."

I already suspected the answer.

"You are all going aboard that ship." Sergkov nodded at the alien. "And the Pariah is going aboard with you."

"No other choice," I whispered, eyes still on the XT. I didn't like this one bit. "Riggs, you're flying."

Less than ten minutes later, we were clad in new skins and loaded for war. I glanced around the Warhawk's cabin—the same cabin in which Riggs and I had rutted only a day ago. I shifted that memory and sealed it way, instead performed a cursory check on the rest of the team.

"Transition confirmed," I said, into the communicator.

The *Santa Fe*'s hangar bay doors soundlessly opened, pressure escaping. Space appeared beyond the lock.

"We hear you, Lieutenant," Zero said. She was back in the SOC, vicariously soaking up every bit of the action. "Your video-feeds are looking good."

"Bridge confirms feeds too," Sergkov said. "Mission is a go."

"I hear that…" Feng muttered, flexing his hands in the armoured combat-suit. "Sure feels good to have the nice toys."

"Although some were luckier than others," Riggs said, turning from the cockpit to grin at me. He was at the flight controls, the only occupant of the shuttle's cockpit.

The inside of the cabin was positively jammed with bodies. Four simulants in full combat-armour were bad enough, but the HURT was enormous. I felt like a goddess, albeit a clumsy one, inside the armour. I fought to control my pulse, to keep in check my eagerness to deploy the HURT again.

The Jackals all wore full combat-suits, cradled plasma rifles on up-armoured legs. I felt a curious mixture of pride and anxiety as I looked on the team. Pride, because they were shaping up. Every suit was marked with the Jackal-head insignia, every weapon primed and tested.

But also anxiety, because of what Riggs had said. Could I trust my own team, and what were we walking into?

Don't think about that now, I insisted to myself. *Concentrate on the mission.*

"Just remember, as I told you: these suits are bigger and more powerful than those you're used to."

"Is not problem," Novak said. "Do not worry."

"I do worry, Novak," I said.

"We did those simulations and drills," Lopez said. "We're ready."

I tapped Lopez's forearm. "The combat-suits have a null-shield generator in the left vambrace. Keep that turned on; the shield will operate as soon as the suit detects an incoming projectile."

The team all nodded and voiced agreement because, of course, we'd been through this a hundred times already.

"I want all suits sealed throughout the operation," Sergkov said over the comm. Each combat-suit was fully pressurised, could act as a space suit if necessary. "No one is to unseal under any circumstances."

"You heard the major," I said. "This is not a combat mission—"

"At least, not yet," Riggs said.

I scowled at Riggs and started again: "This is *not* a combat mission. No one shoots until I give the order. The Krell are friendlies, until I say otherwise."

The Pariah was stooped in one of the crew seats, unharnessed, wearing its bio-suit and helmet: the equipment it had taken from North Star.

"Is the Pariah reading your comms?" Sergkov asked.

"We are," the alien said.

"Will fish survive the vac?" Novak questioned, although the tone of his voice didn't carry any concern for the alien.

"It's wearing Class III bio-armour," Zero said, "which is probably more durable than your combat-suit."

"That told you," Lopez said.

"Hey, you are one sitting next to it," Novak replied.

Lopez was closest to the Pariah, and she cast her eyes sideways. Although it was difficult to fidget in a full combat-suit, Lopez seemed to manage it. She looked less than comfortable.

"Can the chatter," I said. "We've got an objective to secure in there."

New data scrolled across Riggs' control console, and iconography on my HUD gave the all-clear for launch.

"Ready when you are," Carmine said.

"Copy that," Riggs said. "Let's kick the tyres and light the fires."

"What the fuck is that supposed to mean?" I asked.

Riggs flipped control switches on his console, the board illuminating green. "Just an old air force saying."

"Right. Let's launch, shall we?"

"You're the boss," Riggs said. "Launching in three... two... one..."

The Warhawk launched from the *Santa Fe*'s hold. There was a brief tug of resistance as we fired thrusters and cleared the ship's gravitational field, then we were on our own.

"Just keep the *Fe*'s weapons systems hot," I said to Carmine, over a closed channel. "No telling when we might need to use them."

Carmine gave a low, throaty laugh. "Do you even have to ask?" she said.

CHAPTER TWENTY

THE *AZRAEL*

A searchlight mounted on the Warhawk's nose absently scanned the bio-ship's battered exohull. There were muttered curses and exclamations from the squad.

"You receiving this, *Fe*?" I asked.

"We see it," Sergkov said.

"This ship is massive," Feng whispered. "Where do we even start?"

There were no wise quips or comebacks from anyone this time.

The bio-ship was much longer than the *Santa Fe*, and maybe twice as broad. The hull was ribbed with biological armoured plating, pocked here and there with what might have been view-ports. Several larger apertures mimicked airlocks or docking bays, but it was hard to say—everything screamed of the organic, rather than the machined. Save for the nose, all angles were soft and curved, and every portal was circular. As we drew nearer still, I saw that several of those were open.

"Looks dead," Novak offered.

"Or at least dormant…" Zero said. I heard her swallowing as we drifted nearer, and I could feel her apprehension over the comms network. Being so close to the Krell was surely taking its toll on her.

"It can't be dead," Sergkov said, "because it was never really alive."

"Looks like it might've been once," Lopez whispered.

"Bio-ship hulls are composed of an organic polymer, fused to a force-grown spaceframe," Sergkov offered, "but they aren't really alive. Very few of the internal elements are what you would call truly 'living.'"

Novak grunted. "'Grown'? 'Fused'? Sounds like alive to me."

"Alive, dead, whatever," I said. "The ship's drive is inactive."

"How can you tell?" Riggs asked.

The outer hull was speckled—seemingly without reason, in a way that certainly felt biological—with bubbles and sensor-vanes, delicate-looking spines that spread from the aft.

"Experience," I said. "Those things are drive spines; when the engine's active they'll often glow blue. That's plasma discharge."

"Ship is in pain," the Pariah intoned.

The Pariah had no access to the shuttle's vid-feed, but the proximity to the alien ship was affecting it. The xeno squirmed, limbs in constant motion.

"Take the shuttle in closer, Corporal," Sergkov ordered. "And begin transmitting across all frequency ranges."

The shuttle carried a short-ranged but powerful communications array. We were now so close that it would be capable of transmitting our beacon to the bio-ship. Riggs licked his lips, and didn't immediately do as ordered, his gloved finger hovering over the INITIATE TRANS-MISSION key. He paused, half-turning to me.

"You cool with this?" he asked.

I gave a reluctant nod. "Do as he says."

Riggs punched the key. On initiation, the Warhawk's comms beacon began to sing on every frequency we had available, across every comms band. At this range, every xeno-form on the bio-ship would hear us.

I nodded at Pariah. "Is it working?"

"We hear it," the XT said, tentacles writhing across its back. I wondered how it functioned with those appendages exposed to vacuum, outside its bio-suit.

"No obvious sign of response," I said. "*Santa Fe*, you getting anything back there?"

"We're picking up the signal," Zero said, "but so far there's no response from the ship."

Sergkov took over. "Corporal Riggs, are you still reading the Alliance beacon?"

"Affirmative," Riggs answered. "Loud and clear."

"Where's it coming from?" the major asked. "Can you get a fix?"

Riggs paused for a moment, analysed the data on his flight console. "Somewhere in the prow, but I can't be any more specific than that."

"There," the Pariah said. It stirred across the cabin, moving so fast that the HURT suit's target-acquisition software flagged it as a potential hostile. The xeno pointed a webbed hand at the cockpit view-port, at a broad section of the *Azrael*'s hull. "We board there," it said. "Signal comes from near. Go there."

A yawning hangar bay: the entrance to a dark cave. Riggs painted the feature with an objective icon, noting the distance to target.

"Follow the Pariah's instructions," Sergkov ordered. "I want you to take the shuttle into the designated hangar."

"Now we take orders from fish head?" Novak asked.

"I want you to leave all comm lines open," Sergkov ordered, "and maintain that broadcast."

"Whatever you say, Major," Riggs muttered. He turned to me and added, "This guy's going to get us killed."

"Been there too many times already, kemo sabe," I said. "Just keep your mind on the job. Take us in."

The Warhawk glided into a hangar. Riggs deftly pulled back on the acceleration, deployed the skids, and touched down in the centre of the bay.

I accessed the Warhawk's remote eyes, and took in the location: a cavernous hold, big enough to take ten transport shuttles. Lit only by the starlight from the open airlock, the walls and floors vaguely ribbed. I activated my suit's scanner systems. *Let's see what we can see…* I swept the nearby chambers, attempting to map the *Azrael*'s insides. The armour's AI built a rough schematic of the surrounding modules, pinned the maps to my HUD.

Riggs said, "Place is pressurised, according to the boat's instruments."

"You sure about that?" I asked. There was no obvious means of sealing the hold from the vacuum outside. "Nothing closed behind us—"

"Shaped energy field," the Pariah offered. "No airlocks."

"Right…" Lopez said. "And that works *how*, exactly?"

"You can trust the shuttle's readings," Sergkov ordered.

"It gets better," Riggs said. "There's also decent atmosphere in here. The fish's 'shaped energy field' is holding everything in nicely. Air humidity is high, with a reasonable oxygen content."

"But you heard Sergkov," I said. "Everyone should stay buttoned up."

"Beacon is still broadcasting," Riggs replied. "I'm picking up some additional information now."

"Such as?"

"It's definitely from the ECS *Hannover*."

"Well isn't that great," Novak answered.

"This might turn out to be a rescue mission after all," Lopez said. "Maybe we can all go home heroes…"

The squad's vitals were jumpy but controlled. That would have to be enough. "Riggs, I want you to remain on-site," I said.

"You sure about that?" Riggs asked. His expression was almost pleading. "I mean, don't you want more boots on the ground?"

"You think you'll miss out on some of the glory?" Feng suggested, grinning behind his face-plate.

"Fuck you, man," Riggs said.

"You're the only qualified pilot," I said, "and this shuttle is our only way of getting off-ship. We find real skins in there, we might need some way of getting them home."

"But—" Riggs started.

I glared at Riggs with an expression that said *don't argue with me*, and he settled back into the cockpit.

"The rest of you follow me. Tight formation, bio-scanners at max amp."

The troopers unharnessed and conducted weapons checks, readying plasma rifles and pistols. An objective marker appeared on my HUD, transposed over a warren of corridors and chambers. That was the target's location, deep within the bio-ship's guts.

"Execute those orders," Sergkov said.

The design—if you could even call it that—of the Krell bio-ship shared little in common with that of any human starship. Corridors spread—capillary-like—from the hangar bay, both vertically and horizontally, splaying in different directions. Every internal surface appeared to have been bored or grown, covered in organic ridging. The squad painted the insides of the ship with their suit-lamps—more reliable than infrared or night-vision in an alien environment.

"Gravity is lower than expected," I said.

"That's been reported before," Sergkov muttered over the comms. "The Krell appear to prefer a below-standard gravity."

"Our boots aren't working in here," Feng said. "Whatever shit this ship is made of, it isn't metal. Place is creepy as all fuck."

"Take look at this…" Novak suggested.

The walls and floor ahead were composed of a grisly, fibrous material that looked uncomfortably close to exposed muscle fibre. Almost immediately, the tunnels tightened. My armour brushed against the walls.

"There's barely enough space to manoeuvre in here," I complained.

"Well, at least the Pariah seems fine," Feng said, indicating further up the tunnel.

The alien had no lighting rig, but that wasn't slowing it down. Pariah scuttled along the ceiling, using every surface detail for purchase, making the most of all six of its limbs. Even inside the HURT suit, and with reduced gravity, I was struggling to keep up.

"Slow down, Pariah," I ordered. "We need to keep this place covered."

"We hear it," the Krell said.

"Me too," I said, referring to the beacon. "But this place isn't secure."

The alien's crested head creased in a frown—probably the first time I'd seen any actual emotion on the XT's features.

"Just slow down," I ordered again.

The alien paused at the junction, hanging from the wall, as the rest of the team advanced. The Jackals cleared the sector.

"So you've never been onto a bio-ship before?" Feng asked the alien.

"We have memories," Pariah said. "But they are not ours. The Collective's seed runs deep."

"Just like you and the Directorate, huh Feng?" Riggs said over the comm. "Maybe you've got more in common with that xeno than you think."

"Is that moisture on the walls?" Zero asked.

I reached out a hand, drew gloved fingertips across the smooth surface. In the pools of light cast by my lamps, I saw that the walls were a uniform grey-green—bone-like, similar to the carapace of a Krell warrior. When I touched it, I felt a deep vibration through the wall.

"Seems like it," I said.

"You should activate your frequency-beacons," Zero suggested. Her signal was weak, and becoming weaker, an expected consequence of the distance between us and the *Santa Fe*.

"Is that a good idea?" Lopez asked. "We'll be giving away our position to anything in here..."

"Do it," Sergkov said. "Riggs too."

"You hear that, Corporal?" I asked.

"Solid copy," he said. "Even if I don't like it."

"You getting lonely back there, Riggs?" Feng asked.

"I'm not proud," Riggs said, "but a little company wouldn't go amiss. Maybe I'll comm Zero on a private channel..."

"I guess it's easy to make jokes when you're safe and sound on the shuttle," Feng said. Riggs' voice was already gathering interference from the bio-ship's structure. "You're a long way from the shit, Riggs, and I guess you'll be the first to bug out if it goes down..."

All five of the Jackals activated their freq-beacons. A

frequency analysis appeared on my HUD, indicating that I was broadcasting loud and clear.

Lopez froze ahead, her outline stark in the lamplight. "What in the Core is this...?" she asked.

She crouched, the Jackals assembling around her. A pool of something yellow and sickly-looking welled up from the floor, breaching the contoured deck. Reminded me a lot of a boil, the surface covered by a skein of sagging flesh.

"No one touch—" I started.

But Novak reached out and touched the surface of the pool.

"Novak!" Lopez exhorted. "What did you do that for?"

Rifles clattered as they aimed in Novak's direction. An oily yellow fluid coated the outside of his gauntlet, coming free in long, sinewy strands. *Icky*: that was the word for it.

"Stay away from that shit," I said, finally finding my voice. "Could be dangerous."

The Pariah twitched. "Transport," it said, cryptically. "For motion."

"Was experiment," Novak said. "Is not dangerous. See?"

He righted himself, wiped his hand across the wall. His glove was thoroughly coated, and the Russian's face creased in annoyance as he tried to wipe it off.

"I don't care what Sergkov says," Lopez said, "this place is alive, and it's disgusting—"

She backed into a wall, beyond the arc of my suit-lamps—

My bio-scanner flashed with activity—

The wall came alive.

Living tendrils lashed free. Clutched for Lopez, embracing her body, wrapping her limbs. Lifting her off the deck, *into* the wall. Lopez screamed: a short, shrill sound. It was an irrepressible reaction. Can't say that I would have responded in any other way.

"Help!" she called, gasping. Her suit wasn't breached—my HUD confirmed that—but she was panicking.

"Get her down," I said. Clutching for the tendrils, tearing them free. The tissue was soft, wet. Slime-coated.

Lopez thrashed. Feng had his plasma rifle up, but had the sense not to fire. A plasma bolt at this range would likely breach Lopez's armour. Novak abandoned his rifle, and grabbed for Lopez's arms, dragging her back from the living wall.

"I'm slipping!" she said. "Hold tighter!"

Novak grunted, baring his teeth. "You are slimy!" he said. "Is not easy job."

Lopez's armour was covered in the same ooze as from the floor, and her body was sliding back into the morass of heaving tissue.

The Pariah leapt into the mass of tendrils. Reached for Lopez with its middle pair of arms.

"Relax body," it ordered.

Lopez continued to wriggle and writhe for a second, then allowed her body to become limp. To my amazement, she slid free from the wall. Collapsed to her knees.

"You all right?" I asked. I wiped a gauntlet over her face-plate, so that I could see her face inside her helmet. I saw that she was shaking in the suit.

"I . . . I'm okay," she said. Feng passed her plasma rifle to her, and she took it, checked it over. "That was my fault. I should've been watching my scanner."

"It appeared fast," I said.

She got to her feet. "I do not like this place one bit."

"It likes you, Lopez," Novak said.

"It is harmless," the Pariah said, towards the wall. "Just portal."

The living tendrils had retreated now, revealing a passage beyond. Walls threaded with thick, vine-like sinew. Things that looked like veins throbbed to life, pumping something dark and viscous along their length.

"The signal is this way," the Pariah said, scuttling ahead.

"I think that Feng's right," Riggs whispered. "I am *much* safer on the shuttle."

The structure around us changed. Became darker, more fetid. Even by the standards of the Krell, this was bad voodoo.

Stinger-ammo studded the walls. Pools of dark fluid that looked too much like blood lined the deck. Curtains of living tissue that had calcified, turned the colour of offal in the midday sun. All rotten.

"Place has seen a fight," I whispered. The Jackals hadn't spoken for a while, and I needed to hear the sound of my own voice. "Are you still reading me, Zero?"

"I copy," Zero said. "Your visuals are breaking up badly though."

"Take in everything that you can down there," Sergkov said. "I will need some samples from that damaged sector on the way back."

Does he really think that any of us are getting out of here alive? I thought to myself.

The Pariah stooped to touch the nearest damaged deck. The alien glared back at me with blatant anger in its eyes.

"You know what's causing this?" I asked.

"Ship is dying," it said. "Collective is in pain. Bad pain."

The Pariah waved a gauntleted hand ahead. At the edge of my lamp's beam, I made out a number of Krell bodies.

"Shit," Novak said. "Dead fishes ahead. No signs on scanner."

"I don't think that we need a bio-scanner to tell us that," Lopez said.

I stared down at the alien cadavers. Piled on top of each other, limbs twisted at weird angles. Carapaces ruptured, innards scattered across the junction. Literally torn apart. I made out stinger-rifles and shriekers among the miscellaneous body parts.

"They killed each other..." I whispered. "Looks like they were secondary-forms, mainly. Gun-grafts." The bodies were covered in heavy chitinous plates, the organic equivalent of a combat-suit. "An armoured breed."

"Didn't do them much good," Novak said.

"High guard," the Pariah explained. There was a disconnect between the alien's voice and its physical presentation. It seethed—limbs in constant motion, waves of anger coming off the thing like heat from a furnace.

"Those are elite Krell," Sergkov said. "Interesting. The colouration confirms that they are Red Fin Collective."

It was impressive that Sergkov could identify what Collective the Krell belonged to just from their carapace patterning, but I'd noticed something else. I crouched in the HURT suit and poked among the remains.

"They don't look right," I decided. "It's like they're *diseased*, or something..."

Where skin was exposed, it had turned an unhealthy white. I turned one of the bodies over, and saw that it was covered in lesions and wicked lacerations. Even the Krell's armour was algae- and fungi-infested, blooming rampant with white-coloured growths.

"Colonised..." Zero whispered over the comms. "The bodies have been colonised."

A memory came to me: distant and very, very

weak. Newport Beach, SoCal state. With my younger brother—the brother that my parents had doted over, that my father had adored. *Loved*: that was the word. In what felt like a past life, a teenaged Keira Jenkins had taken him down to the seafront, to check out the black waters that populated most of SoCal's shoreline. We'd stood on the coast, watched as the angry foam-flecked tide had thrown in wave after wave of silver bodies.

Fish. Those things had been actual fish. That was the last time I'd seen real aquatic life-forms. We'd picked our way through the blackened sand, through the homeless camp around a local pier. And together, in one of the few memories I had of my brother, we had poked at the dead and dying fish. They had mostly been limpid, listless things, crawling with parasites, gills weeping pus and blood. Gasping for air, covered in something the locals called "red tide," in what the newsfeeds referred to as an "ecological hypoxic event."

"You ever seen a diseased Krell before, ma'am?" Riggs asked, pulling me back to the now. I'd almost forgotten about him, back in the shuttle, but I was glad to hear his voice.

"No," I said. "I don't think I have."

"They have a very high tolerance of biological contagions such as viruses and bacterium," Zero offered.

Which makes this a whole lot worse. But I had no way of knowing if such a thing as a diseased Krell was even possible. Since when did these things look normal, anyhow?

"Leave them," Sergkov said, brusquely. "They're of no use. Do you have a better fix on the beacon?"

My eyes dropped to the scanner graphic on the HURT's HUD. No motion, no life-signs, but the evac-pod's beacon was broadcasting loud and clear now: position visible deeper in the ship.

"That's an affirmative," I said. I stood. "Nothing we can do here." Turning to Feng: "Private, I want you to remain at this junction. Keep the path to the Warhawk clear."

"Copy that," Feng said, taking a post among the shadows.

"Opens into some kind of chamber ahead," Lopez said.

"Keep it covered," I ordered. "Watch our six, Novak."

"Six is watched," Novak said. "Have bead on the Warhawk."

The tunnel branched into a chamber that had once housed a dozen Krell worker-forms, each fused to their workstation, lower bodies meshed with the innards of the bio-ship. They died where they had lived—if you could call their existence *living*.

"Probably a command station or weapons post," Lopez suggested. "But whatever it was, everything in there is dead. Same as the others in the tunnel."

"Anything to add, Pariah?" I asked.

The alien glared at the chamber. "We have nothing."

"O-*kay* …" Lopez said. No one felt the need to ask the alien what it meant by that comment; its mood had descended to the extent that it was almost tangible, a gloom that followed the XT around.

"Christo, how did these things end up on our side?" Novak said.

"Good question," I replied. "I've been asking myself the same thing a lot recently."

"Move on," Sergkov ordered.

Feng's transponder beacon lit on my HUD, flashing intermittently. I nodded at Lopez. "Remain here and stay in comms with me and Feng."

"Copy," Lopez said, quietly. To my surprise, there was no dissent from her. Was she actually learning how to be a soldier? Only time would tell. "Feng, I'm watching the corridor beyond your position."

"I see you on my scanner," he answered. "Let me know if there is any movement."

"If it comes to it," I explained, "we'll use this tunnel as an evacuation route. Straight to the hangar and the Warhawk."

"Sounds like plan," Novak said.

Pariah, Novak, and I moved on. The terrain was much of the same, but we appeared to descend a level or two. Decks were connected with rough-walled shafts, features with which Pariah seemed at ease: climbing and scuttling without complaint. It was slower going for Novak and me, and we clambered down the shafts more cautiously.

"Your...transponder sig...is degrading," Sergkov said, his voice chopped with static. "We...follow your... exact...position."

"That's a negative copy, *Fe*. Say again?"

The line hissed. COMMUNICATIONS NETWORK UNAVAILABLE, my suit said. PLEASE TRY AGAIN LATER.

"Novak, take a post on that spur," I said. "Try to stay in communication with the *Fe*. I'm going deeper."

The big Russian nodded and braced against the wall, covering the open junction. "I do as ordered," he said.

"Pariah, you're with me."

The alien responded by bounding onwards, legs pistoning. To this point, the dark around us had been almost impenetrable, but something glowed ahead. A diffuse light came from the walls, circling a portal lined with living tissue—

"There's liquid in here," I said.

I evaluated my surroundings, my face-plate shifting through vision modes. Fluid lapped gently at my armour plating, catching the glint of my lamps. I was knee-deep in it. The stuff responded sluggishly in low gravity. Reflections in various false shapes drifted across the surface.

"Is normal," Pariah said.

"Nothing about this place is normal... Where are we?"

"On Krell ship," it answered.

"Do you always have to be so fucking literal?"

The Pariah blinked at me. No reply.

"I mean, what is this *sector*?" I enunciated very precisely. "What is it used for?"

"Sleep..." the alien said. "Hibernation chamber."

I recalled our conversation in the brig, and how Pariah had spent the whole night basically alert. "Sleep" obviously didn't mean the same thing to the Krell. This was the largest chamber I'd seen since boarding the ship. The walls were claimed by glossy blisters: what I guessed were hibernation pods. Although most were blackened, filled with oily liquid that made the contents invisible, a handful glowed with an amber translucence.

"The signal is in there," I said. Tried hard to conceal the reluctance from my voice. "I'm going in."

I waded through the open portal, ripples throwing off all around me, giving my position away to anything that might be lying in wait. The entire room was flooded, deep as my waist.

Something dangled from the ceiling. Another blister-pod, much bigger than the others, hanging in a cradle of fleshy cables.

"What the fuck is *that*?" I whispered.

"Red Fin Collective," the Pariah said. "Navigator-form." Tapped a clawed gauntlet to its head, as though mimicking our conversation last night. "Higher function," it said.

There was a black shape inside the pod, held in gel-like suspension fluid. I let my suit-lamps linger on it, and couldn't stifle the gasp of shock at what I saw. The thing's body was distended and warped, six limbs curled around its enormous armoured head. More like a squid than a fish. Maybe an evolutionary offshoot of the main Krell genus, certainly unlike anything I had ever seen before. The creature was connected to the blister-pod by organic piping, its face covered by a respirator of some kind. The big, deep-set eyes were shut.

"It's…navigator-form," Sergkov confirmed. "The Krell equivalent of a starship captain, bred…that purpose."

"Carmine's equal," I muttered.

Sergkov continued his scientific monologue, as though unaware that I had spoken: "…specialised type of leader-form. You're…lucky to glimpse one…only ever… seen a handful…in existence…Highly valued…Krell Collectives."

"I feel so special," I said. "But this thing doesn't look right, Pariah. There's something wrong with it."

Everything about the creature's body was deformed, wasted: all except for the head, which was far out of proportion with the rest of its anatomy. More of the algae-bloom had polluted the navigator-form's pod. In fact, as I looked at the strange aberration, I thought that it had more in common with the mutants we'd seen on North Star than with Pariah.

Pariah stared at the navigator. "Collective speaks across void," it said. "Makes network, but not when ship falls."

"A faster-than-light fish? Very interesting."

"Oh, we found out…the navigators after…Krell War," Sergkov insisted. "We found—"

The connection ended with a spike of white noise that suggested a finality to our communications.

"Major? You read me?"

My suit had lost all contact with the *Santa Fe*. I swept every available comms band. No response. I guessed that we were too far into the ship. Even the Jackals' transponder signals—strung in a thin line across the vessel— were blinking erratically. I repressed the sudden and very intrusive thought that I might get lost, on my own, in the dark...

"Signal is here," Pariah said.

I realised that I was standing right on our objective, that I was exactly where I was supposed to be. An icon flashed across my HUD, updating my mission status.

"Why would they put one of our evac-pods in here?" I asked.

"Do not know," Pariah said.

The evacuation-pod was Alliance standard-issue equipment: spherical, not much bigger than the HURT suit, equipped with a short-range thruster and basic life support package. Carried a broadbeam transmitter that would allow for pick-up by friendly forces. This particular example was half-submerged, lying on its side in the centre of the hibernation chamber. The HURT suit's bio-scanner probed the pod, but came up clear: no readings from inside. Or the chamber around me, for that matter...

"Cover me," I said to Pariah.

The circular entry hatch was marked with various safety warnings: EXPLOSIVE BOLTS, STAND CLEAR ON RELEASE, and so on. I grabbed the manual release valve with one hand, and deployed a suit-gun—ready to fire if there was something waiting for me inside the pod—with the other. *Nothing* about this operation felt right any more, and I wasn't taking any chances. The hatch gave with a burst of escaping atmosphere. Liquid poured inside as I released the door.

"I've opened the pod," I said across the squad channel.

"And?" Lopez asked.

"It appears to be empty."

I leaned into the small craft. Explored the interior with my suit-lamps, my guns tracking possible hostile activity…

"That's a confirm on an empty pod," I said.

"Shit. Long way to come to go home empty-handed," Feng said.

Riggs laughed. "I hear that."

The pod's inside contained two pristine crash-couches. There was no sign of any previous occupation, no indication that anyone had used the pod at all. Could the *Hannover*'s AI have launched the craft by mistake? Possibly. It was unlikely, but no machine was infallible. I felt a mixture of relief and disappointment.

"I'm pulling out," I said. "Not sure if you're copying, *Santa Fe* Command, but there's nothing in here. The pod's empty. No survivors. Chalk it up as another mystery for the Maelstrom—"

I abruptly broke off my report.

Wait a minute.

The pod, I realised, wasn't empty. One of the crash-couches was occupied, though not by any human. My lamps fixed on an item that had been harnessed inside. BLACK BOX, my HUD identified. RECOVERY ESSENTIAL TO MISSION. OBJECTIVE UPDATE: RECOVERY OF FLIGHT DATA NOW PRIORITY OBJECTIVE. ALL OTHER MISSION OBJECTIVES ARE RESCINDED.

I reached inside and touched the sleek black casing. The box wasn't much larger than a data-clip, about the size of my palm. The words ECS *HANNOVER*—RESTRICTED ACCESS—were stamped on the armoured casing.

"Scratch that last report," I said to the squad. "I have something."

"Something *live*?" Riggs asked.

"No. The black box flight data. That's all the evac-pod contains."

"Someone sent out an evac-pod with the black box data?" Feng asked. "That doesn't make much sense."

"We can worry about the reasons later," I said. "Maybe Sergkov has some answers."

I withdrew from the evac-pod and slid the black box into one of the armoured pouches on my HURT suit's belt. In other circumstances, I would've just made a direct link to the *Santa Fe* and beamed the data back: we could've extracted, leaving the sims aboard the *Azrael*. But now that the comms link was down, that was an impossibility. The only way of getting the black box data back to the *Santa Fe* would be to extract it manually, by flying it back. *But it's not just that.* Pariah stirred beside me, doing a very bad job of covering me. The alien would be left on the ship if we extracted. For some reason that I couldn't really explain, I didn't think that it would be right to leave the XT aboard the bio-ship. *I'm getting soft*, I taunted myself. *Just make sure it doesn't get you killed.*

I stood up, servos whining. To be honest with myself, I didn't feel quite ready to give up the HURT suit, either.

"Is it just me," Novak asked, "or is water level rising in here?"

"It's just you," Lopez answered.

But the water level *was* rising. The liquid was staining my armour something chronic, the metallic plating now blackened and coated with wet slime.

"I think it's best that we get out of here," Feng said. "I've had enough of this place—"

There was a flash of motion right in front of me.

The Pariah snapped.

Arm outstretched. Claw closed over something grey and writhing.

"What in all the Core is *that*?" I exclaimed.

An eel. Pariah had intercepted the creature, I realised, mere inches from my face-plate. Its catch flexed violently, tried to escape its webbed fingers.

"Young," Pariah said, in a frighteningly calm voice. "Spawn, but gone wrong."

It crushed the mewling thing in its grip. My pulse had started to rise, the expectation that *something* was about to happen sending my gorge into orbit. Even with my onboard medi-suite, I was struggling to maintain any sort of calm...

Pariah grabbed another eel-thing as it leapt from the water. Crushed it with the same cold indifference. The fry squealed—far too loudly for a creature so small.

"I got signals," Feng said. "I got signals!"

"What's happening in there?" Riggs asked. "Report!"

"They come," Pariah said. It flipped both barb-guns, held them ready gunslinger style. "We fight."

CHAPTER TWENTY-ONE

BUTCHER'S DUE

Feng: "I've got signals inbound on your position!"
Riggs: "Get out of there! Keira, fall back to the shuttle!
          Now!"
Novak: "Fucking fishes everywhere! Kill 'em all!"
Lopez: "Hard contact! Hard contact—"

I fired a burst from my suit-guns. Smart rounds slashed the air and the surface of the water, providing brief flashes of illumination. My suit threw visuals across my HUD, flagging hostiles with coloured icons.

Electric ripples—so similar to moving reflections that I could've easily dismissed them as imagined—circled me. Shark-like, working in concert to close the distance between me and the exit to the room—

Simultaneously, several of the eel-things slammed into me. They slid free, left bloody smears where they made contact with my armour.

"Holy shit," I whispered, as I fought. "There are hundreds of them in here."

ARMOUR INTEGRITY: 93%, my suit told me.

"We go now," Pariah said. "Or we die."

It vaulted through the water, and I followed. Backed towards the portal. A thin, reedy buzz was developing in the air, emanating from the bio-ship itself. Like a million angry insects, contained in a tiny space. My suit applied a noise-reduction filter to my audio channel, so loud was the noise becoming.

"What is that sound?" I said, half-turned to Pariah, but still tracking targets all around.

"Alarm," Pariah said. "Wake ship up."

The room was coming alive. The hibernation pods were now shifting. Shapes the size of fully matured Krell warriors were beginning to break free.

Meanwhile, the water level was rising again. *Please don't let me drown in here!* The HURT suit was sealed, and could surely withstand this sort of pressure, but panic isn't a logical thing. And make no mistake: I was seriously fucking panicking.

Fry swarmed my body, wriggling and putrid, bio-electricity flickering over grafted implants. The HURT's joints were formed of a flexible plastic-steel hybrid, and the thought that the eels might be able to breach the suit—*get into the armour, make contact with my skin*—sent a violent shiver through me. One had attached its wide jaws to the back of my knee, was thrashing to stay attached. I paused to kick the fry free, put it down with a burst from my suit-guns.

ARMOUR INTEGRITY: 72%.

"We're falling back," I said. "Keep the route open for us, Jackals!"

But the comms signal sputtered, whined with static disruption. There were screams coming from the ship, all around. Every XT on the vessel seemed to be converging on our location. Something lashed against my leg with force, made an effort to drag me under.

Behind us, the navigator-pod was beginning to glow.

"This is bad, right?" I asked Pariah.

Pariah nodded. "This is bad."

The thing inside—all twisted and surely, *surely* dead—squirmed, pushing its multiple limbs against the interior of the capsule. The skin-membrane stretched—

Not so fast. I opened fire with both guns. Hit the navigator-pod, face on.

The capsule ruptured. Suspension fluid sloughed out, rapidly polluting the surrounding water. Rounds stitched the navigator's head, ichor spraying from a dozen open wounds—

The navigator thrashed free of the pod.

A dozen rounds to the face and it was still Core-damned *alive*.

It used multiple limbs to anchor itself to the surrounding structures, head lolling, gills throbbing. Raised its enormous bulk up from the remains of the pod.

The universe closed in on me.

The navigator set all six limbs wide. Screamed.

I'd heard Krell scream, but this was something altogether different. It was *horrifying*. When the navigator's cold eyes fixed on me, I could think of only one word: *dead*. Those eyes were dead. They were silvered, mirrored orbs, unlike anything I'd ever seen on a Krell. Something terrible had happened aboard this ship, and I wanted no part of it.

"We go," Pariah reminded me.

Then I was up and moving.

More Krell were breaking out of their hibernation pods, roused by the alarm and the navigator's cry. Scanner returns all around.

"I'm coming in there," I heard Riggs saying, his voice choppy as though he was moving as he spoke. "Hold on!"

"Stay where you are! Keep the shuttle running!"

"I'm getting heavy resistance at my watch-point," Feng said. "I'm hit, but I'm still shooting."

"I don't know how much longer I can hold my post, either!" Lopez said.

I was at the portal now, and was grateful to see that it was still open. I was less thrilled that the liquid was now flooding the sealed compartments of the ship. It occurred to me that the bizarrely arranged tunnel network was perfect for retaining liquid, even in low gravity. A home-away-from-home for the Krell.

Pariah cut through the flood in a sort of combination run-swim. Its barb-guns were akin to a human semi-automatic weapon, spitting bone flechettes across our path. It moved fast and fired with an unerring accuracy.

The HURT was a big, ungainly exo-suit, made with brute force in mind: not well suited to this environment. My progress was painfully slow, and before I could clear the room another half-dozen silver shapes launched after me.

"Stay down, P," I said. "I'm going to try something."

"Understood," the Pariah replied.

INITIATE CLUSTER SHELLS, I directed my suit.

CONFIRMED, the suit said back to me.

There was a gentle tug from the launcher-rig on my shoulders, and a curtain of grenades showered the area. Explosives detonated, covering most of the chamber in razor-sharp debris. While the Krell didn't exactly fall back, I managed to clear a zone safe around us.

ARMOUR INTEGRITY: 69%. NULL-SHIELD COMPROMISED.

I squashed a fry underfoot, made it to the main tunnel. The navigator's life-sign was visible behind us.

"We're leaving the command chamber," I said. "Pariah's on point. Coming up on Novak's location now."

"I'll try not to shoot the fish," Novak said.

The Russian was an angry war-demon, surrounded by Krell bodies. He had a primary-form pinned to the wall with one of his mono-knives: speared through the thorax by the blade.

"Having fun, I see," I said to him.

Novak pulled his powered knife free of the alien's body. Tossed the still-squirming xeno aside.

"Is work," he said, shrugging.

Novak's suit was compromised in ten places, the armour plating ruptured by several angry-looking spines. Those, I knew, would get him soon enough. Each was loaded with bio-toxin, filled with incapacitating poison. Novak's medi-suite would keep him alive—flush his blood for as long as it could—but already he was slowing down. And for every Krell he killed, two took its place. Primary-forms erupted from every possible hiding place. Our survival could now be measured in seconds.

"Not coming back," he said, his words peppered with gasps. There was no time for talk, no time for planning. "Move. I hold position."

I slapped a hand to his shoulder as I passed him. "You did good, Novak. You did good."

He grunted. "Tell to someone who cares."

We left Novak—Russian lifer, general asshole, but more than anything else member of Jenkins' Jackals—to his bloody work. Yet more primary-forms—and even the bigger, angrier outlines of tertiaries and quads—were materialising behind us. Novak's fate was absolutely and utterly sealed, and there wasn't a thing I could do about it.

The water level was now rising faster and faster.

"Coming up on your location, Feng!" I said.

I activated the grenade harness again. More cluster grenades pumped the area, explosions muted by the liquid but no less lethal.

A Krell tertiary-form—almost as big as the HURT—lurched from an open shaft in the deckhead. Used every feature and ridge of the ship's interior for purchase—working in perfect concert with the environment, making rapid progress towards me.

I brought my guns round, fired. The alien evaporated, body parts scattering the tunnel. But the action had slowed me down, and I felt a weight on my back. I glimpsed a primary-form, shape jagged and angry, slashing at my life-support pack. Dragging me back the way we'd come.

ARMOUR INTEGRITY: 60%. SUGGEST DEFENSIVE ACTION.

"P!" I bellowed.

Pariah was on it. These two strains of the same species shared no kinship.

In abject rage, Pariah threw the primary-form against the wall—with enough force that the other alien's body-armour split, squirting ichor. Dead.

At just that moment, Feng swam into view.

"Go!" Feng yelled.

He twisted about, and Pariah worked with him to hold another tertiary-form against the wall. Feng punched the xeno hostile with one fist, again and again, while Pariah put a barb through its face.

ARMOUR INTEGRITY: 50%. AMMUNITION LEVELS CRITICAL.

My panic was blinding. I was completely submerged, visibility was shot, and the current in the ship's life-blood was pulling me back towards the navigator's chamber. My medi-suite had started to administer a steady dose of combat-drugs, just to keep me functional. I kicked out with my feet, tried to move forward.

"I'm not going to make this," I said, panting for breath. "There are too many of them."

"Take the upper shaft," Feng said. "I'm right behind you—"

A volley of bio-flechettes showered the area, a clutch of Krell gun-grafts on our six.

"*Incoming!*" I yelled.

Multiple impacts bounced off the HURT's armour plating. ARMOUR INTEGRITY: 40%.

"Up," Feng said, throwing his head upwards, firing his plasma rifle into the horde of Krell coming down the corridor. "Use that shaft!"

A vertical shaft gaped above me. Dark, tight, empty.

Pariah was already there. Limbs stretched across the tunnel mouth, like some massive spider. Climbing to the next deck.

"Come," it barked.

Feng tossed aside his rifle to give me a leg-up. His null-shield flashed with impacts, taking more heat as the Krell followed up their initial assault.

"I've got this," he said. Blood splattered the inside of his face-plate, foamed his lips. When had he been hit? His vitals were displayed on my HUD, and I knew then that he was as good as dead. "You've put on weight."

"Not funny," I said.

Feng grunted as he took the weight of my armoured foot. Hauled me up into the shaft. I gripped the insides of the tunnel with my fingertips. The sides were slick with algae, but as I drew my body up I used my knees and then my feet to climb.

And not a second too soon.

A brief bloom of light at the bottom of the shaft told me that Feng had gone out in a blaze of glory: as good an end as any sim could ever ask for. The backwash flared up the shaft, made the structure around me shake, but I was almost wedged into position and managed to hold tight.

Feng's bios flatlined on my HUD. Extraction confirmed. ARMOUR INTEGRITY: 32%.

Pariah's shadow was above me—clambering talon over claw despite the explosion. Whatever had happened on this ship had seriously pissed the xeno off...

We cleared the shaft and emerged into another tunnel—still dark, but at least this one was dry. A sickening realisation dawned on me: I didn't know where I was. The geography of this place was almost impossible to follow.

"We hear its signal," Pariah said. Corrected: "*Her* signal."

"Lopez's freq-beacon?" I asked, slamming a fist into the face of a Krell primary-form that dared to follow us up the shaft. The body fell away, back the way that we had come.

"Yes," it said. "This way."

As I hauled myself up into the tunnel, I found that my left leg dragged behind me. *I'm hit*, I registered. When had I suffered that damage? I'd barely noticed the haze of error messages and medical alerts that flooded my HUD, but now I fixed on one. LEFT LEG ATTENUATOR DAMAGED. AUTO-REPAIR SYSTEMS OFFLINE. When I tried to lift the leg, the joint locked up. OPERATIONAL STATUS CRITICAL, my suit told me. I stumbled, grabbed the wall to steady myself. Jesus. It wasn't just the HURT that was in pain. I was injured, and badly.

You cannot let yourself die in here, I thought. *Even if it is only simulated.*

"Suit," I ordered. "Open medi-suite. Give me everything you've got. Keep me alive."

The HURT didn't argue, because we both wanted the same thing: to get off this ship. There was a sudden thickness at the back of my throat, a very familiar reaction caused by dumping excessive combat-drugs into my bloodstream. Time seemed to stretch for a heartbeat...

...then everything snapped into hyper-clarity.

But I was living on borrowed time, and I knew that this body would soon crash and burn. The suit medi-suite was compensating, ruining this disposable skin to achieve the mission objective. With the hyper-alertness came a sense of elation. The limb unlocked, attenuator hissing in protest, and I staggered on with new purpose.

Pariah had been watching me throughout, head cocked.

"I'm good," I said. "For now."

Lopez's post was ahead, and I made out her outline.

"I see you, ma'am!" Lopez said. Her expression was incredulous behind her face-plate. "What happened to your armour?"

"No time to explain." Talking felt superfluous. Every word just took too long to say. "Novak and Feng are gone. Can you get Riggs on the comm?"

"I haven't been able to for a while—"

Lopez's null-shield fizzled as a secondary-form raked the tunnel with boomer-fire. There was an enormous thunderclap—the *boom* from which the weapon got its name—and a wave of heat washed the tunnel. I braced to take the force of the backdraft.

ARMOUR INTEGRITY: 19%.

Pariah ducked, escaping the explosion. Lopez wasn't so lucky. She let out a sick cry, crumpled against the wall, then literally disintegrated under the onslaught. Although it seemed that no one was getting out of this in one piece, some weren't going to get out of it in any pieces at all.

Pariah's bio-suit warped in the intense heat. The

voice-box failed to find any adequate translation as it let out a guttural roar. I fired simultaneous volleys from my guns, hoping to catch the shooter—

Behind me, Krell primaries poured from the shaft.

"P! They're on me!"

Move.

Guns firing.

Krell firing back.

More primaries.

Bodies everywhere.

Screaming.

ARMOUR INTEGRITY: 11%.

CRITICAL ERROR! CRITICAL ERROR! USER EVACUATION RECOMMENDED!

No breath to even scream.

A thatch of black limbs above me.

Krell everywhere.

ARMOUR INTEGRITY: 3%. SUIT COMPROMISED.

I was on my back, the HURT's HUD a mess of fractures. All I could see was an enormous Krell warrior over me, strands of black spittle dripping from its open maw, spattering the HURT's face-plate. The alien raised a claw. Brought it down over my head.

"I'm finished—"

Brilliant white light filled my vision. The sound of the Krell assault became distant and remote.

I expected to feel the pull of extraction, the crash as the neural-link between my real body and the simulant was severed. That was how this usually played out.

But not this time. Instead, my sim-senses began to reboot. I was down, but I wasn't out.

A sour, briny smell filled my helmet. Breached: the suit was breached. The Krell's scent was foreign and familiar and disgusting. Combined with the odour of burning Krell flesh: an unmistakable tang.

Crack-crack-crack.

That sound was just as familiar: a plasma rifle firing on full-auto, the noise so sharp that it was dampened by the suit's auto-senses. The body of my Krell attacker had been split in two, had collapsed across me, pinned me to the floor.

A voice came over the comms link: "Get up, Keira! Get up and get out of here!"

Riggs. Yelling at me. Incessantly.

I stirred from the floor and grappled the Krell's smoking corpse. The body was flecked with silver threads across the hide, eyes pools of mercury, and it felt impossibly heavy. That, I realised, was because my armour's man-amp was blown. My left arm was locked in place, and neither of my legs would function. Every grey plate of the suit was stitched with scars, pocked with stinger-spines, peppered with barbs...

"I...I told you to stay with the shuttle!" I said, my voice warbling in my throat, the words difficult to form properly through the miasma of drugs.

Riggs thrust out a hand in my direction. I went to grasp it, but I couldn't move. I collapsed back into the pile of dead and dying Krell.

"I couldn't let you go down like that," Riggs said.

"You abandoned your post..."

"Don't give me that shit," Riggs said. Already, bio-signs were building all round us: the Krell closing in for another assault. "You okay?"

"I'm still moving."

"Then do just that. Get out of here."

"No," I said. "I can't fly the shuttle!"

"It's automated," Riggs insisted. "I've set the flight controls as best I can."

"You take the black box."

Riggs hesitated for an instant. Mouth open, about to say something.

And that was all it took. A Krell primary lurched from above him, speared him with a talon through the shoulder. Riggs howled. He twisted about, hurled the alien over his shoulder and into the wall. It was a particularly ragged-looking specimen, face a mess of lesions and sores.

Pariah pummelled the infected alien with both barbguns. It was a mercy killing, in a way.

"It was a good plan," Riggs said. "But not so much any more." He slumped against the wall, clutching at the hole in his shoulder. "Fuck, that hurts. Now what are we going to do?"

I went to move again. The HURT's servo systems whined in dissent, sent me back to the floor. The suit wasn't going anywhere. Someone had to get the intel off this ship, but with Riggs and me down...That left only Pariah. No. It had to be me.

Acid rose in my gut, burnt all the way up my trachea.

"I'm bailing out."

"What...?" Riggs asked. His eyes were already unfocused, the blood loss and trauma doing their thing to his sim-skin.

"My armour's too badly damaged," I said.

Without any further delay—because, if I let myself think about it for any more than a split second, I knew that I was going to persuade myself that this was a ridiculous idea—I thought-commanded the HURT to EJECT USER.

GOODBYE, the armour said.

Then the torso cavity opened like a clamshell and spat me out. I smoothly pulled my arms free and flexed them. The rest wasn't quite so easy: my left leg felt numb, almost as unresponsive as the limbs of the HURT suit. *I can't believe I'm doing this.* The corridor was cold, but the air clammy and wet: a weird combination. I had no respirator, and the ship's smell alone was almost enough to stop me in my tracks.

"You're insane," Riggs said.

"I'm completing our objective. I have Pariah for security."

Still, it was hard to argue with him. I yanked at the feedback-cables that tied my stimulant to the HURT, severing any connection with the armour. Pretty much *everything* hurt. I was bleeding from a dozen injuries.

"If a mission's worth doing, it's worth dying for," I said.

"I hear that," Riggs muttered.

Without asking his permission, I leant in, unholstered the Widowmaker pistol at his belt, and checked the load. Full magazine of armour-piercing rounds. Riggs didn't resist, just watched on with awe in his eyes. Soon enough, he wouldn't need it anyway. Then I reached for the HURT suit's storage pouch—where the black box had been stored—and pulled it free. Handled without the HURT's man-amp, the box felt a good deal heavier.

"We go," Pariah insisted.

"One more thing."

There was a small manual control panel just inside the HURT's user compartment. The screen flashed erratically, the text difficult for me to read. But I jabbed at the controls, working fast, and selected the appropriate command. What little power was left in the suit was diverted to the set function.

"What are you doing?" Riggs said.

"You're going to have to take one for the team," I said. "I'm putting the suit's frequency-beacon in overdrive. Absolute amplification."

"Nice," Riggs said. We bumped fists. "I think that you'd better do as Pariah says."

I didn't need any more encouragement.

I turned and ran as fast as I could, down the tunnel. The deck was slippery and wet. I was wearing only a neoprene undersuit, the fabric slashed and torn, and the atmosphere prickled against my flesh. The crawling sensation I'd felt pretty much since we got aboard this ship had returned tenfold.

Then on to the home stretch: the hangar bay. Pariah was beside me, bounding now to cover the distance.

Riggs had left the shuttle's access-ramp deployed. In other circumstances, I'd have rebuked him for that. Right now, it was a godsend.

"In!" I shouted at P, as I leapt inside. Drank in lungfuls of atmosphere: it was mildly more palatable than that aboard the Krell bio-ship. I slipped, skidded, lightweight boots no good against the metal decking.

As soon as the xeno was inside, I slapped a palm on the emergency control. The ramp began to hum shut behind us.

"We're in!" I roared. "We're in the shuttle!"

Took me a moment to realise that I had no communications tech any more, that my rig had gone down with the HURT suit. I stumbled into the cockpit, saw that Riggs had left the transport hot, the control panel still illuminated. Slammed fists against the communicator control, desperate to hear another human voice. The Warhawk's console crackled with static.

"We read you!" said Zero, from the speaker unit. "What's happening? Your suit has gone off the grid."

"Riggs saved me," I said. "I think he's dead."

"Extraction confirmed," Zero said. "They're *all* dead."

"Do you have the black box?" Sergkov asked.

"That's an affirmative. P is with me."

"Then you need to get out of there."

"Double affirmative."

The shuttle rocked back and forth, and through the cockpit view-port I saw flashes of shadow in the hangar outside. Something big and angry thrashed behind the now-closed access-ramp. Had they already finished with the HURT suit, already torn apart the freq-beacon? I had no sense of time any more, only knew that the Krell weren't going to let me escape without another battle.

"Fuck you," I whispered, keying the shuttle's thrust control.

The boat was made for fast activation, and instantly the engine roared to life, spaceframe shuddering. Although I wouldn't have wanted to fly the shuttle with a proper human cargo, Riggs had been right: most of the controls had been pre-set. That would have to do.

More Krell bodies outside. The sound of metal shearing, the shuttle's hull being assaulted. Beyond the cockpit's view-port, the hangar's portal was a wide starfield.

IGNITION CONTROL READY, the shuttle's control panel indicated.

"Here goes."

CHAPTER TWENTY-TWO

CONDITION CRITICAL

The shuttle carried a basic chemical drive—nothing so fancy as a fusion engine or Q-drive, but it was fast enough.

The world shifted. The bio-ship's interior blurred.

We were in space. Outside.

And then came the hard burn.

Thank Gaia I was in a sim. My musculature locked up, the G-force pinning me to the pilot's chair. Every organ was squashed by the enormous pressure. I think that I screamed, but who knows? Everything was happening so fast—too fast—and the pounding in my head was almost unbearable. The comedown on combat-drugs is a bitch, and I knew that I was now riding the tail end of that particular comet: the simulant nearing end of life.

Warnings filled the Warhawk's control console. A siren sounded in the cockpit, the shuttle's AI speaking, but the words were lost to the throb of my own heartbeat.

Were the Krell giving chase? No way of knowing right now. I hadn't seen any aerospace support on the *Azrael*, but we'd only explored a tiny fraction of the ship.

When I tried to lift my arm, to activate the local scanner, it slapped back down, restrained by the G-force.

I couldn't see or sense Pariah's response, and I wondered whether the fish had been crushed by gravity. It was hard to care when I was in this much pain. I ground my teeth. All that kept me going was the assurance that it would soon be finished.

"I'm taking over control from here," Carmine's voice cut in on the comms. She sounded so far away, like she was on a different plane of existence.

"Please do," I managed.

The *Santa Fe*'s battered hull was dead ahead, coming up fast to meet us.

"Don't want you crashing into my ship, after all," she said, in her matronly way. "Not after everything you've just been through."

The shuttle's grav-brakes hit, and the boat began to decelerate. That was almost as unpleasant as the acceleration, but at least it was briefer. The *Fe*'s outer docking door was open, and the shuttle—now slowed to a speed that my simulated skin found far more agreeable—slid into the bay, skids clanking against the deck, generating a dull roar through the Warhawk's cabin.

"You are damaged," Pariah said. Its voice warbled erratically, as though it was speaking to me underwater.

"Huh, you're not dead after all."

I tried to sit up in the cockpit, but the body resisted. Didn't feel like it was mine any longer.

"Do you read me, Lieutenant Jenkins?" came Sergkov's voice, squawking from the console speaker. "Are you still operational?"

"Negative," I slurred. "Multiple injuries. It's over. I'm done…"

There was noise at Sergkov's end of the connection. Something was happening on the bridge. I laughed, but the sound was horrible and wet and sent shivers of pain through my ribcage. How could anything else go wrong? Hadn't I done enough? The black box was suddenly in my hands, slick with my blood.

"Extract," Sergkov ordered. "Feng and Lopez will take care of the Pariah."

I turned to the alien beside me. Parts of its armour had been torn away, revealing charred skin beneath, and it had taken several impacts to the torso, stinger-spines poking through ruptured bio-plate. Dark Krell blood splattered the inside of the Krell's face-plate, had stained every surface it came into contact with.

"You okay?"

The Pariah nodded. "You go now."

"You say that a lot," I said.

Then it raised a barb-gun to my head, and fired.

The neural-link severed, and I jumped the length of the *Santa Fe*, the simulation collapsing around me. I was back in my tank, in the familiar surroundings of the SOC.

Of course, I'd never really left my body. It had been here all along, remotely controlling the sim in the hellish environs of the Krell bio-ship. But it was hard to think that way sometimes, because the memories of what had just happened—like a nightmare, vivid and thick, the product of an overworked imagination—came back with me. My real body carried the agonies of the sim and especially the kiss of the barb-round to my temple, but the sensation was already fading. I rested a hand against the inside of the tank's canopy, felt the conducting gel begin to stir and evacuate the capsule—

The world around me swayed.

"Get dressed!" Zero yelled.

"Wh—what ... ?" I slurred.

I wanted to explain that I needed time to become accustomed to my body again, that whatever she had to tell me could wait, but the urgency in Zero's voice, the expression on her face: those things told me that I should do as she said.

"Just get dressed. Captain Carmine wants us on the bridge."

So I clambered out of the tank. With Riggs at my shoulder, I struggled into a pair of fatigues, still dripping with gel from the simulator. Riggs was in his real skin, but wore a Navy-class flak vest that barely fitted his muscled chest: with the words UAS *SANTA FE* printed in bright white letters across the plate.

"Come on, come on," he urged me.

"Bridge, now!" Novak yelled from the corridor outside.

The ship is moving, I suddenly realised. *And I can feel it.* Except that wasn't possible, not normally. The inertial gravity field held us in a tight envelope, protected us from the effects of acceleration...

"Unless the inertial damper is failing," I decided.

"You got it," Riggs said. "You've got to get moving, Keira!"

Zero and Riggs propped me up. A wave of anxiety came off Zero, her eyes wide. Her command station in the centre of the SOC was long-abandoned, and gone was the sense of adventure.

She isn't just watching this any more. She's living it, and maybe dying it too.

The overhead lamps sputtered, and the deck was plunged into darkness.

Novak grabbed my shoulder, hauled me out of the SOC.

Riggs filled me in on the latest news as I stumbled the distance across the ship. The situation had developed at a terrifying rate: I reckoned that Riggs had extracted from his sim seconds before I'd touched down in the *Fe*'s dock, and yet so much had happened in that brief space of time.

"Deck two is gone," he said, solemnly. "Carmine is calling a ship-wide emergency."

"But we're not bailing out," Zero added, machine-gun rapid.

"Not yet," Riggs said. "While you were on the *Azrael*, the Navy crew have been tracking activity throughout this sector."

"Then who's shooting at us?" I asked.

"Whoa," Novak yelled, almost crashing into Pariah as the xeno rounded the corner. "Easy, fish!"

"I'm watching it," said Feng, holding a sim-class Widowmaker pistol in both hands, trained on the alien. He carried the *Hannover*'s black box in his other hand, and was looking down at the module as though he couldn't quite believe it was here.

Pariah ignored both of them. Cocked its head like it was listening to a distant song that only it could hear. The alien still wore its bio-suit, and although it was oozing ichor from every open wound on the armour, the lacerations were beginning to seal: its blood coagulating. Enhanced regeneration—perhaps another of Dr. Skinner's gifts.

The deck shuddered, a cold gust of atmosphere making my skin tingle.

"Hull breach," Novak declared, as if I hadn't already deduced that for myself. "The missile bay is gone."

"I still haven't heard who is actually firing on us," I said. "Will someone give me a proper sit—"

A siren sounded overhead, cutting off my words, and the ship's PA system crackled.

"All personnel to the bridge," Carmine declared. "*Now*."

The *Santa Fe*'s meagre crew filled the chamber, and worked with a focus that I hadn't witnessed from them so far. Even Carmine: processing data faster than I'd ever seen, hard-jacked to her command console. The captain's eyes flitted between the display unit in front of her, and the *Fe*'s near-space holo, as she babbled commands at her staff.

"Crew to weapons stations!" she barked.

Sergkov appeared from a recess of the bridge. "Where the hell are your people, Captain? We don't have time for this!"

Lieutenant Yukio jabbed keys at her console. "Fabian and Klein were on deck four, checking the missile bay—"

"Then they're gone," Feng said. "We've just passed the missile bay, and it's open to vac."

"That's a confirm on the damaged deck," another officer replied. "We have venting atmosphere in three modules." A wireframe holographic of the *Santa Fe* span in front of the staffer, flashing with numerous red markers, indications that the ship had suffered significant damage. "Missile bay charlie has been hit."

"Jettison the tubes," Carmine said. "We can't risk those warheads cooking off."

"Aye, ma'am."

"That's one of your primary armaments, Captain," Sergkov said. "What are you going to fight them with?"

"It's either that," Carmine said, "or this ship goes up with the missiles. Have you ever experienced the uncontrolled explosion of a high-yield warhead? In your real skin, I mean?"

Sergkov set his jaw. Turned to Feng. "Give me the *Hannover*'s black box, Private."

Feng very reluctantly handed over the memory module, and the MI man took it.

"Hope it was worth it," Feng said.

"It was all we came here for," Sergkov replied.

"All we came here for?" I repeated, letting the words bounce around my head. "We were supposed to be an escort operation, Sergkov. Not recovery."

"This is not the time," Sergkov said.

Riggs met my eyes with a hard glance. "First we've heard about it…"

"Holy shit," Lopez said. Her face was still loaded with lacerations, pocked by the simulated deaths she'd just suffered on the *Azrael*. "How the fuck are we going to fight that thing?"

Then I saw for myself why everyone was so spooked.

The *Azrael* dominated the view-port and the tactical display. The sheer enormity of her bulk suddenly became apparent, but that wasn't the worst of it.

The misleadingly delicate-looking drive spines that ringed the ship's aft—reinforcing the impression that the vessel had more in common with a deep-sea creature than a starship—were no longer a dull grey. They now glowed a pure, eye-watering blue—like the most inviting ocean I'd ever seen: the pictures of the western seaboard's coast my grandpa had kept on his wall. The black hull flickered with sporadic light, bridge-blisters illuminating.

"She's waking up…" I whispered.

Plumes of frozen fluid—ejecta from dormant systems—shot across space, and the ship was caged by debris as it threw off the vestiges of interstellar sleep. Tiny specks of light raced along the hull: attack ships that looked like silver needles, starlight reflecting off their hulls.

"Null-shields up, three-sixty degrees," Carmine ordered.

"Aye, ma'am. Shields up."

Carmine's mechanical leg was jerking uncontrollably, and she was sweating heavily: almost through the back of her fatigues. The hand on her leg carried that crumpled picture of her daughters again, and now she didn't seem to care who saw it.

"What is happening to fish?" Novak said. "Does not look so good."

Pariah's features had adopted a sort of blank serenity. It did not react at all to Novak's comment.

"Maybe it's infected…" Lopez mused. "Jesus, what if the plague, or virus, or whatever it was on the bio-ship… What if the Pariah is infected with it?"

"You aren't paid to think about things like that," Sergkov said. "You're paid to go where I say, and die doing it."

"Not for real, we're not," Riggs said.

Sergkov's nostrils flared. His face was chiselled from stone, his brow determined and resolute. "Turn of phrase, Corporal. Nothing more."

"I think that we can safely say that Pariah is out of the game," Riggs said. He spoke with particular vehemence, a tone that I hadn't heard from him before. I wasn't sure that I liked it much. "Fucking waste of life getting it in the first place. Your plan failed, Major."

"Hostile starship is moving," another officer said. "I'm detecting energy readings consistent with weapons charging…"

"Pull back, maximum thrust," Carmine chanted. "I want as much distance as possible between us and that bio-ship."

"Can we make a quantum-jump from here?" I asked.

Carmine never took her eyes from her terminal. "Not until we clear the Gyre."

A lance of energy speared across space, from the *Azrael*. Met the *Santa Fe*'s null-shield and dispersed, but close enough that several of the *Fe*'s stations reported damage.

"*Azrael* is giving chase," an officer declared. "She's accelerating hard."

"Give me drive control now," Carmine said, the pitch of her voice rising.

"Hostile is targeting us," Yukio declared. "Multiple tracking systems."

"Initiate counter-measures," Riggs said. "Make an evasive manoeuvre!"

"Let the Navy see to it," Feng insisted, holding an open hand on Riggs' chest, pushing him back into his seat. He nodded at me, his expression cool and neutral, half of his features claimed by the glow of the bio-ship's lighting drive, now almost painfully bright through the view-ports.

We're not getting out of this, he silently communicated. *And I know it.*

Just as silently, I found myself pondering whether clones worried about meeting their makers. Feng and I hadn't deigned to discuss his exact religious position. Another question that I'd never get the chance to ask.

Riggs reached over and fleetingly grabbed my hand. I tried to ignore him, pushed it away: felt bad that he was almost certainly going to die out here with a bitch of an older lover.

"Not now," was all I could say. "Not here."

Anything that he might've had to say by way of reply was lost as the *Azrael* attacked. Bio-cannons opened up.

"Brace," Carmine said.

Space was awash with energy discharge, and the view-ports polarised to hold back the glare. The tactical display flickered intermittently.

"Weapons operators!" Carmine yelled. "Get me my weapons trained on that ship!"

Yukio shook her head. "We're all that's left, Captain. I'm not seeing any more life-signs aboard the *Fe*."

This was it, then: the Jackals, and a half-dozen remaining staffers. Everyone else had been caught in the venting decks, in the chaos of the initial attack. *I'm going to have to do something about this*, I thought. I struggled out of my crash-couch.

"Jackals, get to the weapons stations," I said. "We aren't going down without a fight."

Carmine smiled at me. "That's my girl."

The Jackals moved to crew stations, jacking to data-ports.

"Will it do us any good?" Lopez said.

Looking out into space, at the slumbering giant that was the *Azrael*, I honestly couldn't say.

There were five weapons stations arranged around the edge of the bridge: immersion-pods with their own specialised data-ports and sensory-deprivation helms. I slipped into the nearest, was vaguely aware of the rest of the team doing the same, and fastened the helm into place. I swapped my eyes for the *Santa Fe*'s external sensors, immersed myself in the datascape. I was no starship weapons officer—with the exception of maybe Riggs, none of us was qualified for this—but one of the benefits of being simulant-operational is that the technology is universally compatible. A wealth of battle-data flooded my synapses, registered in the machine-implants that every operator carried.

USER RECOGNISED, the *Santa Fe* told me. WEAPONS FREE.

The *Azrael* appeared not as a bio-ship any longer, but as a target. A collection of data on the subject scrolled across my mind's eye, filtered through to the weapons at our disposal. The *Santa Fe* wasn't made for direct combat, but we had some offensive measures. Her most powerful weapon was an ion accelerator. I took that, while

Riggs and Novak were on the railguns, Lopez on the plasma cannon battery, and Feng took point defence lasers.

"Just shoot," I ordered. "And don't stop until you're dead."

Novak grunted across the bridge. "Is not hard."

"Dying or shooting?" Lopez asked.

"Where I come from, is both," Novak said. "Railgun away."

The *Azrael* advanced at a frightening speed now, gaining momentum. Bio-plasma cannons fired from its flanks, picking off incoming railgun munition before it got into range. Offensive weapons packages met defensive counter systems. The Krell had an organic equivalent to everything we had machined.

The *Santa Fe* was smaller, more manoeuvrable, and Carmine did a good job of maximising that advantage. She initiated thrust when she could, giving us the best chance of countering incoming weapons fire.

We scored a couple of hits on the bio-ship, but nothing significant: nothing that would put the ship down. It was a war of attrition. The Krell bio-ship was so much bigger. Although most of the *Azrael*'s return fire was absorbed by the *Fe*'s null-shield, that couldn't go on forever. The *Fe* took at least two hits, suffering damage to non-critical systems.

"Railgun bay beta is empty," said Novak.

"Energy reserve on point defence lasers is reaching critical condition," Feng declared.

"We're going to have to drop shield on the portside—" an anonymous officer said.

"No!" Carmine shouted. "Keep all shields raised!"

Plasma suddenly rippled along the *Azrael*'s hull. A cheer went up across the bridge—the exhausted and beleaguered crew grateful to see any effective action against the monstrous bio-ship. Several further explosions followed.

I looked sideways, to the station next to me: crewed by Lopez. She was on the plasma battery—must've been responsible for the successful hit.

"Well done, Lopez," I said. "Good shot."

Lopez bobbed her head in the sensory-deprivation helm, curls of dark hair escaping beneath the visor. I could only see the lower half of her face inside the helmet. She was biting at the inside of her lip.

"Ah, ma'am, that wasn't me..."

CHAPTER TWENTY-THREE

THE ARK-SHIP

My initial reaction was that Lopez was just wrong.

She was the operator of the plasma battery, and of course she'd fired it! Nervously, I checked the ship's near-space scanner—a projection on my mind's eye, an element of the ship-to-operator interface. There was nothing else within range, but the scopes were scrambled.

"Quit fucking around, Lopez."

"I . . . I'm not."

"Then what just happened?" Sergkov demanded.

"I'm reading an enormous energy discharge . . ." a crewman said.

I tore off my sensory-helm, yanked the jacks from my data-ports. Meanwhile, the tactical display registered another power fluctuation.

"The *Azrael*'s been hit," I said. "*Someone* is firing on her. And if it wasn't us . . ."

The Krell bio-ship had just taken a hit to the bow, and was breached. Frozen liquid sprayed from its insides. Although the engine was still alight, the warship listed precariously. I didn't know exactly what internal systems had been damaged, but the impact had obviously done something to disable the drive function.

"I'm getting more data," Carmine said. "Can someone verify this?"

Yukio swallowed so hard that I thought she might be sick. "Yes, ma'am. It's a quantum-space breach."

As ever, we hadn't detected the ship until it was virtually on top of us—at least in terms of deep-space combat—but now I could see that a *second* Krell warship had breached the quantum barrier.

Not just a second.

A third, then a fourth, appeared on the scanner. All jumping into real-space, making hard-burn towards the diseased bio-ship. A war party of at least six Krell scoutships had soon assembled.

"What are they doing out here on their own?" I asked. "I've seen that ship pattern before, and it doesn't usually sail this deep without support…"

"Don't question our luck," Riggs said. "They're on our side. We've got friendlies inbound!"

The *Azrael* was soon surrounded by the scoutships, coming at her from all angles. The newcomers were fast and well armed. Bio-plasma and seeker missiles poured over the enemy bio-ship.

But the *Azrael* was no easy target, and she fought back. An energy lance punched the dark and hit one of the scoutships. The smaller vessel's null-shield flickered, failed to absorb the impact. The lance-strike was a solid hit—went right through the ship. The vessel exploded instantly. There was, I realised, no telling which way this battle would go.

Pariah loomed over the tactical display. An aura of agitation, of something completely alien, prickled around the creature.

"They fight others," it said.

"The infected?" Zero questioned. "The Krell aboard the *Azrael*?"

"Not of Collective," Pariah said. "Not same. Purging." The Krell nodded its crested head at Zero, and repeated "*Infected.*"

"We can talk about this later," Sergkov broke in.

"Hang on," I said. "We're seeing Krell fighting Krell. That's not normal behaviour. Aren't you a little more surprised by all this?"

"Of course I am," he said. I noticed that he was clutching the *Hannover*'s black box to his chest, the battered case reflecting the bridge's low running lights. "But we remain at risk with enemy Krell in the vicinity."

"'Enemy Krell'?" I said. "Another interesting choice of words, Major."

"Pull us out," Carmine said, her voice quiet and firm. "Leave them to their war."

"Main thrust control engaged," Yukio declared.

The Jackals had by now all disengaged from the weapons stations, and watched our progress on the tactical display. We were pulling back, hard, making decent progress out of the Gyre. We were soon at the edge of the stellar anomaly. The *Santa Fe*'s scanners began to probe space beyond the sensor-void, increasing in efficiency outside the Gyre.

"We're going to make it," Lopez said, balling her hands into fists. There was considerable distance between us and the *Azrael*. The bio-ship was ignoring us. "We're going to be okay."

"Is great story for Senator, yes?" Novak said. "To tell Daddy how we escape the fish heads?"

"We get out of this alive," Lopez replied, "I'll tell anyone who wants to hear."

"Can we jump yet?" I asked.

"Always with the jumping," Carmine said. I caught

the hint of a smile on her lips, but she quickly turned away from me, not willing to give in to hope. "Another few hundred klicks and we can risk it. We've lost two decks to the void, and we'll need to conduct some emergency repairs before we even think about engaging the Q-drive for a longer jump—"

"I've got another incoming signal!" Yukio said, throwing alerts across the bridge again. "Watch your scanners. We're not done yet."

Like a shark following blood, came another signal. On a tight trajectory, the bogie was heading straight towards our position.

"That's a big signal," Feng said.

It had now materialised in frightening detail. A titanic vessel, dwarfing even the *Azrael*, followed the initial war party.

"Ark-ship," I said. "Incoming."

Out of the frying pan and into the fusion reactor.

This is a day of firsts, I thought, as I watched the living biological menace gradually appear on the tactical display.

Two decades and then some, objective, in the Alliance Army, and I'd seen some serious shit. It was easy, some days, to think that I'd seen it all.

Today was *not* one of those days.

I'd never seen an ark-ship up close. Science Division had only glimpsed the arks, received precious snippets of intelligence from those who had been taken prisoner by the Krell during the war. Images of the vast, globular ships had been blasted across briefings—with Navy crew being told to watch for them, to gather intelligence without actually engaging them—but no one I had ever met had seen one for real.

Ark-ships were the very pinnacle of Krell bio-tech, much bigger than anything the Alliance had ever built, made for the singular purpose of transporting Krell colonies through deep-space. The closest analogy in the human lexicon was a mobile space station. This was a star fort designed to skip Q-space.

The ship was vaguely spherical but irregularly shaped, reminding me of an asteroid. Hull a dull charcoal, pocked by a hundred lifetimes' sailing the void, with an engine erupting from the rear that trailed blue light as it cut thrust. The ship was accompanied by a protective escort, some of the scoutships we'd seen earlier breaking off and falling into a safe pattern around her weathered hull. There was enough firepower in that war-fleet to kill us ten times over.

"Can someone please tell me how we missed this coming in on the quantum?" Sergkov yelled.

"Shut the fuck up," Carmine said. "And keep your voice down."

"I don't think we'll ever understand these things…" Feng muttered.

Something that big breaching the Q had consequences. The ark threw out a disruption wave: sent ripples through quantum- and real-space. Electromagnetic disturbance was extreme—equivalent to a dozen Navy EMP mines. The *Santa Fe*'s systems-shielding was no match: all of her weapons died, immediately. Across the bridge, the lights went out.

"We're losing gravity!" Zero exclaimed.

I felt my body gradually lifting from the deck, saw Zero grappling with the edge of a console bank, as the gravity drive gave up.

"Life support is down," Yukio said.

"Initiate reboot," Carmine ordered. "Initiate a reboot now!"

"I…I'm not getting anything from my console," Yukio said, her voice breaking. I'd been here before, seen how the veneer of military discipline could so easily crack. "We've suffered extensive systems damage, and the auto-repair module isn't responding."

"We'll run a cold reboot on the life-support functions," Carmine said. Her unwillingness to give up was quite admirable. "Get a body down to the energy core and run—"

"That thing is advancing on us!" Lopez said, pointing outside.

I lurched across the bridge. Grabbed Zero's shoulder, pulling her into a safer position. She clutched my hand. Sweat had broken across her forehead, tiny droplets of perspiration escaping in zero-G.

"It's going to be okay," I said. "It'll be fine."

"How can you say that?" Zero replied, sounding almost hysterical. "How many of them are there on that ship?"

She looked past me, over my shoulder, at the advancing ark-ship. It filled the view-port now: so close that I could see every crater on its hull, could see the dozens of docking bays that lined its outer skin.

"I don't know," I said, honestly. "I only know that you're going to be okay."

The ark was studded with coral-like protrusions, with bone growths that belied any rhyme or reason. The ship had a randomness to it: as though, whereas humanity had tried to tame nature, to make everything fit just so, the Krell had instead chosen to embrace chaos. As I saw the full scale of the hostile, it struck me that even if we had control of our weapons systems, the *Santa Fe* didn't have enough ordnance to make so much as a scratch on the ark-ship's hide.

But Zero didn't need to hear any of that. She was shaking. Her auburn hair escaped around her head like a halo, uncontrolled, reflecting her state of mind. Feng was at her side now, too, and I let the pair embrace, bodies floating away from me.

"What's happening to the fish?" Lopez asked.

Pariah drifted across the bridge, limbs thrashing against terminals and crew alike. Its voice-box emitted a series of garbled warning messages, as though unable to translate any longer, and it was oil-wet, a repugnant odour washing the bridge.

"It's a two-way mirror," I said, to Sergkov. "That was how Dr. Skinner described the Pariah's connection."

Sergkov hissed. "So?"

"Maybe whatever is aboard that ship is trying to bring Pariah back into the fold," I offered.

"And that's good how?" Lopez asked.

"I didn't say it was good," I replied. "But perhaps we can make contact with them."

Pariah touched a claw to its head. "They are Kindred of the Silver Talon Collective. Our kin."

Was the Pariah tapping into the Collective, becoming lost in the abyss of shared intelligence? I remembered what Dr. Skinner had told me: that the pariah-forms were separate from the rest of the Collective, but still connected to it.

The ark-ship threw a shadow across the *Santa Fe*, cast by the distant stars. One of the many hangar bays, which looked increasingly like an open maw, lined up with our position.

"Gravity readings are fluctuating," Yukio declared. "It's... it's sucking us inside."

"Can it do that?" Lopez said, looking around the room for confirmation that this was in fact possible.

There was no answer to her question.

"It wasn't supposed to be like this," Sergkov said, sighing. "I'm issuing an abandon ship order. All hands make for the evacuation pods. It's over." Sergkov was broken, and his words sent a ripple of hysteria across bridge.

"Bullshit," I said. "We board those pods, we'll die in them."

The ark-ship grew larger with each passing heartbeat. A planet, capable of generating its own gravity field: the *Fe* like a moon, trapped within its orbit.

"I'll escort you to the SOC," I said, "and the Jackals will get skinned up. We'll stand our ground and repel any Krell that try to board the *Fe*."

"My orders are to abandon this ship!" Sergkov said. "Anything else is suicide!"

His hackles rose, eyes burning from across the chamber. No one moved. Sergkov's hand dropped to his pistol, rested on the holster buckle.

Riggs, Lopez, and Feng floated around me. Novak just a little closer, making it plain that if anyone was going to shoot, he'd react soon thereafter.

"No," Carmine said. "Jenkins is right. We have to make a stand."

"Five sims against *that*?" Sergkov said, tossing his head towards the view-port and the advancing ship.

I said nothing but met Sergkov's gaze. He was silent for a moment.

Finally, he said, "Execute the order. We'll repel them."

I nodded. "Very good, sir. Jackals, let's move. Yukio, try to hard-restart all ship's systems."

"You've got some balls on you, Jenkins," Carmine said, a thin smile on her lips. "The SOC is still running. You're on emergency power."

Only then did I notice that Carmine's carbine had been stowed beneath her terminal. She removed the weapon and harnessed herself in her workstation.

"We'll get Pariah down to medical," I said. I glanced at the crumpled, sweated abomination of a xeno. It looked pitiful. "I think that it may be our only method of communication with the ark-ship."

"How long until that thing *swallows* us?" Carmine asked. "I need a number, Yukio."

Yukio shrugged, an exaggerated motion in zero-G. "Two minutes, ma'am. Maybe less."

"You heard that," Carmine said to me. "That's how long you have to make preparations. Crew, you might like to break open the weapons locker. This is New Ohio, all over again." She stroked the stock of her carbine, the arming stud turning green.

"Second time you've said that this mission," I said.

"And yet I've still got my other leg."

"Good luck, Carmine," I said, brushing my hand against her shoulder as I drifted past, already making my way to the hatch.

"I have the distinct feeling that we're all going to need it," Carmine said. "So the same to you too."

Sergkov and I took point, jointly supporting Pariah's bulk—not an easy task in zero-G—and kicked off down the corridor as fast as we could. Feng and Zero stirred close behind, Zero plotting our route through the pressurised decks of the ship. Riggs, Novak, and Lopez took up the rear.

"That way," Zero said, pointing ahead. "Take the main corridor to Junction B-6."

That was the spine linking the command modules such as the bridge, Medical, Engineering. The walls were plastered with words in printed glowing letters: EVACUATION PODS THIS WAY—DECKS 4–19 TO 4–23. Sergkov glanced sidelong at the open doors, at the activated control panels. I could see that he was tempted, but our confrontation on the bridge had put pay to any further discussion about abandoning ship.

I readjusted Pariah's mass under my arm. The xeno was shivering, its voice-box chirping with machine-code that could just as well be an alien language.

The air tasted metallic and cold. Behind us, Riggs, Novak, and Lopez had stopped at a bright red box that was set into the wall. Labelled EMERGENCY, it was loaded with supplies such as respirators, oxygen bottles, flare guns: everything a girl could want in the event of a hull breach. Riggs took to distributing the stash.

"Keep up!" I barked. "Feng, go get them. We don't have time for this."

"Copy that," Feng said. He broke off from Zero, retraced our steps to hurry on the rest of the squad.

Back to Sergkov, I said, "You knew about the *Hannover*, didn't you?"

Sergkov's tongue shot from between his lips, licked them experimentally. Snake-like. When he answered, I was surprised by his honesty.

"Yes. We knew."

"And that was why we came out here, wasn't it? To collect the black box, I mean."

"Not just the black box, but whatever was left of the *Hannover*. That was always our objective. But everything I've done, everything that has happened…It was for the good of the Alliance. You have to believe that."

I shook my head. It wasn't far to Medical now. "That's not how the Jackals will see it."

"I chose you because I knew that I could trust you. I knew that if anyone could get this done, it would be you."

"Flattery will get you everywhere but off this ship. What's really happening out here, Sergkov?"

"I'm trying to stop a war," he said, bluntly. "What you saw on that bio-ship: it's only the beginning. I'm not in this alone."

We were on a roll so far as honesty was concerned,

and it struck me that this was the most intel Sergkov had shared with me the whole mission. I chanced my luck with another question.

"And Cooper?" I asked. "Who is he? How does the Black Spiral fit into this? Don't pretend that you don't know."

"Cooper is a prime target for the Alliance intelligence agencies. He, and the Spiral, are—"

There was a yell from behind us. *"Ma'am!"*

Zero's voice. Shrill, panicked.

I whirled around. Only managing to control the movement of Pariah's bulk with Sergkov's help.

I hadn't realised how far the Jackals had dropped behind. The squad was still back at the evac-pods, encumbered with survival gear—the straps of breather masks and cables from oxy-bottles floating around them like a cloud of flies—made slow by zero-G. Riggs, Novak, Lopez, and Feng.

Zero kicked off after me, pointing at the ceiling frantically. Indicating to something no one else had noticed. I frowned, tried to follow her words as she shouted over the emergency klaxon.

"Hatch!"

The light set into the deckhead had begun to flash.

"Emergency breach detected in module B-13," the AI said. "Please evacuate this corridor. Safety protocols initiated."

The whole ship was subject to emergency safety routines, and a series of bulkhead hatches set across the main decks would seal in the event of decompression. That was basic starship protocol: an age-old method to inhibit the spread of fire, or prevent atmospheric breach across multiple modules. It was supposed to save lives, not take them.

Every face was stricken into a kind of living rigor

mortis. I was paralysed as I played out in my head what was going to happen.

The hatch is going to seal.

That will cut the corridor in two.

The Jackals will be sealed on one side of the ship, and Pariah, Sergkov, Zero, and I on the other.

"Away from the door!" I said, waving at Zero, trying desperately to clear the distance to the hatch.

Already, it was coming down, the hydraulics whining as the six-inch-thick metal panel extended from the deckhead. The AI continued that warning, and the deck rumbled around us.

Sergkov snapped out of it first. He disentangled himself from Pariah, pushed off down the corridor, towards the sealing hatch.

"Get to the SOC!" he shouted as he went, without turning to look at me. "I'll see to the door!"

The Jackals were closing the distance now, abandoning their salvage. Lopez was yelling, Riggs hauling her on.

"Chu!" Zero said, fingers outstretched, clawing at the corridor walls to pull herself towards the door.

"Don't," Sergkov ordered. He stabbed at the console. Swearing in Russian, sweat swelling across his brow. "The lieutenant will need you in the SOC."

"We can't leave them!" Zero wailed back.

The door was closing much faster than the Jackals could move.

"We can use my override code," Sergkov said. The control console was on the Jackals' side; Sergkov ducked beneath the hatch, now almost to the deck, and began operating the terminal.

Novak reached the door, Feng crouching behind him. Eyes on Zero and fingers clutching at the bottom of the closing hatch.

"Get it open!" Lopez said. Now I could only see the lower legs of each trooper, limbs frantically working as they floated.

"I'm trying," Sergkov shouted back. "My override code isn't working."

"Come through!" Zero suggested, clutching at the bottom of the hatch: at the six-inch gap beneath it. The edge was toothed, made to fit into the grooved markings in the deck, to make the seal airtight between sections.

But already that was impossible. I knew then that nothing the squad did would make a difference, that in their real skins and without strength-amplifiers there was no way they were coming back from behind that hatch.

With a resolute, final thud, the security door came down, and Pariah, Zero, and I were sealed on our side of the corridor.

"Is there another way round?" Zero asked.

"You know there isn't," I said.

There was no sound from the other side of the door. Whether that was because the hatch was so thick, or because the rest of the corridor had been exposed to vacuum, I couldn't say. I didn't want to think about that possibility right now. I cancelled the thought-stream: focused on the only objective I could.

Survival.

I grabbed Zero's shoulder, shook it.

"Come on. We need to go."

CHAPTER TWENTY-FOUR

BAD KRELL

It was some small irony that Medical wasn't far from the sealed bulkhead: the Jackals had been so close to making it that it hurt. I dragged both Zero and Pariah as best I could, the stitches to my ribcage from the North Star incident tugging, reminding me that my body had some very real limits that were presently being pushed to the extreme.

"They might be okay," Zero mumbled. "They might've taken an evac-pod…"

I knew the truth. *If the corridor decompressed at their end, there was no way that they made it.*

"They might," I said. Better to humour her than to crush her hopes, no matter how unrealistic. Zero had been through enough. "The best thing that we can do to help them right now is to get the SOC operational."

"Right," Zero said, a manic light glowing behind her eyes. Like this was the first time I had suggested the idea. "Right. Perhaps I can get the ship's security cameras working," she said, speaking more to herself than me. "I can plot the Jackals' position."

"No. You need to get my simulator working, and I'm

going to make transition. Then we can decide how best to help the team."

"But Chu—"

"I need you to hold it together, Zero. For Feng's sake, and for the Jackals' sake. Understand?"

Irrational as it was, Zero looked like she was going to argue with me for an instant, but then the fire left her expression. She was lost. Reminded me of when I'd first set eyes on her.

"I got it," Zero said. "I'm okay."

After the relative dark of the *Santa Fe*'s corridors, the SOC was dazzlingly well lit: every terminal activated, five simulator-tanks throbbing with blue gel. The location felt out of time and place—working technology on an otherwise failing ship. I tried not to take in the Jackals' names printed on each tank, their operating figures on the scoreboard monitor.

Riggs is probably gone.

I was surprised at the sudden rush of emotion that I felt. Whatever I said, whatever I'd done, Riggs meant *something* to me. I couldn't lie to myself about it any more.

"Help me with this," I said.

With obvious unease—brow knitted, lips pressed tight—Zero looped an arm under Pariah and assisted me with the Krell's bulk. I knew I was asking a lot of her, and wanted to tell her how much I appreciated it, but time was quickly evaporating.

"How are we going to treat it?" Zero said. "I mean, I have no training in this field. If only Dr. Skinner had survived, maybe he would've known what to do…"

"Well he didn't, and now we have to do what we can."

"Then what's the plan?"

"First, we secure P. Then I'm getting into the tank."

Pariah slipped from my hands. Spasmodic twitches

rippled over the alien's body, limbs occasionally thrashing as we moved. I had literally no idea how we were going to control whatever medical emergency the Krell was experiencing, but I knew that we had to try. Together, we dragged the alien to a treatment couch. Zero grabbed some archaic-looking straps that dangled from the edges of the couch, used to secure patients during low-G.

"Hey, P," I said, "can you still hear me?"

The alien stared at me as though I were a stranger. "Contact. Coming."

"Yeah, yeah," I said. "That's not what I'm asking. Can you understand me? What do we need to do to make you better?"

There was a mechanical groan from deep inside the *Santa Fe*. The starship shook. Zero slammed into a console, and I only just avoided doing the same. That had to be a significant impact of some kind, although exactly what I couldn't say. Zero made a play for the nearest comms console, leaving a trail of bright blood droplets in her wake.

"It could be good news," I said. "Maybe Carmine has the weapon systems back online."

"The captain does not," Pariah croaked. "We are going aboard the ark-ship."

Pariah stirred. In a single effortless motion, it broke the restraining straps, and briskly sat up.

"How do you know?" Zero said.

"We are they," Pariah said. "We see what they see."

I exchanged a glance with Zero.

"Can you communicate with them?" I asked, aware of how desperate I sounded. "Tell them that we are allies. Tell them what happened on the diseased bio-ship!"

"They know," Pariah said. "They still come."

And in that moment, any prospect of diplomacy—of

negotiating our way out of this—vanished. We were going to have to fight them, just like the old days. The Krell were as unknowable now as they ever were, I realised.

An enormous roar rang throughout the vessel, followed by a deep grinding sound. Much, much worse than anything I'd heard before, sounding through the very structure of the ship. So intense that I could feel the impact through the surrounding atmosphere. Zero and I did as best we could to hold steady, bracing against medical equipment. Pariah just sat there, taking it in. The starship's frame contorted and groaned for several long seconds, making every bone in my body vibrate.

Then, finally, noise and motion ceased. The silence that stretched out around me was almost frightening.

"We've got gravity," Zero said. She let go of the console that she had anchored herself to, tested the strength of the G. "Feels lighter than standard."

I grimaced. "That's because it's not being generated by the *Santa Fe*."

"Have they already taken us aboard the ark?" Zero asked. Horror dawned on her face.

"I think so. That would explain the shift."

I looked at my wrist-comp. The blood-spattered display—and I couldn't even tell *whose* blood that was—indicated that Yukio's two minutes were up.

"We need to move," I said. "They'll be boarding the *Fe* soon."

"None of this feels real," Zero whispered.

"Probably best that you let it stay that way for as long as possible," I said. Unreality was a shield. "I need you icy. Can you do that for me, girl?"

"Like I said, I'm okay," insisted Zero. Nodded. "I'm tougher than I look; that's what Feng told me."

"Well, let's prove him right."

Beyond the infirmary hatch, lurking like the ghost at the feast, was a hulking black shape. Multiple shapes, in fact: several copies of me, wearing standard combat-suits. Each hooked to charging cradles, ready for imme-diate deployment. Zero had prepped them for the *Azrael* mission, had prepped multiple copies of the entire squad.

"I . . . I wish that I could help," Zero said.

"You can. Stay here."

"They will search this ship," Pariah said. "They will find her."

"Not if they have a distraction," I said. My simulator was already booting up: glowing blue, filled with active amniotic fluids. "And that's what I'm going to give them: the biggest fucking distraction that they can imagine."

"Do the Krell have an imagination?" Zero asked absently, as she worked.

"Not much of one," answered Pariah.

"Hey, the fish has a sense of humour," I said. I was stripped naked now, grabbing for the data-cables and plugging them to my ports. I fixed the respirator in place, checked the flow of oxygen through the mask.

"We're good to go over here," Zero said. Her terminal was booted up, flushed with feeds.

A rhythmic pounding had started through the bulk-heads, echoing through the very structure of the ship.

"They board," Pariah said. Whatever affliction it had been suffering from seemed to have cleared, at least for now.

The canopy of the tank slid open, and I stepped inside. Felt the cool liquid lap around me. I popped the comms bead into my ear so that I could hear Zero.

"I want you to initiate my transition," I said, "then get out of sight. Hide."

"Where?"

"Anywhere."

If Zero went down, it would be for good. Whatever my words, however I tried to dress it up, the idea of her dying aboard the *Santa Fe* filled me with dread. She wasn't like the others. She had done nothing to deserve it. The fact was we may not survive this, and the idea of Zero being dragged into the Deep—subjected to whatever horrors Cooper had endured, whatever had turned him from the Alliance—was too much to bear.

The canopy slid shut, and even inside the tank I could feel the violent pounding that shook the *Santa Fe*. Were the Krell already aboard the ship? Only one way to find out. My mind had started to disengage now, and the urge to make transition was overwhelming.

"Let's kick the tyres and light the fires, Zero."

"What?" Zero said, looking at me with a frown.

"Something Riggs said." *Used to say.* "Just make transition."

"Affirmative." Zero raised an open palm and counted off on her fingers. "Commencing in three…two…one…"

I made transition.

The icy spread of combat-drugs coursed through my limbs, chest, and head. My heart rate decreased, became regular and stable.

There was no time to enjoy it. I simply stepped out of the combat-suit's charging dock: new and ready to kill. The suit's HUD initiated with a flood of new messages, linking to whatever remained of the ship's AI, warning me of critical systems failures across the board. I cancelled everything that wasn't essential.

"Zero? You hear me?"

"I copy," she said. "I'm doing as you ordered."

I stomped though the SOC, found that she had vanished. An airshaft cover on one wall had been displaced, suggesting that she had retreated into the network of ventilation tunnels that criss-crossed the ship. It was as good a hiding place as any.

"Remember: go deep. Don't let them find you."

"Understood," she said. There was a bite to her voice, and I only understood why when she added, "It's like Mau Tanis, all over again."

"I hadn't thought of it that way," I said. "Turn off all your radio and comms apparatus. The Krell will use it to track you."

"Solid copy. Zero out."

"Jenkins out."

I switched off my communicator, probably for the last time. Pariah watched me with something like curiosity.

"What does it—*she*—mean to you?" it asked.

"You wouldn't understand," I said. "No one else does."

"We will never understand others."

"You're telling me, huh? Well, we'll never understand you either. But maybe we've got one thing in common."

"We are warriors," Pariah said.

I snapped the M115 plasma rifle from the magnetic plate on my backpack, checked the power cell. The rifle had a full charge, would be good for a hundred shots. It felt reassuringly heavy in my gloved hands, and auto-slaved to the targeting software in my tactical helmet.

Pariah had its own transformation. I watched with sick fascination as the bio-suit it wore became slick with oil, fluid seeping from every broken plate. It looked sinewy and monstrous in the light of the SOC, and I was glad that I was using my internal oxygen supply: that I couldn't smell the thing. The xeno still bore enough scars to indicate that it was not at full fighting strength, but it was close enough.

"Yeah, every fucking one of you fishes is a warrior," I replied.

"Not Collective," Pariah said, putting a hand to its

throax. "We." Paused, as though struggling to enunciate the concept. "You . . . and I."

I laughed. "We'll make a human out of you yet, P."

"We . . . are not sure that is what we . . . want," Pariah said.

"You got ammunition for those pea-shooters of yours?"

The Pariah glared at the barb-guns that had suddenly appeared in its palms, weaponising the limbs. "What is 'pea-shooter'?"

"Never mind."

The thumping had grown all around us: becoming louder, more violent. Whatever was out there was closing in.

"Let's go to work."

We breached the security bulkhead to Medical.

As I decided where best to go, my face-plate was painted with the *Santa Fe*'s internal schematics. There was the bridge: several hundred metres ahead. Life support: two decks down. Engineering: in the aft. Cargo hold: another hundred metres aftward. The evacuation pods . . .

Where was Riggs? I detested the miserable gnawing on the edge of my thought-stream, wished that I could repress it with a shot of combat-drugs from the medi-suite. I didn't want to feel anything for him, because that was a way in, a weakness that I couldn't afford. But I wanted—*needed*—to know what had happened to him. I checked every communications band, searching for some explanation. If he was alive, surely he would've tried to make contact with me. But every band was empty, no sign of comms at all.

"We're heading back through the main corridor," I decided.

"You wish to find your kin?" Pariah guessed.

I want to see if Riggs is really dead.

"I want numbers on our side," I said.

The security hatch that had separated us from the rest of the Jackals was now open. It had been demolished, torn open messily. Smoke streamed from the damaged panel.

"Something's been through here..." I whispered, touching the sharp edge of the hole in the door. "Something big."

"It was not your kind," Pariah said.

I stared down the corridor: so long and straight. The emergency box that had caused the squad to stop—that had tempted them—was still open. The equipment they'd salvaged from there was strewn across the deck. An oxy-bottle. A respirator. A flare gun...

And blood. A streak of brilliant red blood on the wall. Incautiously, irrationally, I stalked onwards: close enough to examine the mark.

A handprint.

My heart leapt. My medi-suite compensated, tried to keep me sharp.

"Riggs?" I shouted, over my suit's external speakers. "Lopez?"

No reaction. My eyes traced the direction of the bloodied print, along the wall panel. The evac-pods sat further along the corridor, warning text still flashing...

The pods hadn't been fired.

"They are gone," Pariah said.

"No," I insisted. Swallowed. "Not like this. Not my squad..."

Each of the Jackals—every member of the Alliance military—carried a personal ID chip. I'd scanned for those on Daktar, used them to find the missing officers—the cadre that had turned out to be composed of simulant decoys. Now, I hurriedly used my suit's systems to look for possible chips in the vicinity, hoping to find some indication of what had happened to the Jackals. But there was nothing, no sign at all.

"They are not here," Pariah said.

"I know. That's not the point."

A bio-sign appeared on my HUD: a shape materialising at the end of the corridor, becoming solid as it advanced through shadow.

But any idea that this could be Riggs, or Lopez, or any of my team, was quickly quelled as a Krell primary-form leapt into view.

"Here goes," I said.

I brought up the plasma rifle. Let the auto-targeter do its thing.

No going back now. They're gone. Keira is gone. I'm a machine, and I'm doing what I do.

The xeno screamed an ungodly war cry, taloned arms outstretched. It was a space-borne variant, bigger, wearing a bulky bio-suit.

It fell into my fire: no challenge to a volley of plasma bolts. The XT split in half, threw boiling ichor across the walls and floor.

"Target neutralised."

But there were more. Always more. Krell poured into the corridor, secondary-forms readying to launch ranged attacks. Threat markers flashed across my face-plate. My null-shield initiated as boomer-fire came from somewhere ahead.

I tossed a frag grenade down the length of the deck. It shook the area as it exploded, stitching the corridor with hot shrapnel and momentarily driving back the boarders.

I knew how this ended. I knew that this was futile.

A primary reached our line, but Pariah was on it. It slammed barbs into the XT's bio-armour, then barrelled into the hostile. The alien squirmed under Pariah's weight, thrashing, and went down in front of me. I stomped it with an armoured boot, splitting the alien's thorax.

"You weren't shitting me about your buddies being aboard the ship," I said. "They're everywhere."

"We were not shitting you," Pariah replied, as though unsure of my meaning. "They are not our 'buddies.'"

"You're learning fast."

"This way," Pariah said. Falling back towards the cargo bay now, away from the bridge. There were simply too many Krell in that direction.

The bulkhead had been ruptured, and through a curtain of live wiring—spitting white sparks—was another module. My suit suggested that we were dangerously close to the outer hull now. Maybe, I decided, this was part of the damage caused by the Krell attack—one of the multiple hull-breaches we'd suffered during the ark-ship's assault. That the *Fe* had stayed space-borne for so long after suffering this sort of damage: that was impressive.

Pariah leapt ahead, monkey-like, into the hole in the bulkhead. I did the same, grazing the edges as I pulled my bulk through. We were in an access shaft: one of the elevator hubs between decks.

"What the damn——?" I started.

A lobster-like claw slashed through the *Santa Fe*'s metal skin. Its tip punctured the hull and emerged in the corridor wall, producing a startling scream as it tore metal.

I turned my rifle on the appendage, but in the blue light of the plasma discharge I saw more of the alien claws. A dozen perforated the metalwork, working fast to open up more holes. The Krell were equipped with specialised ship-boarding enhancements, something I'd never seen before. Bio-electricity danced the alien weapons as they opened the ship like a tin can.

"Stop them, P!" I said, frantically. "We've got to stop them!"

It was then that I noticed that Pariah wasn't moving any more. It had returned to that hypnotised state, grimacing uncomfortably.

"Cannot..." it said. "Collective comes..."

Shafts of light ruptured the outer hull. An opening as big as a man—bigger even—had been created in the passage wall. I went to retreat backwards, firing repeatedly with my plasma rifle. But the tide of bio-signs was closing in behind me, the net tightening.

I was trapped, and I knew it.

"Fight them!" I yelled, spittle flicking across the inside of my face-plate. "We've got to fight them!"

Weapons fire poured in from the opening in the hull. Stinger-spines bounced off the metal walls, boomers sparking my null-shield. Lumbering quad-forms—Krell so big and wide, so fully enclosed in their alien bio-suits, that they resembled living tanks—widened the opening in the hull. Their lobster-like heads turned to me, barking commands at the wall of lesser Krell warriors that encircled the *Santa Fe*.

Through the breach in the hull, I saw flashes of the environment beyond. The *Fe* was inside an enormous cave. Green-black walls that ran with mucous and liquid, shafts that erupted in every direction. Hellish organic geometry, a world within the closed bio-system of the ark-ship. The same warped architecture of the *Azrael*, but on a much bigger scale.

Primary-forms circled Pariah. The alien went down, fate uncertain.

As the Krell closed in on me, I vaguely considered making a jump for one of the tunnels. But even as the thought formed in my mind, I knew that it was fantastical. Impossible. There were hundreds of aliens here: Krell of every variety, carrying nightmarish bio-weapons of every type. *And only one Zero.* She was the only other confirmed survivor of the Jackals, and right now she was somewhere in the *Fe*—hiding from the horde of XTs that were invading our ship.

I fired my plasma rifle into the tide of xenos.

LOW AMMUNITION! my suit warned.

A leader-form—recognisable because it was bigger than the other Krell primaries, because its bio-armour was more ornate in an alien way—waved a webbed claw at me.

"Come on, you fuckers!" I screamed.

I grappled for a grenade from the harness across my chest, readied to activate it.

Then a rain of stinger rounds covered the area. My null-shield finally collapsed, and a round punctured the armoured plating at my chest. I gasped, dropped my rifle, staggered backwards. The flood of bio-toxins into my simulated bloodstream was very nearly instant. I raised my hand, thumb to the grenade's detonator…

But my fingers were numb, unresponsive. Too late. The toxin was already working.

Should've taken my own advice, I thought. *I'm sorry that I let you down, Zero.* No: that wasn't her name. It was just what everyone else called her. Zoe: that was her real name. That was who she was.

The agony of the engineered poison detonated inside of me, and I was screaming, and the lights went out.

Since the war on Mau Tanis began, the nights had become infinite.

Not just darker, but truly limitless: the sky an impenetrable smog, a cloak that was difficult to navigate by day. By night, there was nothing to navigate with. The moons—once ever-present orbs against the silken, Earth-like horizon—were now gone. The stars concealed by the chemical shroud that the Krell War had brought with it.

"I'm clearing Main Street," I said into my combat-suit communicator, my voice a whisper. "These colonists aren't very inventive with their road names."

"Keep radio comms minimal," came Captain Harris, his gruff tone carrying over the short-range comm grid and making it rougher still. "Fishes are out there."

Harris: callsign LAZARUS. No one called him Harris.

"Tell me about it," I said.

"This place is a damned mess," Kaminski muttered. His Standard was branded with a thick Brooklyn accent, impossible to mistake.

I glanced at the bio-scanner in the corner of my HUD. It showed the rest of the Lazarus Legion, spread across the remains of Mau Tanis Main. Felt reassuring to know that at least four of these blips were mine—were friendlies doing just the same as me. Reassuring, but didn't really make this job any easier.

"They don't believe in leaving much behind," Harris said.

"You're breaking your own radio rules," I replied.

"I make 'em, I break 'em."

I plotted my way through the remains of a habitation module. The metal and plastic had been bonded by the intense heat of the bombardment: an assault that had lasted all of two minutes, if Naval intelligence was accurate. Sixteen million people had once lived here—had once called Mau Tanis home. It had been a teeming metropolis, an example of Alliance terraforming to be lauded all the way back to the Core.

Now? It was a few dozen kilometres of dead earth. Of skeletal remains. Of charred derelicts and still-burning forests. Hard to believe that the fishes had done this, but it was nothing new.

"Hold," I said.

My soldier-sense—all the stronger because I was in a simulant—stirred into action milliseconds before I saw the signal on my scanner. Plasma rifle up, panning the gloom of the abandoned hab. If it wasn't for my tactical helmet multi-sense, I wouldn't have been able to see in there at all.

"What have you got?" Harris asked.

"Anyone else in my sector?"

"No. Report?"

"I'm getting a bio-sign. Something weak. Ahead." I picked my way through a room of dead bodies, blast-burnt by the bombardment. Some of those bodies were small, child-sized. I reckoned that this place had once been a family home. "It's in this building."

"Wait for me," Kaminski said. "I can be there in two."

The signal fluctuated just ahead of me. Didn't seem very strong.

"Hold your post, Jenkins," Harris said, gruffly. "I mean it."

"I don't think that it's Krell," I said. "I'm sure that it isn't."

"Doesn't mean that you should be going after it alone," Kaminski said.

I ignored them both. In a full combat-suit and a sim I was heavy, and the structure I walked through groaned sympathetically. Mau Tanis had been built for the future—a world of gleaming metal and plastic alongside habs of dark oak and synthetic wood: an attempt to show that not all colonies had to be impersonal, militarised steel bunkers. When war had come a-calling, that vision had been the planet's undoing.

I cancelled my multi-vision and popped on my suit-lamps. The brilliant beams played around the room, picking out the variety of shades of black that the chamber had become.

"Wait!" Harris ordered. "Jenkins, this isn't—"

I don't know why I did it, but I cancelled my comm. Directed both lamps into the corner of the room. Something stirred there. Something that had remained hidden, had survived the Krell bombardment. Had somehow, against the odds, survived.

"You... you okay?" I asked. The words came out too loud, and I dialled back the volume of my external speakers.

A bundle of rags cowered in the corner. A filthy moon of a face peered out from behind what had once been the arm of a chair: two eyes set deep into the pale-skinned face.

I'd never had much empathy with children. Never really encountered many; in those days, if I wasn't on an operation, I was getting ready for the next. But something about the little girl in the corner of the room, it called out to me. She called out to me.

I crouched. Felt the servos in my legs creaking beneath me, the combat-suit taking the weight.

"You okay?" I repeated.

The girl had a shock of ginger hair. A speckling of freckles across the bridge of her nose, over her cheeks. She held up a hand to her face, shielding her eyes from the light of my lamps.

"I'm sorry, kid," I said. Turned down the lights.

For a long while, she just crouched there, watching me.

I cracked the seal on my tac helmet. Slowly, so as not to freak her out, I removed the helmet. Set it down on the floor between us.

"Hey, kid. You can talk to me. I'm Alliance. I'm here to help."

The girl's face gradually softened. Not by much, but enough.

"What's your name?" I asked.

"Zoe," she whispered. "My name's Zoe."

CHAPTER TWENTY-FIVE

END GAME

Drip-drip-drip.

The shock of being alive was almost as vivid as that of dying.

I was suffering from the worst hangover *ever*. My limbs throbbed, and every beat of my heart was agony. I'd felt plenty of pain before. That wasn't a problem for me. But this? It was something new. My temples ungodly ached, had become deep wells of pain that threatened to suck me in.

I was still skinned—still in a simulant. Surprising. But I wasn't in my combat-suit any more, and only wore my neoprene undersuit; I guessed that the Krell had cut me out of my armour, although for what purpose I didn't know. I'd never seen them do that before.

I realised that I couldn't move, was being held in place by something that bound my legs, arms, body. Only my head and neck were mobile. I was in some sort of cocoon, webbing tight around me. I twisted in my bonds, tried to get some idea of my location, but the pain came back again. Getting free would have to wait.

Where was I? How long had I been here? My eyes

took a while to adjust to my surroundings. Bioluminescent fungus, or at least some alien equivalent, had
collected here and there, casting pale light across the
chamber, but the place was dark. It stank of Krell—the
sickly, briny smell that accompanied them everywhere,
but so much stronger. I fought the urge to gag, to throw
up. I felt my nose wrinkle, twitch. A bug, or something
like it climbed, my face, just visible on my cheek. The
dripping was water, coming from somewhere far above,
running down the slicked walls.

Then it struck me that the room around me was the
wrong way up.

Or, to put it another way, I was upside down. I could
already feel the rush of blood to my head, the pressure
that came with being held in this position for too long.
Probably not fatal, yet, but it would be soon. Without my
armour, I had no medi-suite to rely on. Hysteria gripped
me for a second, and I renewed my efforts to break free
of the cocoon, violently thrashing, wriggling both legs
together. But the cocoon was made from a strong, weed-
like material—something that seemed to constrict the
more I fought.

"Everyone thinks I am bad. But sometimes, when
they think you are bad, it makes you that way."

I strained my neck to find the origin of the voice.

"This is prison, but this is not worst."

Slavic. Russian.

I focused on the shape beside me. I recognised it.

"Novak?" I asked. My throat was dry kindling and it
hurt to talk. "Is that you?"

"Is me," he said. Then continued, as though he wasn't
bothered by my presence: "I know prisons. I know worst
gulag on Old Earth. They ask why I join up. They ask
what I do to make it so. I tell them one day."

Like me, Novak was suspended. Encased in green

webbing. Swaddled all the way to his neck: only his head poking from the cocoon. He turned to me, sharply, visible in outline.

"Fifteen men I kill, and that is truth. But not two women. No women."

Have you gone insane? I wondered. He was babbling, his voice sounding as though his larynx was filled with grit. I could hardly stand to listen to the crack of it as he talked.

"They put me in deepest, darkest hole. No light, never. They accuse me of killing my own wife and child."

"You don't have to tell me this," I said. "We have to get out of—"

"I *do* have to tell you this," Novak pursued. "I have to tell you this because if we die in here, I want you to know truth about me. About Leon Novak."

"Not now, Novak—"

"I was once *bratva*, a member of the Brotherhood. Like your crime rings, yes? An enforcer, is word. I work for them. I go where they say. I do what they tell me. I make money for family. I have wife, I have daughter."

I had no choice but to hang there and listen to the man's ramblings. Who knew whether it was true? It probably didn't much matter now.

"Then one day I decide: no more. I decide will be good man." Novak grinned, and the bioluminescent fungi flashed against his teeth. "I try to. But no one leave *bratva*. Brotherhood, ones I call friends, come after me." He sniffed, and let out a long, pained howl. A cry. "They take them both. Kill them."

"You don't need to tell me this," I said again. Slowly, patiently.

"I am blamed. So they lock me away. And I become the monster they want me to be. And in that hole, in the gulag, I kill the rest. But not because I am bad man, but because I must. To survive, you understand? Only to survive. Fifteen men. No women."

"We don't have time for this," I said. Began to wriggle in the cocoon again, fighting to get free. "We have to get out of here."

Then, as suddenly as a flipped switch, Novak's presentation changed again. The wracking sob that had enveloped him evaporated, was replaced by the cold determination of the killer that I knew. His transformation was terrifying.

"Easy," he said. "Don't want to black out again. You've been under for long time."

"How long?" I asked.

Novak laughed, and because he was upside down the noise came out all weird. "I only know I am here long time before they bring you."

"You're hurt," I said. My eyesight was changing, improving, and I could make out more of Novak's features now. I registered his face: bruised, lacerated all over. Something dark—blood—dripped from the pate of his head.

"Is nothing new," he said. "Is life, or something like it. I saw them bring you in. Is worse for you, yes?"

Sensation was returning to not just my head, but also the rest of my body. Now that Novak mentioned it, I could feel the poisoned throb where the bio-toxin round had hit me. It felt like the undersuit had been torn there.

Memories came flooding back, so fast that I had to close my eyes to ride the pain-wave that accompanied them. The Jackals being cut off. Carmine left on the ship. Pariah. Then, most poignantly: Zero. In the SOC. Alone again.

"Where are the others?" I asked. "Have you seen Zero?"

"The Krell came aboard the *Santa Fe*," Novak

explained, "and took us. I fight back, kill one of fishes." He gave a characteristic grunt, a sound that might've been another laugh. "There were too many of them. The sailors got hit. They won't be coming back."

"Is Riggs . . . ?" I started.

"They took him. They took all others—Sergkov too. But since I am here, I have not seen any others."

"What about Carmine?"

"She was not with us." Novak sighed. "Is good captain."

And just like that, I saw the spark of hope. That, or the blood pooling in my head was making me see flashing lights. Either was possible.

"I'm still on the *Fe*," I said. "My real body, I mean. In the SOC. And if you haven't seen Zero, then she must be there too."

"I hope so," Novak said. "She does not deserve to end up like *them* . . ."

My eyes suddenly focused on the desiccated things at the edge of the cave. Human-sized cocoons that were webbed to the walls, from which pale, atrophied faces peered. I could just make out scraps of uniform, Navy blues and Army khakis. Those poor bastards were long dead. None of the Jackals deserved that fate.

"Prisoners," I whispered to myself. "This is where the Krell must've taken them, during the war."

Dead, black pits stared back from the faces of those corpses, where eyes had once been. I turned away from the bodies, tried not to think about what those servicemen and women had gone through. I hoped beyond hope that Zero was still alive, that she had managed to ride out this catastrophe.

There was a sound—that bizarre shrieking that the Krell sometimes made—somewhere beneath us.

The noise echoed around the chamber, multiplying, as though there were a hundred XTs in there with us.

"Stay sharp," I said.

Blurs of motion polluted my peripheral vision. An alien face appeared in front of me, right side up. Unblinking eyes. Features held in that unknowable expression that the Krell always wore.

"Fucking fish head!" Novak spat into the xeno's face.

The alien did nothing to recognise the tiny act of resistance, not even to wipe the spittle away.

"Save it, Novak," I said. "Don't do anything. Not until I say so."

My simulant-eyes had adjusted to the dark now, and I saw that we were surrounded by Krell. Hanging from the walls, from the ceiling. To fight back would be suicide, and not in a good way.

"Understood," Novak said, begrudgingly.

The alien chirped noisily. Slashed a claw across my chest. Pulled me out of the cocoon. Novak was freed beside me too.

The Krell guards dragged us into one of the many sub-shafts that honeycombed the prison cell. We passed through the organic equivalent of a starship hatch, with one of the Krell pausing to activate it, and out into a wider corridor. A gaggle of familiar figures stood outside our prison.

"Keira!" Riggs exclaimed.

"Corporal," I said, briskly. I struggled to contain the rush of elation that I felt on seeing that he was alive, and resisted the urge to throw my arms around him. "Good to see that you're alive."

Riggs, Lopez and Feng were surrounded by Krell warriors. The Jackals were covered in the vestiges of cocoon-matter, the weed-like material clinging to their fatigues, but as far as I could see none of them appeared seriously injured. Most importantly, none of them had been hit by stingers or barbs: surely a death sentence without a full medi-suite to filter the poison.

"You're skinned," Lopez said. Her hair was plastered to her scalp in thick strands.

"Let's not make a thing of it," I said.

There was no telling how much the Krell actually understood of our communications: no telling what they would do if they knew that I was in a simulant. Although Lopez nodded in agreement, I could see that the information had lit hope in her eyes.

Feng feverishly looked over my shoulder, back the way we had come, and one of the Krell guards prodded him into the group.

"Is Zero with you?" he said, desperately. "Did she make it out?"

"Long story," I said. "No need to go into it now."

"But she's okay?"

"I think so," I said. "What about Sergkov? Where is he?"

"He was with us," Riggs said, "but the fishes took him."

The Krell marched us together. One on each arm, another two ahead of us, heads constantly swivelling to check that we weren't trying anything. Two gun-grafts trailed at the rear, their bio-cannons tracking us with particular menace.

"Maybe we should make a break for it," Riggs suggested, from his position behind me. "This place looks empty except for these bastards."

"Look again," I said, nodding towards the shafts that lined the ceiling and walls. "The Krell are everywhere. They're watching us. This is their habitat."

Eyes peered out at us from darkened shafts. Camouflaged bodies slinked at the edge of my perception.

"You could still make a run for it," Riggs said. "Or let them kill you, and bug out to the *Santa Fe* . . ."

As my feet scraped the wet, smooth floor of the tunnel I realised in just how bad a shape this skin was. The wound in my chest throbbed, pulsing as though I was fighting deep infection, and my limbs felt like they were set in concrete. No doubt being suspended upside down for the last few hours hadn't helped. But if I bugged out now, there was no telling how the Krell might react.

"And you'd all pay the cost," I said. "That's no kind of plan. We're better biding our time. You still got that gun, Lopez?"

"Yeah," she said. "And I even brought some ammo."

"And you have knives, Novak?"

"Have one knife," Novak said. He sounded almost glum.

"That will have to do."

We went through dank, wet corridors, lit only by the soft glow of blue and green fungi that erupted from the walls. Plants and bugs and coral-things sprouted from every available orifice or cavity. The place wasn't so much a ship as a colony: a slice of the Krell's natural bio-system, flying through space. I was struck by how much life there was aboard the ark.

I assessed the Krell guards. The two nearest to me had back-plates lined by antenna-spines, which wriggled and writhed with a life of their own. I'd seen that behaviour before. It suggested that they were particularly agitated, were receiving communication from other bio-forms higher up in the chain of command. The Krell were otherwise healthy, muscular specimens: larger examples of primary-forms. Their colouration was more extreme than those we'd seen on the *Azrael*; instead of muted grey-green, these soldiers wore stippled bio-plate, striped like wasps.

"I don't think that these ones are the same as the Krell aboard the *Azrael*," I whispered.

"All fish heads are same," Novak said.

"That's not right," I said. "Red Fin, Blue Claw: there are tens of Collectives. But that isn't what I mean."

"Then what do you mean, ma'am?" Feng said.

"The ones on the *Azrael* looked wrong," I said. "They looked as though they were infected by something. Diseased."

"That is toxin talking," Novak persisted. "All fish heads are sick."

Lopez barked a laugh, loud enough that her Krell escort responded by shaking her shoulder and hissing at her.

"Fuckers!" Lopez yelped as the Krell touched her. "I'm moving as fast as I can!"

She cursed some more and I heard more scuffling, but she quickly settled down. The Krell went back to their programmed march.

And even from that small detail, I learnt something.

"They don't want to kill us," I decided.

"They're waiting to do that," Riggs muttered.

"I mean it," I said. I stared down at the open wound on my chest, where the stinger-spine had punctured the combat-suit and lodged itself inside me… "They took out the stinger. Since when did the Krell do that?" I looked around, at tunnel walls running with thick fluid. "And they've drained these tunnels."

"Maybe they're trying to make us comfortable," Feng said.

"It isn't working," Lopez added.

The idea that the Krell were deliberately keeping us alive was somehow more terrifying than the idea that they were trying to kill us. I'd spent so long at war with the fishes that nothing else seemed natural.

The tunnel terminated in another living door, and one of the Krell on point activated it. The hatch sucked open, revealing a much larger cavern beyond. The two fish heads at my shoulders pushed me inside, and the Jackals filed in behind me.

The chamber was vast and wide, made from the same bizarre pseudo-organic material as the rest of the ark. It reminded me of a wasps' nest: a big insect hive, teeming with not just Krell life but whatever else they picked up on the way. Whereas the tunnels outside had been dark, this place positively blazed with light. Fungi and glowing barnacle-things covered the walls, illuminating dozens of open shafts that fed into the chamber. Podiums made of coral grew everywhere, interconnected by bone rigging and catwalks of luminous material that looked a lot like a calcified spider's web.

A behemoth of a Krell presided over the alien court.

"What in all the Core is *that?*" Lopez murmured beside me.

"It's a navigator-form," I said.

The xeno shared certain characteristics with the navigator-form I'd seen aboard the *Azrael*, but again I got the distinct impression that this creature was not of the same breed: its colouration was different, the sweep of its head. Its distended body was supported by six spindly, atrophied limbs, and every inch of the creature's skin—if that really was skin, and not some sort of grafted armour—was covered in barnacles and small crustaceans, a pattern made up of a million tiny whorls.

"Just stay quiet," I hissed at the Jackals. "And don't do anything that might get you killed."

"I think that's going to be easier said than done," Riggs replied.

What little energy remaining in this skin ebbed out of

me: as though my life-force was earthed, seeping through the soles of my boots. An aura of age surrounded the navigator—something that I'd never experienced from the Krell before. Perversely, that seemed to do little to reduce its sense of physical threat. Rather, it somehow made it all the more fearsome.

A weird clicking noise echoed around the chamber, and as I gingerly looked upwards I saw that the cavern was filled with further platforms, each spilling with Krell. Shark-eyes gazing down at us.

"That's a shit load of Krell to fight," Riggs whispered.

"You just can't help yourself, can you?" I said. "I told you to be quiet."

Lopez whimpered. "Should've listened to Daddy..."

There were dozens, hundreds of other Krell assembled around the chamber. I recognised leader-forms, secondaries, and tertiaries, but others were more bizarre still. Here were examples of Krell that I had never seen before, had never even been briefed on. Quad-forms— tremendously powerful specimens that reminded me of a combination of gorilla and crustacean—pounded up behind us, closing the only available exit from the chamber. They rested on their forelimbs like crabs, their bio-helmets scanning us. Yet others carried rarefied staves that crackled with bio-energy, sending bright blue sparks through the air.

"They haven't killed the major yet," Feng offered, indicating to the centre of the room.

Major Sergkov was badly dishevelled, covered in more of the living weed from the prison cell. As the guards dragged us into the centre of the chamber, to where Sergkov was kneeling, he half-turned to look at me. His eyes were black wells, and his face was haggard.

"Lieutenant," he said, in greeting.

Just the slightest dip of his head, like he was

frightened to move. Both of the major's hands were on his head, fingers locked. I thought back to when we had first met, on Daktar Outpost. When I had seen him looking down the certainty of death, when he had appeared resolute and determined. Now that he was in his real skin, he didn't seem anywhere near so willing to meet his maker.

"You're injured, sir," I said. I noted a particularly nasty-looking injury on his back, where something sharp had torn his uniform, penetrated skin and bone. Sticky blood coated the fabric of his fatigues.

"Don't be concerned," he said. "I'm fine."

The major knelt in a shallow pool of water, mere metres from the navigator. Krell guards prodded us onwards, then forced us into the same pose as Sergkov.

"I do not take orders from fish," Novak barked.

"Do as they tell you," Sergkov said. "Trust me on this."

I saw then that the walls of the chamber were lined with blisters—pod-like things that were similar to those I'd seen in the *Azrael*'s hibernation chamber, glowing with pale internal light. Except, I realised, these were most certainly not sleeping-capsules.

"Are those…?" Lopez started.

She didn't need to finish the question, and it was better that she didn't. There were vaguely humanoid outlines in the blisters—shapes unmistakable, held like flies in amber. Many of those bodies were still in uniforms.

Army, Navy, Aerospace.

But not all were human. There were some Krell bioforms—usually six-limbed, much bigger than humans. Then more esoteric shapes that I didn't recognise at all: things that were more alien than even the Krell.

Dr. Skinner had used the description "organic computers" back on North Star. Was that what the network of pods was? The idea sent a shiver of revulsion through me—each of these minds networked to the Collective, forced to become part of the Krell's knowledge-base, whether the occupants wanted to be or not.

"This is the Deep," Sergkov said. "This is what they do with prisoners." He added sharply, "Please: don't look. It won't help."

So this was what had happened to Sergeant Cooper, former Alliance Ranger…What was worse: that he had been subjected to forced communion with the Krell Collective, or that he had somehow come back from it? I didn't want to dwell on how such a thing might change a man, or a woman…Sergkov did his best not to look at the walls, or at the enormous navigator in front of him.

"At least now we know what happened to Pariah," Feng said.

Pariah had been woven into the wall, beside the navigator: pinned in place by bundles of vine-like cables. Dozens of bleeding injuries covered the alien's body, and its head lolled to one side. It was easily the smallest bioform in the chamber.

"You okay up there, P?" I asked, despite myself. "What have they done to you?"

Pariah didn't respond, but I noted the gentle rise and fall of the XT's chest. Krell breathed, just like the rest of us.

"It is an abomination," came an electronic voice.

"More talking Krell?" Lopez whispered.

"It's not them," Sergkov said. "It's the pariah-form."

"…a necessary abomination…" the voice completed.

"They're speaking though it?" I asked.

"Yes," Sergkov said. His eyes remained fixed on the floor, on a certain point of focus that it appeared only he could see. "They're tapping into the pariah-form's communication ability."

Skinner's warning: that the Pariah was a two-way mirror. That was exactly how the Krell were using it.

"Answers…" the pariah-form said. "Required."

Whatever they were doing, Pariah was in obvious pain, with creeper-cables plugged to open wounds on its body. *Like being jacked with cables to my data-ports*, I realised, with growing unease.

"It's still Krell," I said to the navigator.

"It is Pariah," the navigator said, through Pariah. "It is not of Collective."

"It's a member of our crew," I said back. "You have no right to take it prisoner."

"Please," Sergkov said. His body shook, quivered. "Don't."

The navigator's forelimbs gently extended, demonstrating the truly threatening scale of the beast. The living antennae on its back writhed, perhaps formulating a response, perhaps communicating with the rest of the ark.

"Others call us Silver Talon," the navigator said. "The Pariah was of us. Now it is not."

I nodded. "He was donated."

"Not donated. Taken." The navigator paused. "Maelstrom: Krell space," the alien said. "This is."

"We know."

"Not us," it said. Thrust a talon in our direction. "Not of Kindred."

"We came here to investigate the loss of a ship." I worked the words around my mouth. "A vessel called the *Hannover*. A human vessel."

I was no xeno-linguist, and I was painfully aware of the importance of this meeting.

"We know of a craft that sails the stars," the navigator replied.

"A ship?"

The alien paused again, then answered. "A craft that sails stars," it agreed.

"Your kind," I said, "did they destroy the craft that sails the stars?"

"Not us. We are Silver Talon."

"Then the Red Fin? The Krell that you just attacked?"

"Was not of Collective. Was of exile."

"You're all Krell!" Riggs barked. "You're all fucking fishes, and you've just attacked your own ship!"

"I've already told you to shut up!" I said, turning to Riggs. "Let me handle this..."

I was just in time to see a dozen Krell descend on the squad. They circled us, limbs always in motion, offering the threat of abrupt and unpredictable violence. My minds-eye was clouded by flashbacks of a hundred deaths at their claws, each bloodier than the last. But they did not attack. The navigator nonchalantly raised a claw, and the swarm retreated.

"I'll be quiet now," Riggs whispered.

"That is best," Novak said.

The truth was that I had no idea how to handle this, whatever *this* actually was. Simulant Operations teams were not briefed on contact scenarios: the only two alien species that we were aware shared our space were not prone to direct communication. I'd fought the Krell for most of my life—been in some of the hottest combat zones that this galaxy had to offer—and yet none of that could ready me for what I was seeing. I had a painful suspicion that whatever happened here would have repercussions for the rest of humanity. The weight of this encounter rested heavily on my shoulders.

I decided to try again. "We were sent on a mission

to find the whereabouts of the…the craft that sails the stars," I explained. "We thought that this craft was here, in this system. We found a…a Kindred ship, but it had something wrong with it."

The navigator exhaled slowly from a series of gills set into its enormous head. The expression reminded me of a sigh. Pale mist bellowed from the creature's bulk. It paused, as though contemplating its response. Although they were of different species, the vibe I picked up from the XT was the same as I'd felt when Major Sergkov had first briefed us. The alien was evaluating me, weighing me up.

"They are dying," it finally said. "Red Fin has rot."

The mention of that word—"rot"—seemed to send a shiver through the gathered aliens. They were frightened of the word, or perhaps its implications.

"Collective dies." The alien's body writhed, as though describing those events was causing it pain. "Crafts that sail stars die."

"We saw you attacking that bio-ship," I said. "We saw your ships chasing it."

"Other carried the rot," the navigator said. "Other should not survive to carry rot."

The wall behind the navigator illuminated with threads of light, generated by the fungi and coral.

"It's a star-map," Feng exclaimed. "A fucking star-map!"

"It's the Gyre," I said, directing my words to the navigator. Several stars had been snuffed out though, and the map showed that detail. "Your home?"

"One time…Not this time…Long ago." It gesticulated at the living map. "Then others came from outer dark."

Sergkov looked up abruptly. "The Shard?" he asked.

"Shard," the navigator repeated. "Inside Gyre. Long ago."

Carmine had described the Gyre as a failed Shard Gate. I'd heard that sort of story before, as explanations of other bizarre features of the Maelstrom. Perhaps, in this instance, there was some truth in the description.

The navigator went on. "Rot spreads. Red Fin carries rot. Worlds die. Collective must kill stars."

It was impossible to tell whether the Krell was talking of current, historic, or recent events. What did time mean to a species that did not record it, that did not understand the importance of individuality? I was witness to a collective intelligence that had occupied the Maelstrom in antiquity, had fought a war against the Machines long before humanity had even existed.

"You destroyed your own stars?" I asked.

"We had…have…no choice. Rot infects…everything."

I saw things in my head. Not really images, but bursts of emotion, of feelings, wrapped in an alienness that was very nearly impenetrable. *Seabeds of kelp on fire. Meteors raining from the sky, leaving fiery trails of destruction in their wake. Entire jungles burning, burning. Oceans running dry. And everywhere the silver-eyed ones. The hungry ones, those who were not of the Collective. A weapon of such power that it pained the Kindred to use it.* I screamed, put my hands to my head. Held them there.

"Keira!" Riggs shouted. He moved beside me. "What's happening to you?"

The sensation was painful, and I suspected that it was even more so in a real skin. It took a while for my head to clear, for my synapses to filter the alien contact. When they did, I was weak and debilitated.

"I don't want to feel that again," I said. "Some things can't be unseen."

I glanced around at the chamber. The Krell watched on. Their anticipation was blood-deep, perhaps pheromonal or even more complicated. Psychic energy seemed to prickle around them, especially the older specimens, and the navigator itself. Everything here was, to one degree or another, alive. The repercussions of a virus or plague or whatever this thing was—actually *infecting* the Krell worlds? I didn't like it one bit.

I sensed how the virus might work. Trickling through the Collective, through the many drones. Infecting the Krell at every level. Taking the navigators and leaderforms, working its way into the spawn, the bio-ships, the arks...

I turned to Sergkov. "This is above my pay grade," I said.

"I have the feeling that it's above even *mine*," he answered.

"We steer the ship that sails stars," the navigator said. "We must cull those that fall from the Kindred mind."

The star-map shifted. Showing not only the Gyre, but also the huge tranche of space that was the Maelstrom. In a reflection of what we had just seen, light winked out across the periphery of the map, leaving black stains. With each that fizzled out, the Krell's psychic hurt accumulated. The experience was almost too much for me to bear. I felt like I was approaching neural overload, that soon the simulant would just give up and the simulation would collapse.

"Why is this happening? Where did this rot come from?" I probed.

"Collective does not know," the navigator said. "Infected worlds cannot speak."

I saw again flashes of the burning planets that this arkship—that a dozen other ark-ships just like it—had put to the flame. As with severing an infected limb, the Krell knew that they had to do it, even if every lance-strike hurt them. The shoal was weaker than ever before. The virus had claimed its dues, and was spreading at an alarming rate.

"What do you want from us?" I said, eager to make this stop.

Two venerable Krell quad-forms lumbered into the middle of the chamber. Between them, they carried my combat-suit. It was battered, worn, and punctured in multiple locations, but to my surprise it was still functional. Activation lights set into the helmet collar flashed intermittently. The quads dropped the suit in the pool in front of me, then withdrew, their weapon-limbs trained on me and the Jackals at all times.

The navigator snarled, head lifted into the air.

"We want help from others who are not us. We want help to remove the rot."

This was massive, bigger than anything I'd faced before. A situation so serious that the Krell couldn't deal with it themselves, that they required our help to solve it.

"We don't owe them," Riggs said. "Think of everything they've done. Think of what they've done to *you*."

I'd seen it all. I'd lived, and died, through the war...

"This isn't about me," I said back to him. "This isn't about us."

Lopez sighed. "Not any more, it isn't."

"We need to find the cure," the navigator said. "We need to find from where the...contagion...comes. We know where it began: the worlds and ships that first... developed...it."

"That has to be a start," Lopez said. "Maybe Science Division: they can work on this information or something."

Sergkov was silent beside me. He added nothing to the discussion: just as on Daktar, this was my call. I only hoped that, this time, I would make the right one.

"We will help you," I decided. "As best we can."

The navigator's body appeared to relax. More gas emitted from its gills and mouth. Jesus, the thing stunk.

"We will need our ship," I said. "We will need to leave here, to travel back to our space."

The navigator nodded. "In craft that sails stars."

"I want my crew back too," I said. Standing now, on shaking legs. My determination was waxing, the repercussions of what we had just been told becoming clearer. "Including him," I said, nodding at Pariah. "Her. Whatever you want to call it."

"Individuality is a curse," the navigator said through Pariah. "Those not of us will see this one day."

"We're fine as we are," I said. "We must leave here."

The navigator raised a claw. Krell approached Pariah, and relaxed the restraints. Bio-fluid dripped from open wounds across the xeno's body, as they began to unplug it from the living machine. Pariah stood alone now, flexing damaged limbs. Testing muscles, inspecting its injured body. It was still connected to the wall by some cables, suggesting that the navigator had not yet finished communicating.

The Jackals were standing too now. Unlocking legs, grateful to no longer be kneeling in the filthy pool. They were a more than a sorry sight: filthy faces, ripped and torn uniforms. Very far from the ideal of an Army operator.

"Not others are pariahs," the navigator said. "All."

"This is too big for us," Sergkov said. "I meant what I said to you: about telling you everything."

I frowned. "Such as?"

"I haven't been completely honest with you about the *Hannover*'s mission," he started. "Once we get back to the *Fe*, we can discuss it."

Sergkov held the black box out in front of him. He stared at it—

I didn't get the chance to ask how he had hidden the drive from the Krell, because Sergkov was suddenly *gone*.

The black box bounced across the algae-slicked floor. Came to a stop just in front of me.

It happened too fast for even my sim-senses to track, but Sergkov was two metres off the deck and being held in a pair of the navigator-form's talons: locked round his neck. His body was rigid, legs flapping. Gasping for breath. Own hands forming into claws, reaching desperately for the air.

"You're killing him!" Lopez said ineffectually.

Pariah snapped back against the wall. The Krell surrounded it, plugging the thing back in.

The navigator stirred angrily. The whole chamber did the same.

"Others must call off attack," it said through Pariah again.

"What attack?" I said, shaking my head. "We only have one ship. Only one thing that sails stars!"

The navigator's communication tendrils waved furiously. Sergkov's face had turned a horrible, mortal shade of purple: verging on blue now. Legs thrashing.

"Others that sail stars come," the navigator said. "Tell others to leave."

Pariah's guardians closed, and it threw them off. It grabbed at the connecting cables, readying to sever the connection between it and the navigator.

"Call off others' attack!" the navigator said again.

The organic wall-screen illuminated with glowing coral. The Gyre provided a backdrop, and a dozen flickering lights in the foreground.

"Incoming ships," Feng said. "Is that what you're trying to tell us?"

"Just our luck, huh?" Novak said. His shoulders tensed as he stood, took in the Krell around him. "So, we go down fighting after all."

"No one is fighting!" I yelled. "Those ships are not ours!"

Faster flashes of light broke away from the attackers.

The chamber shook. A muted explosion sounded from inside the ark-ship, sending droplets of water like rainfall all around us. The pressure dropped: a chamber had been breached somewhere. The Krell broke into agitated rustling, like a million angry locusts.

"Use your shields," I said to the Krell. "Use them! It's not us! We have only one thing that sails stars—"

The navigator raised Sergkov higher, and held him there…

Then snapped his neck. The major's body gave one final twitch, then relaxed.

Lopez's breathing accelerated. "No! It's not us! It wasn't *him*!"

I felt a wave of revulsion from the alien—directed at me, directed at my squad.

"Lopez!" I shouted. "Gun!"

I doubt that Lopez knew what I was about to do, but she didn't question the order. Passed the pistol to me: grip down. She was learning, at least.

"Novak, get ready to use that blade."

"With pleasure," Novak said, producing his Adrianna-knife from a holster tucked into his waistband. "Is good way to die, yes?"

The navigator threw Sergkov aside, and let out a wail of anger and pain. The Krell closed in, surrounding the Jackals.

"Stay sharp," I ordered. Raised the gun to my chin. "Hold tight until I get back."

I pulled the trigger.

CHAPTER TWENTY-SIX

LIGHTING THE FIRE

It took me a moment to recover from the sudden violence of the extraction—the ache in my head was excruciating, and my mind was having a hard time accepting that I hadn't just blown my own brains out, but that I was back in my simulator, on the *Santa Fe*.

The Simulant Operations Centre was in a state of utter disarray: medical equipment strewn across the floor, benches overturned, monitors smashed. The Krell had obviously been through here, searching for survivors, and it was a minor miracle that my simulator-tank was still functional. That stood stalwart, barring some damage to the outer canopy.

No time. Got to act now.

"Zero!" I barked. I still had the respirator over my mouth, and I could feel the pressure of the comms bead in my ear. "Are you out there?"

For a fraught second, my stomach went into turmoil as I scanned the SOC. There was no blood, but that didn't mean much. The idea that the little girl I'd rescued from Mau Tanis had met her end out here, in the dark: it gripped me and wouldn't let go.

Just as panic began to set in, I heard her voice over the comm.

"I'm here," Zero said. She appeared from behind an upturned examination table, somewhere in the adjoining infirmary. Speaking into her headset, she said, "You're back!"

"Damn straight. Are you okay?"

"I'm not hurt. I—I hid. The Krell came aboard the ship. I've managed to get the external security cameras working. I can see them outside."

"Where's Carmine? Is anyone else alive?"

"She's on the bridge," Zero said, nodding. "The Navy crew—what's left of them—barricaded themselves in." She swallowed. "They were searching for something. They came aboard, then backed off again."

Maybe that explained why the Krell had missed Zero, why the *Fe*'s crew were still alive. Perhaps they had intended to make contact, had been searching for the Pariah. I couldn't test that theory right now, not while the Jackals were still stranded aboard the ark-ship.

"We've spoken over the closed comm-net," Zero explained, "but I thought that the Krell might detect the transmissions. The crew took out a fair few xenos, from what Yukio told me. We've remotely booted the ship's engine, but the *Fe*'s taken a lot of damage."

"Can she fly?"

"I think so."

That was unexpected, given what I'd seen of her condition. Maybe Gaia was smiling on us after all. "Good job, Zero."

She pursed her lips, uncomfortable with the praise despite the circumstances. "I was scared, ma'am. Real scared. They searched everywhere. I've only just made it out of the airshafts." Pressed down her uniform again, as though any of that actually mattered given how deep in the shit we were. "Where are the others? Have you seen Feng?"

"He's aboard the ark," I said. "The Jackals are alive, but I don't know for how long. That ship we saw— the *Azrael*—was infected with some sort of virus. The Krell can't engineer a cure for it. They want our help." I punched a fist against the interior of the simulator-tank, fighting a sense of resignation that threatened to claim me. "Or at least, they *wanted* it. One of their navigators communicated through Pariah."

Zero was shaking. I knew that the revelation would have this effect on her. She said nothing, only watched me with red-rimmed eyes.

"I thought that this was going to be tough for you to deal with," I said, speaking fast, "but we can talk about that later. The others are still being held prisoner aboard the ship."

Who was I really kidding? *Riggs* was still aboard the ark-ship. I loathed myself for thinking of him above the others, but it was his face that I saw in my mind's eye—

The *Santa Fe*'s frame shook aggressively. Gravity seemed to shift.

"What was that…?" Zero questioned.

"Another fleet is approaching our location," I said. "Open a communications channel to Carmine, on the bridge."

Zero did as she was asked, moving to her nest of broken monitors. Although the main console had been damaged, she managed to pull up a holo-menu and from there activated a comm-band. That would, I knew, be traceable by the Krell.

"I'm not sure that this is a good idea," Zero said, "but here you go…"

"Carmine? Do you read me?"

The line hissed. "Keira? That you?" came the old

captain's voice. "You're alive, girl! Thanks to Gaia and Christo both!"

"I'm in the SOC. I've been aboard the ark."

"Then you did better than us. We're pinned down on the bridge. I have three officers left—"

"No time, Carmine. I need you to open the scanner-suite."

"Done. What do you want to see?"

"Who's attacking us?"

She paused, worked, for a few seconds. *Come on, come on!* I screamed inwardly. Then I heard a sharp intake of breath, a muttered curse.

"It…it's impossible," she said.

"There's no time, Carmine." Impatient now. Every passing second reduced the prospect of the Jackals making it out of this alive. "Who's attacking the ark?"

"It's the Black Spiral. I'm registering the same starship IDs as those at North Star. Jesus, it's a goddamn fleet. A dozen ships, maybe more."

We'd suspected that Daktar Outpost might be part of some wider, organised plan, and now it seemed undeniable. The Black Spiral was orchestrating something against not just the Alliance, but also the Krell.

"We've got to get out of here," Carmine said. "They're overwhelming the ark-ship's defences, and the *Azrael* is out there somewhere too. I can cold-boot the fusion drive, and we can get out-system: try to repair the Q-drive in space—"

"We're not going anywhere. Not until I exfiltrate the Jackals. Await further orders. I'm pulling the shots now. Sergkov is gone."

"Understood," Carmine said, without hesitation or argument.

I cut the line. Zero hovered outside my tank, wringing her hands nervously.

"You know what I'm going to do," I said over our link. She smiled. "Ready when you are."

Transition was fast and furious: just how I like it.

I was in a fresh simulant-body. And not just a new sim: new armour, new weapons, replenished ammo.

I rolled through the *Santa Fe*'s destroyed corridors, and then out of the open rent in her belly—where Pariah and I had been captured by the Krell. Briefly wondered how in the Core we were going to get the *Fe* space-borne with that much damage, then told myself that I couldn't think about it. Retrieving the Jackals: that was my priority objective. Getting off the ark: that was my secondary objective. Everything else: that could wait.

I got a better look at the hangar in which the *Santa Fe* had been forcibly docked. Space was visible through the shaped energy field at the end of the chamber, the same tech as that we'd seen on the *Azrael*.

"Do you read me, Zero?" I asked, flexing a powered glove.

"Loud and clear, ma'am."

I jumped through an open shaft. It felt damned good to be back in a fresh simulant. The HURT suit might've been flashy, but nothing beats a Class VI combat-suit. It was the military equivalent of a little black dress; it looked good, and it always got results. The armour was online and purring like a kitten, equipped with an M115 plasma rifle. That too felt familiar in a good way. A back-up M63 plasma pistol in my thigh holster: the best personal protection a girl could ask for. Just in case it wasn't enough firepower, I'd strapped grenades—stun, frag, incendiary—to the chest harness. An EVAMP rounded off my inventory.

"I don't think that the Krell will pay much attention to the *Santa Fe* until we start powering her up," I said.

"They have bigger things to worry about," Zero replied.

I could sense the Krell's movements all around: hundreds, if not thousands, of bodies skittering along the open shafts, through the tunnel network. Their biosigns danced across my HUD.

"I'd tend to agree," I said. "Activate the Jackals' tracking devices."

"Done and done. Broadcasting their location to your suit now."

The armour's AI opened and digested the datapacket. Although I had no schematics or maps, my suit had started mapping the locale. The place was vast, but I would have to find my way through it.

I felt yet another impact with the ark-ship. They were coming with increasing, and worrying, frequency now.

"Any idea what that was, Zero? It felt too big to be a missile or a kinetic."

"I think that the Spiral is trying to breach the ark's hull," Zero said, sounding dubious. "This is unbelievable! They've crashed a starship into the flank. Two more ships are breaching the ark's outer defences."

"Black Spiral agents aboard the ark? That's all I need."

A Krell primary lurched from somewhere above me. I ducked back, watched it move off. A swarm of primaries followed, like a trail of ants defending their hive. I slipped on my frequency-beacon, set it to maximum amplification. Although I couldn't rely on its accuracy, it was the only tool I had to distinguish me from the invaders.

"What better way to jeopardise galactic peace than by killing each other," Zero said, wistfully.

"It's the human way. I'm going off comms. Ping me if anything happens."

"Anything 'happens'?" Zero said, with a taut, nervous laugh. "That's pretty open ended."

"All right, anything bad. Anything fatal."

"Still not narrow enough," she said, "but I get the idea. Give 'em hell. Zero out."

"Jenkins out."

Ahead, doors opened to allow streams of Krell warriors through. Armed with stingers and shriekers, chittering to themselves, they scurried past me.

On my HUD, the squad's personal trackers lit.

Alive or dead, they were somewhere beyond this hatch.

Either the Krell didn't have very effective crisis management systems in place, or they'd been knocked offline, because the sector beyond the portal was a complete mess. There were a series of open caverns, very much like those in which we'd met with the navigator. Fire erupted everywhere, had claimed pools of liquid that had gathered on the floor. Whatever that shit was, clearly it was highly flammable. Dead, roasted fry lingered in rock pools. I tried not to look at the rictus corpses in the blister-pods—those prisoners caught in the Deep. At least now they had found release from forced communion with the Krell.

I'm too late. They're already dead. Riggs is gone.

But I couldn't believe it until I'd seen it with my own, simulated, eyes.

Gravity had been cut in the next chamber. Krell bodies in bio-suits floated past me, from a variety of castes. A handful of quad-forms pirouetting in the flickering gloom: shredded by weapons fire. That pretty much answered the question of whether the Black Spiral had made it onto the ship.

I switched to my internal atmosphere supply, drank

in processed oxygen. My grip on the plasma rifle had tightened, and my HUD filled with possible targets. I activated my external suit speakers. Tuned them to maximum gain.

"Jackals! Respond!"

To my utter disbelief, through the crackle and pop of the burning chamber, I heard a voice.

"Here!" came a thick, Slavic accent.

Figures emerged from beneath a burning coral structure. Just because it didn't seem possible that we'd be so damned lucky, I scanned them with my suit's senses. But it was true: Novak, Lopez, Riggs, and Feng, all confirmed by their personal ID chips. Alive and breathing.

"You came back for us," Feng said, his face splitting into a grin.

"We're the Jackals," I said, bouncing to the cavern's base with a burst from my EVAMP pack. "And I'd never leave you."

Riggs reached out a hand to touch the armour plating of my clean new combat-suit. "I never doubted you, Keira."

"How did you find us?" Lopez asked.

"I told you, back on Daktar, that you'd be grateful one day for those ID chip implants. I just followed them."

Another dark shape was strung between Novak and Feng. Ragged as a scarecrow, and dripping life-blood faster than it could probably make it, was Pariah. When it saw me with those big alien eyes, the XT's face seemed to shift.

"Are you trying to smile, P?" I asked.

"We do not smile," Pariah replied.

"Whatever you say. What happened in here?"

"Something big hit the ark, just after you extracted," Lopez said. "Most of the chamber collapsed, took out a lot of Krell. The others ignored us, left this chamber."

"We kind of hoped you'd have some answers," Feng added.

"The Spiral is here," I said. "They're boarding the ark."

"Maybe I'll get to finish this magazine after all..." Lopez said.

She looked a million light-years from the girl I'd known back on Daktar: covered in dirt, uniform tattered, pistol cocked in both hands. The change was impressive.

"That navigator got wasted," Riggs said.

He nodded behind me. The navigator had been caught beneath a falling chunk of black coral: crushed so precisely that its head was almost severed from its torso. Sergkov's body lay beneath the alien, crumpled and useless. Not simulated this time: for real.

"Couldn't have happened to a nicer XT," Riggs said, with a jeering expression on his face. Shrugged. "Sergkov might be gone, but shit comes around."

"The navigator thought that we were attacking the ark," I said. "The Krell don't seem to know the difference between us and the Spiral."

"They can't tell the difference between humans," Lopez pitched in. "Good or bad."

"There are good humans?" Novak said. He had his knife in one hand, the blade dripping with Krell blood.

"Yeah," I said. "And as of now, that's us."

I bent down to inspect the navigator's body. It was one ugly son of a bitch, that was for sure, but it was obviously important to the Krell. To see an apex Krell organism die like this...It didn't feel right. My gloved hand brushed the xeno's skull, the enormous armoured carapace—

The creature's eyes flared suddenly. Black and empty,

they reflected the burning chamber: the heat-quivered outlines of my squad.

"Shit!" Lopez said. "That thing's still alive!"

She aimed her pistol, ready to take a shot, but I was faster. I pushed her aside before she had the chance to fire.

"There's no need for that," I said.

The alien shifted beneath the platform, stirring pieces of rubble, but remained pinned. The debris was too substantial for me to remove, even with the suit's strength-aug.

"I'm sorry," I whispered. "There's nothing that I can do to help you."

Without Pariah's particular abilities, the navigator couldn't vocalise communication, but it still tried to make contact. The connection was sharp, frightening. This creature had sailed the stars for hundreds of years. Anger and then fear washed through me. Fear of the virus, not just of what it was doing—*would do*—but of where it came from.

Worlds on fire. End times. Exodus.

"What are you trying to tell me?" I asked the xeno, bending lower now so that my face-plate was almost against the Krell's head. "I need to know!"

But it was futile. The Krell's great gills fluttered, then flattened to its head. It folded over Sergkov's corpse and went still. LIFE-SIGNS EXTINCT, my HUD confirmed. No bio-sign even lingered on the scanner—

Boom. Boom. Boom.

The chamber shuddered with each impact.

I stood from the corpse. Readied my plasma rifle.

"We should go," Lopez said. "This place is finished."

"Get back to the *Santa Fe*," I ordered.

I unclipped my M63 plasma pistol; that was about the

only weapon I carried small enough for a real skin to use. I tossed it to Riggs, who inspected the gun as though it were the first time he'd ever seen it. Then I unhooked the wrist-computer set into my right vambrace, and gave that to Feng.

"My freq-beacon is broadcasting on my wrist-comp. Keep together, and keep it turned on. I've plotted a route back to the *Santa Fe*. One more thing."

I bent to Sergkov's corpse. In the pool in which his body lay was the *Hannover*'s black box. I picked it up. Handed it to Riggs.

"Take this with you," I said. "And make sure you keep it safe."

"Solid copy," Riggs said.

Lopez nodded. "What about you, ma'am?"

I smiled at her. "I'm going looking for someone. Now get moving."

I bounced off into the smoke, leaving the Jackals to it.

I followed the destruction, further into the nest.

Although I told myself that I was covering the Jackals' retreat, even as that thought formed I knew that it wasn't really that. I don't much know why I felt the need to track him down, but I suspected that he was the key to all this.

Cooper. I was going after the Warlord.

How did I know that he was aboard the ship? I didn't. Not really, but something guided me. Something told me that he would be here: in the thick of it. And if Cooper was aboard the ark, then I wanted to be the one to kill him. I wanted revenge, pure and simple.

Our peace accord with the Krell wasn't perfect, and it wasn't what everyone wanted. But it was the best we had: that was just the way things were. And now Cooper and the Black Spiral, they threatened it. I had no way of knowing whether the navigator finally accepted that we were not the same, that I was different to the Spiral, and that cryptic message that it had thought-pinged in its death-throes hadn't made things any clearer. Perhaps, I considered, I was being guided by the brief mind-communion with the navigator. Cooper had once been in the Deep, once been part of the Collective.

"Maybe stopping Cooper will make a difference…" I whispered to myself.

And maybe this talking to yourself is becoming a thing, I thought.

Finding Cooper wasn't hard. The Black Spiral were invading the ship, and in force.

"Stupid bastards should've turned off their comms systems," I said, again to myself. "That was their first mistake…"

The Black Spiral shed data like proper rookies. I could see their comms, hear them bickering to each other in a variety of Standard dialects. As I got nearer, I detected that three ships had in fact breached the ark.

Now that the Spiral were aboard, they were wreaking havoc. Krell bio-fire stitched the walls, chasing exo-armoured Spiral agents. Quads roared in anger and pain, bodies absorbing volleys of gunfire from the invaders. Secondary-forms popped from shafts all around the tunnels, laying down barriers with their shriekers, sending bolts from boomers.

"*Nuke breaching coordinates alpha-six-nine-three,*" someone said.

The tunnel shook with a not-so-distant explosion. Krell bodies rolled past me, gravity flexing and twisting so that I had to use my EVAMP to keep moving.

"*We've got a tactical plasma charge coming in on your six. Fishy bastards'll never know what hit them.*"

"*Copy that. Praises be to He that Cares.*"

"He'll see you on the other side, Braven."

"Who the damn is He that Cares?" I said, over the open comms.

"Who's this?" someone asked.

"Lieutenant Keira Jenkins."

I jumped into a cavern-space above me. The chamber had taken a direct hit from something—maybe one of the Black Spiral's missiles—and the Krell were fighting to contain a hull breach. Frozen liquid streamed past me in hard spheres, reflecting the destruction.

"What are you still doing here?" a voice asked. "Cut comms, cut the comms!"

A stream of kinetic gunfire hit the floor beside me, and I rolled away. My suit predicted the firer's location. Without conscious thought, I responded with a volley from my plasma rifle. Old faithful did its job, blasting apart several Spiral agents. Another half-dozen were on my six, their jump-packs glowing bright as they closed the distance. I primed an incendiary grenade and tossed it behind me, watched as it caught the invaders in the blast, their bio-signs extinguishing on my HUD.

"I'm here, Cooper," I said. "I just wanted to say thanks."

"Not necessary," came the response. That same raspy voice: as though the speaker was in pain.

"I think that it is. I got this mission after what happened on Daktar. *You* got me this mission."

"We've all got a mission," Cooper said. "Some are just more difficult than others."

"That's right," I said, goading him now. "Some have a cost."

I scanned the devastation. Coral and bone structures rose from the cavern floor like a maze of skeletons. Alien life-forms had been reduced to blackened husks. Krell bodies spiralled past me, twisting to fire at incoming

Black Spiral tangos. Gravity had gone haywire, and as I jumped between structures I felt my centre of balance twisting, shifting. Then I was back on solid ground, landing on another coral platform. I ducked some more gunfire. Took cover behind something that looked like a giant spiked urchin.

"You've done a lot of damage, considering how long you've been on this ship," I said.

My suit was actively tracing Cooper's signal, whenever he spoke with me: all this chat had a purpose. NEGATIVE LOCK, it said. I needed more time, needed to get just a little closer...

"I like to think so," Cooper said. "There's a plan behind it all, Jenkins. *Everything* I am doing here is with reason."

LOCK ACQUIRED. Coordinates flashed across my HUD. Cooper was above me, where the wash of enemy comms traffic was thickest. I let the rangefinder search for the source of that signal.

I was surprised by what I saw. Two plumes of heat appeared on my scanner: a couple of hundred metres overhead, but as dazzling as twin stars. I recognised the distinctive flare-pattern as belonging to the VTOL engine of a starship. It was making a fast but cautious approach into the ark, descending on a white column, manoeuvring around the Krell bio-structures. The engine regularly fired with blue-white emissions, bringing the small vessel further inside the ark, using the cavern as a dock.

"What are you doing here, Cooper?" I said. "After what happened to you, why come back to the Maelstrom?"

"You don't need to know that," Cooper answered. "Not yet."

Black Spiral troopers, wearing exo-assisted survival armour, had assembled all around the cavern. By now,

I was heavily outnumbered. As my HUD flagged the enemy assailants, I realised that the Krell were too.

"What's your objective then, I wonder?"

I dodged back into cover as an assault rifle fired on my location.

"I know what you're doing," Cooper replied. "And I can do just the same."

COMMS LOCK LOST.

Damn.

"Question still stands," I said, trying to track his signal again. I bounced up another level, through more dead coral structures. "You've done a lot of damage here, like I say, but I don't think that is your objective. Not just that, anyway. I know what happened to you. I know all about the Deep."

Cooper's snarl surprised me. "What do you know of the Deep? Nothing! I'm the only one who came back from it!"

"What were you doing on North Star, for that matter?"

Two Black Spiral troopers descended from somewhere above me. I dispatched both with my rifle, plasma bolts punching through their armoured bodies. They were well armed, I noted, carrying zero-G assault rifles with grenade bandoliers over their chests. Even as I killed them, another began to fire on me.

"I see you," Cooper said.

Energy fire raked my location. Above me, the starship descended further. Whatever that ship was doing, it was important to the Spiral, and important to Cooper.

"*Is it in position?*" someone else asked.

"*Not yet. She's holding us up.*"

"Cut your comms," Cooper roared.

"*My apologies, Warlord.*"

"Warlord? That what you make them call you now? Doesn't the name Clade Cooper suit you better?"

Cooper let out an angry roar. "That's not who I am any more."

TRIANGULATING LOCATION, my armour told me. RE-ACQUIRING LOCK …

Good. Keep going.

I bounced upwards again.

"Clade Cooper. Formerly of the 1st Alliance Rangers. Originally MIA on Barain-11. Your whole unit was wiped out."

"Wiped out?" Cooper growled. I could imagine the spittle dripping from his lips, his anger hot enough that I felt it over the comms. "Is that what they told you?"

LOCATION CONFIRMED. LOCK ACQUIRED.

Now I was getting somewhere. I pushed on. "And only you made it out. Did that hurt? I'm an Army brat myself. It's bred into us, isn't it? Maybe we're closer to the Krell than we think."

"They are a virus!" Cooper bellowed. His anger was stronger than the pull of a black hole, drawing me onwards. "They need to be purged from this galaxy, and that is *my mission*!"

"I've read your file," I lied. "You had a mission once, Sergeant Clade Cooper. It was called Operation Pitfall. And you fucked it up."

"You know *nothing* about what happened! I did not fail!"

Then I saw him. Cooper: galactic enemy number one, Warlord of the Drift. Standing on the edge of a precipice, surrounded by a handful of Black Spiral operatives. All wearing heavy survival suits, equipped with thruster packs and rifles.

From my position, through the blackened strands of webbing, they couldn't see me. My combat-suit camouflage was also running active, and I stayed low. The starship was descending the shaft above them, moving slowly, her access ports open. Thrusters on her nacelles fired periodically, their heat muted by the distance. Although I couldn't swear that it was the same, the ship looked very similar to that Cooper had used to escape from Daktar.

"Scared yet?" I asked. "You should be..."

For all his bravado, whoever the fuck Cooper actually was—whoever he *had* been—he was scared now. His bodyguards were about as tetchy as it got.

"Our mission is greater than you could ever imagine," Cooper said. "This is destiny. Whatever happens to me, and whatever happens here, you should know that there are a hundred more like me: that whatever you do, you cannot stop what we've set in motion."

"Right..." I whispered. "Then this won't matter one bit."

I still couldn't get a good shot, not without exposing my position to every Black Spiral in the chamber. So instead I slid a grenade from my harness. High explosive. Grenade damage projections and the likely blast-zone scrolled across my HUD. All good.

I tossed the grenade underarm.

"Goodbye, Cooper."

It hit home. The structure collapsed in near slow motion, an explosion coursing through the chamber. The platform on which Cooper and his men had been standing broke apart. Bodies were thrown against the wall, limbs sagging and useless. Some suits breached. One tango survived for long enough to return fire, but the rounds bounced off my null-shield.

I activated my EVAMP. Bouncing between platforms, I filled the chamber with grenades. Nothing, and nobody, was getting out of here alive.

Cooper's exo-suit was a custom job, of that I was sure. He sailed past me, reacting faster than an unaugmented man really should be able to. We almost passed in mid-air, and he blasted the surrounding area with weapons fire.

I gave chase. The Spiral ship was settling on a platform above us now, and I knew exactly what Cooper was doing.

"Don't run," I said. "It'll only hurt more."

"I'm gone," he said.

"Damn straight you are."

I ran along the coralline structure, gaining speed with each footfall. Felt it shifting beneath me, collapsing. I fired my EVAMP just as it gave way: perfect timing to launch myself to the next structure.

Cooper sailed ahead. He jinked left, right—through another looping bone construction. Smaller than me, as before his greatest advantage was speed. The survival suit's thruster pack fired brightly as he jumped among the dying Krell structures.

Tracking targets on my HUD, I fired my rifle again and again. Plasma bolts clipped possible landing sites, sending a rain of glowing coral shrapnel across Cooper's path. He dodged that. Rolled across an open platform: slammed a powered fist into the skull of a dying Krell primary. He came to a stop atop one of the largest coral structures. Fittingly, surrounded by dead and dying xenos, the latter still clawing for him as though they stood a chance of stopping him.

I followed, landing hard with my weapon trained on him.

"It's over," I said. "I don't know what's happening out here, but I'm shutting you down."

"And how exactly are you going to do that, Lieutenant?"

"You've no right to use my rank," I said. "You lost that when you turned on the Alliance."

"You think that by killing me you'll get a damned medal? That they'll take you back and give you a parade?" Cooper laughed, eyes towards the ship. That was the only part of his face that I could see; the rest was wrapped in filthy rags, inside his helmet.

"Don't even think about it," I said.

Cooper froze. "I really did think that you might see things differently." He sighed, shook his head: helmet bobbing. His entire suit was smoke-stained, covered in Krell blood. "Then I've no other option."

"You've no options at all," I said, advancing on him.

A clean shot at this range would be utterly fatal. I raised my rifle.

"This is all for the Spiral," Cooper said.

He dropped a small silver canister from his belt: the item *clink-clinking* as it hit the hard coral deck.

CHAPTER TWENTY-SEVEN

THE BIG JUMP

And then I was back in the tank.

The simulator canopy cracked open, spilling amniotic, and I stirred inside.

"Get her out!" I heard Riggs yelling, over and over.

"What the fuck, Riggs?" I shouted back. "I *had* him! I had Cooper!"

The *Santa Fe*'s SOC rumbled around me, and I recognised the pull of gravity as the inertial damper activated. We were moving under thrust, and fast.

Riggs hauled me from the tank, my weakened body slipping in his arms. Zero was there too, and the consoles around us squawked with Navy jargon.

"They're blowing the ark-ship, Jenkins," he said. "We can't stay here any longer."

The *Santa Fe*'s frame screamed.

"*That hull patch is holding,*" the console said. I assumed that was from the remains of the bridge crew, directing our escape. "*Thrust control initiated . . .*"

"*Keep it up,*" I heard Carmine's voice.

"I *had* him!" I said again, unable to let it go.

The *Santa Fe*'s PA chimed. "Are we buckled for evac? Because ready or not, we're leaving."

Zero picked her way through the mess that the SOC had become. "We're ready, Captain. Everyone is aboard."

"You could've left me down there!" I insisted. "I would've bugged out when the neural-link broke."

But even so, I collapsed into Riggs' arms.

The *Santa Fe* pulled away from the dying ark-ship, moving at the greatest velocity her spaceframe could withstand. The energy field protecting the ark-ship's hangar had failed, and it was exposed to vacuum. That made evac that little bit easier. The ship accelerated faster and faster as it escaped what was left of the ark's artificial gravity well.

Still aching from the last transition, still rankled by Riggs' unnecessary extraction, I watched the process from the bridge. The view-ports were wide open, and what detail I couldn't make out with the naked eye was filled in by the tac-display.

"The inertial damper is stable, ma'am," Yukio said. "We're approaching the likely blast threshold."

"Good, good," Carmine said. She was, as of now, the mistress of shit: a ship that was virtually flying on spit and duct-tape, and a crew that numbered—including her—four.

"Blast threshold?" Lopez asked.

"I'm reasonably sure the ark-ship is about to go down," Carmine said, with a wave at the holo. "Those Spiral bastards did a proper job on it. See for yourself."

The Krell ark-ship had been torn apart. Huge gouges, marking the detonation of warheads and enemy starships, had been scored into its hull. Great chunks had been ripped from the ark's profile, sufficient to change its shape.

"They were determined," Novak said. His face was a complete mess: one eye bandaged, his chest taped up with medi-packs. "Sometimes is all it takes."

"You okay, Novak?" I asked him. "You look like shit."
He grunted.

"You take some getting used to," I said, "but I think I'm almost there."

"And being cut up is pretty much your regular state," Lopez said, with a grin. She punched the big guy in the arm, and he grunted again.

"Why were the Spiral out here, Keira?" Carmine said, still staring at the imagery on the tac-display. "What was their objective?"

I shrugged. "I'm not sure what they wanted, but I know what they were doing. Cooper used a canister of something, just before Riggs pulled me out."

"A canister?" Lopez asked. "Like, of what?"

"I think that they are responsible for spreading this... this virus, or whatever it is."

"You know that how, exactly?" Carmine said with a raised eyebrow. "Lot of conjecture going on there, girl."

"So what do we do?" Lopez asked.

She sighed, and I was struck again by how different she looked. Her pistol was holstered on her thigh, her face still dirty from the evac. She was Sim Ops, through and through.

"We run back to Alliance space, and we tell someone— anyone—what's happened out here."

Carmine smiled, but it wasn't a happy expression. "And what *has* happened? We were sent out here to investigate a missing starship, and all we've come away with is a black box. What exactly did my crew die for?"

"Sergkov tried to tell me something before he died," I said. Remembering both the flight across the *Santa Fe*, and then the seconds before the navigator's attack. "He said that the *Hannover* had a mission, but that it wasn't what he told us."

"I know that we shouldn't speak ill of the dead," Carmine said, "but why am I not surprised by that?"

Explosions rippled along the ark-ship's flanks. Everyone fell silent and a sombre mood descended over the bridge. It felt wrong to be joking when so many lives were being lost, even if the casualties were Krell. I kept it to myself, but I sensed a sympathetic ache as each biological component exploded inside the Krell vessel.

"The Spiral have suffered their own losses from this battle," Carmine said. "I counted maybe ten ships lost during that exchange. They flew eight into the damned ark."

"Perhaps it will slow the Spiral down," Lopez suggested.

Feng crossed his arms over his chest, his eyes boring into the tac display. "We still don't know what the Spiral is really capable of," he muttered. "They're an unknown quantity."

"I think that they have a plan," I said, remembering Cooper's last words aboard the ark-ship. "And, of course, Cooper is still out there."

Numerous Black Spiral ships had docked with the ark, only to pull out shortly after I'd extracted. There seemed no tactical explanation for that. Tiny streaks of light—rats leaving a sinking ship—were confirmed to be escaping Black Spiral vessels. At least three had left in the last few seconds; and although I couldn't be certain, I was pretty sure that one of those ships had departed from the coordinates of my last extraction. That could only be Cooper's escape ship.

I glared sideways at Riggs. "I could've taken Cooper."

"Bitter much?" Feng asked.

"I'm sorry, Keira," Riggs said, quietly. "I thought that

it was best to extract you. I—I panicked." He exhaled slowly. "It was a rash decision, but we were evacuating."

"You've still got a lot to learn about Sim Ops. You should've just left me there. My real body was aboard the *Santa Fe.*"

But I knew that I wasn't going to be able to stay angry with Riggs. He *had* done what he thought was best, even if it was a bad call. I'd made enough of those in my career.

"Then what's the plan to get us out of here, Carmine?" I asked.

The captain stirred in her throne. Her mechanical leg hadn't stopped twitching since I'd come back aboard the *Santa Fe*, and she still clutched her carbine across her lap, a protective ward against the chaos around us.

"We run as dark as we can, which won't be hard given that only a tenth of our shipboard systems are currently functional," she said, rubbing her chin, "and once we're a safe distance from the Gyre, we activate the quantum-drive."

"And if those infected Krell come after us?" Lopez enquired.

"I think you already know the answer to that," Feng said, with a plaintive grimace.

"Then we die," Carmine said, bluntly. "Simple as that. Our weapons systems are non-functional. Our null-shield is running at twenty per cent efficiency. We have no communication array, and don't even think about going aft of Module A-3..."

"So no hot showers, I guess?" Lopez said. "Which is a shame, because Novak needs one."

The Russian made a noise that could've been a laugh, but it was hard to tell.

I stood from my console, ricked my neck. Looked out

into space, at the whirling miasma of the Gyre, and the incandescent wreck of the ark-ship.

"Anything you need done for launch prep," I said, to Carmine, "let the Jackals help."

Carmine nodded. "We've no navigator. We lost Lieutenant Robinson." She paused. "And so many others."

"Riggs, you up to programming a Q-jump?" I asked. "You can make up for pulling me out too early."

Riggs smiled. "I can try."

"It won't be an easy job," Carmine said. "We'll likely need to loop around the Drift, and in our condition we can't afford to risk using a Shard Gate. A dozen quantum-jumps, at least, before we're on the home stretch."

"See what you can do," I said.

I made off towards the hatch. Novak followed me out of the bridge, wincing just a little as he walked.

"I think that you've earned some downtime, Big Man," I said to him.

Novak's face remained settled. "No need. Would rather work."

I shrugged. "Your call. But listen, when we get back I'll be sure to put in a good word with Command. That sentence: it might not look so long after this."

"Will not change anything," he said. But there was no bluster in his words, and his shoulders sagged.

"I remember well enough what you told me when we were on the ark. And you're okay, Novak. You're okay."

For a fleeting moment, Novak's eyes misted. Perhaps, just perhaps, he wasn't the monster that they thought he was.

"Thank you," he said, haltingly.

Hours after the flight from the ark-ship, the mood aboard the *Santa Fe* had settled into cautious optimism.

Everyone was too busy covering essential maintenance duties, repairing the ship, taking watch, to dwell on our prospects of survival. I spent the time on the bridge.

"It won't save us, you know," Carmine said.

I sipped at my third cup of coffee. It had already grown cold.

"What won't?"

"Staring at the tactical display. It won't save us, if they come after us. The Krell or the Spiral or whoever else is out here. You should get some rest."

"I'm good," I said. "Honestly. I'm good. I'll take watch if you like."

Carmine started to protest, then sighed, and finally gave in. "All right. It has been a while since I've had any beauty-sleep."

I smiled. "Go take forty winks."

"You have the con, Keira."

Carmine stood on shaky legs, clutching her cane to steady herself. I went to help, but she waved me off. Hobbled from her command station, her cane tapping away as she went.

"I didn't think that you'd want to be left alone with me," Riggs said, from across the bridge. His head was buried in the navigation console, data-cables running to his ports.

"Maybe that's why I sent Carmine away," I said.

Riggs gave one of his boyish smiles in my direction, the hint of encouragement enough to brighten his mood. He'd been working on programming the Q-drive for the last two hours, and I hadn't heard so much as a word out of him.

"Really?" he said.

This is an unnecessary complication, Keira. Stop leading him on.

I sighed. "Let's worry about that later."

"Carmine was wrong you know," Riggs said, nodding at the tac-display. "About the ark-ship. Whatever the Black Spiral were doing, they weren't trying to destroy it. Not directly, at least."

"I'd noticed," I said. "They didn't blow it up, in other words."

There had been no tell-tale Q- or other subspace disturbance, no mass energy discharge. The *Santa Fe*'s scanner-suite was pretty trashed, but if the ark had blown, we'd have seen it.

"That's what I was watching for," I said, resting my elbows on the edge of the tac-display. Space was still, quiet. "But you were wrong too, I think."

Riggs looked over at me, with that blank expression that was both cute and infuriating. He looked almost as tired as Carmine: battered and bruised, his face still encrusted with dirt and blood from the ark-ship exfiltration.

"How so?" he asked.

"When you said that there was a traitor on this ship," I said. "You were wrong about that."

Riggs shrugged noncommittally. "I was just worried, is all. Better to raise it than let it stew, right?"

"Of course. But I'd know if any of the Jackals was a traitor." I met his eyes, let a smile creep across my lips. "We've died together, Riggs. All of us. There's a bond there."

Riggs slowly nodded. "Yeah. Yeah, you're right."

"Of course I'm right," I said. "I'm your commanding officer, kemo sabe. Cooper was tracking Sergkov. That's why he was on North Star. I'm not sure how he managed it, but I know my squad, and after what we've just been through, I know that I can rely on you all."

There was a swell of pride in Riggs' chest. "Thanks. That means a lot to me."

"And hey, if you get those Q-jumps programmed, maybe we can take another look at the Warhawk sometime," I said, despite myself.

"I'd like that, ma'am."

The words just tumbled out of my mouth before I'd had a chance to think. "Call me Keira," I said.

I went down to Medical. Took the ladder shaft between decks—because the elevators were still down—and had to take a detour to avoid the depressurised modules.

"You need anything in here?" I asked, hand on hip, as I stood at the hatch and surveyed the damage.

Zero was the only human occupant of the room. She sat in front of a bank of terminals, a mash-up of equipment that looked to have been seized from elsewhere aboard the ship and put to new use. When I entered, she jumped awake.

"Sorry, ma'am," she said. She looked patently exhausted; it wasn't just the black rings under her eyes, but also the coffee cups that lined her terminal. "You startled me there."

"You've done a good job of tidying the place up."

"Liar," she said, with a tired grin.

"I'm serious."

"Well, I've done what I can. The tanks are working."

The simulator-tanks had been powered down for now, their canopies closed, but they were ready for operation should they be required.

"Let's hope that we won't be needing them for a while."

"Some of us will never get to use them," she said.

"I didn't mean it like that."

"I know, and I agree. Let's hope," Zero echoed. She stared around the room: at the vandalised equipment, at the smashed terminals and monitors. The damage caused by the Krell attack was plain to see. "We're still in Krell space though. We're still in the Maelstrom."

"We're doing okay."

Zero repressed a shiver. "You know what? I never thought that something could frighten me more than the Krell. After what happened at home, after Mau Tanis. But the *diseased* Krell…"

This time she couldn't repress her reaction, and I wished that I could do something to make it better.

"To think," she went on, "before all this, I thought I was missing out on something by not going into the field. Being a simulant operator was all I'd ever wanted to be."

I nodded. "I know, Zero."

"Well things have changed. When we get back, I'm going to think very hard about that desk job."

"Whatever you want to do, I'll be behind you. Not everyone is cut out for the field, even if they can do it."

"It's taken a near-death experience to teach me that." Zero rubbed her eyes, sighing to herself. "This thing— this virus, whatever it is—it's major, isn't it?"

"I think so," I said. "And I expect High Command will say the same. That the navigator spoke to us…The Krell obviously think that it's big."

"What about the *Hannover*'s black box?" Zero said. "Have you analysed it yet?"

"Not yet," I said.

"Are you going to?"

"I'm not sure. The data is heavily encrypted."

Zero watched me carefully. "Aren't you curious about what the box contains?"

"Of course I am."

The data-drive—the *Hannover*'s black box—was safely locked away in my quarters, and I wasn't even sure if the *Fe*'s systems would be able to access it. Something about the entire mission, about the importance that Sergkov had attached to that box, made me wary of opening it. Somehow, it was easier to just leave it for others to examine.

"It's someone else's problem," I said, definitively.

"I understand," Zero said.

"Glad to see you're doing okay."

"Is that why you came down here?" Zero asked, with a knowing grin.

"Maybe," I said.

"It's through there."

She nodded towards the infirmary.

Pariah was in a converted cryogenic capsule. The device was big enough to hold the XT's body, and it floated inside the tube, suspended in fluid. Brackish and green, it looked almost the same consistency as the stuff aboard the Krell bio-ship. I placed a hand against the outside of the glass, held it there for a moment. There was a warmth coming from inside the tank.

Pariah had stripped off its bio-suit, and folded its limbs so that it was almost half its usual size. The xeno's head nuzzled against the inner glass, a respirator plugged over its mouth and nose.

"Can you hear me?"

The alien nodded.

"We can," it said. The voice-box was still grafted to its neck, and had been tuned to a speaker in the capsule's control console.

"How's the hurt?"

"We do not understand."

"The injuries, I mean. Are you going to pull through?"

"Define 'pull through.'"

"You know what I mean. Quit fucking with me."

Pariah paused, then said, "We will try."

It, too, looked tired, if that were possible. Although

many wounds pocked its body, most had been stapled shut to stem the flow of blood.

"Zero's handiwork, huh?"

The alien blinked. "Zero's handiwork," it repeated. "Yes."

"This shit going to help?" I gestured to the tube.

"We are being stored in a chemically balanced electrolyte mix," Pariah explained. "It will increase our capacity to self-heal, and allow us to enter hibernation in due course."

"Good, good," I said. "I know that you didn't have a choice back there aboard the ark-ship. I know that the, ah, *other*, Krell were trying to control you."

"They are of our Collective," it said. "Very old."

"But I saw you fighting it too. I saw that you didn't want to let them take control."

"That is true," Pariah said. The alien appeared to shiver, in a gesture that struck me as peculiarly human. "We are Kindred, but we have no experience of being part of the Collective mind. It was unpleasant."

"What you did—acting as a bridge between us and the navigator: it was very helpful. More than you can imagine."

Pariah nodded. "We are all pariahs, now."

"I'll never understand your kind," I said.

"Nor I yours," Pariah said.

"But maybe there is hope. If we can work together."

"Perhaps."

"When you were aboard the *Azrael*, why weren't you infected?"

I could still recall every detail of the nightmarish attack by the infected Krell. The smell. The snapshot images. That final primary-form: its jaws open wide, ready to stream black fluid into my face. Could I have been infected too?

"We are not native Kindred," Pariah said.

"Can you be infected?"

"We do not know. Dr. Skinner made us more resilient than the wild strain."

Despite old animosities, I found myself hoping that Pariah was okay. What other secrets were locked inside the alien's body?

Our conversation was interrupted by a chime from the bridge.

"*Q-jump in T minus two minutes,*" the ship's AI declared.

I left the alien in its hibernation cell.

As Carmine had promised, we made multiple Q-jumps across the Maelstrom. Time-dilation did its thing, the ship's quantum-clock ticking away, indicating that with every jump the universe was moving closer to forgetting us.

After each jump, I got that little tummy-roll as we breached the real-space barrier. That second of doubt: was the Q-drive going to give up? Was the hull going to breach? Thankfully, as we made our way across the Maelstrom and towards the Former Quarantine Zone, none of those things happened. There were no Krell: diseased or otherwise. No Black Spiral. Just us and the stars.

And then finally the day came. After many short quantum-skips, we were ready to commence the big jump across the FQZ and into Alliance space. Because it felt like an occasion, the Jackals gathered on the bridge.

Carmine eased herself into her command station. "Your Corporal Riggs has been very helpful in plotting our Q-jumps," she said. Winked at me. "He's quite a catch."

I tried my best not to make eye contact with her. "I don't know what you're talking about."

"Of course you don't," the old captain said. "All squared away for the next jump?"

"Aye, ma'am," Yukio said. "I'm getting some error messages from the cargo deck, but it's nothing we can't fly on."

Carmine clapped her hands together. Rubbed the picture of her daughters for luck. "Good, good. I, for one, can't wait to see some friendly stars. Initiate the jump on my command."

"Talking of Riggs," Zero said, "has anyone seen him?"

"He was down in the shuttle bay," Feng said. "Last I saw, anyhow. Said something about fixing the bay door sensor."

"Jesus, is that still playing up?" I asked. It had been a recurring fault throughout the journey, and not just as a cover for my covert meetings with Riggs...

"Looks that way," Carmine said. "Someone should go get the corporal though. He should be here for the big jump."

"Novak, you're on it," I said.

The Russian nodded. "I go," he said, shambling out of the bridge.

"Hurry, lifer," Carmine said. "We're jumping in two."

"So we risked our asses for the *Hannover*'s black box?" Feng said, with a tone of exasperation in his voice.

"That's about the size of it," I said.

"And they say that the Directorate are crazy..." he replied, shaking his head.

"I'm sure that they would kill for whatever is on the *Hannover*'s drive," Lopez said.

"Thankfully we don't have to worry about that," I said.

"*Commencing jump in T minus two minutes...*" the ship's AI declared.

But the cheer of relief that went up around the bridge was abruptly interrupted by an alert chime.

Carmine frowned down at her console. "That cargo bay really is playing up."

Yukio continued the countdown, but I turned to Carmine. "What's the sitrep?"

"The bay reports it has been unsealed," Carmine said, "which patently cannot be true. Computer says that the Warhawk's drive has been activated."

Sudden and cold realisation hit me.

"Abort the jump," I said. I scrambled for Carmine's console, watching as the pre-launch sequence began to accelerate. "*Now.*"

"*T minus twenty seconds…*" the AI declared, skipping through the usual launch countdown.

Carmine shook her head at me. "There's no problem here. It's just a glitch."

One of the bridge's consoles crackled with an incoming report from elsewhere on the *Fe*.

"*Ma'am!*" Novak's voice, thick with panic. "*Shuttle bay will not open! Someone is in there, but cannot get hatch open!*"

"Abort launch," I insisted. "Do something!"

Yukio looked at Carmine for approval, and the captain nodded. "Do it."

But when Yukio reported, I wasn't surprised. "I'm locked out of the system, ma'am!"

"*Jump imminent,*" the AI declared. "*All hands prepare.*"

Traitor. Onboard the ship.

How had I been so stupid?

"What's all this about?" Carmine said.

An amber security lamp had started flashing overhead. "*Jump. Jump. Jump.*"

Space outside had already started to warp, to twist as the *Santa Fe* created its own time-space breach.

Riggs. It was Riggs all along.

"Novak!" I yelled into the communicator. "Stop that shuttle from launching!"

I heard the pitched hum of the ship's Q-drive igniting. The gut-roll, space shifting. The console crackled again, but when it spoke it wasn't Novak's voice.

"I'm sorry," Riggs mumbled. "I'm sorry!"

"*Jump complete,*" the ship's AI said.

Zero's face was a paler shade of white. "Where are we?" she managed.

I shook my head. Panic gripped me. "H—he programmed the Q-jump…"

"*Shuttle bay open,*" the AI reported. "*Warhawk deployed.*"

Feng slipped into the station Riggs had been manning.

"Oh shit…" he whispered.

The stars settled around us. The tactical display repopulated, astrogation data flooding in.

"We're in Asiatic Directorate space," Feng said. "Riggs has jumped us directly into Directorate space."

Outside, a fleet of black shapes had already collected, and were moving on our position.

EPILOGUE

"There's a storm coming," Lieutenant Runweizer said.

"Yep," replied Captain Uzbek. "Looks that way."

It was hard to argue with the black clouds that gathered in the distance. They were a bruise across the horizon: massed and rolling.

"Although," Runweizer said, turning the aerocar's steering column so that the vehicle entered an approach pattern, gliding cross-country, "it's rarely ever nice out here. Not any more. Not after the war, that is."

The car's engine gave a throaty roar as the vehicle reached ground level, and found an overgrown highway between two grey fields. Like most of the roads in this region, it could hardly be described as that. Uzbek didn't like this place much.

"Spells rain, I'd say," Runweizer added.

Uzbek didn't like Runweizer much, either. He was a mouth-breather, and a noisy one at that. Coupled with his poor conversation skills, it made him a bad travel companion. His every driving habit, over the last few hours, had grown to rile Uzbek. Annoy him.

"Yep," Uzbek said. "War did a lot of things for this place, even if it never reached it."

"Wasn't the chick French or something?"

"So the files say," Uzbek answered.

"What, you don't believe them?"

"I only believe what I can see with my own eyes. And I've never met her."

"Who has? They're recluses."

"So I read."

Runweizer gave a deep belly laugh and sat back in his seat. "I could probably learn a thing or two from you German guys. We run things differently out my way."

The journey had been long, and Uzbek was tired of Runweizer's constant small talk. Chatter that seemed formulated to irritate—a relatively easy task, given that the pair had taken a non-stop military transport from Berlin Central to Paris, then broken early to commence the cross-country drive to Normandy.

Runweizer slid the aerocar into a low gear, climbing the hillside. He sighed to himself. "If I ever retire, I'm going to choose a better place to do it than here. Somewhere warm. Off-world."

"Yep," Uzbek said, staring out of the window of the car, wishing that the Americans hadn't insisted that he be accompanied by this cretinous fool. "I'll bet."

"Mmmm," Runweizer said. "I'd go somewhere real nice."

The car's navigation system began to chime, zeroing in on the coordinates. "It's up there."

The house on the hillside wasn't much. Small, stone-clad. Dark.

Runweizer pulled the car into a badly maintained paddock outside the building, and Uzbek got out before the vehicle had stopped moving. Felt the bracing wind cut into his uniform, pulled his tunic a little higher. Had he been an off-world operative, the Alliance would've provided an environment-controlled uniform. Because he was only local, based in Euro-Confed Germany, things were different.

Uzbek positively raced towards the door, so glad was he to be free of the confines of the car. The little house's porch was wooden-slatted, and as the deck took Uzbek's weight the building groaned. As he got closer still, he noticed that the structure looked rotted. How could anyone live like this? This wasn't what he had expected, not at all. With mounting concern, he rapped a knuckle on the metal-grilled door.

"Doesn't look good, boss," Runweizer said. His heavier build made the whole porch shake as he padded up behind Uzbek, shadow falling across the door. "Doesn't look as though there's anyone here."

Uzbek frowned. "Shut up, Lieutenant."

He tried again. The door creaked, the house murmuring as it caught the wind blowing in across the surrounding farmland.

"Colonel?" Uzbek called.

"No one's home," Runweizer said, in his blunt American accent. He stooped at a window beside the door, hand to his forehead as he peered inside. "Take a look for yourself."

The idiot-lieutenant was right. The inside of the farmhouse was semi-gutted, derelict. One of the window-panes had been smashed, a curtain inside fluttering lazily in the wind. It looked as though the place had been abandoned for a long time.

Uzbek frenziedly circled the house. Checked every window, hammered on every door. No response. He found that the rear entrance had been prized open by someone or something, the thin wooden door slamming rhythmically against the rotted frame, caught by the wind. The room inside had once been a kitchen, but now no one lived here: a cloak of dust over the empty table, the barren work surfaces.

"Hello?" Uzbek called out.

No answer.

"This what you were expecting?" Runweizer asked. He'd tapped a cigarette from a packet in his lapel pocket, and commenced dragging on the stick noisily.

"No, Lieutenant. It is not."

Runweizer grinned, let out a muted laugh. "Maybe someone else got here first."

"This was a secret location. This is where he was supposed to be!"

"Things change."

Uzbek froze. His burning indignation was dowsed—and suddenly—by the fact that Runweizer had unholstered his pistol. The arming stud was lit.

"I don't think that will help..." he started.

"Oh, I think it will," Runweizer said. "I think it will help a lot."

The gun barked twice.

Uzbek grabbed for his stomach when the first shot was fired, but the second hit him in the temple. He just managed to let his jaw drop open, to form the remains of his forehead into a frown, when consciousness left him.

He collapsed on the porch.

Dead.

Runweizer finished his cigarette, then searched the rest of the house. When he tried the taps, he found that they were dry too. Although surely no one would see Captain Uzbek's body—not for several days, at least—he took the time to drag the corpse into the abandoned living room. That was about as depressing as the kitchen. Threadbare furniture covered in a thick layer of dust, curtains so thin that they barely held out the grey light of the coming dawn.

Nothing here. No sign of anyone, either. No paperwork, no electronic devices. Runweizer used his wrist-comp to run a scan of the property—searching for listening and seeing bugs—but found nothing. Hardly surprising, really, if even a tenth of the stories they told about the man were true. He'd cover his tracks, for sure.

The lieutenant smoked another cigarette out on the porch. It was a long drive cross-country, and without any company this time. So he took his time smoking the cigarette, and then dropped it to the floor. Snubbed it out with the toe of his boot. This wasn't a forensic job, and he didn't care what evidence he left behind at the scene. There were some benefits to being outside usual structures.

Once he had finished, he sauntered down the porch steps to the waiting aerocar. Pulled the collar of his uniform a little higher to his neck. Those clouds on the horizon looked darker. It might even be raining in the distance.

"Storm's breaking, all right," Runweizer said to himself. "And we're all going to suffer."

He fished in his pocket for the icon—tiny and insignificant as it was—and held it tightly in his hand. An eternity spiral. A silly, sentimental trinket: something that would surely get him killed if he was ever found with it. No matter. Runweizer was a man who liked a little risk in his life.

Then he slid the car into gear, and reached for the altitude controller, leaving behind the abandoned farmhouse.

extras

orbit

meet the author

JAMIE SAWYER was born in 1979 in Newbury, Berkshire. He studied law at the University of East Anglia, Norwich, acquiring a master's degree in human rights and surveillance law. Jame is a full-time barrister, practising in criminal law. When he isn't working in law or writing, Jamie enjoys spending time with his family in Essex. He is an enthusiastic reader of all types of SF, especially classic authors such as Heinlein and Haldeman.

if you enjoyed

THE ETERNITY WAR: PARIAH

look out for

THE RULE OF LUCK

A Felicia Sevigny Novel

by

Catherine Cerveny

Year 2950. Humanity has survived devastating climate shifts and four world wars, coming out stronger and smarter than ever. Incredible technology is available to all, and enhancements to appearance, intelligence, and physical ability are commonplace.

In this future, Felicia Sevigny has built her fame reading the futures of others.

Alexei Petriv, the most dangerous man in the TriSystem, will trust only Felicia to read his cards. But the future she sees is darker than either of them could ever have imagined. A future that pits them against an all-knowing government, almost superhuman criminals, and something from Felicia's past that she could never have predicted, but that could be the key to saving—or destroying—them all.

CHAPTER ONE

I've always been a big fan of eyeliner. The darker, the better. Growing up, I'd heard the expression "Pretty is as pretty does" almost every day of my life—but I believe that sometimes pretty needs help. Since I've decided against tattooing my way to beauty or using gene modification, I do things the old-fashioned way. And as one of the only Tarot card readers in Nairobi, I've cultivated a certain look that is as much personal choice as mysterious mask. So the fact that I stood in the tiny bathroom of my card reading shop and scrubbed my face clean, opting for tasteful over flashy, made me feel like I'd sold out.

"All for the greater good," I mumbled, examining my nearly naked face. "I can look straitlaced and respectable for an hour. Two, tops."

A quick time check showed it was nearly seven in the morning. It made me glad I'd decided to close up shop early at two and catch some sleep on the reception room couch. At least I didn't look like complete garbage, even if my sleep was more tossing and turning than actual shut-eye.

I hightailed it to the front door. I needed to be on the other side of the city by nine sharp. To do that in an hour using the unreliable Y-Line would take all the prayers and karmic brownie points I had to spare. Maybe if I lit some incense sticks and offered a prayer for guidance... but no, no time for that.

Then I had to stop, my hand frozen in mid-reach on the way to the doorknob. Standing in the entranceway of my shop was the most beautiful man I'd ever seen. I know it's shallow to focus on looks since they are so easily bought and modified, and yet...

"I'd like a Tarot card reading, please," he said, his voice so deep, I was certain the windows rattled.

"I'm sorry, but we're closed. I can take your information and schedule an appointment for later this week." I infused my voice with as much formality as I could muster. Anything to prevent stammering like a drooling idiot in front of such a good-looking man. Even though "good-looking" barely covered it.

"This won't take long and I'm prepared to pay generously," he said, as if he'd already dropped gold notes into my account. Wonderful—arrogant enough to assume money buys everything and he thinks his time is more valuable than mine. Well, that was exactly the shot of ice water I needed to break the spell.

"I appreciate your offer, but I'm afraid you'll have to book an appointment." *Like everybody else.*

"Unfortunately, I'm leaving Nairobi today. This is my last stop before my flight. I've heard of your reputation as a card reader. My research says you're quite accurate."

And just like that, he pierced the proverbial chink in my armor. When people said they'd heard of me, I felt honor-bound to accept. If word got back to the source that I was ungracious or unobliging, I could lose business. Damn it, why had I let my receptionist, Natty, leave early? She could have dealt with this situation. Oh right, it was so I could sleep and get ready in private with no one the wiser. But why had I forgotten to lock up? I did not have time for this.

I studied him. He wore reflective sunshades that prevented me from getting the full picture, but there were still plenty of other clues to give me a sense of what I was dealing with. A well-cut carbon-gray suit and scuff-free shoes screamed gold notes and good taste. He was tall, very tall. His fashionably scruffy, thick black hair brushed his suit collar and nearly met his very nicely broad shoulders. He was clean-shaven, with chiseled cheekbones and a slight tan that had to be Tru-Tan since no one exposed themselves to the sun anymore. Good tans cost a fortune. But his accent was the real giveaway. His deep voice carried a lilt that made it clear he was from the Russian Federation of Islands. In a word— money. Lots and lots of money.

But I wouldn't reschedule my appointment for all the money, contacts, or goodwill in the tri-system. I gestured toward the door, intending to walk him out. "I'm sorry, but perhaps next time you're in town."

He looked as if he hadn't the slightest intention of leaving. "If you're concerned about the time, my people can ensure you arrive at the fertility clinic before nine this morning."

I froze. "Excuse me, but that information is classified."

"And so it will remain. It would be a shame for One Gov to learn the true nature of your appointment, after all."

My eyes narrowed. "It's just a routine fertility consultation."

"Of course," he agreed. "I ask only for a brief reading. Surely you can spare a moment?"

I should have been both angry and terrified that he knew my plans. Hell, I hadn't even told my boyfriend, Roy! His words stopped just short of blackmail. And yet... I found myself intrigued, damn it. What would this Tarot reading show me? I had that odd feeling again— the one that hit deep in my gut and paid no attention to what I had lined up for the rest of the day, let alone my life. It demanded I follow through on whatever happened next. Over the years I'd learned never, and I mean *never*, to ignore that feeling no matter how pesky it might be.

He removed his sunshades and I was snared by blue eyes so intense I wondered if he had to hide them or risk turning people to stone—or women to mush. I peered closer, considering the whole package. The looks. The play of his muscles beneath his clothes when he moved. The symmetry. I wasn't sure why I hadn't caught it earlier: His MH Factor—Modified Human—was turned up high enough to scorch.

Out of my mouth came: "I can fit you in now with a short reading."

"Wonderful." He offered a smile that had no doubt removed numerous panties. Nice to know one of us was having a good time.

"I don't see many advanced stage Modified Humans in my shop. Are you fifth generation?" My question was beyond rude. Asking about genetic modifications was worse than asking how much money someone made. But if he knew my business, I didn't see why I couldn't know his. "I heard it's less invasive to upgrade technological modifications later in life rather than opting for full pre-birth gene manipulation. The t-mods are supposed to be less expensive too."

"Perhaps it depends on how many gold notes exchange hands and how natural you want it to look," he said, noncommittally.

So there was some genetic manipulation involved. I knew it! But how much? Some people went overboard with their upgrades and the results weren't always as advertised.

I waited for more follow-up from him. Instead, the silence stretched. Okay, then. "Is there a particular aspect of your life you want to know about? Or an issue that's troubling you?"

"I'm concerned about a meeting and its success. Should I continue on my current path, or cut my losses and run? You no doubt receive many similar requests."

He was right; I'd built my business on less. I had a steady clientele including a few minor celebrities, but nothing had really launched my career. Not that I wanted to be a card reader to the stars, but I definitely wanted to ensure I never had to worry about money.

"Follow me," I said, and with those words went my last lick of common sense.

I removed the c-tex bracelet I'd put on—so that no one could accuse me of skimming the Cerebral Neural Net and faking a reading—then led him through the shop. Gentle lighting flicked on as we entered the back room. Soft music began, the automatic soundtrack set to a Mars chill funk vibe. The room was decorated with thick Venusian carpets, decadent pillows on velvet chaise lounges, and paintings of exotic Old Earth terrain and new-world Martian landscapes. Rich colors that begged to be touched—a tactile experience for the senses. Customers had certain expectations as to how a Tarot card shop on Night Alley, the most exclusive and decadent street in Nairobi, should appear. If my Russian stranger had been there the night before when business was in full swing, he would have seen my designer silk print dress and makeup just this side of too much, instead of the prim beige knee-length skirt and sky-blue blouse I now wore. I looked overdressed, conservative, and slightly out of style.

Oddly, the idea that he'd caught me this way made me feel vulnerable, like I'd allowed him to see the real me instead of the persona I wore when I cast a reading. That woman didn't care what her clients thought because she knew they were all in awe of her. In those silk dresses she was untouchable. She held their future in her hands. This stripped-down me was too exposed, too likely to get caught up in things that didn't concern her. Well, too bad. I wasn't letting a hot guy and an off-the-chart gut feeling get the best of me. What I wore now was just another disguise. After all, how could I convince the Shared Hope program's fertility Arbiter I should be allowed to have a baby if I didn't look like a respectable member of society?

"Have a seat." I directed him to one of the chaise lounges with an ornate gold-leaf table beside it. A chandelier that appeared to drip with gemstones, which were really artfully colored glass, hung overhead.

"Interesting décor," he said.

"Would you be as impressed with a rickety table and some collapsible benches?" I asked as I took the chaise across from him.

He laughed. "I suppose not. I understand the need for showmanship. At times, it can be as important as the act itself."

"Hence the décor." I gestured around us.

I smiled, so did he, and suddenly the table between us seemed ridiculously small. The feeling in my gut grew, paired now with a growing sense that this man, whoever the hell he was, held some significance for me. It hung in the air.

I took a breath to center myself and refocused on the box in the middle of the table. Whatever designs were once painted on its black lacquered wood surface had long since faded. What it contained was easily the most valuable thing I owned.

I opened the box and removed the Tarot cards. They'd been in my family for generations, dating back to a time before the Earth's axis shifted thanks to a series of massive global quakes, polar melts, and then the two wars of succession that followed. Family lore claimed they came from the Old World—an all-but-forgotten place that existed only in history books and on the bottom of the ocean floor.

"Since we're pressed for time, I'll do a five-card spread using only the Major Arcana," I explained. "They are the heart of the Tarot. Each card represents a different state of being. I'm forgoing a Significator since you're asking about yourself, but I want you to select five cards from the deck which represent what may or may not happen, what will prevent it from happening, why you're in this situation, what you can do to either encourage or change it, and finally, depending on the steps you take, what will happen."

As I shuffled, I fell into my usual banter where I reassured the client they were in capable hands. Its familiarity made me feel more secure. I could do this. No need to panic because I was looking into the bluest eyes I'd ever seen. Once done shuffling, I fanned out the cards, let him pick his five, then arranged and flipped them over.

I'd been doing this too long to gasp, but that was what I wanted to do. I had a bizarre affinity with this set of cards—more so than anyone in the family according to my dearly departed Granny G. In fact, the cards had bypassed two disgruntled and pissed off generations of Romani to come directly to me, per her wishes. So when I examined the cards, I never lost my smile, even though I'd cast this identical reading for myself only an hour earlier.

I've always believed that things happen for a reason, and when the universe taps you on the shoulder, you pay attention. This was the equivalent of the universe punching me in the face.

He leaned forward. "What does it mean?"

"This is the Emperor, reversed." I pointed to the first card. "You have goals, but waste energy on pointless things that get in the way. You have the will and strength to fight, but aren't using those gifts properly. Next, the Moon. You want to shape events, not be shaped by them. You need to learn to read what's happening around you and act accordingly. However, you also need caution. You have hidden enemies who've yet to reveal themselves. The third card is the Falling Tower. It's the destruction of everything you've built because of your own misunderstanding and lack of judgment. Your bad choices may have put you in a situation where you could lose everything."

The man laughed. It didn't sound forced nor did he look worried, but at the same time, I could tell something was going on in his head. "So far it appears I shouldn't have gotten out of bed this morning."

"It's not all bad," I said consolingly. "Fourth is the Lovers. It could mean attraction or love, but given the other cards, it appears to be a partnership and mutual commitment. This connection will help you overcome your difficulties and further your control of the events. Lastly, the Judgment. It represents the end of an old life, and the beginning of a new one. It's a radical change, but one you will need if you are to overcome your situation."

When I looked up, he was gazing at me with such an intent expression that I worried I'd offended him. Well, I didn't have time to couch the reading in the prettiest of terms; he got what he got. He had to smarten up or he'd lose everything. Sadly, the same applied to me as well. Quickly, I swept the cards back into their box.

"I hope you found it useful."

"Very. I appreciate you making the time to see me."

He was still looking at me. I mean, *really* looking. Looking at me the way a man did when he wondered how a woman looked naked or was considering ways to get her naked. I wondered if he was thinking about the Lovers. Or maybe I was the one thinking that? My throat went dry. I hadn't been studied like that in a long time and it felt better than it should. Even if I didn't have an active MH Factor, I was no slouch. My almost-black hair reached mid-back, my olive skin held tones of Old World ancestry, and I could make my green eyes pop by dressing in shades of blue-green. My figure and height also fit One Gov's genetic specification guidelines, hence putting me in the Goldilocks zone: just right.

No, enough of this. What was I thinking? I had a boyfriend. I had plans for the future. In an hour, my whole world could change. And yet...

I stood. He stood with me. Even in my metal-clad high-heeled boots, my eyes were barely level with his shoulder. I felt feminine in ways I hadn't in years. The air felt charged with potential. My gut jerked again, reminding me to act before the moment disappeared. What the hell did it want me to do? Jump him? Rip his clothes off?

He held out his hand. I shook it. It swallowed mine. "Thank you, Felicia. I know how I need to conduct my future affairs now."

I froze when he said my name. Not that him knowing it was a surprise; it was how he'd said it. If I tried to describe it I'd sound crazy. He said it like he knew me. Or, had made it his business to know me. Or, planned on knowing me so well, I would someday learn what his body pressed against mine would actually feel like.

I flushed and released his hand as if it burned. "Feel free to leave your payment on the way out."

He laughed and a bolt of heat shot through me. "As I said earlier, my people can ensure you make your appointment at the clinic if you're concerned about time."

Again, I should have been terrified. If he contacted One Gov, getting arrested would be the least of my problems. Yet I had the oddest feeling that whatever this stranger knew, he'd keep it to himself. Still, I had to make some sort of a token protest, didn't I? "My private schedule is just that—private. I understand your investigating my flat-file avatar on the CN-net. Many clients do and access is always open. However, any personal information I've logged is off-limits. I would appreciate it if you left my shop now."

He seemed amused instead of angry. "My apologies. I'm glad to have made your acquaintance. Hopefully, we will have other dealings in the future."

Gut feeling be damned, I sincerely hoped not. However, I must not have managed to school my expression well enough since he added, "Despite what you may believe, the future isn't decided yet. There are always gray areas left to explore."

He turned on his heel to leave. Bemused, I followed. Outside, I found two personal bodyguards—all muscle and matching suits. They fell into step behind him as he continued down the sidewalk to the street. I saw four more musclemen at either end of the block, and a helicon hovering overhead in the dull gray sky. Street-side were two flight-limos ready for takeoff, one with its windows down. I could see the pilot in front while in back sat a gorgeous redhead. My mouth fell open. I know it did— just open and flapping in the breeze.

He paused before he climbed inside the first flight-limo. "Ms. Sevigny, you'll find my payment inside, as well as my halo should you need to get in touch. Your reputation is well deserved. Feel free to use me as a reference."

With that, he got into the flight-limo. I saw the redhead attempt to climb onto his lap and watched him push her away before the windows rolled up. The security detail ducked into the second flight-limo as the helicon zipped away. In a few seconds, the street was empty.

I ran back inside. On the reception desk was a blue chip wafer used to transfer funds between locked CN-net accounts. It was old tech, the kind used by people who didn't have direct CN-net t-mods. People like me. I tapped its face and the readout displayed an obscene amount of money. I charged seventy gold notes a reading. The readout said ten thousand—very near to the amount that had been in the savings account I'd recently decimated. I almost fainted. Beside the chip was the promised halo. Like the blue chip, it was also old tech. I touched it and watched the name unfurl in bold script.

So I'd been right about the accent. I knew the name. Who didn't? I'd just never seen his face. He rarely surfaced in public, and when he did, he came and went like smoke.

Alexei Petriv. Crown Prince of the Tsarist Consortium—though "crime lord" and "thug" would also be accurate descriptors. Robin Hood too, in some circles. Thorn in the side of One Gov. Pirate of the tri-system. In my office. Wanting a reading. The need to faint grew stronger. So did the feeling in my gut.

I had a terrible suspicion I was about to be made an offer I could not refuse.

if you enjoyed
THE ETERNITY WAR: PARIAH

look out for

FORSAKEN SKIES

Book One of the Silence

by

D. Nolan Clark

Sometimes the few must stand against the many.

From the dark, cold void came an unknown force.

*Their target a remote planet, the home for a
group of people distancing themselves from mankind
and pursuing a path of piety and peace.*

*If they have any chance at survival a disparate
group of pilots must come together to fight
back any way they can.*

*But the best these aces can do might
not be good enough.*

CHAPTER ONE

Flying down a wormhole was like throwing yourself into the center of a tornado, one where if you brushed the walls you would be obliterated down to subatomic particles before you even knew it happened.

Racing through a wormhole at this speed was suicide. But the kid wouldn't slow down.

Lanoe thumbed a control pad and painted the yacht's backside with a communications laser. A green pearl appeared in the corner of his vision, with data on signal strength rolling across its surface. "Thom," he called. "Thom, you've got to stop this. I know you're scared, I know—"

"I killed him! I can't go back now!"

Lanoe muted the connection and focused for a second on not getting himself killed. The wormhole twisted and bent up ahead, warped where it passed under some massive gravity source, probably a star. Side passages opened in every direction, split by the curvature of spacetime. Lanoe had lost track of where, in real-space terms, they were—they'd started back at Xibalba but they could be a hundred light-years away by now. Wormspace didn't operate by Newtonian rules. They could be anywhere. They could theoretically be on the wrong end of the universe.

The yacht up ahead was still accelerating. It was a sleek spindle of darkness against the unreal light of the tunnel walls, all black carbon fiber broken only by a set of airfoils like flat wings spaced around its thruster. At his school Thom had a reputation as some kind of hotshot racer—he was slated to compete in next year's Earth Cup—and Lanoe had seen how good a pilot the kid was as he chased him down. He was still surprised when Thom twisted around on his axis of flight and kicked in his maneuvering jets, nearly reversing his course and sending the yacht careening down one of the side tunnels.

Maybe he'd thought he could escape that way.

For all the kid's talent, though, Lanoe was Navy trained. He knew a couple of tricks they never taught to civilians. He switched off the compensators that protected his engine and pulled a right-hand turn tighter than a poly's purse. He squeezed his eyes shut as his inertial sink shoved him hard back into his seat but when he looked again he was right back on the yacht's tail. He thumbed for the comms laser again and when the green pearl popped up he said, "Thom, you can't outfly me. We need to talk about this. Your dad is dead, yes. We need to think about what comes next. Maybe you could tell me why you did it—"

But the green pearl was gone. Thom had burned for another course change and surged ahead. He'd pulled out of the maze of wormspace and back into the real universe, up ahead at another dip in the spacetime curve.

Lanoe goosed his engine and followed. He burst out of the wormhole throat and into searing red light that burned his eyes.

———

Centrocor freight hauler 4519 approaching on vector 7, 4, −32.

Wilscon dismantler ship Angie B, you are deviating from course by .02. Advise.

Traffic control, this is Angie B, we copy. Burning to correct.

The whispering voices of the autonomic port monitors passed across Valk's consciousness without making much of an impression.

Orbital traffic control wasn't an exacting job. It didn't pay well, either. Valk didn't mind so much. There were fringe benefits. For one, he had a cramped little workstation all to himself. He valued his privacy. Moreover, at the vertex between two limbs of the Hexus there was no gravity. It helped with the pain, a little.

Valk had been in severe pain for the last seventeen years, ever since he'd suffered what he always called his "accident." Even though there'd been nothing accidental about it. He had suffered severe burns over his entire body and even now, so many years later, the slightest weight on his flesh was too much.

His arms floated before him, his fingers twitching at keyboards that weren't really there. Lasers tracked his fingertip movements and converted them to data. Screens all around him pushed information in through his eyes, endless columns of numbers and tiny graphical displays he could largely ignore.

The Hexus sat at the bottom of a deep gravity well, a place where dozens of wormhole tunnels came together, connecting all twenty-three worlds of the local sector. A thousand vessels came through the Hexus every day, to offload cargo, to undertake repairs, just so the crews could stretch their legs for a minute on the way to their destinations. Keeping all those ships from colliding with each other, making sure they landed at the right docking berths, was the kind of job computers were built for, and the Hexus's autonomics were very, very good at it. Valk's job was to simply be there in case something happened that needed a human decision. If a freighter demanded priority mooring, for instance, because it was hauling hazardous cargo. Or if somebody important wanted the kid glove treatment. It didn't happen all that often.

Traffic, this is Angie B. We're on our way to Jehannum. Thanks for your help.

Civilian drone entering protected space. Redirecting.

Centrocor freight hauler 4519 at two thousand km, approaching Vairside docks.

Vairside docks report full. Redirect incoming traffic until 18:22.

Baffin Island docks report can take six more. Accepting until 18:49.

Unidentified vehicle exiting wormhole throat. No response to ping.

Unidentified vehicle exiting wormhole throat. No response to ping.

Maybe it was the repetition that made Valk swivel around in his workspace. He called up a new display with imaging of the wormhole throat, thirty million kilometers away. The throat itself looked like a sphere of perfect glass, distorting the stars behind it. Monitoring buoys with banks of floodlights and sensors swarmed around it, keeping well clear of the opening to wormspace. The newcomers were so small it took a second for Valk to even see them.

But there—the one in front was a dark blip, barely visible except when it occluded a light. A civilian craft, built for speed by the look of it. Expensive as hell. And right behind it—there—

"Huh," Valk said, a little grunt of surprise. It was an FA.2 fighter, cataphract class. A cigar-shaped body, one end covered in segmented carbonglas viewports, the other housing a massive thruster. A double row of airfoils on its flanks.

Valk had been a fighter pilot himself, back before his accident. He knew the silhouette of every cataphract, carrier scout, and recon boat that had ever flown. There had been a time when you would have seen FA.2s everywhere, when they were the Navy's favorite theater fighter. But that had been more than a century ago. Who was flying such an antique?

Valk tapped for a closer view—and only then did he see the red lights flashing all over his primary display. The two newcomers were moving *fast,* a considerable chunk of the speed of light.

And they were headed straight toward the Hexus.

He called up a communications panel and started desperately pinging them.

Light and heat burst into Lanoe's cockpit. Sweat burst out all over his skin. His suit automatically wicked it away but it couldn't catch all the beads of sweat popping out on his forehead. He swiped a virtual panel near his elbow and his viewports polarized, switching down to near-opaque blackness. It still wasn't enough.

There was a very good reason you didn't shoot out of a wormhole throat at this kind of speed. Wormhole throats tended to be very close to very big stars.

He could barely see—afterimages flickered in his vision, blocking out all the displays on his boards. He had a sense of a massive planet dead ahead but he couldn't make out any details. He tapped at display after display, trying to get some telemetry data, desperate for any information about where he was.

Then he saw the Hexus floating right in front of him. Fifty kilometers across, a vast hexagonal structure of concrete and foamsteel, like a colossal dirty benzene ring. Geryon, he thought. The Hexus orbited the planet Geryon, a bloated gas giant that circled a red giant star. That explained all the light and heat, at least.

He tried to raise Thom again with his comms laser but the green pearl wouldn't show up in his peripheral vision. Little flashes of green came from his other eye and he realized he was being pinged by the Hexus. He thumbed a panel to send them his identifying codes but didn't waste any time talking to them directly.

The Hexus was getting bigger, growing at an alarming rate. "Thom," he called, whether the kid could hear him or not, "you need to break off. You can't fly through that thing. Thom! Don't do it!"

His vision had cleared enough that he could just see the yacht, a dark spot visible against the brighter skin of the station. Thom was going to fly straight through the Hexus. At first glance it looked like there was plenty of room—the hexagon was wide open in its middle—but that space was full of freighters and liners and countless drones, a bewilderingly complex interchange of ships jockeying for position, heading to or away from docking facilities, ships being refueled by tenders, drones checking heat shields or scraping carbon out of thruster cones. If Thom went through there it would be like firing a pistol into a crowd.

Lanoe cursed under his breath and brought up his weapon controls.

~~~

Centrocor freight hauler 4519 requesting berth at Vairside docks.

Vairside docks report full. Redirect incoming traffic until 18:22.

Valk ignored the whispering voices. He had a much bigger problem.

In twenty-nine seconds the two unidentified craft were going to streak right through the center of the Hexus, moving fast enough to obliterate anything in their way. If there was a collision the resulting debris would have enough energy to tear the entire station apart. Hundreds of thousands of people would die.

Valk worked fast, moving from one virtual panel to the next, dismissing displays and opening new ones. His biggest display showed the trajectory of the two newcomers, superimposed on a diagram of every moving thing inside the Hexus. Tags on each object showed relative velocities, mass and inertia quantities, collision probabilities.

Those last showed up in burning red. Valk had to find a way to get each of them to turn amber or green before the newcomers blazed right through the Hexus. That meant moving every ship, every tiny drone, one by one—computing a new flight path for each craft that wouldn't intersect with any of the others.

The autonomic systems just weren't smart enough to do it themselves. This was exactly why they still had a human being working Valk's job.

If he moved this liner here—redirected this drone swarm to the far side of the Hexus—if he ordered this freighter to make a correction burn of fourteen milliseconds—if he swung this dismantler ship around on its long axis—

One of the newcomers finally responded to his identification requests, but he didn't have time to look. He swiped that display away even while he used his other hand to order a freighter to fire its positioning jets.

Civilian drone entering protected space. Redirecting.

Centrocor freight hauler 4519 requesting berth at Vairside docks.

The synthetic voices were like flies buzzing around inside Valk's skull. That freight hauler was a serious pain in the ass—it was by far the largest object still inside the ring of the Hexus, the craft most likely to get in the way of the incoming yacht.

Valk would gladly have sent the thing burning hard for a distant parking orbit. It was a purely autonomic vessel, without even a pilot onboard, basically a giant drone.

Who cared if a little cargo didn't make it to its destination in time? But for some reason its onboard computers refused to obey his commands. It kept demanding to be routed to a set of docks that weren't even classified for freight craft.

He pulled open a new control pad and started sending override codes.

The freighter responded instantly.

Instructed course will result in distress to passengers. Advise?

Wait. Passengers?

Up ahead the traffic inside the ring of the Hexus scattered like pigeons from a cat, but still there were just too many ships and drones in there, too many chances for a collision. Thom hadn't deviated even a fraction of a degree from his course. In a second or two it would be too late for him to break off—at this speed he wouldn't be able to burn hard enough to get away.

On Lanoe's weapons screen a firing solution popped up. He could hit the yacht with a disruptor. One hit and the yacht would be reduced to tiny debris, too small to do much damage when it rained down on the Hexus. His thumb hovered over the firing key—but even as he steeled himself to do it, a second firing solution popped up.

A ponderous freighter hung there, right in the middle of the ring. Right in the middle of Thom's course.

It was an ugly ship, just a bunch of cargo containers clamped to a central boom like grapes on a vine. It had thruster packages on either end but nothing even resembling a crew capsule.

Lanoe had enough weaponry to take that thing to pieces.

He opened a new communications panel and pinged the Hexus. "Traffic control, you need to move that freighter right now."

The reply came back instantly. At least somebody was talking to him. "FA.2, this is Hexus Control. Can't be done. Are you in contact with the unidentified yacht? Tell that idiot to change his trajectory."

"He's not listening," Lanoe called back. Damn it. Thom was maybe five seconds from splattering himself all over that ugly ship. "Control, move that freighter—or I'll move it for you."

"Negative! Negative, FA.2—there are people on that thing!"

What? That made no sense. A freight hauler like that would be controlled purely by autonomics. It wasn't classified for human occupation—it wouldn't even have rudimentary life support onboard.

There couldn't possibly be people on that thing. Yet he had no reason to think that traffic control would lie about that. And then—

In Lanoe's head the moral calculus was already working itself out. People, control had said—meaning more than one person.

If he killed Thom, who he knew was a murderer, it would save multiple innocent lives.

He reached again for the firing key.

～～

There had to be an answer. There had to be.

Instructed course would result in distress to passengers. Advise?

Valk could see six different ways to move the freighter. Every single one of them meant firing its main thrusters for a hard burn. Accelerating it at multiple g's.

If he did that, anybody inside the freighter would be reduced to red jelly. Unlike passenger ships, the cargo ship didn't carry an inertial sink. The people in it would have no protection from the sudden acceleration.

Centrocor freight hauler 4519 requesting berth at Vairside docks.

The ship was too stupid to know it was about to be smashed to pieces. Not for the first time he wished he could switch off the synthetic voices that reeled off pointless information all around him. He opened a new screen and studied the freighter's schematics. There were maneuvering thrusters here, and positioning jets near the nose, but they wouldn't be able to move the ship fast enough, there were emergency retros in six different locations, and explosive bolts on the cargo containers—

Yes! He had it. "FA.2," he called, even as he opened a new control pad. "FA.2, do not fire!" He tapped away at the pad, his fingers aching as he moved them so quickly.

Instructed action may cause damage to Centrocor property. Advise?

"I advise you to shut up and do what I say," Valk told the freighter. That wasn't what it was looking for, though. He looked down, saw a green virtual key hovering in front of him, and stabbed at it.

Out in the middle of the ring, the freight hauler triggered the explosive bolts on all of its port side cargo containers at once. The long boxes went tumbling away with aching slowness, blue and yellow and red oblongs dancing outward on their own trajectories. Some smashed into passing drones, creating whole new clouds of debris. Some bounced off the arms of the Hexus, obliterating against its concrete, the goods inside thrown free in multicolored sprays.

On Valk's screens a visual display popped up showing him the chaos. The yacht was a tiny dark needle lost in the welter of colorful boxes and smashed goods, moving so fast Valk could barely track it. But this was going to work, a gap was opening where the yacht could pass through safely, this was going to—

There was no sound but Valk could almost feel the crunch as one of the cargo containers just clipped one of the yacht's airfoils. The cargo container tore open, its steel skin splitting like it was a piece of overripe fruit. Barrels spilled out in a broad cloud of wild trajectories. The yacht was thrown into a violent spin as it shot through the Hexus and out the other side.

A split second later the FA.2 jinked around a flying barrel and burned hard to follow the yacht on its new course, straight down toward Geryon.